SHE WON THE WEST

By the same Editors

THE WEB SHE WEAVES
An Anthology of Mystery & Suspense Stories by
Women

SHE WON THE WEST

AN ANTHOLOGY OF
WESTERN & FRONTIER STORIES
BY WOMEN

EDITED BY
MARCIA MULLER & BILL PRONZINI

William Morrow and Company, Inc.
New York

Library of Congress Cataloging in Publication Data
Main entry under title:

She won the West.

1. Western stories. 2. American fiction—Women authors. 3. Frontier and pioneer life—Fiction.
I. Muller, Marcia. II. Pronzini, Bill.
PS648.W4S53 1985   813'.0874'089287   84–20789
ISBN 0-688-04701-7

Printed in the United States of America

First Edition

1 2 3 4 5 6 7 8 9 10

BOOK DESIGN BY JAYE ZIMET

Contents

7

8

Introduction

___

Although the winning of the American West was largely accomplished by men, women played a crucial, if subtle, role. Rather than being the lusty conquerors, the large-scale movers and shapers, they were (in more ways than one) the settlers—those who established the home and brought a measure of order to the wild frontier.

Thus it is, too, in the fiction that chronicles the westward expansion of the late 1800s. While men have dominated the various forms of western literature, the works of women constitute a small but important segment, and each major contributor has brought her special viewpoint to this uniquely American art form.

The introduction of the dime novel in the latter half of the nineteenth century first brought the frontier story widespread attention. And it was a woman, magazine editor Mrs. Ann Sophia Winterbotham Stephens, who wrote the very first dime novel: *Maleska: The Indian Wife of the White Hunter* (1860). A romance set in the Hudson River valley of the 1700s, it is a work of considerable quality. Its popularity paved the way for the mass-produced nickel and dime novels and the story weeklies of such firms as Beadle & Adams which dominated the American publishing scene for the next fifty years; many of these books were also written by women, sometimes hidden behind male pseudonyms.

Over the years critics have complained that dime novels and much other early western fiction (by both men and women) were tinged with condescension for their subject matter and characters. Indeed, some early works *were* written from a decidedly eastern viewpoint, seeming to smile down upon the rough-edged ways and odd attitudes of those who surged across the prairies and flooded the mining camps and new towns of the western frontier. As the western story matured, however, even eastern writers began to view their material much more sympathetically, and women were in the forefront of this change.

In the late 1800s serious western fiction emerged from women who lived in the West and used its vast spaces as backdrops for their novels—women such as Gertrude Atherton, Mary Austin, Willa Cather, Eleanor Gates, Mary Hallock-Foote, and Marah Ellis Ryan. Similarly, more accomplished popular westerns also emerged, as the new century arrived and readers began to demand more than the highly melodramatic situations and superhuman characters of the dime novel era. One of the earliest of these writers of realistic westerns, whose sales compared favorably with those of Owen Wister and Zane Grey, was B. M. Bower—a woman born and reared in the West, whose "Flying U" stories remain some of the best ever written about the working cowboy.

Though their numbers remain small, women have continued throughout this century to give us outstanding western fiction of all types—stories set in the mountains and on the plains and deserts, against the backgrounds of mining, ranching, town life, and pioneer travel, featuring explorers and trappers, cowboys and cavalrymen, lawmen and outlaws, Indians and whites. They have portrayed both the hardships and high hopes of the westward expansion as well as the triumph of the human spirit over adversity. And they have done so with sensitivity, drama, and high good humor.

Mainstream westerns of substantial merit have been written by Mari Sandoz, Martha Ostenso, Jane Gilmore Rushing, Dorothy Scarborough, Marilyn Durham (the best sellers *The Man Who Loved Cat Dancing* and *Dutch Uncle*), and, to some extent, Jessamyn West. The work of Dorothy M. Johnson bridges the gap between the literary and popular western; "A Man Called Horse," "Lost Sister," and the novels *Buffalo Woman* and *All the Buffalo Returning* are among the finest portrayals of the Indian consciousness in American literature. Eli Colter and Elsa Barker competed favorably with male writers in the demanding pulp magazine markets of the period 1920–1950. And such contemporary writers as Peggy Simson Curry, Jeanne Williams, Lee Hoffman *(The Valdez Horses)*, Ann Ahlswede, Amelia Bean, P. A. Bechko, and Carla Kelly have produced western fiction of power and imagination, a not inconsiderable number of which have won Golden Spur Awards from the Western Writers of America (WWA) in the best novel, best juvenile, and best short story categories.

The stories in these pages have been selected to provide the reader with, first, a high level of entertainment; secondly, a historical perspective on women whose work has had an impact on the field of western writing; and thirdly, a cross section of story types encompassing the literary, the popular, and a blending of the two. We think you'll agree, after reading them, that they are indeed among the finest of western stories and that they prove conclusively women have won—and are continuing to win—the fictional West.

—MARCIA MULLER and BILL PRONZINI
San Francisco, California
July 1984

SHE WON THE WEST

The era of los ranchos grandes was a short but fabled one in the history of California, and "The Conquest of Doña Jacoba" is rich in the details and romance of those brief years. The scene is a grand hacienda, filled with guests for the marriage of one of the daughters; the characters range from Doña Jacoba, the stern mistress of the rancho, to her lovely young daughter, Elena, a girl who is hopelessly in love with an unsuitable man; and the resolution of the conflict produced by this passion says much about the people of this golden age. Gertrude Atherton (1857–1948) was a keen observer of the people of her native state, in both the era described in this story and later periods. A leader of San Francisco society, she portrayed her fellow citizens' lives and times in such historically accurate collections and novels as The Californians *(1898),* The Splendid Idle Forties *(1902),* The Sophisticates *(1931), and* The Horn of Life *(1942).*

The Conquest of Doña Jacoba

GERTRUDE ATHERTON

I

A forest of willows cut by a forking creek, and held apart here and there by fields of yellow mustard blossoms fluttering in their pale green nests, or meadows carpeted with the tiny white and yellow flowers of early summer. Wide patches of blue where the willows ended, and immense banks of daisies bordering fields of golden grain, bending and shimmering in the wind with the deep even sweep of rising tide. Then the lake, long, irregular, half choked with tules, closed by a marsh. The valley framed by mountains of purplish gray, dull brown, with patches of vivid green and yellow; a solitary gray peak, barren and rocky, in sharp contrast to the rich Californian hills; on one side fawn-coloured slopes, and slopes with groves of crouching oaks in their

17

hollows; opposite and beyond the cold peak, a golden hill rising to a mount of earthy green; still lower, another peak, red and green, mulberry and mould; between and afar, closing the valley, a line of pink-brown mountains splashed with blue.

Such was a fragment of Don Roberto Duncan's vast rancho, Los Quervos, and on a plateau above the willows stood the adobe house, white and red-tiled, shaped like a solid letter *H*. On the deep veranda, sunken between the short forearms of the *H*, Doña Jacoba could stand and issue commands in her harsh imperious voice to the Indians in the rancheria among the willows, whilst the long sala behind overflowed with the gay company her famous hospitality had summoned, the bare floor and ugly velvet furniture swept out of thought by beautiful faces and flowered silken gowns.

Behind the sala was an open court, the grass growing close to the great stone fountain. On either side was a long line of rooms, and above the sala was a library opening into the sleeping room of Doña Jacoba on one side, and into that of Elena, her youngest and loveliest daughter, on the other. Beyond the house were a dozen or more buildings: the kitchen; a room in which steers and bullocks, sheep and pigs, were hanging; a storehouse containing provisions enough for a hotel; and the manufactories of the Indians. Somewhat apart was a large building with a billiard-room in its upper story and sleeping rooms below. From her window Elena could look down upon the high-walled corral with its prancing horses always in readiness for the pleasure-loving guests, and upon the broad road curving through the willows and down the valley.

The great house almost shook with life on this brilliant day of the month of June, 1852. Don Roberto Duncan, into whose shrewd Scotch hands California had poured her wealth for forty years, had long ago taken to himself a wife of Castilian blood; to-morrow their eldest remaining daughter was to be married to a young Englishman, whose father had been a merchant in California when San Francisco was Yerba Buena. Not a room was vacant in the house. Young people had come from Monterey and San Francisco, Santa Barbara and Los Angeles. Beds had been put up in the library and billiard-room, in the store-rooms and attics. The corral was full of strange horses, and the huts in the willows had their humbler guests.

Francisca sat in her room surrounded by a dozen chattering girls. The floor beneath the feet of the Californian heiress was bare, and the heavy furniture was of uncarved mahogany. But a satin quilt covered the bed, lavish Spanish needlework draped chest and tables, and through the open window came the June sunshine and the sound of the splashing fountain.

Francisca was putting the last stitches in her wedding-gown, and the girls were helping, advising, and commenting.

"Art thou not frightened, Panchita," demanded one of the girls, "to go away and live with a strange man? Just think, thou hast seen him but ten times."

"What of that?" asked Francisca, serenely, holding the rich corded silk at arm's length, and half closing her eyes as she readjusted the deep flounce of Spanish lace. "Remember, we shall ride and dance and play games together for a week with all of you, dear friends, before I go away with him. I shall know him quite well by that time. And did not my father know him when he was a little boy? Surely, he cannot be a cruel man, or my father would not have chosen him for my husband."

"I like the Americans and the Germans and the Russians," said the girl who had spoken, "particularly the Americans. But these English are so stern, so harsh sometimes."

"What of that?" asked Francisca again. "Am I not used to my father?"

She was a singular-looking girl, this compound of Scotch and Spanish. Her face was cast in her father's hard mould, and her frame was large and sturdy, but she had the black luxuriant hair of Spain, and much grace of gesture and expression.

"I would not marry an Englishman," said a soft voice.

Francisca raised her eyebrows and glanced coldly at the speaker, a girl of perfect loveliness, who sat behind a table, her chin resting on her clasped hands.

"Thou wouldst marry whom our father told thee to marry, Elena," said her sister, severely. "What hast thou to say about it?"

"I will marry a Spaniard," said Elena, rebelliously. "A Spaniard, and no other."

"Thou wilt do what?" asked a cold voice from the door. The girls gave a little scream. Elena turned pale, even Francisca's hands twitched.

Doña Jacoba was an impressive figure as she stood in the doorway; a tall unbowed woman with a large face and powerful penetrating eyes. A thin mouth covering white teeth separated the prominent nose and square chin. A braid of thick black hair lay over her fine bust, and a black silk handkerchief made a turban for her lofty head. She wore a skirt of heavy black silk and a shawl of Chinese crêpe, one end thrown gracefully over her shoulder.

"What didst thou say?" she demanded again, a sneer on her lips.

Elena made no answer. She stared through the window at the servants laying the table in the dining room on the other side of the court, her breath shortening as if the room had been exhausted of air.

"Let me hear no more of that nonsense," continued her mother. "A strange remark, truly, to come from the lips of a Californian! Thy father has said that his daughters shall marry men of his race—men who belong to that island of the North; and I have agreed, and thy sisters are well married. No women are more virtuous, more industrious, more religious, than ours; but our men—our young men—are a set of drinking gambling vagabonds. Go to thy room and pray there until supper."

Elena ran out of an opposite door, and Doña Jacoba sat down on a high-backed chair and held out her hand for the wedding-gown. She examined it, then smiled brilliantly.

"The lace is beautiful," she said. "There is no richer in California, and I have seen Doña Trinidad Iturbi y Moncada's and Doña Modeste Castro's. Let me see thy mantilla once more."

Francisca opened a chest nearly as large as her bed, and shook out a long square of superb Spanish lace. It had arrived from the city of Mexico but a few days before. The girls clapped their admiring hands, as if they had not looked at it twenty times, and Doña Jacoba smoothed it tenderly with her strong hands. Then she went over to the chest and lifted the beautiful silk and crêpe gowns, one by one, her sharp eyes detecting no flaw. She opened another chest and examined the piles of underclothing and bed linen, all of finest woof, and deeply bordered with the drawn work of Spain.

"All is well," she said, returning to her chair. "I see nothing more to be done. Thy brother will bring the emeralds, and the English plate will come before the week is over."

"Is it sure that Santiago will come in time for the wedding?" asked a half-English granddaughter, whose voice broke suddenly at her own temerity.

But Doña Jacoba was in a gracious mood.

"Surely. Has not Don Roberto gone to meet him? He will be here at four to-day."

"How glad I shall be to see him!" said Francisca. "Just think, my friends, I have not seen him for seven years. Not since he was eleven years old. He has been on that cold dreadful island in the North all this time. I wonder has he changed!"

"Why should he change?" asked Doña Jacoba. "Is he not a Cortez and a Duncan? Is he not a Californian and a Catholic? Can a few years in an English school make him of another race? He is seven years older, that is all."

"True," assented Francisca, threading her needle; "of course he could not change."

Doña Jacoba opened a large fan and wielded it with slow curves of her strong wrist. She had never been cold in her life, and even a June day oppressed her.

"We have another guest," she said in a moment—"a young man, Don Dario Castañares of Los Robles Rancho. He comes to buy cattle of my husband, and must remain with us until the bargain is over."

Several of the girls raised their large black eyes with interest. "Don Dario Castañares," said one; "I have heard of him. He is very rich and very handsome, they say."

"Yes," said Doña Jacoba, indifferently. "He is not ugly, but much too dark. His mother was an Indian. He is no husband, with all his leagues, for any Californian of pure Castilian blood."

II

Elena had gone up to her room, and would have locked the door had she possessed a key. As it was, she indulged in a burst of tears at the prospect of marrying an Englishman, then consoled herself with the thought that her best-beloved brother would be with her in a few hours.

She bathed her face and wound the long black coils about her shapely head. The flush faded out of her white cheeks, and her eyelids were less heavy. But the sadness did not leave her eyes nor the delicate curves of her mouth. She had the face of the Madonna, stamped with the heritage of suffering; a nature so keenly capable of joy and pain that she drew both like a magnet, and would so long as life stayed in her.

She curled herself in the window-seat, looking down the road for the gray cloud of dust that would herald her brother. But only black flocks of crows mounted screaming from the willows, to dive and rise again. Suddenly she became conscious that she was watched, and her gaze swept downward to the corral. A stranger stood by the gates, giving orders to a vaquero but looking hard at her from beneath his low-dropped sombrero.

He was tall, this stranger, and very slight. His face was nearly as dark as an Indian's, but set with features so perfect that no one but Doña Jacoba had ever found fault with his skin. Below his dreaming ardent eyes was a straight delicate nose; the sensuous mouth was half parted over glistening teeth and but lightly shaded by a silken mustache. About his graceful figure hung a dark red serape embroidered and fringed with gold, and his red velvet trousers were laced, and his yellow riding-boots gartered, with silver.

Elena rose quickly and pulled the curtain across the window; the blood had flown to her hair, and a smile chased the sadness from her mouth. Then she raised her hands and pressed the palms against the slope of the ceiling, her dark upturned eyes full of terror. For many moments she stood so, hardly conscious of what she was doing, seeing only the implacable eyes of her mother. Then down the road came the loud regular hoof-falls of galloping horses, and with an eager cry she flung aside the curtain, forgetting the stranger.

Down the road, half hidden by the willows, came two men. When they reached the rancheria, Elena saw the faces: a sandy-haired hard-faced old Scotsman, with cold blue eyes beneath shaggy red brows, and a dark slim lad, every inch a Californian. Elena waved her handkerchief and the lad his hat. Then the girl ran down the stairs and over to the willows. Santiago sprang from his horse, and the brother and sister clung together kissing and crying, hugging each other until her hair fell down and his hat was in the dust.

"Thou hast come!" cried Elena at last, holding him at arm's length that she might see him better, then clinging to him again with all her strength. "Thou never wilt leave me again—promise me! Promise me, my Santiago! Ay, I have been so lonely."

"Never my little one. Have I not longed to come home that I might be with you? O my Elena! I know so much. I will teach you everything."

"Ay, I am proud of thee, my Santiago! Thou knowest more than any boy in California—I know."

"Perhaps that would not be much," with fine scorn. "But come, Elena mia, I must go to my mother; she is waiting. She looks as stern as ever; but how I have longed to see her!"

They ran to the house, passing the stranger, who had watched them with folded arms and scowling brows. Santiago rushed impetuously at his mother; but she put out her arm, stiff and straight, and held him back. Then she laid her hand, with its vice-like grip, on his shoulder, and led him down the sala to the chapel at the end. It was arranged for the wedding, with all the pomp of velvet altar-cloth and golden candelabra. He looked at it wonderingly. Why had she brought him to look upon this before giving him a mother's greeting?

"Kneel down," she said, "and repeat the prayers of thy Church—prayers of gratitude for thy safe return."

The boy folded his hands deprecatingly.

"But, mother, remember it is seven long years since I have said the Catholic prayers. Remember I have been educated in an English college, in a Protestant country."

Her tall form curved slowly toward him, the blood blazed in her dark cheeks.

"What!" she screamed incredulously. "Thou hast forgotten the prayers of thy Church—the prayers thou learned at my knee?"

"Yes, mother, I have," he said desperately. "I cannot—"

"God! God! Mother of God! My son says this to me!" She caught him by the shoulder again and almost hurled him from the room. Then she locked her hand about his arm and dragged him down the sala to his father's room. She took a greenhide reata from the table and brought it down upon his back with long sweeps of her powerful arm, but not another word came from her rigid lips. The boy quivered with the shame and pain, but made no resistance—for he was a Californian, and she was his mother.

III

Joaquin, the eldest son, who had been hunting bear with a number of his guests, returned shortly after his brother's arrival and was met at the door by his mother.

"Where is Santiago?" he asked. "I hear he has come."

"Santiago has been sent to bed, where he will remain for the present. We have an unexpected guest, Joaquin. He leans there against the tree—Don Dario Castañares. Thou knowest who he is. He comes to buy cattle of thy father, and will remain some days. Thou must share thy room with him, for there is no other place—even on the billiard-table."

Joaquin liked the privacy of his room, but he had all the hospitality of his race. He went at once to the stranger, walking a little heavily, for he was no longer young and slender, but with a cordial smile on his shrewd warmly coloured face.

"The house is at your service, Don Dario," he said, shaking the newcomer's hand. "We are honoured that you come in time for my sister's wedding. It distresses me that I cannot offer you the best room in the house, but, Dios! we have a company here. I have only the half of my poor bed to offer you, but if you will deign to accept that—"

"I am miserable, wretched, to put you to such inconvenience—"

"Never think of such a thing, my friend. Nothing could give me greater happiness than to try to make you comfortable in my poor room. Will you come now and take a siesta before supper?"

Dario followed him to the house, protesting at every step, and Joaquin threw open the door of one of the porch rooms.

"At your service, señor—everything at your service."

He went to one corner of the room and kicked aside a pile of saddles, displaying a small hillock of gold in ten- and

fifty-dollar slugs. "You will find about thirty thousand dollars
there. We sold some cattle a few days ago. I beg that you will
help yourself. It is all at your service. I will now go and send
you some aguardiente, for you must be thirsty." And he
went out and left his guest alone.

Dario threw himself face downward on the bed.
He was in love, and the lady had kissed another man as
if she had no love to spare. True, it was but her brother
she had kissed, but would she have eyes for any one else
during a stranger's brief visit? And how, in this crowded
house, could he speak a word with her alone? And that
terrible dragon of a mother! He sprang to his feet as an
Indian servant entered with a glass of aguardiente.
When he had burnt his throat, he felt better. "I will stay
until I have won her, if I remain a month," he vowed. "It
will be some time before Don Roberto will care to talk
business."

But Don Roberto was never too occupied to talk business. After he had taken his bath and siesta, he sent a servant
to request Don Dario Castañares to come up to the library,
where he spent most of his time, received all his visitors,
reprimanded his children, and took his after-dinner naps. It
was a luxurious room for the Californian of that day. A thick
red English carpet covered the floor; one side of the room
was concealed by a crowded bookcase, and the heavy mahogany furniture was handsomely carved, although uphol-
stered with horse-hair.

In an hour every detail of the transaction had been
disposed of, and Dario had traded a small rancho for a herd
of cattle. The young man's face was very long when the last
detail had been arranged, but he had forgotten that his host
was as Californian as himself. Don Roberto poured him a
brimming glass of angelica and gave him a hearty slap on the
back.

"The cattle will keep for a few days, Don Dario," he
said, "and you shall not leave this house until the festivities
are over. Not until a week from to-morrow—do you hear?

I knew your father. We had many a transaction together, and I take pleasure in welcoming his son under my roof. Now get off to the young people, and do not make any excuses."

Dario made none.

IV

The next morning at eight, Francisca stood before the altar in the chapel, looking very handsome in her rich gown and soft mantilla. The bridegroom, a sensible-looking young Englishman, was somewhat nervous, but Francisca might have been married every morning at eight o'clock. Behind them stood Don Roberto in a new suit of English broadcloth, and Doña Jacoba in heavy lilac silk, half covered with priceless lace. The six bridesmaids looked like a huge bouquet, in their wide delicately coloured skirts. Their dark eyes, mischievous, curious, thoughtful, flashed more brilliantly than the jewels they wore.

The sala and Don Roberto's room beyond were so crowded that some of the guests stood in the windows, and many could not enter the doors; every family within a hundred leagues had come to the wedding. The veranda was crowded with girls, the sparkling faces draped in black mantillas or bright rebosos, the full gay gowns fluttering in the breeze. Men in jingling spurs and all the bravery of gold-laced trousers and short embroidered jackets respectfully elbowed their way past brown and stout old women that they might whisper a word into some pretty alert little ear. They had all ridden many leagues that morning, but there was not a trace of fatigue on any face. The court behind the sala was full of Indian servants striving to catch a glimpse of the ceremony.

Dario stood just within the front door, his eyes eagerly fixed upon Elena. She looked like a California lily in her white gown; even her head drooped a little as if a storm had passed. Her eyes were absent and heavy; they mirrored nothing of the solemn gayety of the morning; they saw only the welts on her brother's back.

Dario had not seen her since Santiago's arrival. She had not appeared at supper, and he had slept little in consequence; in fact, he had spent most of the night playing *monte* with Joaquin and a dozen other young men in the billiard-room.

During the bridal mass the padre gave communion to the young couple, and to those that had made confession the night before. Elena was not of the number, and during the intense silence she drew back and stood and knelt near Dario. They were not close enough to speak, had they dared; but the Californian had other speech than words, and Dario and Elena made their confession that morning.

During breakfast they were at opposite ends of the long table in the dining room, but neither took part in the songs and speeches, the toasts and laughter. Both had done some manoeuvring to get out of sight of the old people, and sit at one of the many other tables in the sala, on the corridor, in the court; but Elena had to go with the bridesmaids, and Joaquin insisted upon doing honour to the uninvited guest. The Indian servants passed the rich and delicate, the plain and peppered, dishes, the wines and the beautiful cakes for which Doña Jacoba and her daughters were famous. The massive plate that had done duty for generations in Spain was on the table; the crystal had been cut in England. It was the banquet of a grandee, and no one noticed the silent lovers.

After breakfast the girls flitted to their rooms and changed their gowns, and wound rebosos or mantillas about their heads; the men put off their jackets for lighter ones of flowered calico, and the whole party, in buggies or on horseback, started for a bull-fight which was to take place in a field about a mile behind the house. Elena went in a buggy with Santiago, who was almost as pale as she. Dario, on horseback, rode as near her as he dared; but when they reached the fence about the field careless riders crowded between, and he could only watch her from afar.

The vaqueros in their broad black hats shining with varnish, their black velvet jackets, their crimson sashes, and short, black velvet trousers laced with silver cord over spotless linen, looked very picturesque as they dashed about the field jingling their spurs and shouting at each other. When the bulls trotted in and greeted each other pleasantly, the vaqueros swung their hissing reatas and yelled until the maddened animals wreaked their vengeance on each other, and the serious work of the day began.

Elena leaned back with her fan before her eyes, but Santiago looked on eagerly in spite of his English training.

"Caramba!" he cried, "but that old bull is tough. Look, Elena! The little one is down. No, no! He has the big one. Ay! yi, yi! By Jove! he is gone—no, he has run off—he is on him again! He has ripped him up! Brava! brava!"

A cheer as from one throat made the mountains echo, but Elena still held her fan before the field.

"How canst thou like such bloody sport?" she asked disgustedly. "The poor animals! What pleasure canst thou take to see a fine brute kicking in his death-agony, his bowels trailing on the ground?"

"Fie, Elena! Art thou not a Californian? Dost thou not love the sport of thy country? Why, look at the other girls! They are mad with excitement. By Jove! I never saw so many bright eyes. I wonder if I shall be too stiff to dance to-night. Elena, she gave me a beating! But tell me, little one, why dost thou not like the bull-fight? I feel like another man since I have seen it."

"I cannot be pleased with cruelty. I shall never get used to see beasts killed for amusement. And Don Dario Castañares does not like it either. He never smiled once, nor said 'Brava!' "

"Aha! And how dost thou know whether he did or not? I thought thy face was behind that big black fan."

"I saw him through the sticks. What does 'By Jove' mean, my Santiago?"

He enlightened her, then stood up eagerly. Another bull had been brought in, and one of the vaqueros was to fight him. During the next two hours Santiago gave little thought to his sister, and sometimes her long black lashes swept above the top of her fan. When five or six bulls had stamped and roared and gored and died, the guests of Los Quervos went home to chocolate and siesta, the others returned to their various ranchos.

But Dario took no nap that day. Twice he had seen an Indian girl at Elena's window, and as the house settled down to temporary calm, he saw the girl go to the rancheria among the willows. He wrote a note, and followed her as soon as he dared. She wore a calico frock, exactly like a hundred others, and her stiff black hair cut close to her neck in the style enforced by Doña Jacoba; but Dario recognized her imitation of Elena's walk and carriage. He was very nervous, but he managed to stroll about and make his visit appear one of curiosity. As he passed the girl he told her to follow him, and in a few moments they were alone in a thicket. He had hard work to persuade her to take the note to her mistress, for she stood in abject awe of Doña Jacoba; but love of Elena and sympathy for the handsome stranger prevailed, and the girl went off with the missive.

The staircase led from Don Roberto's room to Doña Jacoba's; but the lady's all-seeing eyes were closed, and the master was snoring in his library. Malia tiptoed by both, and Elena, who had been half asleep, sat up, trembling with excitement, and read the impassioned request for an interview. She lifted her head and listened, panting a little. Then she ran to the door and looked into the library. Her father was sound asleep; there could be no doubt of that. She dared not write an answer, but she closed the door and put her lips to the girl's ear.

"Tell him," she murmured, horrified at her own boldness—"tell him to take me out for the contradanza tonight. There is no other chance." And the girl went back and delivered the message.

V

The guests and family met again at supper; but yards of linen and mounds of plate, spirited, quickly turning heads, flowered muslin gowns and silken jackets, again separated Dario and Elena. He caught a glimpse now and again of her graceful head turning on its white throat, or of her sad pure profile shining before her mother's stern old face.

Immediately after supper the bride and groom led the way to the sala, the musicians tuned their violins and guitars, and after an hour's excited comment upon the events of the day the dancing began. Doña Jacoba could be very gracious when she chose, and she moved among her guests like a queen to-night, begging them to be happy, and electrifying them with her brilliant smile. She dispelled their awe of her with magical tact, and when she laid her hand on one young beauty's shoulder, and told her that her eyes put out the poor candles of Los Quervos, the girl was ready to fling herself on the floor and kiss the tyrant's feet. Elena watched her anxiously. Her father petted her in his harsh abrupt way. If she had ever received a kiss from her mother, she did not remember it; but she worshipped the blinding personality of the woman, although she shook before the relentless will. But that her mother was pleased to be gracious to-night was beyond question, and she gave Dario a glance of timid encouragement, which brought him to her side at once.

"At your feet, señorita," he said; "may I dare to beg the honour of the contradanza?"

She bent her slender body in a pretty courtsy. "It is a small favour to grant a guest who deigns to honour us with his presence."

He led her out, and when he was not gazing enraptured at the graceful swaying and gliding of her body, he managed to make a few conventional remarks.

"You did not like bull-fighting, señorita?"

"He watched me," she thought. "No, señor. I like nothing that is cruel."

"Those soft eyes could never be cruel. Ay, you are so beautiful, señorita."

"I am but a little country girl, señor. You must have seen far more beautiful women in the cities. Have you ever been in Monterey?"

"Yes, señorita, many times. I have seen all the beauties, even Doña Modeste Castro. Once, too—that was before the Americans came—I saw the Señorita Ysabel Herrera, a woman so beautiful that a man robbed a church and murdered a priest for her sake. But she was not so beautiful as you, señorita."

The blood throbbed in the girl's fair cheeks. "He must love me," she told herself, "to think me more beautiful than Ysabel Herrera. Joaquin says she was the handsomest woman that ever was seen."

"You compliment me, señor," she answered vaguely. "She had wonderful green eyes. So has the Señora Castro. Mine are only brown, like so many other girls'."

"They are the most beautiful eyes in California. They are like the Madonna's. I do not care for green eyes." His black ones flashed their language to hers, and Elena wondered if she had ever been unhappy. She barely remembered where she was, forgot that she was a helpless bird in a golden cage. Her mate had flown through the open door.

The contradanza ends with a waltz, and as Dario held her in his arms his last remnant of prudence gave way.

"Elena, Elena," he murmured passionately, "I love thee. Dost thou not know it? Dost thou not love me a little? Ay, Elena! I have not slept one hour since I saw thee."

She raised her eyes to his face. The sadness still dwelt in their depths, but above floated the soft flame of love and trust. She had no coquetry in her straightforward and simple nature.

"Yes," she whispered, "I love thee."

"And thou art happy, querida mia? Thou art happy here in my arms?"

She let her cheek rest for a moment against his shoulder. "Yes, I am very happy."

"And thou wilt marry me?"

The words brought her back to reality, and the light left her face.

"Ay," she said, "why did you say that? It cannot ever be."

"But it shall be! Why not? I will speak with Don Roberto in the morning."

The hand that lay on his shoulder clutched him suddenly. "No, no," she said hurriedly; "promise me that you will not speak to him for two or three days at least. My father wants us all to marry Englishmen. He is kind, and he loves me, but he is mad for Englishmen. And we can be happy meanwhile."

The music stopped, and he could only murmur his promises before leading her back to her mother.

He dared not take her out again, but he danced with no one else in spite of many inviting eyes, and spent the rest of the night on the corridor, where he could watch her unobserved. The walls were so thick at Los Quervos that each window had a deep seat within and without. Dario ensconced himself, and was comfortable, if tumultuous.

VI

With dawn the dancing ended, and quiet fell upon Los Quervos. But at twelve gay voices and laughter came through every window. The family and guests were taking their cold bath, ready for another eighteen hours of pleasure.

Shortly after the long dinner, the iron-barred gates of the corral were thrown open and a band of horses, golden bronze in colour, with silvern mane and tail, silken embroidered saddles on their slender backs, trotted up to the door. The beautiful creatures shone in the sun like burnished armour; they arched their haughty necks and lifted their small feet as if they were Californian beauties about to dance El Son.

The girls wore short riding-skirts, gay sashes, and little round hats. The men wore thin jackets of brightly coloured silk, gold-laced knee-breeches, and silver spurs. They tossed the girls upon their saddles, vaulted into their own, and all started on a wild gallop for the races.

Dario, with much manoeuvring, managed to ride by Elena's side. It was impossible to exchange a word with her, for keen and mischievous ears were about them; but they were close together, and a kind of ecstasy possessed them both. The sunshine was so golden, the quivering visible air so full of soft intoxication! They were filled with a reckless animal joy of living—the divine right of youth to exist and be happy. The bars of Elena's cage sank into the warm resounding earth; she wanted to cry aloud her joy to the birds, to hold and kiss the air as it passed. Her face sparkled, her mouth grew full. She looked at Dario, and he dug his spurs into his horse's flanks.

The representatives of many ranchos, their wives and daughters, awaited the party from Los Quervos. But none pushed his way between Dario and Elena that day. And they both enjoyed the races; they were in a mood to enjoy anything. They became excited and shouted with the rest as the vaqueros flew down the field. Dario bet and lost a ranchita, then bet and won another. He won a herd of cattle, a band of horses, a saddle-bag of golden slugs. Surely, fortune smiled on him from the eyes of Elena. When the races were over they galloped down to the ocean and over the cliffs and sands, watching the ponderous waves fling themselves on the rocks, then retreat and rear their crests, to thunder on again.

"The fog!" cried some one. "The fog!" And with shrieks of mock terror they turned their horses' heads and raced down the valley, the fog after them like a phantom tidal wave; but they outstripped it, and sprang from their horses at the corridor of Los Quervos with shouts of triumph and lightly blown kisses to the enemy.

After supper they found eggs piled upon silver dishes in the sala, and with cries of "Cascarón! Cascarón!" they flung them at each other, the cologne and flour and tinsel with which the shells were filled deluging and decorating them.

Doña Jacoba again was in a most gracious mood, and leaned against the wall, an amused smile on her strong serene face. Her husband stood by her, and she indicated Elena by a motion of her fan.

"Is she not beautiful to-night, our little one?" she asked proudly. "See how pink her cheeks are! Her eyes shine like stars. She is the handsomest of all our children, viejo."

"Yes," he said, something like tenderness in his cold blue eyes, "there is no prettier girl on twenty ranchos. She shall marry the finest Englishman of them all."

Elena threw a cascarón directly into Dario's mouth, and although the cologne scalded his throat, he heroically swallowed it, and revenged himself by covering her black locks with flour. The guests, like the children they were, chased each other all over the house, up and down the stairs; the men hid under tables, only to have a sly hand break a cascarón on the back of their heads, and to receive a deluge down the spinal column. The bride chased her dignified groom out into the yard, and a dozen followed. Then Dario found his chance.

Elena was after him, and as they passed beneath a tree he turned like a flash and caught her in his arms and kissed her. For a second she tried to free herself, mindful that her sisters had not kissed their lovers until they stood with them in the chapel; but she was made for love, and in a moment her white arms were clinging about his neck. People were shouting around them; there was time for but few of the words Dario wished to say.

"Thou must write me a little note every day," he commanded. "Thy brother's coat, one that he does not wear, hangs behind the door in my room. To-morrow morning thou wilt find a letter from me in the pocket. Let me find one there, too. Kiss me again, consuelo de mi alma!" and they separated suddenly, to speak no more that night.

VII

The next morning, when Elena went to Joaquin's room to make the bed, she found Dario's note in the pocket of the coat, but she had had no opportunity to write one herself. Nor did she have time to read his until after dinner, although it burned her neck and took away her appetite. When the meal was over, she ran down to the willows and read it there, then went straight to the favourite lounging-place of an old vaquero who had adored her from the days when she used to trot about the rancho holding his forefinger, or perch herself upon his shoulder and command him to gallop.

He was smoking his pipe, and he looked up in some wonder as she stood before him, flushed and panting, her eyes darting apprehensive glances.

"Pedro," she said imperiously, "get down on thy hands and knees."

Pedro was the colour of tanned leather and very hairy, but his face beamed with good-nature. He put his pipe between his teeth and did as he was bidden. Elena produced the pencil and paper she had managed to purloin from her father's table, and kneeling beside her faithful vaquero, wrote a note on his back. It took her a long time to coin that simple epistle, for she never had written a love-letter before. But Pedro knelt like a rock, although his old knees ached. When the note was finished she thrust it into her gown, and patted Pedro on the head.

"I love thee, my old man. I will make thee a new salve for thy rheumatism, and a big cake."

As she approached the house her mother stood on the corridor watching the young people mount, and Elena shivered as she met a fiery and watchful eye. Yesterday had been a perfect day, but the chill of fear touched this. She sprang on her horse and went with the rest to the games. Her brother Joaquin kept persistently by her side, and Dario thought it best not to approach her. She took little interest in the games.

The young men climbed the greased pole amidst soft derisive laughter. The greased pig was captured by his tail in a tumult of excitement, which rivalled the death of the bull, but Elena paid no attention. It was not until Dario, restive with inaction, entered the lists for the buried rooster, and by its head twisted it from the ground as his horse flew by, that she was roused to interest; and as many had failed, and as his was the signal victory of the day, he rode home somewhat consoled.

That night, as Dario and Elena danced the contradanza together, they felt the eyes of Doña Jacoba upon them, but he dared to whisper:—

"To-morrow morning I speak with thy father. Our wedding-day must be set before another sun goes down."

"No, no!" gasped Elena; but for once Dario would not listen.

VIII

As soon as Elena had left his room next morning, Dario returned and read the note she had put in her brother's pocket. It gave him courage, his dreamy eyes flashed, his sensitive mouth curved proudly. As soon as dinner was over he followed Don Roberto up to the library. The old man stretched himself out in the long brass and leather chair which had been imported from England for his comfort, and did not look overjoyed when his guest begged a few moments' indulgence.

"I am half asleep," he said. "Is it about those cattle? Joaquin knows as much about them as I do."

Dario had not been asked to sit down, and he stood before Don Roberto feeling a little nervous, and pressing his hand against the mantelpiece.

"I do not wish to speak of cattle, señor."

"No? What then?" The old man's face was flushed with wine, and his shaggy brows were drooping heavily.

"It is—it is about Elena."

The brows lifted a little.

"Elena?"

"Yes, señor. We love each other very much. I wish to ask your permission that we may be married."

The brows went up with a rush; the stiff hairs stood out like a roof above the cold angry eyes. For a moment Don Roberto stared at the speaker as if he had not heard; then he sprang to his feet, his red face purple.

"Get out of my house, you damned vagabond!" he shouted. "Go as fast as God Almighty'll let you. You marry my daughter—you damned Indian! I wouldn't give her to you if you were pure-blooded Castilian, much less to a half-breed whelp. And you have dared to make love to her. Go! Do you hear? Or I'll kick you down the stairs!"

Dario drew himself up and looked back at his furious host with a pride that matched his own. The blood was smarting in his veins, but he made no sign and walked down the stair.

Don Roberto went at once in search of his wife. Failing to find her, he walked straight into the sala, and taking Elena by the arm before the assembled guests, marched her upstairs and into her room, and locked the door with his key.

Elena fell upon the floor and sobbed with rebellious mortification and terror. Her father had not uttered a word, but she knew the meaning of his summary act, and other feelings soon gave way to despair. That she should never see Dario Castañares again was certain, and she wept and prayed with all the abandon of her Spanish nature. A picture of the Virgin hung over the bed, and she raised herself on her knees and lifted her clasped hands to it beseechingly. With her tumbled hair and white face, her streaming upturned eyes and drawn mouth, she looked more like the Mater Dolorosa than the expressionless print she prayed to.

"Mary! Mother!" she whispered, "have mercy on thy poor little daughter. Give him to me. I ask for nothing else in this world. I do not care for gold or ranchos, only to be his wife. I am so lonely, my mother, for even Santiago thinks of so many other things than of me. I only want to be loved, and no one else will ever love me who can make me love him. Ay! give him to me! give him to me!" And she threw herself on her face once more, and sobbed until her tears were exhausted. Then she dragged herself to the window and leaned over the deep seat. Perhaps she might have one glimpse of him as he rode away.

She gave a little cry of agony and pleasure. He was standing by the gates of the corral whilst the vaqueros rounded up the cattle he had bought. His arms were folded, his head hung forward. As he heard her cry, he lifted his face, and Elena saw the tears in his eyes. For the moment they gazed at each other, those lovers of California's long-ago, while the very atmosphere quivering between them seemed a palpable barrier. Elena flung out her arms with a sudden passionate gesture; he gave a hoarse cry, and paced up and down like a race-horse curbed with a Spanish bit. How to have one last word with her? If she were behind the walls of the fort of Monterey it would be as easy. He dared not speak from where he was. Already the horses were at the door to carry the eager company to a fight between a bull and a bear. But he could write a note if only he had the materials. It was useless to return to his room, for Joaquin was there; and he hoped never to see that library again. But was there ever a lover in whom necessity did not develop the genius of invention? Dario flashed upward a glance of hope, then took from his pocket a slip of the rice-paper used for making cigaritos. He burnt a match, and with the charred stump scrawled a few lines.

> Elena! Mine! Star of my life! My sweet! Beautiful and idolized. Farewell! Farewell, my darling! My heart is sad. God be with thee.
>
> DARIO

He wrapped the paper about a stone, and tied it with a wisp of grass. With a sudden flexile turn of a wrist that had thrown many a reata, he flung it straight through the open window. Elena read the meaningless phrases, then fell insensible to the floor.

IX

It was the custom of Doña Jacoba personally to oversee her entire establishment every day, and she always went at a different hour, that laziness might never feel sure of her back. To-day she visited the rancheria immediately after dinner, and looked through every hut with her piercing eyes. If the children were dirty, she peremptorily ordered their stout mammas to put them into the clean clothes which her bounty had provided. If a bed was unmade, she boxed the ears of the owner and sent her spinning across the room to her task. But she found little to scold about; her discipline was too rigid. When she was satisfied that the huts were in order, she went down to the great stone tubs sunken in the ground, where the women were washing in the heavy shade of the willows. In their calico gowns they made bright bits of colour against the drooping green of the trees.

"Maria," she cried sharply, "thou art wringing that fine linen too harshly. Dost thou wish to break in pieces the bridal clothes of thy señorita? Be careful, or I will lay the whip across thy shoulders."

She walked slowly through the willows, enjoying the shade. Her fine old head was held sternly back, and her shoulders were as square as her youngest son's; but she sighed a little, and pressed a willow branch to her face with a caressing motion. She looked up to the gray peak standing above its fellows, bare, ugly, gaunt. She was not an imaginative woman, but she always had felt in closer kinship with that solitary peak than with her own blood. As she left the wood and saw the gay cavalcade about to start—the burnished horses, the dashing caballeros, the girls with their radiant faces and jaunty habits—she sighed again. Long ago she had been the bride of a brilliant young Mexican officer for a few brief years; her youth had gone with his life.

She avoided the company and went round to the buildings at the back of the house. Approving here, reproaching
there, she walked leisurely through the various rooms where
the Indians were making lard, shoes, flour, candles. She was
in the chocolate manufactory when her husband found her.

"Come—come at once," he said. "I have good news for
thee."

She followed him to his room, knowing by his face that
tragedy had visited them. But she was not prepared for the
tale he poured forth with violent interjections of English
and Spanish oaths. She had detected a flirtation between her
daughter and the uninvited guest, and not approving of
flirtations, had told Joaquin to keep his eyes upon them
when hers were absent; but that the man should dare and
the girl should stoop to think of marriage wrought in her a
passion to which her husband's seemed the calm flame of a
sperm-candle.

"What!" she cried, her hoarse voice breaking. "What! A
half-breed aspire to a Cortez!" She forgot her husband's
separateness with true Californian pride. "My daughter and
the son of an Indian! Holy God! And she has dared—she has
dared! The little imbecile! The little—But," and she gave a
furious laugh, "she will not forget again."

She caught the greenhide reata from the nail and went
up the stair. Crossing the library with heavy tread, as if she
would stamp her rage through the floor, she turned the key
in the door of her daughter's room and strode in. The girl
still lay on the floor, although consciousness had returned. As
Elena saw her mother's face she cowered pitifully. That
terrible temper seldom dominated the iron will of the
woman, but Santiago had shaken it a few days ago, and
Elena knew that her turn had come.

Doña Jacoba shut the door and towered above her
daughter, red spots on her face, her small eyes blazing, an
icy sneer on her mouth. She did not speak a word. She
caught the girl by her delicate shoulder, jerked her to her
feet, and lashed her with the heavy whip until screams min-

gled with the gay laughter of the parting guests. When she had beaten her until her own arm ached, she flung her on the bed and went out and locked the door.

Elena was insensible again for a while, then lay dull and inert for hours. She had a passive longing for death. After the suffering and the hideous mortification of that day there seemed no other climax. The cavalcade rode beneath her windows once more, with their untired laughter, their splendid vitality. They scattered to their rooms to don their bright evening gowns, then went to the dining room and feasted.

After supper Francisca unlocked Elena's door and entered with a little tray on her hand. Elena refused to eat, but her sister's presence roused her, and she turned her face to the wall and burst into tears.

"Nonsense!" said Francisca, kindly. "Do not cry, my sister. What is a lover? The end of a little flirtation? My father will find thee a husband—a strong fair English husband like mine. Dost thou not prefer blondes to brunettes, my sister? I am sorry my mother beat thee, but she has such a sense of her duty. She did it for thy good, my Elena. Let me dress thee in thy new gown, the white silk with the pale blue flowers. It is high in the neck and long in the sleeves, and will hide the marks of the whip. Come down and play cascarones and dance until dawn and forget all about it."

But Elena only wept on, and Francisca left her for more imperative duties.

The next day the girl still refused to eat, although Doña Jacoba opened her mouth and poured a cup of chocolate down her throat. Late in the afternoon Santiago slipped into the room and bent over her.

"Elena," he whispered hurriedly. "Look! I have a note for thee."

Elena sat upright on the bed, and he thrust a piece of folded paper into her hand. "Here it is. He is in San Luis Obispo and says he will stay there. Remember it is but a few miles away. My—"

Elena sank back with a cry, and Santiago blasphemed in English. Doña Jacoba unlocked her daughter's hand, took the note, and led Santiago from the room. When she reached her own, she opened a drawer and handed him a canvas bag full of gold.

"Go to San Francisco and enjoy yourself," she said. "Interfere no farther between your sister and your parents, unless you prefer that reata to gold. Your craft cannot outwit mine, and she will read no notes. You are a foolish boy to set your sense against your mother's. I may seem harsh to my children, but I strive on my knees for their good. And when I have made up my mind that a thing is right to do, you know that my nature is of iron. No child of mine shall marry a lazy vagabond who can do nothing but lie in a hammock and bet and gamble and make love. And a half-breed! Mother of God! Now go to San Francisco, and send for more money when this is gone."

Santiago obeyed. There was nothing else for him to do.

Elena lay in her bed, scarcely touching food. Poor child! her nature demanded nothing of life but love, and that denied her, she could find no reason for living. She was not sport-loving like Joaquin, nor practical like Francisca, nor learned like Santiago, nor ambitious to dance through life like her many nieces. She was but a clinging unreasoning creature, with warm blood and a great heart. But she no longer prayed to have Dario given her. It seemed to her that after such suffering her saddened and broken spirit would cast its shadows over her happiest moments, and she longed only for death.

Her mother, becoming alarmed at her increasing weakness, called in an old woman who had been midwife and doctor of the county for half a century. She came, a bent and bony woman who must have been majestic in her youth. Her front teeth were gone, her face was stained with dark splashes like the imprint of a pre-natal hand. Over her head she wore a black shawl; and she looked enough like a witch to frighten her patients into eternity had they not been so well used to her. She prodded Elena all over as if the girl were a loaf of bread and her knotted fingers sought a lump of flour in the dough.

"The heart," she said to Doña Jacoba with sharp emphasis, her back teeth meeting with a click, as if to proclaim their existence. "I have no herbs for that," and she went back to her cabin by the ocean.

That night Elena lifted her head suddenly. From the hill opposite her window came the sweet reverberation of a guitar: then a voice, which, though never heard by her in song before, was as unmistakable as if it had serenaded beneath her window every night since she had known Dario Castañares.

EL ÚLTIMO ADIÓS

Si dos con el alma
Se amaron en vida,
Y al fin se separan
En vida las dos;
Sabeis que es tan grande
Le pena sentida
Que con esa palabra
Se dicen adiós.
Y en esa palabra
Que breve murmura,
Ni verse prometen
Niamarse se juran;
Que en esa palabra
Se dicen adiós.
No hay queja mas honda,
Suspiro mas largo;
Que aquellas palabras
Que dicen adiós.
Al fin ha llegado,
La muerte en la vida;
Al fin para entrambos

Muramos los dos:
Al fin ha llegado
La hora cumplida,
Del último adiós.
Ya nunca en la vida,
Gentil compañera
Ya nunca volveremos
A vernos los dos:
Por eso es tan triste
Mi acento postrere,
Por eso es tan triste
El último adiós.—

They were dancing downstairs; laughter floated through the open windows. Francisca sang a song of the bull-fight, in her strong high voice; the frogs chanted their midnight mass by the creek in the willows; the coyotes wailed; the owls hooted. But nothing could drown that message of love. Elena lit a candle and held it at arm's length before the window. She knew that its ray went straight through the curtains to the singer on the hill, for his voice broke suddenly, then swelled forth in passionate answer. He sat there until dawn singing to her; but the next night he did not come, and Elena knew that she had not been his only audience.

X

The week of festivity was over; the bridal pair, the relatives, the friends went away. Quiet would have taken temporary possession of Los Quervos had it not been for the many passing guests lavishly entertained by Don Roberto.

And still Elena lay in her little iron bed, refusing to get out of it, barely eating, growing weaker and thinner every day. At the end of three weeks Doña Jacoba was thoroughly alarmed, and Don Roberto sent Joaquin to San Francisco for a physician.

The man of science came at the end of a week. He asked many questions, and had a long talk with his patient. When he left the sick-room, he found Don Roberto and Doña Jacoba awaiting him in the library. They were ready to accept his word as law, for he was an Englishman, and had won high reputation during his short stay in the new country.

He spoke with curt directness. "My dear sir, your child is dying because she does not wish to live. People who write novels call it dying of a broken heart; but it does not make much difference about the name. Your child is acutely sensitive, and has an extremely delicate constitution—predisposition to consumption. Separation from the young man she desires to marry has prostrated her to such an extent that she is practically dying. Under existing circumstances she will not live two months, and, to be brutally frank, you will have killed her. I understand that the young man is well-born on his father's side, and possessed of great wealth. I see no reason why she should not marry him. I shall leave her a tonic, but you can throw it out of the window unless you send for the young man," and he walked down the stair and made ready for his departure.

Don Roberto translated the verdict to his wife. She turned very gray, and her thin lips pressed each other. But she bent her head. "So be it," she said; "I cannot do murder. Send for Dario Castañares."

"And tell him to take her to perdition," roared the old man. "Never let me see her again."

He went down the stair, filled a small bag with gold, and gave it to the doctor. He found Joaquin and bade him go for Dario, then shut himself in a remote room, and did not emerge until late that day.

Doña Jacoba sent for the maid, Malia.

"Bring me one of your frocks," she said, "a set of your undergarments, a pair of your shoes and stockings." She walked about the room until the girl's return, her face terrible in its repressed wrath, its gray consciousness of defeat. When Malia came with the garments she told her to follow, and went into Elena's room and stood beside the bed.

"Get up," she said. "Dress thyself in thy bridal clothes. Thou art going to marry Dario Castañares to-day."

The girl looked up incredulously, then closed her eyes wearily.

"Get up," said her mother. "The doctor has said that we must let our daughter marry the half-breed or answer to God for her murder." She turned to the maid: "Malia, go downstairs and make a cup of chocolate and bring it up. Bring, too, a glass of angelica."

But Elena needed neither. She forgot her desire for death, her misgivings of the future; she slipped out of bed, and would have taken a pair of silk stockings from the chest, but her mother stopped her with an imperious gesture, and handed her the coarse shoes and stockings the maid had brought. Elena raised her eyes wonderingly, but drew them on her tender feet without complaint. Then her mother gave her the shapeless undergarments, the gaudy calico frock, and she put them on. When the maid returned with the chocolate and wine, she drank both. They gave her colour and strength; and as she stood up and faced her mother, she had never looked more beautiful nor more stately in the silken gowns that were hers no longer.

"There are horses' hoofs," said Doña Jacoba. "Leave thy father's house and go to thy lover."

Elena followed her from the room, walking steadily, although she was beginning to tremble a little. As she passed the table in the library, she picked up an old silk handkerchief of her father's and tied it about her head and face. A smile was on her lips, but no joy could crowd the sadness from her eyes again. Her spirit was shadowed; her nature had come to its own.

They walked through the silent house, and to Elena's memory came the picture of that other bridal, when the very air shook with pleasure and the rooms were jewelled with beautiful faces; but she would not have exchanged her own nuptials for her sister's calm acceptance.

When she reached the veranda she drew herself up and turned to her mother with all that strange old woman's implacable bearing.

"I demand one wedding present," she said. "The green-hide reata. I wish it as a memento of my mother."

Doña Jacoba, without the quiver of a muscle, walked into her husband's room and returned with the reata and handed it to her. Then Elena turned her back upon her father's house and walked down the road through the willows. Dario did not notice the calico frock or the old handkerchief about her head. He bent down and caught her in his arms and kissed her, then lifting her to his saddle, galloped down the road to San Luis Obispo. Doña Jacoba turned her hard old face to the wall.

"On the Divide" is one of the earliest stories penned by the celebrated Willa Cather (1873–1947), having first appeared in the Overland Monthly *in 1896. A simple, powerful tale of a Nebraska farmer named Canute Canuteson, it foreshadows such of her major works as* O Pioneers! *(1913) and* My Ántonia *(1918), which deal with similar material in much the same locale. The vast midwestern prairie is also the setting of her Pulitzer Prize-winning novel* One of Ours *(1922). A different western background, that of New Mexico and its Indian population, is the focal point of Miss Cather's most famous novel,* Death Comes for the Archbishop *(1927).*

On the Divide

WILLA CATHER

Near Rattlesnake Creek, on the side of a little draw stood Canute's shanty. North, east, south, stretched the level Nebraska plain of long rust-red grass that undulated constantly in the wind. To the west the ground was broken and rough, and a narrow strip of timber wound along the turbid, muddy little stream that had scarcely ambition enough to crawl over its black bottom. If it had not been for the few stunted cottonwoods and elms that grew along its banks, Canute would have shot himself years ago. The Norwegians are a timber-loving people, and if there is even a turtle pond with a few plum bushes around it they seem irresistibly drawn toward it.

As to the shanty itself, Canute had built it without aid of any kind, for when he first squatted along the banks of Rattlesnake Creek there was not a human being within twenty miles. It was built of logs split in halves, the chinks stopped with mud and plaster. The roof was covered with earth and was supported by one gigantic beam curved in the shape of a round arch. It was almost impossible that any tree had ever grown in that shape. The Norwegians used to say that Canute had taken the log across his knee and bent it into the shape he wished. There were two rooms, or rather there was one room with a partition made of ash saplings interwoven and bound together like big straw basket work. In one corner there was a cook stove, rusted and broken. In the other a bed made of unplaned planks and poles. It was fully eight feet long, and upon it was a heap of dark bed clothing. There was a chair and a bench of colossal proportions. There was an ordinary kitchen cupboard with a few cracked dirty dishes in it, and beside it on a tall box a tin washbasin. Under the bed was a pile of pint flasks, some broken, some whole, all empty. On the wood box lay a pair of shoes of almost incredible dimensions. On the wall hung a saddle, a gun, and some ragged clothing, conspicuous among which was a suit of dark cloth, apparently new, with a paper collar carefully wrapped in a red silk handkerchief and pinned to the sleeve. Over the door hung a wolf and a badger skin, and on the door itself a brace of thirty or forty snake skins whose noisy tails rattled ominously every time it opened. The strangest things in the shanty were the wide window-sills. At first glance they looked as though they had been ruthlessly hacked and mutilated with a hatchet, but on closer inspection all the notches and holes in the wood took form and shape. There seemed to be a series of pictures. They were, in a rough way, artistic, but the figures were heavy and labored, as though they had been cut very slowly and with very awkward instruments. There were men plowing with little horned imps sitting on their shoulders and on their horses' heads. There were men praying with a skull hanging over their heads and little demons behind them mocking their attitudes. There were men fighting with big serpents, and skeletons dancing together. All about these pictures were blooming vines and foliage such as never grew in this world, and coiled among the branches of the vines there was always the scaly body of a serpent, and behind every flower there was a serpent's head. It was a veritable Dance of Death by one who had felt its sting. In the wood box lay some boards, and every inch of them was cut up in the same manner. Sometimes the work was very rude and careless, and looked as though the hand of the workman had trembled. It would sometimes have been hard to distinguish the men from their evil geniuses but for one fact, the men were always grave and were either toiling or praying, while the devils were always smiling and dancing. Several of these boards had been split for kindling and it was evident that the artist did not value his work highly.

It was the first day of winter on the Divide. Canute stumbled into his shanty carrying a basket of cobs, and after filling the stove, sat down on a stool and crouched his seven foot frame over the fire, staring drearily out of the window at the wide gray sky. He knew by heart every individual clump of bunch grass in the miles of red shaggy prairie that stretched before his cabin. He knew it in all the deceitful loveliness of its early summer, in all the bitter barrenness of its autumn. He had seen it smitten by all the plagues of Egypt. He had seen it parched by drought, and sogged by rain, beaten by hail, and swept by fire, and in the grasshopper years he had seen it eaten as bare and clean as bones that the vultures have left. After the great fires he had seen it stretch for miles and miles, black and smoking as the floor of hell.

He rose slowly and crossed the room, dragging his big feet heavily as though they were burdens to him. He looked out of the window into the hog corral and saw the pigs burying themselves in the straw before the shed. The leaden gray clouds were beginning to spill themselves, and the snow flakes were settling down over the white leprous patches of frozen earth where the hogs had gnawed even the sod away. He shuddered and began to walk, trampling heavily with his ungainly feet. He was the wreck of ten winters on the Divide and he knew what that meant. Men fear the winters of the Divide as a child fears night or as men in the North Seas fear the still dark cold of the polar twilight.

His eyes fell upon his gun, and he took it down from the wall and looked it over. He sat down on the edge of his bed and held the barrel towards his face, letting his forehead rest upon it, and laid his finger on the trigger. He was perfectly calm, there was neither passion nor despair in his face, but the thoughtful look of a man who is considering. Presently he laid down the gun, and reaching into the cupboard, drew out a pint bottle of raw white alcohol. Lifting it to his lips, he drank greedily. He washed his face in the tin basin and combed his rough hair and shaggy blond beard. Then he stood in uncertainty before the suit of dark clothes that hung on the wall. For the fiftieth time he took them in his hands and tried to summon courage to put them on. He took the paper collar that was pinned to the sleeve of the coat and cautiously slipped it under his rough beard, looking with timid expectancy into the cracked, splashed glass that hung over the bench. With a short laugh he threw it down on the bed, and pulling on his old black hat, he went out, striking off across the level.

It was a physical necessity for him to get away from his cabin once in a while. He had been there for ten years, digging and plowing and sowing, and reaping what little the hail and the hot winds and the frosts left him to reap. Insanity and suicide are very common things on the Divide. They come on like an epidemic in the hot wind season. Those scorching dusty winds that blow up over the bluffs from Kansas seem to dry up the blood in men's veins as they do the sap in the corn leaves. Whenever the yellow scorch creeps down over the tender inside leaves about the ear, then the coroners prepare for active duty; for the oil of the country is burned out and it does not take long for the flame to eat up the wick. It causes no great sensation there when a Dane is found swinging to his own windmill tower, and most of the Poles after they have become too careless and discouraged to shave themselves keep their razors to cut their throats with.

It may be that the next generation on the Divide will be very happy, but the present one came too late in life. It is useless for men that have cut hemlocks among the mountains of Sweden for forty years to try to be happy in a country as flat and gray and as naked as the sea. It is not easy for men that have spent their youth fishing in the Northern seas to be content with following a plow, and men that have served in the Austrian army hate hard work and coarse clothing on the loneliness of the plains, and long for marches and excitement and tavern company and pretty barmaids. After a man has passed his fortieth birthday it is not easy for him to change the habits and conditions of his life. Most men bring with them to the Divide only the dregs of the lives that they have squandered in other lands and among other peoples.

Canute Canuteson was as mad as any of them, but his madness did not take the form of suicide or religion but of alcohol. He had always taken liquor when he wanted it, as all Norwegians do, but after his first year of solitary life he settled down to it steadily. He exhausted whisky after a while, and went to alcohol, because its effects were speedier and surer. He was a big man and with a terrible amount of resistant force, and it took a great deal of alcohol even to move him. After nine years of drinking, the quantities he could take would seem fabulous to an ordinary drinking man. He never let it interfere with his work, he generally drank at night and on Sundays. Every night, as soon as his chores were done, he began to drink. While he was able to sit up he would play on his mouth harp or hack away at his window sills with his jack knife. When the liquor went to his head he would lie down on his bed and stare out of the window until he went to sleep. He drank alone and in solitude not for pleasure or good cheer, but to forget the awful loneliness and level of the Divide. Milton made a sad blunder when he put mountains in hell. Mountains postulate faith and aspiration. All mountain people are religious. It was the cities of the plains that, because of their utter lack of spirituality and the mad caprice of their vice, were cursed of God.

Alcohol is perfectly consistent in its effects upon man. Drunkenness is merely an exaggeration. A foolish man drunk becomes maudlin; a bloody man, vicious; a coarse man, vulgar. Canute was none of these, but he was morose and gloomy, and liquor took him through all the hells of Dante. As he lay on his giant's bed all the horrors of this world and every other were laid bare to his chilled senses. He was a man who knew no joy, a man who toiled in silence and bitterness. The skull and the serpent were always before him, the symbols of eternal futileness and of eternal hate.

When the first Norwegians near enough to be called neighbors came, Canute rejoiced, and planned to escape from his bosom vice. But he was not a social man by nature and had not the power of drawing out the social side of other people. His new neighbors rather feared him because of his great strength and size, his silence and his lowering brows. Perhaps, too, they knew that he was mad, mad from the eternal treachery of the plains, which every spring stretch green and rustle with the promises of Eden, showing long grassy lagoons full of clear water and cattle whose hoofs are stained with wild roses. Before autumn the lagoons are dried up, and the ground is burnt dry and hard until it blisters and cracks open.

So instead of becoming a friend and neighbor to the men that settled about him, Canute became a mystery and a terror. They told awful stories of his size and strength and of the alcohol he drank. They said that one night, when he went out to see to his horses just before he went to bed, his steps were unsteady and the rotten planks of the floor gave way and threw him behind the feet of a fiery young stallion. His foot was caught fast in the floor, and the nervous horse began kicking frantically. When Canute felt the blood trickling down into his eyes from a scalp wound in his head, he roused himself from his kingly indifference, and with the quiet stoical courage of a drunken man leaned forward and wound his arms about the horse's hind legs and held them against his breast with crushing embrace. All through the darkness and cold of the night he lay there, matching strength against strength. When little Jim Peterson went over the next morning at four o'clock to go with him to the Blue to cut wood, he found him so, and the horse was on its fore knees, trembling and whinnying with fear. This is the story the Norwegians tell of him, and if it is true it is no wonder that they feared and hated this Holder of the Heels of Horses.

One spring there moved to the next "eighty" a family that made a great change in Canute's life. Ole Yensen was too drunk most of the time to be afraid of any one, and his wife Mary was too garrulous to be afraid of any one who listened to her talk, and Lena, their pretty daughter, was not afraid of man nor devil. So it came about that Canute went over to take his alcohol with Ole oftener than he took it alone. After a while the report spread that he was going to marry Yensen's daughter, and the Norwegian girls began to tease Lena about the great bear she was going to keep house for. No one could quite see how the affair had come about, for Canute's tactics of courtship were somewhat peculiar. He apparently never spoke to her at all: he would sit for hours with Mary chattering on one side of him and Ole drinking on the other and watch Lena at her work. She teased him, and threw flour in his face and put vinegar in his coffee, but he took her rough jokes with silent wonder, never even smiling. He took her to church occasionally, but the most watchful and curious people never saw him speak to her. He would sit staring at her while she giggled and flirted with the other men.

Next spring Mary Lee went to town to work in a steam laundry. She came home every Sunday, and always ran across to Yensen's to startle Lena with stories of ten cent theaters, firemen's dances, and all the other esthetic delights of metropolitan life. In a few weeks Lena's head was completely turned, and she gave her father no rest until he let her go to town to seek her fortune at the ironing board. From the time she came home on her first visit she began to treat Canute with contempt. She had bought a plush cloak and kid gloves, had her clothes made by the dress-maker, and assumed airs and graces that made the other women of the neighborhood cordially detest her. She generally brought with her a young man from town who waxed his mustache and wore a red necktie, and she did not even introduce him to Canute.

The neighbors teased Canute a good deal until he knocked one of them down. He gave no sign of suffering from her neglect except that he drank more and avoided the other Norwegians more carefully than ever. He lay around in his den and no one knew what he felt or thought, but little Jim Peterson, who had seen him glowering at Lena in church one Sunday when she was there with the town man, said that he would not give an acre of his wheat for Lena's life or the town chap's either; and Jim's wheat was so wondrously worthless that the statement was an exceedingly strong one.

Canute had bought a new suit of clothes that looked as nearly like the town man's as possible. They had cost him half a millet crop; for tailors are not accustomed to fitting giants and they charge for it. He had hung those clothes in his shanty two months ago and had never put them on, partly from fear of ridicule, partly from discouragement, and partly because there was something in his own soul that revolted at the littleness of the device.

Lena was at home just at this time. Work was slack in the laundry and Mary had not been well, so Lena stayed at home, glad enough to get an opportunity to torment Canute once more.

She was washing in the side kitchen, singing loudly as she worked. Mary was on her knees, blacking the stove and

scolding violently about the young man who was coming out
from town that night. The young man had committed the
fatal error of laughing at Mary's ceaseless babble and had
never been forgiven.

"He is no good, and you will come to a bad end by
running with him! I do not see why a daughter of mine
should act so. I do not see why the Lord should visit such a
punishment upon me as to give me such a daughter. There
are plenty of good men you can marry."

Lena tossed her head and answered curtly, "I don't
happen to want to marry any man right away, and so long
as Dick dresses nice and has plenty of money to spend, there
is no harm in my going with him."

"Money to spend? Yes, and that is all he does with it I'll
be bound. You think it very fine now, but you will change
your tune when you have been married five years and see
your children running naked and your cupboard empty. Did
Anne Hermanson come to any good end by marrying a town
man?"

"I don't know anything about Anne Hermanson, but I
know any of the laundry girls would have Dick quick
enough if they could get him."

"Yes, and a nice lot of store clothes huzzies you are too.
Now there is Canuteson who has an 'eighty' proved up and
fifty head of cattle and—"

"And hair that ain't been cut since he was a baby, and
a big dirty beard, and he wears overalls on Sundays, and
drinks like a pig. Besides he will keep. I can have all the fun
I want, and when I am old and ugly like you he can have me
and take care of me. The Lord knows there ain't nobody else
going to marry him."

Canute drew his hand back from the latch as though it
were red hot. He was not the kind of man to make a good
eavesdropper, and he wished he had knocked sooner. He
pulled himself together and struck the door like a battering
ram. Mary jumped and opened it with a screech.

"God! Canute, how you scared us! I thought it was crazy

Lou—he has been tearing around the neighborhood trying to convert folks. I am afraid as death of him. He ought to be sent off, I think. He is just as liable as not to kill us all, or burn the barn, or poison the dogs. He has been worrying even the poor minister to death, and he laid up with the rheumatism, too! Did you notice that he was too sick to preach last Sunday? But don't stand there in the cold, come in. Yensen isn't here, but he just went over to Sorenson's for the mail; he won't be gone long. Walk right in the other room and sit down."

Canute followed her, looking steadily in front of him and not noticing Lena as he passed her. But Lena's vanity would not allow him to pass unmolested. She took the wet sheet she was wringing out and cracked him across the face with it, and ran giggling to the other side of the room. The blow stung his cheeks and the soapy water flew in his eyes, and he involuntarily began rubbing them with his hands. Lena giggled with delight at his discomfiture, and the wrath in Canute's face grew blacker than ever. A big man humiliated is vastly more undignified than a little one. He forgot the sting of his face in the bitter consciousness that he had made a fool of himself. He stumbled blindly into the living room, knocking his head against the door jamb because he forgot to stoop. He dropped into a chair behind the stove, thrusting his big feet back helplessly on either side of him.

Ole was a long time in coming, and Canute sat there, still and silent, with his hands clenched on his knees, and the skin of his face seemed to have shriveled up into little wrinkles that trembled when he lowered his brows. His life had been one long lethargy of solitude and alcohol, but now he was awakening, and it was as when the dumb stagnant heat of summer breaks out into thunder.

When Ole came staggering in, heavy with liquor, Canute rose at once.

"Yensen," he said quietly, "I have come to see if you will let me marry your daughter today."

"Today!" gasped Ole.

"Yes, I will not wait until tomorrow. I am tired of living alone."

Ole braced his staggering knees against the bedstead, and stammered eloquently: "Do you think I will marry my daughter to a drunkard? a man who drinks raw alcohol? a man who sleeps with rattle snakes? Get out of my house or I will kick you out for your impudence." And Ole began looking anxiously for his feet.

Canute answered not a word, but he put on his hat and went out into the kitchen. He went up to Lena and said without looking at her, "Get your things on and come with me!"

The tones of his voice startled her, and she said angrily, dropping the soap, "Are you drunk?"

"If you do not come with me, I will take you—you had better come," said Canute quietly.

She lifted a sheet to strike him, but he caught her arm roughly and wrenched the sheet from her. He turned to the wall and took down a hood and shawl that hung there, and began wrapping her up. Lena scratched and fought like a wild thing. Ole stood in the door, cursing, and Mary howled and screeched at the top of her voice. As for Canute, he lifted the girl in his arms and went out of the house. She kicked and struggled, but the helpless wailing of Mary and Ole soon died away in the distance, and her face was held down tightly on Canute's shoulder so that she could not see whither he was taking her. She was conscious only of the north wind whistling in her ears, and of rapid steady motion and of a great breast that heaved beneath her in quick, irregular breaths. The harder she struggled the tighter those iron arms that had held the heels of horses crushed about her, until she felt as if they would crush the breath from her, and lay still with fear. Canute was striding across the level fields at a pace at which man never went before, drawing the stinging north winds into his lungs in great gulps. He walked with his eyes half closed and looking straight in front of him, only lowering them when he bent his head to blow away the snow flakes that settled on her hair. So it was that Canute took her to his home, even as his bearded barbarian ancestors took the fair frivolous women of the South in their hairy arms and bore them down to their war ships. For ever and anon the soul becomes weary of the conventions that are not of it, and with a single stroke shatters the civilized lies with which it is unable to cope, and the strong arm reaches out and takes by force what it cannot win by cunning.

When Canute reached his shanty he placed the girl upon a chair, where she sat sobbing. He stayed only a few minutes. He filled the stove with wood and lit the lamp, drank a huge swallow of alcohol and put the bottle in his pocket. He paused a moment, staring heavily at the weeping girl, then he went off and locked the door and disappeared in the gathering gloom of the night.

Wrapped in flannels and soaked with turpentine, the little Norwegian preacher sat reading his Bible, when he heard a thundering knock at his door, and Canute entered, covered with snow and his beard frozen fast to his coat.

"Come in, Canute, you must be frozen," said the little man, shoving a chair towards his visitor.

Canute remained standing with his hat on and said quietly, "I want you to come over to my house tonight to marry me to Lena Yensen."

"Have you got a license, Canute?"

"No, I don't want a license. I want to be married."

"But I can't marry you without a license, man. It would not be legal."

A dangerous light came in the big Norwegian's eye. "I want you to come over to my house to marry me to Lena Yensen."

"No, I can't, it would kill an ox to go out in a storm like this, and my rheumatism is bad tonight."

"Then if you will not go I must take you," said Canute with a sigh.

He took down the preacher's bearskin coat and bade

him put it on while he hitched up his buggy. He went out and closed the door softly after him. Presently he returned and found the frightened minister crouching before the fire with his coat lying beside him. Canute helped him put it on and gently wrapped his head in his big muffler. Then he picked him up and carried him out and placed him in his buggy. As he tucked the buffalo robes around him he said: "Your horse is old, he might flounder or lose his way in this storm. I will lead him."

The minister took the reins feebly in his hands and sat shivering with the cold. Sometimes when there was a lull in the wind, he could see the horse struggling through the snow with the man plodding steadily beside him. Again the blowing snow would hide them from him altogether. He had no idea where they were or what direction they were going. He felt as though he were being whirled away in the heart of the storm, and he said all the prayers he knew. But at last the long four miles were over, and Canute set him down in the snow while he unlocked the door. He saw the bride sitting by the fire with her eyes red and swollen as though she had been weeping. Canute placed a huge chair for him, and said roughly —

"Warm yourself."

Lena began to cry and moan afresh, begging the minister to take her home. He looked helplessly at Canute. Canute said simply,

"If you are warm now, you can marry us."

"My daughter, do you take this step of your own free will?" asked the minister in a trembling voice.

"No, sir, I don't, and it is disgraceful he should force me into it! I won't marry him."

"Then, Canute, I cannot marry you," said the minister, standing as straight as his rheumatic limbs would let him.

"Are you ready to marry us now, sir?" said Canute, laying one iron hand on his stooped shoulder. The little preacher was a good man, but like most men of weak body he was a coward and had a horror of physical suffering, although he had known so much of it. So with many qualms of conscience he began to repeat the marriage service. Lena sat sullenly in her chair, staring at the fire. Canute stood beside her, listening with his head bent reverently and his hands folded on his breast. When the little man had prayed and said amen, Canute began bundling him up again.

"I will take you home, now," he said as he carried him out and placed him in his buggy, and started off with him through the fury of the storm, floundering among the snow drifts that brought even the giant himself to his knees.

After she was left alone, Lena soon ceased weeping. She was not of a particularly sensitive temperament, and had little pride beyond that of vanity. After the first bitter anger wore itself out, she felt nothing more than a healthy sense of humiliation and defeat. She had no inclination to run away, for she was married now, and in her eyes that was final and all rebellion was useless. She knew nothing about a license, but she knew that a preacher married folks. She consoled herself by thinking that she had always intended to marry Canute someday, any way.

She grew tired of crying and looking into the fire, so she got up and began to look about her. She had heard queer tales about the inside of Canute's shanty, and her curiosity soon got the better of her rage. One of the first things she noticed was the new black suit of clothes hanging on the wall. She was dull, but it did not take a vain woman long to interpret anything so decidedly flattering, and she was pleased in spite of herself. As she looked through the cupboard, the general air of neglect and discomfort made her pity the man who lived there.

"Poor fellow, no wonder he wants to get married to get somebody to wash up his dishes. Batchin's pretty hard on a man."

It is easy to pity when once one's vanity has been tickled. She looked at the window sill and gave a little shudder and wondered if the man were crazy. Then she sat down again and sat a long time wondering what her Dick and Ole would do.

"It is queer Dick didn't come right over after me. He surely came, for he would have left town before the storm began and he might just as well come right on as go back. If he'd hurried he would have gotten here before the preacher came. I suppose he was afraid to come, for he knew Canuteson could pound him to jelly, the coward!" Her eyes flashed angrily.

The weary hours wore on and Lena began to grow horribly lonesome. It was an uncanny night and this was an uncanny place to be in. She could hear the coyotes howling hungrily a little way from the cabin, and more terrible still were all the unknown noises of the storm. She remembered the tales they told of the big log overhead and she was afraid of those snaky things on the window sills. She remembered the man who had been killed in the draw, and she wondered what she would do if she saw crazy Lou's white face glaring into the window. The rattling of the door became unbearable, she thought the latch must be loose and took the lamp to look at it. Then for the first time she saw the ugly brown snake skins whose death rattle sounded every time the wind jarred the door.

"Canute, Canute!" she screamed in terror.

Outside the door she heard a heavy sound as of a big dog getting up and shaking himself. The door opened and Canute stood before her, white as a snow drift.

"What is it?" he asked kindly.

"I am cold," she faltered.

He went out and got an armful of wood and a basket of cobs and filled the stove. Then he went out and lay in the snow before the door. Presently he heard her calling again.

"What is it?" he said, sitting up.

"I'm so lonesome, I'm afraid to stay in here all alone."

"I will go over and get your mother." And he got up.

"She won't come."

"I'll bring her," said Canute grimly.

"No, no. I don't want her, she will scold all the time."

"Well, I will bring your father."

She spoke again and it seemed as though her mouth was

close up to the key-hole. She spoke lower than he had ever heard her speak before, so low that he had to put his ear up to the lock to hear her.

"I don't want him either, Canute—I'd rather have you."

For a moment she heard no noise at all, then something like a groan. With a cry of fear she opened the door, and saw Canute stretched in the snow at her feet, his face in his hands, sobbing on the door step.

A Yellow Man and a White

ELEANOR GATES

Fong Wu sat on the porch of his little square-fronted house, chanting into the twilight. Across his padded blouse of purple silk lay his *sam-yen* banjo. And as, from time to time, his hymn to the Three Pure Ones was prolonged in high, fine quavers, like the uneven, squeaky notes of a woman's voice, he ran his left hand up the slender neck of the instrument, rested a long nail of his right on its taut, snake's-skin head, and lightly touched the strings; then, in quick, thin tones, they followed the song to Sang-Ching.

The warm shadows of a California summer night were settling down over the wooded hills and rocky gulches about Fong Wu's, and there was little but his music to break the silence. Long since, the chickens had sleepily sought perches in the hen yard, with its high wall of rooty stumps and shakes, and on the branches of the Digger pine that towered beside it. Up the dry creek bed, a mile away, twinkled the lights of Whiskeytown; but no sounds from the homes of the white people came down to the lonely Chinese. If his clear treble was interrupted, it was by the cracking of a dry branch as a cottontail sped past on its way to a stagnant pool, or it was by a dark-emboldened coyote, howling, dog-like, at the moon which, white as the snow that eternally coifs the Sierras, was just rising above their distant, cobalt line.

One year before, Fong Wu, heavily laden with his effects, had slipped out of the stage from Redding and found his way to a forsaken, ramshackle building below Whiskeytown. His coming had proved of small interest. When the news finally got about that "a monkey" was living in "Sam Kennedy's old place," it was thought, for a while, that laundering, thereafter, would be cheaply done. This hope, however, was soon dispelled. For, shortly after his arrival, as Fong Wu asked at the grocery store for mail, he met Radigan's inquiry of "You do my washee, John?" with a grave shake of the head. Similar questions from others were met, later, in a similar way. Soon it became generally known that the "monkey at Sam Kennedy's" did not do washing; so he was troubled no further.

Yet if Fong Wu did not work for the people of Whiskeytown, he was not, therefore, idle. Many a sunrise found him wandering through the chaparral thickets back of his house, digging here and there in the red soil for roots and herbs. These he took home, washed, tasted, and, perhaps, dried. His mornings were mainly spent in cooking for his abundantly supplied table, in tending his fowls and house, and in making spotless and ironing smooth various undergarments —generous of sleeve and leg.

But of an afternoon, all petty duties were laid aside, and he sorted carefully into place upon his shelves numerous little bunches and boxes of dried herbs and numerous tiny phials of pungent liquid that had come to him by post; he filled wide sheets of foolscap with vertical lines of queer characters and consigned them to big, plainly addressed, well-stamped envelopes; he scanned closely the last newspapers from San Francisco, and read from volumes in divers tongues, and he pored over the treasured Taoist book, "The Road to Virtue."

Sunday was his one break in the week's routine. Then, the coolies who panned or cradled for gold in the tailings of near-by abandoned mines, gathered at Fong Wu's. On such occasions, there was endless, lively chatter, a steady exchange of barbering—one man scraping another clean, to be, in turn, made hairless in a broad band about the poll and on cheek and chin—and much consuming of tasty chicken, dried fish, pork, rice, and melon seeds. To supplement all this, Fong Wu recounted the news: the arrival of a consul in San Francisco, the raid on a slave- or gambling-den, the progress of a tong war under the very noses of the baffled police, and the growth of Coast feeling against the continued, quiet immigration of Chinese. But of the social or political affairs of the Flowery Kingdom—of his own land beyond the sea—Fong Wu was consistently silent.

Added to his Sunday responsibilities as host and purveyor of news, Fong Wu had others. An ailing countryman, whether seized with malaria or suffering from an injury, found ready and efficient attention. The bark of dogwood, properly cooked, gave a liquid that killed the ague; and oil from a diminutive bottle, or a red powder whetted upon the skin with a silver piece, brought out the soreness of a bruise.

Thus, keeping his house, herb-hunting, writing, studying, entertaining, doctoring, Fong Wu lived on at Whiskeytown.

Each evening, daintily manipulating ivory chopsticks, he ate his supper of rice out of a dragon-bordered bowl. Then, when he had poured tea from a pot all gold-encrusted —a cluster of blossoms nodding in a vase at his shoulder the while—he went out upon the porch of the square-fronted house.

And there, as now, a scarlet-buttoned cap on his head, his black eyes soft with dreaming, his richly wrought sandals tapping the floor in time, his long queue—a smooth, shining serpent—in thick coils about his tawny neck, Fong Wu thrummed gently upon the three-stringed banjo, and, in peace, chanted into the twilight.

Flying hoofs scattered the gravel on the strip of road before Fong Wu's. He looked through the gloom and saw a horse flash past, carrying a skirted rider toward Whiskeytown. His song died out. He let his banjo slip down until its round head rested between his feet. Then he turned his face up the gulch.

Despite the dusk, he knew the traveler: Mrs. Anthony Barrett, who, with her husband, had recently come to live in a house near Stillwater. Every evening, when the heat was over, she went by, bound for the day's mail at the post-office. Every evening, in the cool, Fong Wu saw her go, and sometimes she gave him a friendly nod.

Her mount was a spirited, mouse-dun mustang, with crop-ears, a roached mane, and the back markings of a mule. She always rode at a run, sitting with easy erectness. A wide army hat rested snugly on her fair hair, and shaded a white forehead and level-looking eyes. But notwithstanding the sheltering brim, on her girlish face were set the glowing, scarlet seals of wind and sun.

As he peered townward after her, Fong Wu heard the hurrying hoof-beats grow gradually fainter and fainter—and cease. Presently the moon topped the pines on the foot-hills behind him, bathing the gulch in light. The road down which she would come sprang into view. He watched its farthest open point. In a few moments the hoof-beats began again. Soon the glint of a light waist showed through the trees. Next, horse and rider rounded a curve at hand. Fong Wu leaned far forward.

And then, just as the mustang gained the strip of road before the square-fronted house, it gave a sudden, unlooked-for, outward leap, reared with a wild snort, and, whirling, dashed past the porch—riderless.

With an exclamation, Fong Wu flung his banjo aside and ran to the road. There under a manzanita bush, huddled and still, lay a figure. He caught it up, bore it to the porch, and put it gently down.

A brief examination, made with the deftness practise gives, showed him that no bones were broken. Squatting beside the unconscious woman, he next played slowly with his long-nailed fingers upon her pulse. Its beat reassured him. He lighted a lamp and held it above her. The scarlet of her cheeks was returning.

The sight of her, who was so strong and active, stretched weak and fainting, compelled Fong Wu into spoken comment. "The petal of a plum blossom," he said compassionately, in his own tongue.

She stirred a little. He moved back. As, reviving, she opened her eyes, they fell upon him. But he was half turned away, his face as blank and lifeless as a mask.

She gave a startled cry and sat up. "Me hurtee?" she asked him, adopting pidgin-English. "Me fallee off?"

Fong Wu rose. "You were thrown," he answered gravely.

She colored in confusion. "Pardon me," she said, "for speaking to you as if you were a coolie." Then, as she got feebly to her feet—"I believe my right arm is broken."

"I have some knowledge of healing," he declared; "let me look at it." Before she could answer, he had ripped the sleeve away. "It is only a sprain," he said. "Wait." He went inside for an amber liquid and bandages. When he had laved the injured muscles, he bound them round.

"How did it happen?" she asked, as he worked. He was so courteous and professional that her alarm was gone.

"Your horse was frightened by a rattler in the road. I heard it whir."

She shuddered. "I ought to be thankful that I didn't come my cropper on it," she said, laughing nervously.

He went inside again, this time to prepare a cupful of

herbs. When he offered her the draught, she screwed up her face over its nauseating fumes.

"If that acts as strongly as it tastes," she said, after she had drunk it, "I'll be well soon."

"It is to keep away inflammation."

"Oh! Can I go now?"

"Yes. But tomorrow return, and I will look at the arm." He took the lamp away and replaced his red-buttoned cap with a black felt hat. Then he silently preceded her down the steps to the road. Only when the light of her home shone plainly ahead of them, did he leave her.

They had not spoken on the way. But as he bowed a good night, she addressed him. "I thank you," she said. "And may I ask your name?"

"Kwa"—he began, and stopped. Emotion for an instant softened his impassive countenance. He turned away. "Fong Wu," he added, and was gone.

The following afternoon the crunch of cart wheels before the square-fronted house announced her coming. Fong Wu closed "The Book of Virtue," and stepped out upon the porch.

A white man was seated beside her in the vehicle. As she sprang from it, light-footed and smiling, and mounted the steps, she indicated him politely to the Chinese.

"This is my husband," she said. "I have told him how kind you were to me last night."

Fong Wu nodded.

Barrett hastened to voice his gratitude. "I certainly am very much obliged to you," he said. "My wife might have been bitten by the rattler, or she might have lain all night in pain if you hadn't found her. And I want to say that your treatment was splendid. Why, her arm hasn't swollen or hurt her. I'll be hanged if I can see—you're such a good doctor—why you stay in this—"

Fong Wu interrupted him. "I will wet the bandage with medicine," he said, and entered the house.

They watched him with some curiosity as he treated the

sprain and studied the pulse. When he brought out her second cup of steaming herbs, Mrs. Barrett looked up at him brightly.

"You know we're up here for Mr. Barrett's health," she said. "A year or so after we were married, he was hurt in a railway collision. Since then, though his wounds healed nicely, he has never been quite well. Dr. Lord, our family physician, prescribed plenty of rough work, and a quiet place, far from the excitement of a town or city. Now, all this morning, when I realized how wonderful it was that my arm wasn't aching, I've been urging my husband— what do you suppose?—to come and be examined by you!"

Fong Wu, for the first time, looked fully at the white man, marking the sallow, clayey face, with its dry, lined skin, its lusterless eyes and drooping lids.

Barrett scowled at his wife. "Nonsense, dear," he said crossly; "you know very well that Lord would never forgive me."

"But Fong Wu might help you," she declared.

Fong Wu's black eyes were still fixed searchingly upon the white man. Before their scrutiny, soul-deep, the other's faltered and fell.

"You might help him, mightn't you, Fong Wu?" Mrs. Barrett repeated.

An expression, curious, keen, and full of meaning, was the answer. Then, "I might if he—" Fong Wu said, and paused.

Past Mrs. Barrett, whose back was toward her husband, the latter had shot a warning glance. "Come, come, Edith," he cried irritably; "let's get home."

Mrs. Barrett emptied her cup bravely. "When shall we call again?" she asked.

"You need not come again," Fong Wu replied. "Each day you have only to dampen the bandages from these." He handed her a green-flowered box containing twelve tiny compartments; in each was a phial.

"And I sha'n't have to take any more of this—this

awful stuff?" she demanded gaily, giving back the cup.
"No."

"Ah! And now, I want to thank you again, with all my
heart. Here"—she reached into the pocket of her walking-
skirt—"here is something for your trouble." Two double-
eagles lay on her open palm.

Fong Wu frowned at them. "I take no money," he said,
a trifle gruffly. And as she got into the cart, he closed the
door of his home behind him.

It was a week before Mrs. Barrett again took up her
rides for the mail. When she did, Fong Wu did not fail to be
on his porch as she passed. For each evening, as she cantered
up the road, spurring the mustang to its best paces, she
reined to speak to him. And he met her greetings with
unaccustomed good humor.

Then she went by one morning before sunrise, riding
like the wind. A little later she repassed, whipping her horse
at every gallop. Fong Wu, called to his door by the clatter,
saw that her face was white and drawn. At noon, going up
to the post-office, he heard a bit of gossip that seemed to bear
upon her unwonted trip. Radigan was rehearsing it excit-
edly to his wife, and the Chinese busied himself with his mail
and listened—apparently unconcerned.

"I c'n tell you she ain't afraid of anythin', that Mrs.
Barrett," the post-master was saying; "neither th' cayuse she
rides or a critter on two legs. An' that fancy little drug-clerk
from 'Frisco got it straight from th' shoulder."

"S-s-sh!" admonished his wife, from the back of the
office. "Isn't there some one outside?"

"Naw, just th' chink from Kennedy's. Well, as I remarked, she did jus' light into that dude. 'It was criminal!'
she says, an' her eyes snapped like a whip; 'it was criminal!
an' if I find out for sure that you are guilty, I'll put you where
you'll never do it again.' Th' young gent smirked at her an'
squirmed like a worm. 'You're wrong, Mrs. Barrett,' he says,
lookin' like th' meek puppy he is, 'an' you'll have t' look some
place else for th' person that done it.' But she wouldn't

talk no longer—jus' walked out, as mad as a hornet."

"Well, well," mused Mrs. Radigan. "I wonder what 'twas all about. 'Criminal,' she said, eh? That's funny!" She walked to the front of the office and peeked through the wicket. But no one was loitering near except Fong Wu, and his face was the picture of dull indifference.

That night, long after the hour for Mrs. Barrett's regular trip, and long past the time for his supper-song, Fong Wu heard slow, shuffling steps approach the house. A moment afterward, the knob of his door was rattled. He put out his light and slipped a knife into his loose sleeve.

After some fumbling and moving about on the porch, a man called out to him. He recognized the voice.

"Fong Wu! Fong Wu!" it begged. "Let me in. I want to see you; I want to ask you for help—for something I need. Let me in; let me in."

Fong Wu, without answering, relit his lamp, and, with the air of one who is at the same time both relieved and a witness of the expected, flung the door wide.

Then into the room, writhing as if in fearful agony, his hands palsied, his face a-drip and, except for dark blotches about the mouth, green-hued, his eyes wild and sunken, fell, rather than tottered, Anthony Barrett.

"Fong Wu," he pleaded, from the floor at the other's feet, "you helped my wife when she was sick, now help me. I'm dying! I'm dying! Give it to me, for God's sake! give it to me." He caught at the skirt of Fong Wu's blouse.

The Chinese retreated a little, scowling. "What do you want?" he asked.

A paroxysm of pain seized Barrett. He half rose and stumbled forward. "You know," he panted, "you know. And if I don't have some, I'll die. I can't get it anywhere else. She's found me out, and scared the drug-clerk. Oh, just a little, old man, just a little!" He sank to the floor again.

"I can give you nothing," said Fong Wu bluntly. "I do not keep—what you want."

With a curse, Barrett was up again. "Oh, you don't," he

screamed, leering frenziedly. "You yellow devil! You al-
mond-eyed pigtail! But I know you do! And I must have it.
Quick! quick!" He hung, clutching, on the edge of Fong
Wu's wide ironing-table, an ashen wreck.

Fong Wu shook his head.

With a cry, Barrett came at him and seized his lean
throat. "You damned highbinder!" he gasped. "You saddle-
nosed monkey! You'll get me what I want or I'll give you
away. Don't I know why you're up here in these woods, with
your pretty clothes and your English talk? A-*ha!* You bet I
do! You're hiding, and you're wanted"—he dropped his
voice to a whisper—"the tongs would pay head-money for
you. If you don't give it to me, I'll put every fiend in 'Frisco
on your trail."

Fong Wu had caught Barrett's wrists. Now he cast him
to one side. "Tongs!" he said with a shrug, as if they were
beneath his notice. And "Fiends!" he repeated contemptuously, a taunt in his voice.

The white man had fallen prone and was grovelling
weakly. "Oh, I won't tell on you," he wailed imploringly. "I
won't, I won't, Fong Wu; I swear it on my honor."

Fong Wu grunted and reached to a handy shelf. "I will
make a bargain with you," he said craftily; "first, you are to
drink what I wish."

"Anything! anything!" Barrett cried.

From a box of dry herbs, long untouched, the Chinese
drew out a handful. There was no time for brewing. Out-
raged nature demanded instant relief. He dropped them
into a bowl, covered them with water, and stirred swiftly.
When the stems and leaves were broken up and well mixed,
he strained a brown liquid from them and put it to the
other's lips.

"Drink," he commanded, steadying the shaking head.

Barrett drank, unquestioningly.

Instantly the potion worked. Calmed as if by a miracle,
made drowsy to a point where speech was impossible, the
white man, tortured but a moment before, tipped sleepily
into Fong Wu's arms. The Chinese waited until a full effect

was secured, when he lifted his limp patient to the blanket-covered ironing-table. Then he went out for fuel, built a fire, and, humming softly—with no fear of waking the other—sat down to watch the steeping of more herbs.

What happened next at the square-fronted house was the unexpected. Again there was a sound of approaching footsteps, again some one gained the porch. But this time there was no pausing to ask for admission, there were no weak requests for aid. A swift hand felt for the knob and found it; a strong arm pushed at the unlocked door. And through it, bareheaded, with burning eyes and blanched cheeks, her heavy riding-whip dangling by a thong from her wrist, came the wife of Anthony Barrett.

Just across the sill she halted and swept the dim room. A moment, and the burning eyes fell upon the freighted ironing-table. She gave a piercing cry.

Fong Wu neither spoke nor moved.

After the first outburst, she was quiet—the quiet that is deliberative, threatening. Then she slowly closed her fingers about the whip butt. Fixing her gaze in passionate anger upon him, she advanced a few steps.

"*So it was you,*" she said, and her voice was hollow.

To that he made no sign, and even his colorless face told nothing.

She came forward a little farther, and sucked in a long, deep breath. "You *dog* of a Chinaman!" she said at last, and struck her riding-skirt.

Fong Wu answered silently. With an imperative gesture, he pointed out the figure on the ironing-table.

She sprang to her husband's side and bent over him. Presently she began to murmur to herself. When, finally, she turned, there were tears on her lashes, she was trembling visibly, and she spoke in whispers.

"Was I wrong?" she demanded brokenly. "I *must* have been. He's not had it; I can tell by his quick, easy breathing. And his ear has a faint color. You are trying to help him! I know! I know!"

A gleaming white line showed between the yellow of Fong Wu's lips. He picked up a rude stool and set it by the table. She sank weakly upon it, letting the whip fall.

"Thank God! thank God!" she sobbed prayerfully, and buried her face in her arms.

Throughout the long hours that followed, Fong Wu, from the room's shadowy rear, sat watching. He knew sleep did not come to her. For now and then he saw her shake from head to heel convulsively, as he had seen men in his own country quiver beneath the scourge of bamboos. Now and then, too, he heard her give a stifled moan, like the protest of a dumb creature. But in no other ways did she bare her suffering. Quietly, lest she wake her husband, she fought out the night.

Only once did Fong Wu look away from her. Then, in anger and disgust his eyes shifted to the figure on the table. "The petal of a plum blossom"—he muttered in Chinese—"the petal of a plum blossom beneath the hoofs of a pig!" And again his eyes dwelt upon the grief-bowed wife.

But when the dawn came stealing up from behind the purple Sierras, and Mrs. Barrett raised her wan face, he was studiously reviewing his rows of bottles, outwardly unaware of her presence.

"Fong Wu," she said, in a low voice, "when will he wake?"

"When he is rested; at sunrise, maybe, or at noon."

"And then?"

"He will be feeble. I shall give him more medicine, and he will sleep again."

He rose and busied himself at the fire. Soon he approached her, bringing the gold-encrusted teapot and a small, handleless cup.

She drank thirstily, filling and emptying the cup many times. When she was done, she made as if to go. "I shall see that everything is all right at home," she told him. "After that, I shall come back." She stooped and kissed her husband tenderly.

Fong Wu opened the door for her, and she passed out. In the road, unhitched, but waiting, stood the mustang. She mounted and rode away.

When she returned, not long afterward, she was a new woman. She had bathed her face and donned a fresh waist. Her eyes were alight, and the scarlet was again flaming in her cheeks. Almost cheerfully, and altogether hopefully, she resumed her post at the ironing-table.

It was late in the afternoon before Barrett woke. But he made no attempt to get up, and would not eat. Fong Wu administered another dose of herbs, and without heeding his patient's expostulations. The latter, after seeking his wife's hand, once more sank into sleep.

Just before sunset, Fong Wu, who scorned to rest, prepared supper. Gratefully Mrs. Barrett partook of some tender chicken and rice cakes. When darkness shut down, they took up their second long vigil.

But it was not the vigil of the previous night. She was able to think of other things than her husband's condition and the doom that, of a sudden, had menaced her happiness. Her spirits having risen, she was correspondingly impatient of a protracted, oppressive stillness, and looked about for an interruption, and for diversion. Across from her, a celestial patrician in his blouse of purple silk and his red-buttoned cap, sat Fong Wu. Consumed with curiosity —now that she had time to observe him closely—she longed to lift the yellow, expressionless mask from his face —a face which might have patterned that of an oriental sphinx. At midnight, when he approached the table to satisfy himself of Barrett's progress, and to assure her of it, she essayed a conversation.

Glancing up at his laden shelves, she said, "I have been noticing your medicines, and how many kinds there seem to be."

"For each ailment that is visited upon man, earth offers a cure," he answered. "Life would be a mock could Death, unchallenged, take it."

"True. Have you found in the earth, then, the cure for each ailment of man?"

"For most, yes. They seek yet, where I learned the art of healing, an antidote for the cobra's bite. I know of no other they lack."

"Where you were taught they must know more than we of this country know."

Fong Wu gave his shoulders a characteristic shrug.

"But," she continued, "you speak English so perfectly. Perhaps you were taught that in this country."

"No—in England. But the other, I was not."

"In England! Well!"

"I went there as a young man."

"But these herbs, these medicines you have—they did not come from England, did they?"

He smiled. "Some came from the hills at our back." Then, crossing to his shelves and reaching up, "This"—he touched a silk-covered package—"is from Sumbawa in the Indian Sea; and this"—his finger was upon the cork of a phial —"is from Feng-shan, Formosa; and other roots are taken in winter from the lake of Ting-ting-hu, which is then dry; and still others come from the far mountains of Chamur."

"Do you know," Mrs. Barrett said tentatively, "I have always heard that Chinese doctors give horrid things for medicine—sharks' teeth, frogs' feet, lizards' tails, and—all sorts of dreadful things."

Fong Wu proffered no enlightenment.

"I am glad," she went on, "that I have learned better."

After a while she began again: "Doubtless there is other wonderful knowledge, besides that about doctoring, which Chinese gentlemen possess."

Fong Wu gave her a swift glance. "The followers of Laou-Tsze know many things," he replied, and moved into the shadows as if to close their talk.

Toward morning, when he again gave her some tea, she spoke of something that she had been turning over in her mind for hours.

"You would not take money for helping me when I was hurt," she said, "and I presume you will refuse to take it for what you are doing now. But I should like you to know that Mr. Barrett and I will always, always be your friends. If"— she looked across at him, no more a part of his rude surroundings than was she—"if ever there comes a time when we could be of use to you, you have only to tell us. Please remember that."

"I will remember."

"I cannot help but feel," she went on, and with a sincere desire to prove her gratitude, rather than to pry out any secret of his, "that you do not belong here—that you are in more trouble than I am. For what can a man of your rank have to do in a little town like this!"

He was not displeased with her. "The ancient sage," he said slowly, "mounted himself upon a black ox and disappeared into the western wilderness of Thibet. Doubtless others, too, seek seclusion for much thinking."

"But you are not the hermit kind," she declared boldly. "You belong to those who stay and fight. Yet here you are, separated from your people and your people's graves— alone and sorrowful."

"As for my living people, they are best without me; as for my people dead, I neither worship their dust nor propitiate devils. The wise one said, 'Why talk forever on of men who are long gone?' "

"Yet—" she persisted.

He left the stove and came near her. "You are a woman, but you know much. You are right. My heart is heavy for a thing I cannot do—for the shattered dreams of the men of Hukwang." He beat his palms together noiselessly, and moved to and fro on soft sandals. "Those dreams were of a young China that was to take the place of the old—but that died unborn."

She followed his words with growing interest. "I have heard of those dreams," she answered; "they were called 'reform.' "

"Yes. And now all the dreamers are gone. They had voyaged to glean at Harvard, Yale, Cornell, and in the halls of Oxford. There were 'five loyal and six learned,' and they shed their blood at the Chen Chih Gate. One there was who died the death that is meted a slave at the court of the Son of Heaven. And one there was"—his face shrank up, as if swiftly aging; his eyes became dark, upturning slits; as one who fears pursuit, he cast a look behind him—"and one there was who escaped beyond the blood-bathed walls of the Hidden City and gained the Sumatra Coast. Then, leaving Perak, in the Straits Settlements, he finally set foot upon a shore where men, without terror, may reach toward higher things."

"And was he followed?" she whispered, comprehending.

"He fled quietly. For long are the claws of the she-panther crouched on the throne of the Mings."

Both fell silent. The Chinese went back to the stove, where the fire was dying. The white woman, wide awake, and lost in the myriad of scenes his tale had conjured, sat by the table, for once almost forgetful of her charge.

The dragging hours of darkness past, Anthony Barrett found sane consciousness. He was pale, yet strengthened by his long sleep, and he was hungry. Relieved and overjoyed, Mrs. Barrett ministered to him. When he had eaten and drunk, she helped him from the table to the stool, and thence to his feet. Her arm about him, she led him to the door. Fong Wu had felt his pulse and it had ticked back the desired message, so he was going home.

"Each night you are to come," Fong Wu said, as he bade them good-by. "And soon, very soon, you may go from here to the place from which you came."

Mrs. Barrett turned at the door. A plea for pardon in misjudging him, thankfulness for his help, sympathy for his exile—all these shone from her eyes. But words failed her. She held out her hand.

He seemed not to see it; he kept his arms at his sides.

"A dog of a Chinaman" had best not take a woman's hand.

She went out, guiding her husband's footsteps, and helped him climb upon the mustang from the height of the narrow porch. Then, taking the horse by the bridle, she moved away down the slope to the road.

Fong Wu did not follow, but closed the door gently and went back to the ironing-table. A handkerchief lay beside it —a dainty linen square that she had left. He picked it up and held it before him by two corners. From it there wafted a faint, sweet breath.

Fong Wu let it flutter to the floor. "The perfume of a plum petal," he said softly, in English; "the perfume of a plum petal."

First published in 1909, "The Walking Woman" is one of Mary Austin's best, if little known, stories. Like much of her work, it deals with Indians and the California wilderness, and like all her work, it is sensitive, mysterious, and quite powerful. Mary Hunter Austin (1868–1934) wrote many fine books about the early American West, among them The Land of Little Rain *(1903),* Lost Borders *(1909), and* One-Smoke Stories *(1934). The noted western writer Jack Schaefer once said about her, "It is impossible to read any [fiction] by Mary Austin and not know at once that there was greatness in her."*

The Walking Woman

MARY AUSTIN

The first time of my hearing of her was at Temblor. We had come all one day between blunt, whitish cliffs rising from mirage water, with a thick, pale wake of dust billowing from the wheels, all the dead wall of the foothills sliding and shimmering with heat, to learn that the Walking Woman had passed us somewhere in the dizzying dimness, going down to the Tulares on her own feet. We heard of her again in the Carrisal, and again at Adobe Station, where she had passed a week before the shearing, and at last I had a glimpse of her at the Eighteen-Mile House as I went hurriedly northward on the Mojave stage; and afterward sheepherders at whose camps she slept, and cowboys at rodeos, told me as much of her way of life as they could understand. Like enough they told her as much of mine. That was very little. She was the Walking Woman, and no one knew her name, but because she was a sort of whom men speak respectfully, they called her to her face Mrs. Walker, and she answered to it if she was so inclined. She came and went about our western world on no discoverable errand, and whether she had some place of refuge where she lay by in the interim, or whether between her seldom, unaccountable appearances in our quarter she went on steadily walking, was never learned. She came and went, oftenest in a kind of muse of travel which the untrammeled space begets, or at rare intervals flooding wondrously with talk, never of herself, but of things she had known and seen. She must have seen some rare happenings, too—by report. She was at Maverick the time of the Big Snow, and at Tres Piños when they brought home the body of Morena; and if anybody could have told whether De Borba killed Mariana for spite or defence, it would have been she, only she could not be found when most wanted. She was at Tunawai at the time of the cloudburst, and if she had cared for it could have known most desirable things of the ways of trail-making, burrow-habiting small things.

All of which should have made her worth meeting, though it was not, in fact, for such things I was wishful to meet her; and as it turned out, it was not of these things we talked when at last we came together. For one thing, she was a woman, not old, who had gone about alone in a country where the number of women is as one in fifteen. She had eaten and slept at the herders' camps, and laid by for days at one-man stations whose masters had no other touch of human kind than the passing of chance prospectors, or the halting of the tri-weekly stage. She had been set on her way by teamsters who lifted her out of white, hot desertness and put her down at the crossing of unnamed ways, days distant from anywhere. And through all this she passed unarmed and unoffended. I had the best testimony to this, the witness of the men themselves. I think they talked of it because they were so much surprised at it. It was not, on the whole, what they expected of themselves.

Well I understand that nature which wastes its borders
with too eager burning, beyond which rim of desolation it
flares forever quick and white, and have had some inkling
of the isolating calm of a desire too high to stoop to satisfaction. But you could not think of these things pertaining to
the Walking Woman; and if there were ever any truth in the
exemption from offense residing in a frame of behavior
called ladylike, it should have been inoperative here. What
this really means is that you get no affront so long as your
behavior in the estimate of the particular audience invites
none. In the estimate of the particular audience—conduct
which affords protection in Mayfair gets you no considera-
tion in Maverick. And by no canon could it be considered
ladylike to go about on your own feet, with a blanket and a
black bag and almost no money in your purse, in and about
the haunts of rude and solitary men.

There were other things that pointed the wish for a
personal encounter with the Walking Woman. One of them
was the contradiction of reports of her—as to whether she
was comely, for example. Report said yes, and again, plain
to the point of deformity. She had a twist to her face, some
said; a hitch to one shoulder; they averred she limped as she
walked. But by the distance she covered she should have
been straight and young. As to sanity, equal incertitude. On
the mere evidence of her way of life she was cracked; not
quite broken, but unserviceable. Yet in her talk there was
both wisdom and information, and the word she brought
about trails and water-holes was as reliable as an Indian's.

By her own account she had begun by walking off an
illness. There had been an invalid to be taken care of for
years, leaving her at last broken in body, and with no recourse but her own feet to carry her out of that predicament. It seemed there had been, besides the death of her
invalid, some other worrying affairs, upon which, and the
nature of her illness, she was never quite clear, so that it
might well have been an unsoundness of mind which drove
her to the open, sobered and healed at last by the large

soundness of nature. It must have been about that time that she lost her name. I am convinced that she never told it because she did not know it herself. She was the Walking Woman, and the country people called her Mrs. Walker. At the time I knew her, though she wore short hair and a man's boots, and had a fine down over all her face from exposure to the weather, she was perfectly sweet and sane.

I had met her occasionally at ranch-houses and road-stations, and had got as much acquaintance as the place allowed; but for the things I wished to know there wanted a time of leisure and isolation. And when the occasion came we talked altogether of other things.

It was at Warm Springs in the Little Antelope I came upon her in the heart of a clear forenoon. The spring lies off a mile from the main trail, and has the only trees about it in that country. First you come upon a pool of waste full of weeds of a poisonous dark green, every reed ringed about the water-level with a muddy white incrustation. Then the three oaks appear staggering on the slope, and the spring sobs and blubbers below them in ashy-colored mud. All the hills of that country have the down plunge toward the desert and back abruptly toward the Sierra. The grass is thick and brittle and bleached straw-color toward the end of the season. As I rode up the swale of the spring I saw the Walking Woman sitting where the grass was deepest, with her black bag and blanket, which she carried on a stick, beside her. It was one of those days when the genius of talk flows as smoothly as the rivers of mirage through the blue hot desert morning.

You are not to suppose that in my report of a Borderer I give you the words only, but the full meaning of the speech. Very often the words are merely the punctuation of thought; rather, the crests of the long waves of inter-communicative silences. Yet the speech of the Walking Woman was fuller than most.

The best of our talk that day began in some dropped word of hers from which I inferred that she had had a child.

I was surprised at that, and then wondered why I should have been surprised, for it is the most natural of all experiences to have children. I said something of that purport, and also that it was one of the perquisites of living I should be least willing to do without. And that led to the Walking Woman saying that there were three things which if you had known you could cut out all the rest, and they were good any way you got them, but best if, as in her case, they were related to and grew each one out of the others. It was while she talked that I decided that she really did have a twist to her face, a sort of natural warp or skew into which it fell when it was worn merely as a countenance, but which disappeared the moment it became the vehicle of thought or feeling.

The first of the experiences the Walking Woman had found most worth while had come to her in a sand-storm on the south slope of Tehachapi in a dateless spring. I judged it should have been about the time she began to find herself, after the period of worry and loss in which her wandering began. She had come, in a day pricked full of intimations of a storm, to the camp of Filon Geraud, whose companion shepherd had gone a three days' *pasear* to Mojave for supplies. Geraud was of great hardihood, red-blooded, of a full laughing eye, and an indubitable spark for women. It was the season of the year when there is a soft bloom on the days, but the nights are cowering cold and the lambs tender, not yet flockwise. At such times a sand-storm works incalculable disaster. The lift of the wind is so great that the whole surface of the ground appears to travel upon it slantwise, thinning out miles high in air. In the intolerable smother the lambs are lost from the ewes; neither dogs nor man make headway against it.

The morning flared through a horizon of yellow smudge, and by mid-forenoon the flock broke.

"There were but the two of us to deal with the trouble," said the Walking Woman. "Until that time I had not known how strong I was, nor how good it is to run when running is worth while. The flock travelled down the wind, the sand bit our faces; we called, and after a time heard the words broken and beaten small by the wind. But after a while we had not to call. All the time of our running in the yellow dusk of day and the black dark of night, I knew where Filon was. A flock-length away, I knew him. Feel? What should I feel? I knew. I ran with the flock and turned it this way and that as Filon would have.

"Such was the force of the wind that when we came together we held by one another and talked a little between pantings. We snatched and ate what we could as we ran. All that day and night until the next afternoon the camp kit was not out of the cayaques. But we held the flock. We herded them under a butte when the wind fell off a little, and the lambs sucked; when the storm rose they broke, but we kept upon their track and brought them together again. At night the wind quieted, and we slept by turns; at least Filon slept. I lay on the ground when my turn was and beat with the storm. I was no more tired than the earth was. The sand filled in the creases of the blanket, and where I turned, dripped back upon the ground. But we saved the sheep. Some ewes there were that would not give down their milk because of the worry of the storm, and the lambs died. But we kept the flock together. And I was not tired."

The Walking Woman stretched out her arms and clasped herself, rocking in them as if she would have hugged the recollection to her breast.

"For you see," said she, "I worked with a man, without excusing, without any burden on me of looking or seeming. Not fiddling or fumbling as women work, and hoping it will all turn out for the best. It was not for Filon to ask, Can you, or Will you. He said, Do, and I did. And my work was good. We held the flock. And that," said the Walking Woman, the twist coming in her face again, "is one of the things that make you able to do without the others."

"Yes," I said; and then, "What others?"

"Oh," she said, as if it pricked her, "the looking and the seeming."

And I had not thought until that time that one who had the courage to be the Walking Woman would have cared! We sat and looked at the pattern of the thick crushed grass on the slope, wavering in the fierce noon like the waterings in the coat of a tranquil beast; the ache of a world-old bitterness sobbed and whispered in the spring. At last—

"It is by the looking and the seeming," said I, "that the opportunity finds you out."

"Filon found out," said the Walking Woman. She smiled; and went on from that to tell me how, when the wind went down about four o'clock and left the afternoon clear and tender, the flock began to feed, and they had out the kit from the cayaques, and cooked a meal. When it was over, and Filon had his pipe between his teeth, he came over from his side of the fire, of his own notion, and stretched himself on the ground beside her. Of his own notion. There was that in the way she said it that made it seem as if nothing of that sort had happened before to the Walking Woman, and for a moment I thought she was about to tell me of the things I wished to know; but she went on to say what Filon had said to her of her work with the flock. Obvious, kindly things, such as any man in sheer decency would have said, so that there must have something more gone with the words to make them so treasured of the Walking Woman.

"We were very comfortable," said she, "and not so tired as we expected to be. Filon leaned upon his elbow. I had not noticed until then how broad he was in the shoulders, and how strong in the arms. And we had saved the flock together. We felt that. There was something that said together, in the slope of his shoulders toward me. It was around his mouth and on the cheek high up under the shine of his eyes. And under the shine the look—the look that said, 'We are of one sort and one mind'—his eyes that were the color of the flat water in the toulares—do you know the look?"

"I know it."

"The wind was stopped and all the earth smelled of

dust, and Filon understood very well that what I had done with him I could not have done so well with another. And the look—the look in the eyes—"

"Ah-ah—!"

I have always said, I will say again, I do not know why at this point the Walking Woman touched me. If it were merely a response to my unconscious throb of sympathy, or the unpremeditated way of her heart to declare that this, after all, was the best of all indispensable experiences; or if in some flash of forward vision, encompassing the unimpassioned years, the stir, the movement of tenderness were for *me*—but no; as often as I have thought of it, I have thought of a different reason, but no conclusive one, why the Walking Woman should have put out her hand and laid it on my arm.

"To work together, to love together," said the Walking Woman, withdrawing her hand again, "there you have two of the things; the other you know."

"The mouth at the breast," said I.

"The lips and the hands," said the Walking Woman. "The little, pushing hands and the small cry." There ensued a pause of fullest understanding, while the land before us swam in the noon, and a dove in the oaks behind the spring began to call. A little red fox came out of the hills and lapped delicately at the pool.

"I stayed with Filon until the fall," said she. "All that summer in the Sierras, until it was time to turn south on the trail. It was a good time, and longer than he could be expected to have loved one like me. And besides, I was no longer able to keep the trail. My baby was born in October."

Whatever more there was to say to this, the Walking Woman's hand said it, straying with remembering gesture to her breast. There are so many ways of loving and working, but only one way of the first-born. She added after an interval that she did not know if she would have given up her walking to keep at home and tend him, or whether the thought of her son's small feet running beside her in the trails would have driven her to the open again. The baby had not stayed long enough for that. "And whenever the wind blows in the night," said the Walking Woman, "I wake and wonder if he is well covered."

She took up her black bag and her blanket; there was the ranch-house at Dos Palos to be made before night, and she went as outliers do, without a hope expressed of another meeting and no word of good-bye. She was the Walking Woman. That was it. She had walked off all sense of society-made values, and, knowing the best when the best came to her, was able to take it. Work—as I believed; love—as the Walking Woman had proved it; a child—as you subscribe to it. But look you: it was the naked thing the Walking Woman grasped, not dressed and tricked out, for instance, by preju-dices in favor of certain occupations; and love, man love, taken as it came, not picked over and rejected if it carried no obligation of permanency; and a child; *any* way you get it, a child is good to have, say nature and the Walking Woman; to have it and not to wait upon a proper concur-rence of so many decorations that the event may not come at all.

At least one of us is wrong. To work and to love and to bear children. *That* sounds easy enough. But the way we live establishes so many things of much more importance.

Far down the dim, hot valley, I could see the Walking Woman with her blanket and black bag over her shoulder. She had a queer, sidelong gait, as if in fact she had a twist all through her.

Recollecting suddenly that people called her lame, I ran down to the open place below the spring where she had passed. There in the bare, hot sand the track of her two feet bore evenly and white.

B. M. (for Bertha Muzzy) Bower was the first woman, and one of the few women altogether, to write traditional cowboy stories. Beginning with Chip of the Flying U *(1906), she published more than seventy novels of the old and new West, most of them featuring the often humorous adventures of Chip and his comrades on the Flying U Ranch. Bower (1871–1940) was extremely popular during the first four decades of this century, but at her best she was more than simply an entertainer. Her depiction of western women and of the day-to-day working conditions of cowboys provides a vivid and realistic picture of life on a large Montana cattle ranch circa 1880–1910. (She knew whereof she wrote: She herself was born and reared on just such a ranch.) Among the best of her novels are* Lonesome Land *(1912),* The Flying U's Last Stand *(1915), and* The Haunted Hills *(1934).*

The Lamb of the Flying U

B. M. BOWER

———————◆———————

With disgust in his heart, Chip Bennett rode to town. It was not that he disliked either the trip or the town, but that worry had taken some of the joy out of life for the Flying U's new foreman and unforeseen responsibilities were heavy upon him.

For two days the Flying U herd had grazed within five miles of Dry Lake waiting for box cars along the Montana Central line, which had never come. Then two of his men had gone to town on a spree and continued missing. They were not top hands, but every hand is vital in shipping time so Chip rode forth to bring them back, or acquire reasonable facsimiles thereof.

He found the two deserters in Rusty Brown's place. One was blissfully snoring an alcoholic snore in the back room, clearly hopeless. The other was holding down a poker table with his elbows and taking money from everyone in sight.

To him, Chip addressed himself, his temper even more irritated by the railway agent's report that no box cars had yet split the horizon.

"Are you goin' to quit this foolishness and come back to camp?" Chip demanded.

The request was more righteous than diplomatic. The poker fiend leered at Chip from under his tilted hat brim and suggestively rattled an astonishing pile of blue chips.

"Go back to camp?" he mocked. "What for? Forty a month, when I'm four hundred to the good since last night an' folks just forcin' money on me with both hands? Why shucks, I just found my true vocation."

"You mean vacation," said Chip and turned away with finality. He dismissed both men from his mind and cast around for substitutes as he went through the door.

" 'Scuse me," said a voice behind him. "Are you lookin' for men?"

Chip twisted his head to look down at a dandified little fellow who was staring up at him with bright blue eyes. He wore a silk shirt, neatly pressed gray trousers held up by a russet belt and gleaming tan shoes. Golden hair, freshly barbered, just showed its edges under an immaculate Panama hat. The foreman was slightly taken aback.

"Sorry, son," he muttered. "I want men to *work*."

The fashion plate flashed a pair of dimples that any woman would have envied.

"My mammy done tol' me," he murmured, "never to judge a book by its cover."

"We were speakin' of *men*," Chip reminded him. "And work. I can't quite see you punchin' cows in them duds. Look me up when you've growed a bit, son."

A hand on his arm stopped him as he was turning away again.

"Say, did you ever hear of old Eagle Creek Smith of the Cross L?"

"Why, sure," said Chip. "I—"

"—Or of Rowdy Vaughan, or a fellow up on Milk River they call Pink?"

"I'll say!" Chip turned back. "I've heard tell of Eagle Creek Smith. And Pink—they say he's a bronc fighter and a little devil. Why?"

The blonde shoved his Panama back and grinned into Chip's face.

"Nothin'," he said. "I'm glad to meet yuh. I'm Pink."

Chip digested that in silence, his suddenly alerted eyes measuring the slender figure from Panama to polished shoe tips.

"You travelin' in disguise?" he asked.

"It's a long story," Pink said, and sighed. He found an empty case, upended it in the shade and sat down to roll a cigarette. "I helped Rowdy Vaughan trail a herd of Cross L stock across the Canadian line, bein' a friend of his an' anxious to do him a favor. But I ain't long in our friendly neighbor country to the north when one of them bone-headed grangers gets unfriendly and I has to scatter his features around a bit to pound some sense into his skull.

"Then up rises a bunch of redcoats and I fogs it back across the line just about one jump ahead of the Mounties. I headed back to the Upper Milk River, but the old bunch was gone and it was plumb lonesome, so I sold my saddle an' gatherin' and reformed from punchin' cows."

He grinned his engaging, dimpled grin. "Well, I took the rattlers back to Minnesota and spent all winter with the home folks chewin' the fatted calf. It was mighty nice, too, except that the female critters outnumbered the males back there and each one carries a bear trap an' a pair of handcuffs. I dodged the traps as long as I could, but I seen I was gettin' right gun-shy, so I sloped.

"Besides, even though I'd swore off cowpunchin', I was gettin' plumb mad at all the fences surroundin' everything, and lonesome to straddle a cayuse again. Seems like cow nursin' is in my blood after all. For Pete's sake, old-timer, stake me to a string! You won't be sorry."

Chip sat down on a neighboring case and regarded the dapper little figure. Such words, coming from those girlishly rosy lips, had an odd effect of unreality. But Pink plainly was in earnest. His eyes were pleading and wistful.

"You're it!" said Chip. "You can go right to work. Seems you're the man I've been looking for, only I didn't recognize yuh on sight. We've got a heap of work ahead, and only five decent men in the outfit. It's the Flying U. Those five have worked years for the outfit."

"I sure savvy that bunch," Pink declared sweetly. "I've heard of the Happy Family before. Ain't you one of them?"

Chip grinned. "I was," he admitted, a shade of regret in his voice. "But last spring I got married, and settled down. I'm one of the firm now, so I had to reform. The rest are a pretty salty bunch, but you'll get on all right, seein' you're not the pilgrim you look. Got an outfit?"

"Sure. Bought one, brand new, in the Falls. It's over at the hotel now, with a haughty, buckskin-colored suitcase." Pink pulled the silver belt-buckle of his russet belt straight and patted his pink and blue tie.

"Well, if you're ready, I'll get the horses and we'll drift. By the way, how shall I write you on the book?"

Pink stooped and with his handkerchief carefully wiped the Dry Lake dust from his shiny shoes.

"Yuh won't crawfish on me, if I tell yuh?" he inquired anxiously, standing up.

"Of course not." Chip looked his surprise.

"Well, it ain't *my* fault, but my lawful, legal name is Percival Cadwallader Perkins."

"Wha-at?"

"Percival Cad-*wall*-ader Perkins. Shall I get yuh something to take with it?"

Chip, with his pencil poised in air, stared again. "It's sure a heavy load to carry," he observed solemnly. "How do you spell that second shift?"

Pink told him. "Ain't it fierce?" he wanted to know. "My mother must have sure been light-minded when I was born, but there are two grandfathers who wanted a kid named after 'em. Them two names sure make a combination. You know what Cadwallader means, in the dictionary?"

"Lord, no!" said Chip, putting away his book.

"Battle arranger," Pink told him sadly. "Now, wouldn't that jostle yuh? It's true, too. It has sure arranged a lot of battles for me. When I went to school, I had to lick about six kids a day. At last, seein' the name was mine and I couldn't chuck it, I throwed in with an ex-pugilist and learned how to fight proper. Since then things come easier. I ain't afraid now to wear my name on my hatband."

"I wouldn't," said Chip dryly. "Hike over and get your haughty new war-bag. We've got to be in camp by dinner time."

A mile out Pink looked down at his festal garments and smiled. "I expect I'll be pickings for your Happy Family when they see me in these war-togs," he remarked.

Chip studied him meditatively. "I was just wondering," he said slowly, "if the Happy Family wouldn't be pickings for *you.*"

Pink dimpled and said nothing.

The Happy Family were at dinner when Chip and Pink dismounted by the bed-tent and went over to where the men were sitting. The Happy Family received them with decorous silence. Chip got plate, knife, fork, and spoon and started for the stove.

"Help yourself to the tools, then come over here and fill up," he invited Pink, over his shoulder. "You'll soon get used to things here."

The Happy Family looked guardedly at one another. This wasn't a chance visitor, then. He was going to work!

Weary Davidson, sitting cross-legged in the shade of a wagon wheel, looked at Pink, fumbling shyly among the knives and forks, and whistled absently:

Oh, tell me, pretty maiden,
Are there any more at home like you?

Pink glanced at him quickly and retreated inside the tent. Every man of them knew the stranger had caught Weary's meaning. They smiled discreetly at their plates.

Pink came out with heaped plate and brimming cup, and retired diffidently to the farthest bit of shade, close to Cal Emmett, where he sat down gingerly.

"Going to work for the outfit?" asked Cal politely.

"Yes, sir," answered Pink in his soft treble. "Is it very hard work?"

"It sure is," said Cal plaintively. "What with taming wild broncos and trying to keep the cattle from stampeding, it's a tough life." He sighed deeply and emptied his cup of coffee.

"I—I thought I'd like it," ventured Pink wistfully.

"Purty soon yuh won't. None of us like it."

"Why don't you give it up and get a position doing something else?" Wide-eyed, Pink looked over the rim of his cup.

"Can't. We're most of us escaped desperadoes with a price on our heads." Cal pursed his lips lugubriously. "We're safe here and, if a posse showed up, there's plenty of horses and saddles to make a getaway. We can keep on the dodge a long time, working on roundup, and earn a little money at the same time, so we won't be dead broke."

"Oh!" Pink looked properly impressed. "If it isn't too personal—er—that is, are you—"

"An outlaw?" Cal assisted. "I sure am. I'm wanted for perjury in South Dakota, manslaughter in Texas, and bigamy in Utah. I'm sure bad."

"Oh, I hope not!" Pink looked distressed. "I'm very sorry. I hope the posses won't chase you."

Cal shook his head gravely. "You can't most always tell," he declared gloomily. "I reckon they'll give me a necktie-party some day."

"I've been to necktie-parties myself." Pink brightened visibly. "I don't like them; you always get the wrong girl."

"I don't like 'em either," agreed Cal. "Were you ever lynched?"

Pink moved uneasily. "Not that I remember."

"I was. My gang come along and cut me down just in time. I was leading a gang—"

"Excuse me a minute," Pink interrupted. "I think the overseer is motioning for me."

He hastened to Chip who was standing alone, and asked if he should change his clothes and get ready to go to work.

Chip told him it wouldn't be a bad idea, and Pink, carrying his haughty suitcase and another bulky bundle, disappeared into the bed-tent.

"By golly!" spoke up Slim.

"Where did you pluck that modest flower, Chip?" Jack Bates wanted to know.

Chip sifted some tobacco into a paper. "I picked it in town," he told them. "I hired it to punch cows, and its name is—wait a minute." He put away the tobacco sack, got out his book, and turned the leaves. "Its name is Percival Cadwallader Perkins."

"Oh, mamma! Percival Cadwolloper Perkins!" Weary looked stunned. "Yuh want to double the guard tonight, Chip. That name'll sure stampede the bunch."

"He's sure a sweet young thing—mamma's precious lamb broke out of the home corral!" said Jack Bates. "I'll bet yuh a tall, yellow-haired mamma with flowing widow's weeds'll be out here hunting him up inside a week. We got to be gentle with Cadwolloper."

The reappearance of Pink cut short the discussion. Pink as he had looked before was pretty as a poster. Pink as he reappeared would have driven a rodeo crowd wild with enthusiasm. In the Flying U camp the Happy Family stared at him and drew a long breath. When his back was turned, they shaded their eyes ostentatiously from the blaze of his splendor.

He still wore his Panama, and the dainty pink-and-white striped silk shirt, the gray trousers, and russet-leather belt with silver buckle. But around his neck, nestling under his rounded chin, was a gorgeous rose-pink silk handkerchief, of the hue that he always wore, and that had given him the nickname of "Pink."

His white hands were hidden in a pair of wonderful silk-embroidered buckskin gauntlets. His gray trousers were tucked into number four tan riding boots, with silk-stitched tops. A shiny, new pair of silver-mounted spurs jingled from his heels.

He smiled trustfully at Chip Bennett, got out papers and tobacco and rolled a cigarette. Inwardly he hoped this would not give him away to the Happy Family, whom he felt in honor bound to deceive, and bewailed the smoke-hunger that drove him to take the risk.

The Happy Family, however, was unsuspicious. His pink-and-white prettiness, his clothes, and the baby innocence of his dimples branded him unequivocally in their eyes as the tenderest sort of tenderfoot.

"Get onto the way he rolls 'em—backward!" murmured Weary into Cal's ear.

"If there's anything I hate," Cal remarked irrelevantly to the crowd, "it's to see a girl smoke!"

Pink looked up and opened his lips to speak, then thought better of it. The cavvy came jingling up, and Pink turned to watch. To him the thudding hoofs were sweet music for which he had hungered long.

"Weary, you and Cal better relieve the boys on herd," Chip called. "I'll get you a horse, P—Perkins"—he had almost said "Pink"—"and you can go along with Cal."

"Yes, sir," said Pink, with a docility that would have amazed any who knew him well. He followed Chip out to the corral, where Cal and Weary were already inside with their ropes, among the circling mass.

Chip led out a little cow-pony that could almost day-herd without a rider of any sort, and Pink bridled him before the covertly watching crew. He did not do it as quickly as he might have done, for he deliberately fumbled the buckle and pinned one ear of the pony down flat with the head-stall.

A new saddle, stiff and unbroken, is ever a vexation to

its owner, and its proper adjustment requires time and much language. Pink omitted the language, so that the process took much longer than it should have done. But Cal and Weary, upon their mounts, made cigarettes and waited, with an air of endurance, and gave Pink advice. Somehow he got into the saddle and rode off, with flapping elbows, beside them.

Happy Jack, who had been standing herd disconsolately with two aliens, stared open-mouthed at Pink's approach and rode hastily to camp, fair bursting with questions and comments.

The herd, twelve hundred range-fattened steers, grazed quietly on a hillside a half mile from camp. Pink ran a quick, appraising eye over the bunch estimating correctly the number, and noting their splendid condition.

"Never saw so many cattle in one bunch before, did yuh?" queried Cal, misinterpreting the glance.

Pink shook his head. "Does one man own all those cows?" he wanted to know.

"Yeah—and then some. This is just a few that we're shipping to get 'em out of the way of the real herds."

"How many are there?" asked Pink.

Cal turned his back upon his conscience and winked at Weary. "Oh, only nine thousand, seven hundred and twenty-one," he lied boldly. "Last bunch we gathered was fifty-one thousand six hundred and twenty-nine and a half. Er—the half," he explained hastily in answer to Pink's look of unbelief, "was a calf that we let in by mistake. I caught it and took it back to its mother."

"I should think," Pink ventured hesitatingly, "it would be hard to find its mother. I don't see how you could tell."

"Well," said Cal gravely, sliding sidewise in the saddle, "it's this way. A calf is always just like its mother, hair for hair. This calf had white hind feet, one white ear, and the deuce of diamonds on its left side. All I had to do was ride the range till I found the cow that matched."

"Oh!" Pink looked convinced.

Weary, smiling to himself, rode off to take his station at the other side of the herd. Even the Happy Family must place duty before pleasure, and Cal started down along the nearest edge of the bunch. Pink showed inclination to follow.

"You stay where you're at, Sonny," Cal told him over his shoulder.

"What must I do?" Pink straightened his Panama.

Cal's voice came back to him faintly: "Just don't bother the cattle."

"Good advice, that," Pink commented amusedly. He prepared for a lazy afternoon, and enjoyed every minute.

On the way back to camp at supper time, Pink looked as if he had something on his mind. Cal and Weary exchanged glances.

"I'd like to ask," Pink began timidly, "How you fed that calf—before you found his mother. Didn't he get pretty hungry?"

"Why, I carried a bottle of milk along," Cal lied fluently. "When the bottle went empty I'd catch a cow and milk her. All range cows'll gentle right down, if yuh know the right way to approach 'em. That's a secret that we don't tell everybody."

Pink went diplomatically back to the calf. "Did you carry it in your arms?"

"The calf? Sure. How else would I carry it?" Cal's big, baby-blue eyes matched Pink's for innocence. "I carried that bossy in my arms for three days before I found a cow with white hind feet, one white ear, and the deuce of—er—clubs."

"Diamonds," corrected Pink, drinking in each word greedily.

"That's it: diamonds, on its right hind—er—shoulders."

"The calf's was on its left side," reminded Pink reproachfully. "I don't believe you found the right mother, after all!"

"Yeah, I sure did, all right," contended Cal earnestly. "I know, 'cause she was grateful. When she seen me heave into sight, she come up on the gallop, a-bawling and licked my hand!"

That settled it, of course. Pink dismounted stiffly and walked painfully to the cook-tent. Ten months out of saddle told even upon Pink, and made for extreme discomfort.

When he had eaten hungrily, responding to the ironical sociability of his fellow with a brevity which only his soft voice saved from brusqueness, he unrolled his new bed and lay down with not a thought for the part he was playing. He heard with indifference Weary's remark outside, that "Cadwolloper's about all in. Dayherding's too strenuous for him." The last that came to him, someone was chanting:

> Mamma had a precious lamb,
>   his cheeks were red and rosy;
> And when he rode the festive bronc,
>   he tumbled on his nosey. . . .

There was more, but Pink had gone to sleep, and so missed it.

At sundown he awoke and saddled the night horse Chip Bennett had caught for him, then went to bed again. When shaken gently for middle guard, he dressed sleepily, donned a pair of white angora chaps, and stumbled out into the moonlight.

Guided and coached by Cal, he took his station and began that monotonous round which had been a part of the life he loved best. Though stiff and sore from unaccustomed riding, Pink felt content to be where he was, watching the quiet land and the slumbering herd, with the moon swimming through the drifting gray clouds above. Twice in a complete round, he met Cal going in the opposite direction. At the second round Cal stopped him. "How yuh coming?" he queried cheerfully.

"All right, thank you," said Pink.

"Yuh want to watch out for a lophorned critter over on the other side," Cal went on, in confidential tone. "He keeps trying to sneak out of the bunch. Don't let him get away. If he goes, take after him and fog him back."

"He won't get away from me, if I can help it," Pink promised, and Cal rode on, with Pink smiling maliciously after him.

As Pink neared the opposite side, a dim shape angled slowly out before him, moving aimlessly away from the sleeping herd. Pink followed. Further they moved, and faster. Into a little hollow went the critter and circled. Pink took down his rope, let loose a good ten feet of it, and spurred unexpectedly close.

Whack! The rope landed with precision on the bowed shoulders of Cal. "Yuh will try to fool me, will yuh?" *Whack!* "I guess I can point out a critter that won't stray out uh the bunch again fer a spell!" *Whack!*

Cal straightened in the saddle, gasping astonishment, pulled up with a jerk, and got off in unlovely mood.

"Here's where yuh git yourn, yuh little Mamma's lamb!" Cal cried angrily. "Climb down and get your ears cuffed proper, yuh pink little smart Aleck! Thump *me* with a rope, will yuh."

Pink got down. Immediately they mixed. Presently Cal stretched the long length of him in the grass with Pink sitting comfortably upon his middle. Cal looked up at the dizzying swim of the moon, saw new and uncharted stars, and nearer, dimly revealed in the half-light, the self-satisfied, cherubic face of Pink.

Cal tried to rise and discovered a surprising state of affairs. He could scarcely move. The more he tried the more painful became Pink's hold of him. He blinked and puzzled over the mystery.

"Of all the bone-headed, feeble-minded sons-uh-guns," announced Pink melodiously, "you sure take the sourdough biscuit. For a man who's been lynched and cut down, waitin' for another yank, you certainly are mild! You're plumb tame. A lady could handle yuh. A deep-dyed desperado, wanted for manslaughter in Texas, perjury in South Dakota, and bigamy in Utah! *You* cuff my ears proper? That's a laugh."

Cal, battered as to features and bewildered as to mind, blinked again and grinned feebly.

"Yuh try an old gag that I wore out in Wyoming," went on Pink, warming to the subject. "Loadin' me with stuff that wouldn't bring the heehaw from a sheep-herder! Bah! You're extinct. Say"—Pink's fists kneaded Cal's diaphragm —"are yuh *all* ba-a-d?"

"Oh, Lord! No. I'm dead gentle. Lemme up."

"D'yuh think that critter will quit the bunch ag'in to-night?"

"He ain't liable to," Cal assured him. "Say, who are yuh, anyhow?"

"I'm Percival Cadwallader Perkins. Do you like that name?"

"Ouch! It—it's *bully!*"

"You're a liar," declared Pink, getting up. "Further-more, yuh old chuckle-head, yuh ought to know better than try to run a blazer on me. Yore best girl happens to be my cousin."

Cal scrambled slowly and painfully to his feet. "Then you're Milk River Pink!" He sighed. "I might of guessed it."

"I cannot tell a lie," Pink said. "Only, plain Pink'll do for me. Where do yuh suppose the bunch is by this time?"

They mounted and rode back together. Cal was deeply thoughtful.

"Say," he said suddenly, just as they parted to ride their rounds, "the boys'll be tickled plumb to death. We've been wishin' you'd blow in here ever since the Cross L quit the country."

Pink drew rein and looked back, resting one hand on the cantle. "Yuh needn't break your neck spreading the glad tidings," he warned. "Let 'em find out, the same as you done."

"Sure," agreed Cal, passing his fingers gingerly over his swollen face. "I ain't no hog. I'm willin' for 'em to have some sport with yuh, too."

Next morning, when Cal appeared at breakfast with a slight limp and several inches of cuticle missing from his features, the Happy Family learned that his horse had fallen down with him as he was turning a stray back into the herd.

Chip hid a smile behind his coffee cup.

It was Weary Davidson that afternoon on dayherd who indulged his mendacity for the benefit of Pink. His remarks were but paving-stones for a scheme hatched overnight by the Happy Family.

Weary began by looking doleful and emptying his lungs in sorrowful sighs. Pink rose obediently to the bait and asked him if he felt bad, but Weary only sighed the more. Then, growing confidential, he told how he had dreamed a dream the night before. With picturesque language, he detailed the horror of it. He was guilty of murder, he confessed, and the crime weighed heavily on his conscience.

"Not only that," he went on, "but I know that death is camping on my trail. That dream haunts me. I feel that my days are numbered in words of one syllable. That dream'll come true. You see if it don't!"

"I—I wouldn't worry over just a bad dream, Mr. Weary," comforted Pink.

"But that ain't all. I woke up in a cold sweat, and went outside. And there in the clouds, perfect as life, I seen a posse of men gallopin' up from the South. Down South," he explained sadly, "sleeps my victim—a white-headed, innocent old man. That posse is sure headed for me, Mr. Perkins."

"Still, it was only clouds."

"Wait till I tell yuh," persisted Weary, stubbornly refusing comfort. "When I got up this morning I put my boots on the wrong feet. That's a dead certain sign that my dream'll come true. At breakfast I upset the can of salt, which is bad luck. Mr. Perkins, I'm a lost man."

Pink's eyes widened. He looked like a child listening to a story of goblins. "If I can help you, Mr. Weary, I will," he promised generously.

"Will yuh be my friend? Will yuh let me lean on yuh in my dark hours?" Weary's voice shook with emotion.

Pink said that he would, and he seemed very sympathetic and anxious for Weary's safety. Several times during their shift Weary rode around to where Pink was sitting his horse, and spoke feelingly of his crime and the black trouble that loomed so close and told Pink how much comfort it was to be able to talk confidentially with a friend.

When Pink went out that night to stand his shift, he found Weary at his side instead of Cal. Weary explained that Cal was feeling shaky on account of that fall he had got, and, as Weary couldn't sleep, anyway, he had offered to stand in Cal's place. Pink scented mischief.

This night the moon shone brightly at intervals, with patches of silvery clouds racing before the wind and chasing black splotches of shadows over the sleeping land. For all that, the cattle lay quiet, and the monotony of circling the herd was often broken by Weary and Pink with little talks, as they turned and rode together.

"Mr. Perkins, fate's a-crowding me close," said Weary gloomily, when an hour had gone by. "I feel as if—what's that?"

Voices raised in excited talk came faintly on the wind. With a glance toward the cattle, Weary turned his horse and, beckoning Pink to follow, rode out to the right.

"It's the posse!" he growled. "They'll go to the herd to look for me. Mr. Perkins, the time has come to fly. If only I had a horse that could drift!"

Pink thought he caught the meaning. "Is—is mine any good, Mr. Weary?" he quavered. "If he is, you can have him. I—I'll stay and fool them as—long as I can."

"Perkins," said Weary solemnly, "you're sure all right! Let that posse think you're the man they want for half an hour, and I'm safe. I'll never forget yuh!"

He had not thought of changing horses, but the tempta-
tion mastered him. He was riding a little sorrel, Glory by
name, that could beat even the Happy Family itself for
unexpected deviltry. Yielding to Pink's persuasions, he
changed mounts, clasped Pink's hand affectionately, and
sped away just as the posse appeared over a rise, riding
furiously.

Pink, playing his part, started toward them, then
wheeled and sped away in the direction that would lead
them off Weary's trail. That is, he sped for ten rods or so.
After that he seemed to revolve on an axis. And there was
an astonishing number of revolutions to the minute.

The stirrups were down in the dark somewhere below
the farthest reach of Pink's toes—he never once located
them. But Pink was not known all over Northern Montana
as a bronc peeler for nothing. He surprised Glory even more
than that deceitful bit of horseflesh had surprised Pink.
While his quirt swung methodically, he looked often over his
shoulder for the posse, and wondered why it did not appear.

The posse, however, at that moment had run into trou-
bles of its own. Happy Jack, not having a night horse saddled,
had borrowed one not remarkable for its surefootedness. No
sooner had they sighted their quarry than Jack's horse
stepped in a hole and went headlong—which was bad
enough. When the horse got up, he planted a foot hastily on
Jack's diaphragm and then bolted straight for the peacefully
slumbering herd—which was worse.

With stirrup straps snapping like pistol shots, he tore
down through the dreaming cattle, with nothing to stop
him. The herd did not wait for explanations. As the posse
afterward said, it quit the earth, while they gathered around
the fallen Jack and tried to discover whether it was a doctor
or coroner who was needed.

It was neither, cowboys being notoriously tough. Jack
rebounded from the earth, spitting out sand and a choice
collection of words which he had been saving for just such
an occasion. The other cowboys would have admired to stay

and listen, but stern duty called. The herd was gone, the horse was gone and so was Pink.

Hoofbeats heralded Weary's return, already laughing at his joke and expecting to see a crestfallen Pink surrounded by his captors. Instead he saw Jack emitting language and the cowboys scrambling for their horses to go hunt for the herd.

"Mamma mine!" said Weary feebly. He knew at once that it was useless to try and compete with Jack when that worthy was going at full steam. Instead he turned his horse and headed back to camp as fast as he could go.

Chip woke up as Weary crawled into the tent and grabbed the foreman by the shoulder.

"Saddle muh horse," he mumbled. "I'm ready."

"Chip!" Weary gasped. "Cadwolloper's gone!"

"Huh Who? Oh." Chip's face showed disgust as he removed his shoulder gently and lay down again. "Hell, don't let that worry yuh."

Weary was puzzled but game. "Then it's all right," he said. And added as an afterthought, "The herd's gone too."

"What!" Chip bounded out of bed like an uncoiled spring. Language began to pour out of him and the blushing Weary afterwards testified that when really wound up, he far outclassed Jack.

By sunrise, the hard riding members of the once-Happy Family came upon the herd. It was quietly grazing in a little coulee and Pink was holding them, all by his lonesome.

"Yuh low-down, spavined, wind-broke, jug-headed bunch of locoed sheep-herders!" Pink roared, his blue eyes flashing. "If yuh think the whole bunch of yuh are capable of holding these critters now that they've run theirselves out, you can take over an' let me go get some breakfast! When I took this job, Chip told me I'd be workin' with men! Why, you dirt farmers couldn't hold a baby chick inside a henhouse with the door locked and a rock on the roof!

"On Milk River they'd tie a picket rope to everyone of yuh to keep you from gettin' lost between the bunkhouse and the cook shack. And jokes!—Oh, Mother! Next time you try to play a joke on somebody, *Mister* Weary, don't pick out a horse so feeble that he's like to fall down before anybody climbs aboard him. I thought this Glory would put on a show from all the braggin' about him. What a disappointment. I'm plumb wore out, but not from his buckin'. From tryin' to keep him awake! Come get him and give me somethin' that's half alive!"

The erstwhile Happy Family gulped, blinked and shuffled its feet under this tirade. The joke had backfired with a crash and they wanted nothing now but holes to crawl into.

Then amazingly, the fire died out of Pink's voice and eyes. He slid to the ground and came forward. The dimples flashed as he held out his hand to Weary.

"Meet Milk River Pink," he said.

Then the uproar broke loose as the Happy Family crowded around to pound his back and shake his hand.

Although best known for her nonfiction, Mari Sandoz (1901–1966) was also a consummate writer of fiction for both adults and young readers. Such novels as The Tom-Walker *(1947),* Winter Thunder *(1954), and* Son of the Gamblin' Man *(1960) have been widely praised, and her 1963 juvenile about an Indian youth,* The Story Catcher, *won the WWA Spur Award the following year. Among her nonfiction are the 1935 biography of her Nebraska pioneer father,* Old Jules, *which was the recipient of the* Atlantic Monthly *Press Award, and such other biographies and histories as* Crazy Horse, the Strange Man of the Oglalas *(1942) and* The Buffalo Hunters *(1954). While the bulk of her work deals with historical themes, notably the plight of Indians and the struggles of pioneers, "The Girl in the Humbert" has a twentieth-century western ranching background.*

The Girl in the Humbert

MARI SANDOZ

It was the city nephews who first saw smoke in the Humbert. They came galloping home through the oppressive spring heat, bouncing together on the barebacked old pinto, Down's short arms tight around the middle of his nine-year-old brother before him. Together they kicked the old mare at every jump, the reins flapping loose.

When they saw their tall, browned uncle at the ranch-yard gate, the boys let the pinto drop into a walk. Sliding off on the far side, they started reluctantly toward him. But almost at once their eager young legs betrayed them, their legs and the need to tell the news before they were scolded for running the old mare.

"Somebody's—somebody's in the old house!" Down shouted, to beat his brother in the telling.

"There's smoke coming from the chimney in the Humbert," Dickup said, deliberately explicit.

But Jack Pulmer only snapped Down's transparent ear and picked beggar lice from the older boy's tousled hair. So his two young cowpunchers had been seeing a whirlwind and the dust it can raise?

"But there's a car—there is," they cried together.

The uncle nodded a little, and thumbed imperatively toward the lathered old mare, standing head down, sides heaving. So the boys fetched clean corn-cobs from a manger and started to rub her down, one on a side, while they watched their fine big uncle swing his empty car away through the sandpass.

Jack Pulmer hoped that it was only dust and a whirlwind the boys had seen. The Humbert, apparently never Spurwheel ranch property except by claim of occupation, was his best meadow, its hay essential if he was to hold off foreclosure on the ranch another year. Otherwise it would be the last ending of a long descent since Colonel Pulmer, Jack's grandfather, was killed by Frenchy Humbert, over thirty years ago. Families and times both change and the sons of the ruthless old cowman couldn't keep together much of the empire the old colonel cut from the public domain and held against all settlement until Frenchy appeared.

But the free range pinched out, the days of cheap beef and wild cow towns passed. Five years ago, what was left of the Spurwheel and its mortgages fell to young Jack, who had studied voice instead of ranching. In those five years the colonel's grandson learned about cattle markets and stock diseases and that a frozen bit will burn the mouth of a horse. He learned, too, that he couldn't risk a late April prairie fire from any tin-can tourist, particularly not through the Humbert.

By the time the rancher emerged from the pass no smoke darkened the early green of the meadow, the winter-bleached rushes of the swamp, or the high ridge of hills beyond, tawny in the hot sun. But the windmill at the head of the valley was in gear, the wheel turning slowly, lopsided and awkward as a tumbleweed on the prairie, the water gathering in the reservoir Frenchy threw up years ago. There was a car, too, as the boys had said, and new shingle patches shone yellow on the roof of the old sod house.

At the door Jack Pulmer was faced by a cool-eyed young woman in overalls and striped jersey, a worn rifle in her hand. Without greeting, she listened to what he had to say over the gray cowman's hat in his hand.

"No," she told him, when he was done. "I do not think I would be more comfortable at the Spurwheel ranch house."

When he attempted a little firmness, she let her palm slide down to the trigger guard of the rifle and pointed out that she was not trespassing here. She was Arille Hombiert, *h* and *t* silent, please, and she happened to own this place he called the Humbert.

So there was nothing for the young rancher to do but to go, heading away toward the county seat to check up on the claims of this girl with the name something like Frenchy's. She couldn't be much over twenty, slim as September bluestem, with hair bright and free as its ripening seed. And on the sill of the window beside her was a small statuette, a mule-deer doe carved from some light-colored wood, the head delicate and shy, the wide ears alert. Alone, poised for flight, the little animal stood silvery pale against the full-drawn curtain of solid black.

At the courthouse Jack Pulmer discovered that Frenchy's name was really Hombiert and that the girl's title to the deserted meadow was as solid as the earth from which the old sod house grew. So went the Spurwheel's last bit of free grass and left the young rancher owing several thousand dollars in back rent to a cool-eyed girl named Arille, granddaughter of a murderer.

But because he had to know what his chances of leasing this year's hay were, he came back through the low-clouded dusk by way of the Humbert. The soddy was a dark blur beside the road, with no ray of light anywhere. Yet some-body seemed to be working at the old outside chimney, somebody who stood against the blackness of the earthen wall until the car was past.

Around midnight the drizzle turned to a light, rattling sleet. Jack Pulmer drew on his sheepskin and went out to throw the gates of the winter pasture, where a few of the older cows, smelling snow, were already breaking through and bawling for their calves to follow them to the corrals. When he came in, the ground was covered, soft-cushioned and silent under his boots.

By morning the wind was up, the air thick and white and sharp with driving snow that shut in the ranch house all around. The two boys ran for the door, incredulous and excited. But the great-aunt who cared for them was a sister of the old colonel's, and they got no farther than the win-dows.

Three days later the sun was out, the long drifts mush-ing under the feet of bawling cattle, just right for snow forts. The old aunt sent the boys out, even though she had brought them West to recover from scarlet fever while their mother, not a Pulmer, got a summer's rest.

On his way back from the north range, his sorrel horse dark with snow water to the flanks, Jack Pulmer cut through the Humbert. But the storm hadn't discouraged the pale-skinned Eastern girl. She was out in sunglasses and boots, shooting at a soup can on a gatepost, the bullets well bunched in the center.

"This snow'll be flooding your hay land," the rancher called from the road.

"I suspect it's been flooded before," the girl replied, her teeth white and derisive in her tanning face.

But the man had to have the hay secure, and so he swung a leg over the horn and dickered. The girl from the Humbert was fair enough: Standing hay at the going price, to be measured and paid for after stacking. And before the rancher could unlimber his leg from the horn, the girl was gone through the door of the soddy, leaving only her tracks to show that anyone lived there—firm tracks, some large and deep, as though she had worn big overshoes and carried a heavy load.

As soon as the dark velvet of the earth pushed up wet between the shrinking drifts, Dickup and Down got the old pinto out. They had to see what the storm did to their swamp and the open water in its center, where their uncle had a duck boat they might hope to reach along in July. Jack Pulmer knew the boys shouldn't be playing in the Humbert, no matter how much they liked the chattering ducks along the rising water edge, the flooding muskrat houses, the acres of dead rushes still under snow. But the old aunt was down with a bilious attack and so the man slapped the bony hip of the pinto and let them go.

"Tie your horse solid to a hackberry tree on the slope or you'll be a couple cowpunchers hoofing it in. And don't go near the soddy."

Promising everything, the boys got away. They kicked the old mare and yelled, "Yip-pi!" but hung on tight, Dickup holding the reins close, with both hands buried in the mane, Down's arms gripping his brother's middle. They remembered from the day they got their nicknames, the first time they tried the pinto. Dick had pushed Don up and climbed on behind, the reins hanging loose. The old mare dropped her head, kicked up her heels high and both boys slid off over her ears.

"It's Dickup behind and his brother Down in front!" old Pete roared. When the smaller boy began to cry, the chore man stopped. "Why, sa-ay, all a them old-timers had nicknames—like Lame Johnny an' Fly Speck Billy," he complained.

After that it was all right, with Dickup sitting in front, to pull on the reins, Down hanging on behind, the old pinto plodding along with half-closed eyes.

In the Humbert, summer came hard upon the storm, the greening swamp of evening alive with the soft quack of ducks, the late song of blackbirds and the croak of the awakening frogs. As the noise swelled into night, a thin, white old man often slipped out to sit beside the girl. It was old Frenchy, free after ten years of solitary darkness for successive attempts at prison break and twenty years of darkness by choice when his urge to freedom was stilled at last. In those years he went back to the old, old craft of his people, wood carving. With a knife improvised from a broken hinge, and pieces of his plank bunk for material, he formed little wooden statuettes, mostly small, wild, free things—a saucy prairie dog poised at the mouth of his hole, a young gray wolf trying his voice against the sky, the wide-eared doe on the window sill in the Humbert. All this grew up in darkness, by touch, with the simplicity of line that pleased the fingertips, mass that satisfied the palm.

Free now, and back on his homestead, he returned to his earlier craft, the soil, and when powdery dusk filled the valley and the swamp song began he sat upon the doorstep with his rifle beside him. Sometimes he talked a little to his granddaughter, of plants and weather and earth, with slow, spare words, for speech, too, was almost lost to him in those long years of silence.

In the darkness he chopped up the sod of his old garden plot that the girl hired rebroken. With hoe and rake he worked the soil into a fine seed bed, smooth as any done by light of day, and level for irrigation from the old reservoir. Later he crept along the sprouting rows of green, thinking, transplanting, weeding. He did all these things in darkness, in paths his feet remembered, within the bonds of long, long habit.

And in the meantime he taught his granddaughter to shoot the old rifle, for, to his light-blinded eyes, the Spurwheel ranch over the hill was unchanged, and a settler's risk as great as ever.

One cloudy afternoon the boys came riding home just ahead of a rain. They had a little mud turtle, moss-backed, not as big as a saucer, in Dickup's handkerchief, held safely by the corners. They had news too. There had been hammering all day in the Humbert, somebody on the roof, and the house looking different.

Jack Pulmer poked the wet, soiled handkerchief with a finger. "Hadn't you better keep to your livestock, and not be bothering strangers?"

"Yes, uncle," the boys said together, dutifully. Holding the turtle away from them, the claws coming through the cloth like thorns, they went to turn the old mare out to grass. Jack Pulmer watched them go, saw their heads come together, their faces turn slyly back to look at him. Then they started to run, kicking up like colts.

The young rancher knew about the night construction of the extension to the soddy and the buttressing of the four corners of the house like a Southwest 'dobe church, stout and lasting. He had heard the girl shingling the new roof all this cool day and he didn't understand how she could plan and do these things, all the things of the Humbert, this spring. He remembered the time he found her planting late sweet corn across the Spurwheel road to the summer pasture. He stopped the car and went over to the girl.

"It is customary in this country to leave public highways passable," he announced, but smilingly.

"So-o?" she inquired politely, driving her spade into the sod, dropping two kernels in the crevice, stepping on it. "I was informed at the courthouse that this is not a laid-out road."

The way back to the car was a long and awkward one, but the young rancher made himself seem unhurried, flattening an uptilted sod or two with his boot, tossing a clod at a ground squirrel. And when he sneaked a look back, Arille Hombiert was far down the row, wasting no time.

It was after this that Jack Pulmer paid her as much of the back rent as he could, using what he had laid aside for the mortgage. Even if the girl had known about the debts, she could not have forgotten the face of Frenchy Hombiert the day she took him from the prison office, his eyes closed as the dark curtains of the soddy. Only his hands seemed alive at all.

So she took the money and then couldn't tell the old man, afraid he would call it a bribe to forget a great wrong, one miserable thousand dollars for each ten years in a black hole—and a lifetime in the habit of darkness.

The girl still shot target every day, but a little shame-facedly now, putting the rifle away among the flowers about the soddy if she saw the boys come plowing through the rushes, or heard the young rancher's car in the sand pass. But in the evenings old Frenchy still liked to touch his fingers to the centered bullet holes in her target. Yes, this Arille, the only one left to him now, was a true Hombiert, like those old ones who came pushing up the Mississippi two hundred years ago.

It was late in June, when the spiderwort lay blue along the slopes of the Humbert, the yellow currants in the brush sweetening to honey, that Dickup and Down reported see-ing a man's foot sticking from behind a curtain at the soddy. Now the uncle discovered, too, that there was lemonade with cookies almost every day, and 'Reel, the girl, waving a dish towel to the boys when it was ready.

The uncle ordered them to stay away from people, and took to watching the Humbert from closer. Finally, one windy night, when the sound of his motor was blown behind him, his unexpected headlight shot through the north pass and cut the figure of an old man from the darkness about the reservoir. Blinded eyes closed, the man waited for the light to pass, motionless, gaunt and white as some lightning-charred tree, long standing. But by then young Jack knew that the girl in the Humbert could sing, too, and once he saw her dance on a knoll in the pale light of a summer moon, a wild, beautiful dance. And finally sink, light as cottonwood down, to the sand where he had killed a rattlesnake the summer before.

* * *

Now more and more often the old man stopped between the lush green rows to listen, to move swiftly toward his rifle. Then one Sunday an old open car piled full of ranch hands came through the Humbert. Noisily, with a loud "Whoa-o-o!" they jerked to a stop before the soddy. Hard at one another's heels they trooped up between the flower beds to pound on the old door, pretending a great thirst and wanting to borrow a dipper, please, ma'am.

The girl pointed out that the windmill, in plain sight, was running strong.

"It is quite possible to obtain a good drink from the pipe, you know, by just holding your hand against the flow," she explained carefully, as though they were visiting dudes.

The younger of the hands started to talk up to this pretty girl, but the others nudged their ribs, motioning to Frenchy's old rifle standing in the hollyhocks beside the door, ready at her hand. Silenced, the men fell back and hustled off toward the mill. Pretending to drink, they wiped their mouths and then drove away, the backs of their necks red above the clean work shirts.

When the car was gone, Frenchy began to talk from the darkness of his bunk. "Once more they come," he said slowly, painfully. "Hired men smelling out. We better carry automatics, plenty of shells."

In the dusk of the curtained soddy Arille brought pen and ink, but almost at once the old man started again, weary, defeated. "I don't know—maybe we better get out."

At this his granddaughter stopped, her hands tense. "You mean let them drive us away? No!"

So the guns came. They really sagged the pocket very little and fitted the palm as well as the little wooden statuettes.

Late one evening the Spurwheel hay crew moved into the Humbert, creeping through the pass like a long worm, the tall stacker first, then the mowers, the rakes and the sweeps. It was hard to explain their coming to the old settler, but he knew they must have money, and so he gave in to

Arille. For two weeks the humming mowers swung around the meadow, the rakes rolled the new hay into windrows close-ribbed as corduroy and the groaning stacker threw it high. All these days Frenchy sat stiff and awake on his bunk, his rifle across his knees.

But no one came near the soddy, the cold stream of the windmill or the wide patch of watermelons ripening. Not even the two boys, who followed their uncle's sickle bar as he led the mowers, or rode the piles of hay he swept in from the far ends of the meadow.

When the valley was friendly once more, the rancher drew his horse up before the girl, waist deep in her moon poppies, stringing the finest blooms for seed. He had brought the check for the hay, with a notation of his measurements.

"I can't say anything definite about next year," he told her regretfully, "but for this year I'm grateful—"

Without finishing he touched the sorrel into a lope, and for once the girl from the Humbert stood to look after him, the white slip of paper blowing in her hand.

The day of the rodeo and county fair in late August, Arille came into town early to deliver her melons, early cabbage, wild plums and green wild grapes for jelly to the stores. She had hoped to be away before ten and the packing crowd, but at eight the little town was already jammed, its one traffic light and the sweating deputy marshals lost in the honking, the shoutings and the dust. Only the Indians, painted, feathered, in bead-and-scalp-trimmed shirts for the dance in the square, got through the crowd—the Indians and the few grizzled old cowmen, thick-shouldered and heavy-hipped now, driving their cars as they once spurred mustang cow ponies through the border towns on pay day.

When Arille came out of the last store, her errands done, Jack Pulmer stood at her running board, waiting. The girl was in dull blue, soft as fall asters against a far hill. The man had never seen her so fragile and lovely, so far from anything like shingle laying, or target shooting with a rifle that had killed a man. He had never seen her in a dress.

"Not going home so soon?" he asked, making talk.

Yes, she was.

"But it isn't much after noon, and there's the rodeo and —well, I was hoping you'd see it with me," he trailed off, without confidence as the girl turned the car switch and moved her foot toward the starter.

But she really ought to stay, he urged, have a bite at the barbecue pit, see the bronco busting, not like the show business, with chutes and only ten seconds to ride. This was wild horses, eared down, saddled, the blindfold jerked away and the whole world wide open for man and horse to fight it out. He was alone, the boys chasing off after old Pete, who'd bulldogged some mean steers in his day. And besides, it might be hours before she could get her car out.

As he talked the girl considered the young cowman, saw that the sweep of his cheek had gaunted much this summer, his jaw line leaned, his mouth thinned. But his shoulders were still square as good oak beams, his fingers straight-boned and true. And when she finally had to meet the grave brown of his eyes, she jerked the key from the lock.

"For an hour," she agreed.

Together they climbed over bumpers, slipped between running boards and were lost in the packed mass at the intersection. And everywhere around them mouths opened to exclaim above the noise, arms lifted to point them out. A Pulmer and a Humbert together!

"If you want to back out—" the man whispered to the girl. But Arille Hombiert looked straight before her, pushing on as though through a deep tangle of brush or rushes noisy in the wind.

Suddenly the center lane of cars began to move, making way for the high-school band in blue-and-white, marching double file, led by a red-headed girl in a towering white shako. The crowd broke from the street and the barbecue pit, following toward the fairgrounds; past pine booths selling red hamburgers, chances at pillow tops or looks at the headless woman, the petrified man or Popeye; past bingo stands and the agricultural exhibits to the weathered old grandstand. Jack Pulmer stuck a note for Pete in a crack in the Spurwheel section and took Arille away from the gawking crowd toward the grassy oval inside the race track. At the gate they passed a slim-hipped youth twirling a loop about himself, stepping daintily in and out as he sang in a tuneless monotone for the grandstand:

> I'm a kissin', cussin' son of a gun,
> I'm the kid from Powder River.

"Face-Powder River, N.Y.," Arille laughed, inanely, and the rancher knew how deep the looks, the pointing out, the talk had gone. He tried to pretend too. Yes, the singing kid was an import all right, but with top contest money only twenty-five dollars, the riders out here in the oval were fresh off the range hereabouts.

They did look authentic, with their wind-burnt faces, their easy levis, standing around licking cigarettes and considering a blindfolded smoke roan. The wild horse was sagging groundward under the saddle leather, puffing himself against the tightening cinch, dust rolling before his stubborn nose.

Now the rider, a lanky, weather-beaten old cow hand from the Spurwheel, tucked in his plaid shirt and climbed awkwardly to the saddle. The hazers pulled in closer, the blind was jerked away and the sky opened.

"Ride 'im, Stovepipe!" somebody yelled from the crowd.

When three or four straight high bucks and stiff-legged landings showed no daylight between the rider and his saddle, the horse stopped. Then suddenly he shot ahead, bucking, swapping ends, spinning, sunfishing, bellowing out over the dusty plain.

The crowd was up. "Whoopee, listen at him bawl!"

The rider's teeth still gleamed in his dark face, his old

hat pounding the dusty withers, his spurred heels raking.
Finally the smoke roan quieted, hanging his head sullenly,
swaying lower and lower, his sunken flanks heaving, his
wide nostrils bloody.

"He's done! You got him licked, Stovepipe!" the crowd
yelled. But over them all old Pete roared out a warning.
"Watch 'im, cowboy, watch 'im!"

Pete was right. Already the horse was gathering himself
into a knot. Then his forefeet snapped out, up. The riders
stumbled back, their cigarettes slipping from their open lips.
The hazers spurred forward. A moment the horse and rider
teetered, then, with a whinny wild as a scream, the smoke
roan went over backward, shaking the earth.

A groan swept the grandstand. Arille's hand clutched
the rancher's arm. But old Stovepipe was free. Coolly he had
waited to slide beyond the crushing horn until the last possible moment, ready now to fall back into the saddle as swiftly.
But the smoke roan was done. The taut hide rippled a little,
a hind foot straightened.

From a gateway a tractor came coughing, swinging
around to drag the horse aside. But the girl from the Humbert had seen enough, was hurrying away, the young
rancher beside her. On the way out the boys came running,
leaving Pete behind. Little Down buried his face in the blue
of the girl's dress. "Oh, 'Reel, it's dead! The poor horse is
dead!" he sobbed, while Dickup stood close to his uncle's
hand, white-faced and silent.

But before the next saddle was on, the boys were impatient to find Pete again, to see the bulldogging, the wild-cow
milking, the Indian races. So the girl sent the rancher back
with them and went to her car alone.

That night she sat late in the dim light of the new moon,
watching her grandfather's bent back among the tomatoes,
his head up at the slightest sound that was unusual. Later she
listened to his sure hands move over his supper tray in the
darkness, stop at the far rise of a little wind and move again
when it was past.

The next day the rancher from the Spurwheel found

the road past the soddy posted with No Trespassing signs.

Now at last he had to go to the court records of the trial of Frenchy. It was not the story of a lawless invader he had heard from his father, but a story of long persecution of a lone settler, ending in a gate thrown back, a herd of Pulmer cattle eating his corn and garden. When he took them up for damages, men came creeping through the dusk to turn them out. Frenchy, watching, fired over their heads. When a bullet from the buckbrush grazed his arm, he fired point-blank into the stream of red still on his retina and got Colonel Pulmer through the chest. For this he was given ten years for manslaughter and dragged away.

Slowly Jack Pulmer closed the courthouse door and plodded across the street to his car, his boots heavy as iron in the dust.

All through the drought of August, thunderheads had piled high. Lightning flashed rose-red through the clouds; thunder shook the earth, a few drops of rain fell and the wind blew the storm away. In the meantime the prairie was browning, the swamp in the Humbert drying up. The day after the rodeo, Dickup and Down came home shouting they could walk into the very middle, where the boat was, without getting their shoes muddy, hardly. And now their uncle wouldn't let them go back, not with all their pleading that they could be finding a lot of shells for their collection, that next week it would be town and school again.

The rancher was firm until the old aunt had to be taken to the doctor for her gall bladder and he was busy culling stock for shipment. So he let the boys make one more trip to the swamp, just one more, and no going near anybody. The boys nodded and, with their lunch in their pockets, rode away into the hot, quiet morning.

Around noon a little cloud like a fluff of dandelion started at the zenith and spread white and high over the east, dark olive underneath. A bolt or two of lightning fell, thunder rolled. Then the wind came up and blew the smell of ozone away.

Half an hour later a shouting puncher spurred through the dust and bawling cattle to Jack Pulmer. His arm in the air, he pointed off into the east, toward the Humbert, where white smoke billowed up, twisted into yellow, blue and black, and rolled away over the hills.

Letting the cattle spread, the hands whirled their horses toward the Spurwheel. Under pressure of his knee, Jack's sorrel shot ahead for the Humbert, three miles away, while already dark specks moved in over the far hills—fire fighters in answer to the smoke signal of the range country.

At the line fence the rancher found three posts splintered and scorched, the grass blackened, and from it a widening tongue of burnt prairie spreading away toward the meadow. He spurred his winded horse on, to see that the farther swamp was a towering mass of smoke, cut by flames leaping high from the piles of dead rushes, the near end only gray ashes, reddening in the wind. The whole meadow was black, the stackyards smoldering piles, the gardens of Frenchy Hombiert cooked dark as by frost, about the sod house and the car. Otherwise there was nothing—nothing except the old pinto tied to a hackberry far up the slope and jerking to get free.

In the dark soddy Jack found only the shadowy figure of an old man, still clutching his rifle against his enemy, but begging him to find Arille, his Arille, who had run out into the smoke and did not return.

Of the boys he knew nothing, nothing at all.

While the Spurwheel outfit drove hard toward the head fire, Pete, in the ranch car, turned off to find his boss.

"The boys?" he yelled from far off. At sight of the rancher's face he jerked a gun from the car pocket and fired three rapid shots into the air-the old, old, distress signal of the hills. Then Jack slid under the wheel and headed for the narrowest strip of rushes between the meadow and the open place in the center, still veiled in curling heat and thin blue smoke.

Here the rancher leaped from the car, began kicking a path into the swamp. Old Pete jerked him back, pounded out the fire in his clothes as two, three, half a dozen cars drew up, the men out before the wheels stopped rolling. In relays of three they shoveled glowing ashes down the wind, running back to soak their burning clothes, shoveling again, driving a path into the swamp.

Jack Pulmer was the first to break through into the little quarter-acre open space, baked hard, drifted white in wind-blown ashes. There was nothing here, nothing except the boat out in the center, turned upside down, the water-logged bottom smoldering.

And face down under it lay the two boys, Arille between them, holding them safe, her own clothing scorched, her overalls burnt off above her knees.

Carefully Jack lifted the girl, brushing the hair from her soil-streaked face. Pete yanked the boys up. They looked with awed faces at the singed, blackened, sweating men about them, over the ruins of their beloved swamp, at the girl limp in their uncle's arms. Quietly Down began to cry, while Dickup ran at the heels of his uncle. "Is 'Reel," he whispered—"is she—dead?"

Pete pulled him back, sent a hand for a telephone and a doctor by plane and got the rest to the soddy. There Jack Pulmer carried the girl away, the boys hanging to Pete, afraid of this silent, terrible man who was their uncle. Inside, old Frenchy peered from the darkness of his room, squinting as the curtains at the windows were jerked back, his tongue as helpless as his eyes. But his hands were swift and sure as he helped the rancher cut away the burnt shoes, the scorched tatters of the overalls, laying bare the flesh, seared as the girl ran through the burning grass to save the boys of the Spurwheel.

The next morning, when the doctor was gone and the girl lay quiet at last, only half awake, the boys were permitted to see her. They forgot the little wooden animals they had to show her, their uncle's careful cautioning, in their excitement to tell their news. That dust cloud 'Reel had seen had been a fire, a terrible fire. "All the swamp burned up while we were hid under the boat," they cried together. "Even the grass."

Then suddenly they saw that the girl's face was very white and drawn, sick-looking, and remembering the plane and the doctor, they were quiet, afraid again. But the old man behind them spoke. Yes, the grass was gone, but it would come again.

"Already it is growing at the roots, finer, greener—"

With the boys pulling at him to show them, he started to the door. A moment he hesitated there, to look back to his Arille and this grandson of Colonel Pulmer. Then, still squinting, old Frenchy stepped out into the sunlight for the first time in thirty years, to show two small boys the grass growing new in the Humbert.

The number of women who wrote for the western pulp magazines of the period 1920–1950 was quite small, and those who contributed a large and significant body of work may be counted on the fingers of one hand. New Mexican Elsa Barker is one of those few, having published some 200 stories in such periodicals as Ranch Romances *and* All Western—*everything from short-shorts to full-length novels. Mrs. Barker, whose husband is the well-known western writer and poet S. Omar Barker, also wrote fiction for newspaper syndication and once created the text for a romantic western comic book. "First Notch," about a pioneer family named Malone, is one of her best stories.*

First Notch

ELSA BARKER

At the mouth of a little canyon where a clear spring bubbled up out of great white rocks and a wide green *vega* fanned out below, Ben Malone had stopped the two covered wagons and pitched camp.

Originally from the Kentucky bluegrass country, the Malones had tarried for two years in Texas, then finally pushed on westward to New Mexico Territory where they had heard there was still good homestead land within sight of green-timbered mountains.

So today Ben Malone had ridden back to Los Charcos to find out what he could about this little *rincón.* At the camp Mrs. Malone and Molly heated a big black kettle of water over an open fire and did the family wash for the first time since they had left Texas. That done, they drove stakes in the ground and set up a portable chicken pen they had brought with them.

During the long trek west the big red chickens that were Mrs. Malone's pride had dwindled to eight molting, ailing hens and a single rooster. But now in the warm sunshine they fluffed out their remaining feathers and began pecking at knee-high clover heads.

Mrs. Malone eyed them with some satisfaction. Those chickens had been the one bone of contention between her and her husband through the weary weeks of covered-wagon travel. They would not, she was sure, be able to buy hens like those in the new country. Besides, chickens and a milk cow were a badge of respectability—a sign that they weren't ordinary; no-count nester folks.

Down below in the *vega* twelve-year old Jody sat under a pine and kept an eye on their twenty-odd head of cows and five horses. Not that they really needed much watching, for here was better grass than they had known for weeks.

It was Molly who first saw her father returning, and saw that another man and a boy on a little brown mule rode with him. Excitement, partially mixed with dismay, kindled in her gray eyes as she recognized the second man.

She grabbed an armload of the clothes they had left to dry on bushes and ran to her wagon with them. There was time in there for a quick smoothing of the brown braids she wore coiled around her head, time to realize with further dismay that her old blue-calico dress was wrinkled and a little dirty. Traveling in a covered wagon, cooking over campfires, it [sic] was hard for a woman to keep neat.

What she didn't realize was that no man was going to pay much attention to a dress—old calico or new silk—when something as neat and well turned as Molly Malone was inside of it. Her eyes were wide-set and gray, with a sparkling hint of laughter always just ready to break through. Her skin, always dark, was tanned now almost to an Indian-brown, but in spite of the hot winds across the dry prairies, her rosy cheeks looked as satiny smooth as flower petals.

In short, Molly Malone was young. She was full of fun and laughter—and she was close to being beautiful.

The young man with Ben Malone jumped off his horse to help her climb down out of the big wagon. Molly took his hand and let him help her, just as if she weren't used to swinging agilely over those wagon wheels a dozen times a day.

Ben Malone watched with a kind of dry amusement in his eyes.

"Molly," he said, "this is Casey Holloway—the town marshal of Los Charcos. You remember we talked to him as we came through?"

Molly's pulses were already reminding her how well she remembered, but the demure flick of black lashes showed only polite interest. Any girl in her right mind would remember this tall, blond cowboy officer! She wondered if he was married. The good-looking ones usually were, she reflected.

Ben Malone turned to his wife. "Mr. Holloway rode out with me to ask us to a dance in town tomorrow night."

Mrs. Malone looked doubtful. Los Charcos was a mining boom town, and they had noticed as they drove through that the streets were filled with rough-looking men in high lace boots.

Casey Holloway spoke quickly: "It'll be a plumb respectable party, ma'am. It's my job to see to that—an' anyhow Los Charcos is getting civilized. We're having this dance to raise money toward a schoolhouse." He smiled as he looked at Molly. "The only trouble is—there ain't anywheres near enough pretty girls to go around!"

In spite of herself Molly blushed. "I saw posters in town yesterday advertising Alida Farrington and her troupe of Shakespearean players for tomorrow night. Will she be at the dance?"

"That's right, ma'am. The dance will start right after the show—an' she's promised to come. It'll be in Dub Maddix's hotel ballroom."

Molly sighed, her gray eyes getting bigger.

"I'd sure love to go," she said.

The older Malones looked at each other.

"We couldn't all go," Mrs. Malone said. "Somebody's got to stay and watch the stock."

"I'd be mighty proud to take Miss Molly to the show and dance," Casey Holloway said quickly.

Ben Malone looked him in the eye and shook his head.

"I don't mean no offense," he said quietly, "but I reckon if my daughter goes to this dance—I'd better take her."

For just a moment the tall young officer looked set back on his heels. Then he nodded politely.

"If I was her pa, I expect I'd say the same."

Around the wagon came Jody and his visitor. The kid who had ridden out with Casey Holloway was leading his little brown mule, talking fast in a high, shrill voice, waving his arms for emphasis. Probably not more than two years younger than Jody Malone, he was hardly more than half as tall. His small body was thin, his face wizened and hard-looking. Jody's face wore a pained, disgusted look.

Casey Holloway put his hand on the smaller boy's shoulder. "Mrs. Malone—this is Tony Ballou. He's been helping Dub Maddix run his hotel this summer."

"He said his name was Kit Carson," Jody said disgustedly. "An' that he's a famous Indian scout!"

The boy's thin face flushed. He aimed a kick at Jody's shin, but missed.

Casey Holloway grinned. "I'm sorry, Kit," he said. "I thought maybe you didn't want these folks to know who you really was."

The kid's scowl changed to a grin—and suddenly he didn't look so hard. The smile sweetened his thin face, making him young and vulnerable. His eyes dropped. He dug one bare toe into the soft grass.

"Aw, shucks!" he said. He raised embarrassed eyes. "We better be gittin' on back. Ol' Dub'll be mad if I'm not there in time to do the chores. He's shore a heller!"

Casey Holloway dropped his hand to the kid's shoulder again, his eyes sober.

"All right, Kit. Well—so long, folks!" He let his eyes rest a long instant on Molly Malone. "You'll save me some dances, Miss Molly?"

She nodded, smiling. He turned and boosted the kid into his worn old saddle, and stepped across the back of his own tall sorrel.

Afterward Molly couldn't have said at just what moment the dance began to turn sour. Maybe it was right at first, when Dub Maddix met them at the door to take their fifty-cent admission fee.

Maddix was a big man, heavy-cheeked and frog-eyed. He had eyed them from the lofty altitude of a man who owns a hotel, a couple of stores, a bank, a ranch, and several mines. For just a moment Molly's cheeks had turned hot, and the new dress that had seemed so pretty was after all just a flower-sprinkled red calico. Her father's homemade haircut seemed shabby. So did the heavy everyday shoes he had worn because the only other pair he owned needed half-soling.

Then she had looked up at Ben Malone and that part was suddenly all right. She saw him as others must be seeing him—tall and handsome, his gray eyes calm and steady—carrying his broad shoulders proudly. The Malones might be humble farmer folk, but they were good, honest folks, too—folks who could hold up their heads in any company.

Molly let her eyes drift around the dance room, already crowded, but she didn't see Casey Holloway. The orchestra was playing a tricky little Spanish waltz, *La Varsoviana*. A young miner stepped out of the stag line along the wall. He had a round, sunburned face and a shy smile.

"My name's Bidge Crocker," he said, looking up at Ben Malone rather than his daughter.

Ben Malone smiled. "My name's Malone," he said. "This is my daughter, Molly. She likes to dance."

The young miner grinned and held out his hand. "Let's go!"

After that dance—and after every other—there was a small-sized stampede around Molly Malone. Present were about half a dozen other girls her own age, maybe as many young married women, and a dozen or so older women who were sometimes persuaded out on the floor for a turn or two. Any woman who was able to walk without a crutch got a rush. But Molly was also young and pretty.

It would have been fun if something contrary in her heart hadn't made her keep looking for Casey Holloway. She had been so sure yesterday that there was something special in the way he looked at her. She hadn't thought she could be wrong about that.

When he finally did come in, it was with Alida Farrington and her troupe. There were two other young women in the party and four men, including the fussy, nervous-looking little stage manager. They came in with a wave of laughter and gay chatter, all of them a little flushed of face, as if they had stopped somewhere for a drink or two before coming to the dance.

Alida Farrington was a tall, full-bodied woman, with a deep voice used to making itself heard. Maybe not as glamorous and beautiful as she had looked on the stage, she seemed human and likable. She had on a dark-green satin dress, cut low enough to show off to full advantage a double rope of magnificent pearls. More pearls dripped from her ears.

The stag line promptly closed in around her. Over the hum of male voices her rich laugh rolled out frequently and pleasantly.

Casey Holloway had stopped in the doorway for an instant, his eyes going around the room. Molly's chin had lifted a little, and she had turned her head quickly away, looking up and laughing in answer to some remark of Bidge Crocker's that she hadn't even fully heard.

It was several dances later that she felt a hand on her shoulder, cutting in on the tail end of a waltz. She changed partners smoothly, scarcely missing a step.

Casey Holloway said softly, "I'm very sorry I couldn't make it earlier, Molly."

Molly felt that she would have cut out her tongue, an inch at a time, rather than let him know she cared. She looked up at him, giving him a strictly routine smile. She sighed.

"I've been having a wonderful time, Mr. Holloway."

She thought she saw a little of that falsely intimate smile leave his face.

"I'd sorta hoped you weren't," he said. "I hoped you'd be mad. Give me hell."

Molly widened her eyes innocently. "But why?"

Just then Bidge Crocker touched Molly's shoulder. Molly shifted partners again, giving Casey another bright routine smile as she danced away.

That was the real moment when Molly knew the party had gone flat, and decided she had a bad headache.

She refused all claimants for the next dance and started around the room toward her father, who was talking to a group of older men near the door. Through one of the French windows opening onto the long *portal* she caught a glimpse of a small figure, big-eyed, and with tear-stained cheeks.

She stopped and called softly, "Hello, Tony. Or should I say Kit?"

The big blue eyes looked at her sullenly for a moment, then an impudent smile broke over his tough little face.

"Hi, Lily Langtry!"

Molly laughed. "I'm going home in a minute—but why don't you come in and dance this one with me? I'd like to tell my grandchildren that I once danced with a famous Indian fighter!"

"Aw-w-w-w-w!" said Tony.

Behind Molly a man swore. "Tony—you little sneak! I told you to stay away from this crowd! You know why! Now git—before I tan the seat of your britches again!"

The boy only heard the first part of it. He gave a little

yelp like a hurt pup, jumped off the porch, and scuttled out of sight. Molly turned on big Dub Maddix, fury in her eyes.

"Why—you great big, bullying baboon!" she stormed.

She felt somebody take gentle hold of her arm. Casey Holloway spoke quietly:

"Dub—will you stay with Miss Farrington awhile? I want to talk to Miss Malone."

Dub Maddix gave the girl an angry, half-contemptuous look, then nodded to Casey, and turned away through the crowd. Molly transferred her anger to the young marshal.

"There's nothing you need to say to me," she said shortly.

Casey batted his eyes at her, as if her anger halfway pleased him. She started on but he kept hold of her arm and stayed at her side.

"Molly—listen! I'm marshal of this town. That damn actress is wearing a fortune in pearls. They think somebody might try to steal them. Think what a reputation it would give Los Charcos if somebody did! It's my job to—"

Molly laughed. "I noticed," she said. "A lot of other men seem to have the same job!"

Casey gave her arm a little tug. "Don't talk that way!" he said. "I'm sorry, I tell you. I counted on this dance. You don't know—"

"No," said Molly. "I don't!"

They were nearly to the door now, and Ben Malone turned around to meet them.

"Can I come out and see you tomorrow?"

"No!" said Molly, her chin in the air.

Molly opened her eyes, thinking crossly that Jody and the pup didn't have to make so darned much noise. She heard her mother come around the side of the wagon and speak sharply:

"Jody—you play a little more quiet so Molly can sleep!"

Molly smiled and snuggled down under the covers. But now, contrarily, she wasn't sleepy. She heard her father and mother talking, and some of what they said reached her ears.

She decided she might as well get up. She reached first for the old blue dress, then hung it back against the bows of the wagon, and took down the new red one.

It wasn't like Pa and Ma to be sitting this late around the breakfast fire when there was work to be done. But now they were both looking worried. Molly poured herself a cup of coffee.

"Did I hear you folks saying just now that Tony Ballou joined us last night after we got home?"

Mrs. Malone nodded. "The poor little thing. He wants to stay with us. He claims he ran away from Mr. Maddix because he beat him. He started out on that little mule, but it balked and got loose, so he walked the rest of the way."

"He's an awful little liar," Ben Malone said; "you can't believe anything he tells you."

"I know," Mrs. Malone said. "He hasn't been raised right. He'd get over that."

"Dub Maddix throws a lot of weight around Los Charcos," Ben Malone said slowly. "If we aim to stay here—an' get him down on us—he could make it rough. Besides—I ain't sure I want the danged kid around anyhow! You don't know what sort of stunt he may have pulled off last night that gave him cause to run off."

Mrs. Malone got up. "Come here," she said.

She led the way over to the wagon where she and her husband slept. She opened the canvas at the end, where Jody's short bed was placed crosswise.

Little Tony Ballou was asleep in it. Somehow with his eyes closed, peaceful and relaxed, his face was softened, almost babyish.

Mrs. Malone gently pulled the covers back off his thin, bare shoulders, showing a mass of old black bruises on the soft skin and half a dozen fresh, angry-looking red welts.

Molly caught her breath in shocked unbelief. Behind

her she heard Ben Malone curse softly. His wife drew the covers back gently and they all stepped down from the wagon again.

"You see," she said softly. "Maybe he's bad, Ben—but no *little* boy is *that* bad. And if he wants to stay with us— he knows we're poor, hard-working folks—that's a good sign! We've got to keep him, Ben!"

Ben Malone looked helplessly at his wife. "I don't know what the law out here in the Territory is, Ma. Maybe Maddix is his legal guardian. Like I said—you can't believe a thing the kid tells you."

"You can believe those bruises!" his wife said sharply. "He'll be lots of company for Jody."

Jody had come around the corner of the wagon in time to hear that last. Now he kicked at the ground disgustedly.

"He's an awful liar," he said. "He told me yesterday that he was Billy the Kid, too. He said he had eighteen notches on his gun."

Tony suddenly stuck his head out through the draw hole. He made a face at Jody.

"I *am* Billy the Kid!" he bragged fiercely. "An' for that crack—I'll just shoot you!"

A sling shot appeared suddenly in his hand. He aimed it at Jody's head, pulled the rubber back, and released it suddenly.

"Bang! You're dead!" he shouted.

There wasn't a rock in it—but there might have been. Jody ducked. Tony laughed shrilly.

Mrs. Malone reached up and rapped his knuckles sharply.

"Now here—none of that!" she said. "If you are going to stay with us *you won't ever point a gun,* even a play gun or a sling shot, at anybody! Do you hear me?"

Tony stuck out his underlip rebelliously. He climbed down from the wagon, the sling shot in his hip pocket.

"I'm hungry as a bitch wolf!" he announced.

Molly, Ben Malone, and Jody eyed him dubiously. Mrs.

Malone didn't seem to share their worry. Cheerfully, she set about stirring up the campfire again.

Tony watched Molly set the old black skillet over the coals and break eggs into it. His underlip was still sticking out in a challenge to anyone who might presume to scold him again. Mrs. Malone came over and took him by the arm.

"We're going to the spring and wash that dirty face," she said firmly. "Nobody sits down to eat—even around a campfire—looking like that!"

Tony pulled away from her. "Look here, squaw, d'you know who—" He broke off suddenly, and a sheepish but somehow happy grin broke over his face. "All right, ma'am," he agreed.

A dozen yards on the path toward the spring they suddenly turned around and came hurrying back to the camp.

"There's three men coming on horses," Mrs. Malone said quietly. "Do you reckon it's Mr. Maddix, Pa?"

Tony stood a little away from them. His underlip was threatening to quiver now, his face was white, his eyes scared, but he kept his thin shoulders straight.

"I didn't aim to git you-all in no trouble," he said. "I thought I fixed it so no one could track me—even ol' Casey."

Ben Malone's face was still troubled. He laid a hand on the kid's shoulder.

"I reckon they didn't have much trouble figgerin' out where you'd come, son." He turned to his wife. "What you want me to do?"

There wasn't much question about what Mrs. Malone's answer would have been, but Molly didn't give her a chance. She moved quickly, and caught the boy's arm.

"We don't have to make up our minds about that right now," she said. "Come on, you little squirt! Up in the wagon with you!"

Tony didn't hold back. He scrambled like a chipmunk over the wheel of Molly's wagon and she followed him. Molly rolled out a pile of extra bedding from the space alongside her narrow bed.

"Get under these quilts!" she ordered. "You won't have much air, but there's cracks in the floor you can breathe through. If you wiggle or make any noise—I'll—I'll let Dub Maddix have you—and welcome!"

Tony looked at her despairingly. "The sheriff's with 'em," he said. "He'll search the wagons an' find me—sure!"

Molly's lips set tight. "He won't find you in this wagon," she promised him grimly. "Now get hid! We haven't got much time!"

Tony squeezed his thin body down into the narrow space between bed and wagon frame, pressed his nose down tight to a crack in the bed of the wagon. Molly rolled the bedding back over him. She reached over her head to loosen the draw ropes so the wagon sheet could be opened enough to let her listen. She stuck her head out briefly.

"I forgot to tell you, Ma," she called softly. "I'm sick abed. I caught an awful bad cold last night."

She heard her mother's soft chuckle of understanding as she ducked into her bed and pulled up the covers.

In a few minutes she heard the thud of horses' hoofs, her father's voice pleasantly greeting the newcomers, then her mother cheerfully offering them coffee and a bite of breakfast.

After that they moved over near the campfire, and in spite of the opening she had left in the canvas, she could hear only the murmur of their voices, catching an occasional word.

The heap of bedding alongside her wiggled. Evidently Tony wanted to listen, too. Molly thumped the top of the bedding.

"You lay still!" she hissed.

Now the voices were coming closer to the wagons again. Molly heard one say quietly:

"I hope you won't take it amiss, ma'am. It's my duty as sheriff to look your outfit over. You see—Miss Farrington's pearls were stolen from her hotel room last night an' the boy Tony is missin'. It looks like he took 'em an' skipped out."

"There ain't no doubt about it!" That was Dub Maddix's rumbling voice. "You want me to search this wagon, Sheriff?"

"I'll do the searchin', Dub." The sheriff's voice was polite but firm.

Mrs. Malone spoke up quickly. "You'll go easy in this one, Sheriff, won't you? My daughter's in there sick abed. She caught a terrible cold last night."

The sheriff cleared his throat. "Why, yes, ma'am," he said. "I won't disturb her no more than I can help."

Inside the wagon Molly caught a deep breath. She didn't know what to think—she didn't know what she ought to do. Telling big lies, swearing, those were bad enough sins in a little boy—but stealing—that seemed almost beyond the rim of forgiveness.

"Tony—you little devil!" she whispered softly.

His ear wasn't buried too deep to hear. She felt the bedding wiggle in protest. She thumped it hard.

Then as she felt the faint jar of the sheriff's foot on the wagon step, she gave the covers another tug over her shoulders and closed her eyes.

Now she was scared—scared plenty! What was the penalty here in the Territory for hiding a thief? It seemed impossible to believe now that the sheriff wouldn't search the wagon. What had seemed so smart a trick a few minutes ago seemed plain dumb now.

She opened her eyes dazedly to the brighter light of the opening canvas. She blinked at the sheriff and didn't have to try to look startled. She tugged the covers up with seeming embarrassment.

The sheriff was a tall, thin man in his sixties—a cowman-gentleman of the old school who respected women. He looked as embarrassed as she was trying to look.

"I'm sorry you're sick, Miss Molly," he said.

"Th-thank you!"

His eyes swept around the inside of the wagon, resting for a second on the roll of quilts so arranged that he couldn't move them without disturbing her bed. The girl's heart seemed to stop beating for a second. Then as she met the sheriff's eyes again, she drew in a quick breath of relief, knowing that he wasn't going to search the wagon now, even if he guessed that Tony might be in here.

His position gave him little room for a polite bow, but the sheriff managed to make one.

"I'm sure sorry I disturbed you, Miss Molly."

She smiled at him, and drew another breath of relief as he backed away. Beside her she felt Tony wiggle. She gave the bedding another warning whack, then turned her head quickly as sunlight gleamed in again through the opening canvas.

This time it was Casey Holloway's face looking down at her.

"I'm sorry you're sick, Molly."

Molly stared at him without answering, aware that an arm in a red-calico sleeve was out from under the covers. Quick, hot color came up into her cheeks, anger into her gray eyes.

Casey Holloway eyed her speculatively, then suddenly smiled.

"You don't look awful sick, though," he said. "Not too sick to listen, anyway. An' I don't reckon you'll walk away from me like you did last night."

Still Molly didn't say anything.

"That fussy little manager with Miss Farrington's company last night is her husband. He asked me if I wouldn't hang around close an' keep an eye on them pearls. She insists on wearin' them everywhere—an' he was all tied up in knots for fear someone might try to steal them. They both kept insistin' they couldn't stay at the dance but a few minutes—an' I kept thinkin' they meant it—then you and me would have the rest of the evening together."

He stopped. Molly didn't say anything. She turned it over in her mind, wondering whether she ought to make him sweat a little longer. Alida Farrington was a mighty pretty woman—and some of the glances Casey had bent on her last night hadn't looked like admiration for her pearls.

Tony Ballou squirmed under the roll of bedding again, but now she couldn't give him a warning whack. Casey Holloway's eyes flicked over to the bedding a moment, then back to Molly. Suddenly he grinned.

Molly's face turned white, her gray eyes scared. Casey had seen that stir of movement, and guessed what it meant. There wasn't any doubt about that! Maybe the penalty for deliberately hiding a thief would be a jail sentence!

Molly swallowed hard. She ran her tongue over suddenly dry lips. She gave him a wavering smile.

"You—you won't tell the sheriff, Casey?"

He leaned against the bow and rolled a smoke.

"I could stay for dinner if I was asked—an' maybe go for a hossback ride up Siruela Canyon this afternoon—if I had a real purty girl to go along with me."

Molly's eyes dropped. Color came back to her cheeks. "You're a brute!"

"Born thataway," said Casey, "an' never got over it."

A dimple appeared at one corner of the girl's mouth. She sighed. "There might be wild plums up Siruela Canyon. I'll bet Ma would sure like to have some."

Casey's grin got even wider. "I ain't much of a hand to pick plums," he said, "but I reckon I could hold down the bushes for you!"

Outside, the sheriff called loudly, "Come on, Casey! Quit pesterin' that young lady an' let's go!"

"I'll be around," smiled Casey and jumped off the wagon.

In a sudden panic of fear that he might be smothering, Molly sat up and yanked the heavy roll of bedding off of Tony. He sat up, sweating and sputtering.

"The lyin' ol' devil!" he said. "I never stole nothin' from nobody! Honest, Molly, I didn't! I ran away because he beats me!"

Molly knew he fibbed as easily and readily as he talked,

but somehow this time she believed him. She gave his shoulder a little shake.

"Well, hush now! They aren't gone yet! They'll hear you!"

Tony said a bad word under his breath, but loud enough that Molly heard. She shook him again.

"And you better hush that kind of talk before *Ma* hears you!"

The girl started straightening up the bed and putting the wagon in order. She smoothed down the skirt of the red dress, noting with satisfaction that it hardly looked wrinkled at all.

Some little sound from the other end of the wagon turned her. For a moment she was paralyzed with horror. Then she jumped for the boy.

He had pulled the wagon sheet up to open a crack between it and the wagon bed. He had the sling shot in his hand, and was taking careful aim. Before Molly reached him, he let the rock fly.

Outside Molly heard sudden shouts, her mother's scream, what was probably Casey Holloway's laugh, and a rattle-banging of pots and pans.

For just a moment Molly Malone longed to reach out and smack the part of Tony Ballou that was up-ended in front of her—hard. But it was too late for that to do any good now. The fat was already in the fire.

Tony gave a short, raucous little chortle of glee. Molly ran to look out the end of the wagon.

The rock had hit the big brown horse Dub Maddix was riding, and he had spooked into a bucking fit straight through the neat array of the Malone camp. As Molly looked, Maddix was slowly picking himself up from an ignominious, nose-rooting position smack up against the chicken pen.

Mrs. Malone gave a little startled yelp. "Ben! Ben! The pearls! The chickens are eating the pearls! They spilled out of Mr. Maddix's pocket! Do something!"

She grabbed the broken string that had caught on the

chicken-wire fence and was still slowly dribbling pearls into the pen. Inside the chickens pecked merrily away at the few remaining bright bits.

Tony Baliou gave another squeal of delight that was too wild for him to contain.

"The ol' devil!" he said. "I sure fixed him that time!"

Molly Malone suddenly laughed.

"You sure did," she said. "You can cut another notch on that sling shot—Natty Bumppo!"

She swung down out of the wagon, and Tony scrambled after her.

By that time things had quieted down some. Casey Holloway had caught Dub Maddix's big bay and led him back to camp. Dub himself seemed to have lost most of his big behavior.

Ben Malone looked at his wife, amusement glinting in his gray eyes. "Looks like we're goin' to have to eat them chickens of yours after all, Bessie."

Mrs. Malone bit her lips, nodding regretfully.

Molly smiled across at Casey Holloway. "Maybe we could have one for dinner," she said. "I've invited company."

Casey smiled back at her. He and Molly Malone had known each other less than twenty-four hours, but now, right out in front of God and everybody, he came over and put his arm around her shoulders.

Tony fidgeted with his sling shot. "I'll shoot them ol' chicken's heads off for you!" he offered eagerly.

The sheriff chuckled and put his hand on the kid's arm, not seeming too surprised at seeing him—or that Molly was suddenly over her cold.

"Hold your fire, son," he said. "I reckon Mrs. Malone can keep her chickens. Miss Farrington told us this morning that them pearls was just imitation stuff that she had made up for her recent without even telling her husband. But Casey and me thought if the boy had stolen them, he ought to be found and give a good talkin'-to. He ain't a bad kid, Mr.

Malone. He ran away from an orphanage in Kansas City. He ain't got no folks—so if you-all want to keep him—an' he wants to stay—I reckon there ain't no law against it."

Tony didn't say anything. He had borrowed Jody's pocket knife and was busy cutting a notch—a big one—in the handle of his sling shot.

Peggy Simson Curry's prose is straightforward and lively, as is the theme of "The Brushoff"—the transformation of a boy into a man who "stands for something." A poet as well as a short-story writer and novelist, Curry was the second woman to be awarded the Western Writers of America Spur Award for best short story (in 1957, for this story) and was honored again in 1970 for "In the Silence." In 1981 she was accorded the honor of being named Poet Laureate of Wyoming. Her work has appeared in such publications as the New York Times, Saturday Evening Post, Christian Science Monitor, *and* Boys' Life. *She is also the editor of one of the WWA's annual anthologies of western fiction,* Western Romances *(1973).*

The Brushoff

PEGGY SIMSON CURRY

It was a summer when ranchers in the valley wrote to relatives they didn't give a darn about, and asked them to come for a visit. The ranchers mentioned how good the fishing was and how many young sage chickens had hatched out and would be of eating size by haying season. The idea was that some of these shirttail relations might be persuaded to hook up a team and help put up hay, for hired men were hard to find.

The boss didn't write any letters. He said all his relatives were women and scared of horses. Instead, we went to Denver when we got ready to put up the hay. We had some men at the ranch, but not enough. We had the old steadies—the Madson brothers from Steamboat Springs, Slim the stacker, the Swede sickle grinder, and Old Jack Patton, who drove a lead rake. And we had our share of the drifters who'd happened along at the right time.

The boss and I went down on the street in Denver where the newspaper had said men would be waiting for hire, and there they were, standing around in the sun. It was a seedy-looking outfit, I can tell you—some sobering up from the night before, some too old and frail for any kind of work, and some who looked as if they'd walked out of the hoboes' jungle.

The boss gave them the eye and was about to go on past when this kid came walking up the street and stood off by himself near the other men. He was a big, mean-looking kid with thick blond hair that was greased flat to his head, and eyes that were as clear and cold as our mountain lakes. He took out the makings and built himself a cigarette and let it hang in the corner of his mouth while he sized us up. His overalls were clean and faded, and I judged him to be around seventeen. He didn't have any fuzz on his cheeks yet.

"Well," the boss said in a low tone, "it's husky and alive. Wadda you think, Jeff?"

"Y'know that wild steer that was always bustin' outta the pasture? That's what it is, only two-legged. You finally had to butcher that steer, boss."

"Yeah," the boss muttered, "and even the meat was tough." He gave a tired sigh and started to move away.

Just then a little girl came running up the street, with her mother yelling behind her. The little girl was carrying a small doll, and when she got in front of the kid she dropped it. The doll broke and the little girl began to cry. The kid got down on his knees and tried to put the doll's head together, but it kept falling apart. The little girl kept watching him and whimpering, and the little girl's mother said, "Oh, shut up, Lindy! I'll buy you another doll."

The kid got up and looked at the broken pieces on the sidewalk. "It don't stay together no more," he said. Then he reached in his pocket and brought out a tiny figure of an Indian doll. It looked old and dirty and he handed it to the little girl and said, "Here, you keep this."

The little girl smiled, and her mother yelled, "Put that filthy rag down!" But the little girl went skipping on up the street with the Indian doll in her hands, and the mother ran after her.

The kid looked at us, and his lips drew tight and thin. "It didn't cost me nothin'," he said coldly. "I swiped it at a carnival."

The boss walked over to him and said casually, "Ever make any hay, stranger?"

"Yep," the tight lips barely moved.

"Know how to handle horses?"

"Yep."

"You want a job working in the hayfield up at my ranch?" the boss asked.

The kid shrugged. "Why not? I got nowhere else to go."

"Well," the boss said, "we'll pick up your stuff, then."

"You're lookin' at it," the kid said, and something glared at us from the green eyes, a light that dared us to ask if he didn't have a coat or a jacket or a suitcase or something.

"Let's get moving," the boss said, and the three of us walked up the hot, bright street to where we'd parked our car. The kid got in and he never said a word all the way to Laramie, Wyoming. We picked up three men in Laramie; they were talkative, smelled like whisky, and had battered suitcases. They spoke to the kid, but he just gave them a nod and acted as if they weren't around.

We went to the café to eat, and the boss said the meal was on him. The kid looked at the menu a long time, and finally the boss said, "Order anything you want, boy."

The kid finally said to the waitress, "Just a hamburger. I don't care how it's cooked."

He tried to eat it without hurrying and his face got red. He didn't order any pie and, when the pie was in front of the other men, the kid got up and walked out to the car.

"He's been in reform school," one of the new men said. "I can spot 'em a mile off."

"That so?" the boss asked politely.

"Why, sure. And if you don't mind, mister, I ain't bunking in the same place with that kid."

It turned out that nobody had to sleep near the kid. When we got to the ranch, he took a shine to the old sheep wagon the boss had parked by the river. "Anybody livin' in that wagon?" the kid asked.

"No, it's not much of a wagon any more," the boss replied.

"I'd like to be by myself," the kid said.

"Help yourself," the boss answered. "I'll rustle you up some bedding."

The next morning at the corral, the boss said to the kid, "You know how to harness a team, boy?"

The kid nodded, but when he got in the barn he put the first collar on upside down, and the men began to snicker and make talk. Old Jack Patton straightened the kid out. He came walking through the barn, thin and sour and bowlegged. A scowl settled over his lined face, and his gray hair stuck out in uncombed tufts above his ears.

"Well," he said dryly, "at least you got it on the right end of the horse, and that's more than some dumb city kids know." Old Jack Patton set the collar right and said, "You and me are going to be lead rakin' in the hayfield. I give the orders. You take 'em, see?"

Nobody in the hay crew ever got along with Old Jack Patton, but he was the best hayraker in the country. When a man worked with him Old Jack set the pace; if he drove slowly, he wanted the man following him to go at the same pace; if he speeded up, he expected the man with him to speed up. Old Jack Patton said when it was time to start and when to quit.

That first day the kid raked he was as mad as a hornet when we stopped for the noon meal that was always sent out hot in the lunch wagon. "What's goin' on around here?" the kid asked angrily. "Everybody else gets to quit and gets their teams unhooked and we make two or three more passes at that grass."

"Old Jack Patton believes in outworkin' the rest of the crew," I said. "He wants to keep a lot of hay raked up so the stackers can be busy."

"Bossy old devil," the kid muttered.

We didn't see Old Jack Patton come up beside us until he spoke.

"Listen, you city punk," he said harshly to the kid, "if you don't like the way I do it, you can quit—see? I don't need you. I don't need anybody. I can handle any job and handle it myself—see? Don't get the idea I want you around."

"And I don't want to be around you," the kid shouted back at him.

Old Jack Patton's strange yellow eyes glinted. "Good! Suits me. Run and cry to the boss, then. You tough reform-school kids gotta cry about the world."

The kid stiffened and his fists came up. His face was mean and ugly. "You call me that again and I'll beat your head in!"

Old Jack Patton spat at the kid's feet. Then he turned with slow deliberation and sauntered toward the lunch wagon.

The kid stood clenching and unclenching his fists. "I could break that old man in two," he said.

"Wouldn't change him none," I said. "He'd be the same in two pieces or one."

That night the kid was late for supper. As usual, Old Jack Patton made a couple of rounds with his rake after the other men had unhooked their teams and started for the house. When the kid came into the cookshack, the crew began to ride him about playing nursemaid to Old Jack Patton. Lola, the peroxide-blond cook, said, "You guys shut up. Lay off." And she let her big blue eyes get soft as she looked at the kid.

Everybody knew what was happening; wasn't that she felt sorry for the kid or anything like that. She just had him marked for a sucker, and Lola always had suckers in every hay crew. I figured since the kid was so tough and had been in reform school, he wouldn't fall for the line. But he looked up at her as if she might be some kind of angel.

Old Patton leaned close to me and muttered, "Reform school didn't teach him nothing. He's so soft inside it's pitiful."

It seemed to me that, after that, Old Jack Patton set out to make life hell for the kid. He worked the tail off him and bawled him out in front of the men. The kid didn't say a word, but his eyes got hotter and brighter, and sometimes the look in them scared me. Every night at the supper table Lola gave the kid the soft soap plus an extra-big piece of pie. And the first chance he had to go to town, he spent all his wages buying her candy and perfume and a red silk handkerchief.

"I'm gonna ask her to go to the haymaker's ball next week," he told me one night when I stopped by the sheep wagon. He was sprawled out on the bunk. In the light from the kerosene lamp, he didn't look mean and hard. He only looked young and lonely.

"Look, kid," I said, "there's some women do a man good because they want good to come to a man. And there's other women who don't care a hang for anything but the money that's spent on 'em."

"Lola's not what you think," he said in a low tone. "She's had a hard time, like me. And nobody understands her, just like nobody understands how I am inside. She stands for something; she's not fulla lies, like most people. She stands for being good to me."

"I guess if a man's thirsty enough he'll drink poison and think it's good," I muttered. I sat quiet and still and heard the river murmuring by, and the river said that some people were born to trouble and had it always because they never got things straightened out. I looked at the kid again and I knew he was thinking of Lola and how, to him, her greedy eyes looked kind. I said, "Ain't you got no folks, kid?"

He made a choked-off sound, and for a while there was silence. Then he said, keeping his voice low and steady, "If

I still got 'em, I wouldn't know where they are. Both of 'em run off with other people. That's when I got drunk, and I don't mind tellin' you I broke in a liquor store to find the whisky. After I had enough of it, I stole the cash I could find. That's why I got sent to reform school." Again he was quiet. Then he said in a small tone, "Yeah, and when Christmas come, neither one of 'em even sent me a card. Every other kid there—no matter what bad thing he had done—got something from someone who remembered him, a card or a present or something." He began to laugh. "I made myself a card, but it didn't fool nobody."

Old Jack Patton stuck his head in the doorway then and said in his usual hard tone, "You didn't bathe the horses' shoulders. You drive a team with me and you take some care of your horses or I'm askin' the boss to tie a can on you."

I heard Old Jack Patton's footsteps echo away. The kid said, "I hate the old buzzard! If he wasn't so sure he could make me quit, I'd have gone long ago."

"Better men than you have quit because of him," I said. "But I want to tell you something, kid; Old Jack's not hard inside. He's only lean and tough and honest. He wants to make a man out of you."

"Yeah?" The kid laughed. "Don't give me that stuff. He's like all the rest of 'em around here. I smell reform school and no matter what I do, it won't make any difference. But I can be as mean as he can." The kid rolled off the bunk. "I'll see to those horses, but I swear there ain't a mark on their shoulders. They don't need their shoulders bathed any more than I do."

The next week was the haymaker's ball in town, and the kid asked a couple of days in advance to borrow my car. "Lola said she'd go with me," he said, "and I'll be real careful with your car."

We were standing by the barn, and the evening light was creeping in over the meadows. "Sure," I said, "sure, kid." He walked away toward the sheep wagon, and Old Jack Patton came out of the barn and stood beside me.

"I wonder where he'll get a suit," Old Jack Patton said. "He can't take her in them thin overalls he's been washing out at night and putting on half wet in the mornin'."

"I've got no suit," I said.

The next night I stopped by the sheep wagon, and the kid was whistling and polishing his old work shoes. "I'm gonna clean your car early in the mornin' so's it'll look nice," he said.

"That's good," I said.

"Hey, kid!" It was Old Jack Patton calling from outside.

"Yeah? What do you want?"

"Just wanted to be sure you're there." And Old Jack Patton tossed a big box into the sheep wagon. I heard him walk away.

"What's that?" the kid asked suspiciously.

"You can look," I said.

It was what I had figured. It was a fancy suit and it was the right size. The kid kept turning it over and over and staring at it. Finally he said, "Where'd he get it, anyhow?"

"I figure he had the boss's wife buy it for him in town," I said. "Lord, kid, Old Jack Patton hasn't put on a suit in forty or fifty years."

The kid's head went down and he said in a low voice, "I guess he wanted me to look right, didn't he?"

"I guess he did."

"A fella's father wouldn't do more," the kid said wonderingly.

The next morning at the corral the kid tried to thank Old Jack Patton, and Old Jack glared at him and said, "It's mothy. Only time I ever wore it was to a funeral. It's ready to fall apart. I'd a-given it to the trash barrel before now if I'd thought about it." And he turned and led his team from the corral, shouting back at the kid, "Get the lead out! We got hay to rake."

When we came in from work that night, all the younger men started cleaning up for the haymaker's ball. They shaved and scrubbed themselves in the creek and took their good pants or suits out of their suitcases. Slim, the pusher driver, was the handsomest man in the outfit, and that night he spent a lot of time sizing himself up in the mirror. "A big night coming," he said. "I'm taking cooky."

"You mean our cooky?" I asked.

"Only one around here, ain't she?" Slim asked innocently.

"Don't, Slim. Don't take her."

His mouth came open and he stared at me. "Why? You got a shine for her, Jeff?"

"She promised the kid," I said.

"Y'mean the reform bird? I'm not steppin' aside for that stuff."

"I'm asking you to, Slim."

Slim put down the comb. "You want me to tell you something, Jeff? You're a softhearted old fool. You been kiddin' yourself along, telling yourself he isn't so bad. Well, you're wrong. That kind don't change."

"Who don't change?" The words came cold and hard from the doorway of the bunkhouse, and there stood the kid in his fine suit and his hair all slicked down and his eyes ablaze like July lightning.

Slim told him and told him hard and fast. The kid went after Slim, then. We got them separated, but not before the kid's eye was black and his lip cut and blood spattering the white shirt that had come with the suit. The kid started for the cookhouse and I ran after him, shouting, "Wait a minute, kid!" He went up the steps in two long strides and me right after him.

Lola was frying the supper potatoes. She turned and looked at us, and the kid blurted out, "You're goin' with me to the dance. You promised!"

Lola yawned and stretched and she looked like a sleek, happy cat. "That was a while ago, honey," she said. "I got a right to change my mind."

The kid turned and walked out. He went to the sheep wagon and he didn't come in for supper. I told Lola off in

words a gentleman don't use to a lady, but as the boss sometimes says, "A man can't spit enough to water a dry ground."

I waited around the bunkhouse that night until they'd
all gone, and in the quiet there was only the smell of hair
tonic and shoe polish and whisky. I waited until Lola had
gone with Slim, and the darkness lay deep on the meadows
that smelled of the cut hay. Then I walked down by the river
to the sheep wagon. There wasn't any light, but I knew he
was there. I said, "Kid?" There was no answer, and I stepped
inside and sat in the dark and I could hear him breathing
there on the bunk.

After a while I said, "You may not think it, but you're
better off she turned you down. She never was anything but
a—"

"Shut up!" It was a snarl of sound. "I get it, see? I get
the picture like I got it before. Nobody tells the truth; nobody stands for what they pretend to stand for. Nobody's
anything real and steady; they all change into something
lyin' or mean or ugly. They told me in reform—the big guy
said, 'The world will treat you right. Nobody'll hold a mistake against you.' He lied and he knew it, see? First I believed him, and then I believed Lola, and it was the same.
Nobody's what they pretend. It's all pretend."

"Wait a minute, kid. Not all of us. The boss and I and Old
Jack—some people stand for things they believe. Some people—"

"Get out! Get out and leave me alone."

I went back to the bunkhouse, and there sat Old Jack
Patton reading a story about cowboys and rustlers. He
looked up and said, "Well, she give him the run-around,
didn't she?"

"He didn't have it coming," I said.

"A man's got to have enough inside to take anything
that's coming—trouble, death, and lyin' women. Until he's
got that inside, he don't amount to nothing."

"But he's only a kid," I said.

"The hand of cards life dealt him, he better grow up

fast," Old Jack Patton said, and went back to his reading.

The next morning the kid got some whisky from the men and got drunk. He was already sick when we reached the hayfield. He hooked up his team and then he leaned against the wheel of the rake and looked terrible.

Old Jack Patton walked up to him and grabbed him by the shoulders and shook him hard. He said, "Get on that rake and rake hay. If you got a job to do, you do it, see? You do it whether you're sick in the belly or in the head. And you do it right. Straighten up, you weak punk! Straighten up, damn you!"

The kid called him names, and Old Jack Patton laughed in his face and said, "Get on that rake and get to work." The kid dragged himself onto the rake and began to make the windrows.

We had only a few days of work left, and the kid and Old Jack Patton were just as they had been in the beginning, the man driving the boy as hard as he could, and the boy hating him. The kid looked more mean and sullen than when he'd first come to the ranch, and even the boss thought Old Jack was going too far.

"Lay off the kid, Jack," he said. "He can only take so much."

"He's got to take everything," Old Jack Patton said grimly.

That was the day Lola quit, and the boss sent the kid to the house to help get supper for the men. "My wife needs you," he told the kid. "You give her a hand. Old Jack can finish up that piece of meadow he's laid off to work."

The kid nodded and said, "Well, this is one day I'll get to leave the field ahead of time, and it's killin' that old buzzard's soul."

"He won't have nobody to chew on the rest of the afternoon," I said.

"Tough, huh?" And the kid suddenly grinned at me.

Old Jack Patton was still raking, as usual, when we left the field. The kid helped the boss's wife dish up supper, and we finished eating, but Old Jack hadn't come. The men went back to the bunkhouse, and the boss and I stood by the cookstove while the kid washed dishes.

"I better have a look," the boss said. "Old Jack didn't have much raking left to do. It's taken too long."

The kid swung around from the dishpan. There was something I had never seen before in his green eyes. "Nothing's wrong with him, is there?"

"I couldn't say, kid," the boss answered. . . . "You want to come with me, Jeff?" he said, turning to me.

Before I could answer, the kid had yanked off the dish towel he had tied around his middle. "I'm a-goin' with you," he said.

"I reckon that's all right," the boss replied.

There was moonlight, the kind of moonlight that makes the world almost as bright as in daytime. We rode up the meadow in the wagon and none of us said anything. Then we saw the team standing dark and still, and we saw the little piece of meadow where the cut grass was flat and silvery between the shining waves of the windrows. There wasn't much left to rake there, maybe half a dozen trips back and forth with the rake.

The boss stopped the wagon and wound the lines around the wheel so the team wouldn't walk off. We went across the little space between us and the rake, our feet swishing through the grass. It was so still I could hear my heart beating loud. Or maybe I was just scared.

Old Jack Patton lay by the rake wheel, and the lines were there in his hand. His face was toward the sky, and it was so peaceful that I knew before the boss knelt beside him that he'd never cuss the kid out again.

The boss didn't speak for quite a while, and when he did his voice was husky. "He was a good man, one of the best I ever had. And he was old—older than he ever let on to any of us. It came to him where he would have wanted it, and it came easy and natural." And the boss gently took the lines from Old Jack Patton's quiet hand, and he lifted Old Jack

Patton in his arms and carried him to the wagon.

The kid stooped and picked up the lines. He climbed on the seat of the rake and just sat there. After a while he said, "I'll finish up what he started." And then I saw the shine on the kid's cheeks, and I heard the sound he was trying so hard to hold in. "He was a man stood for something," the kid said. "Like you—and the boss."

As the boss and I drove down the meadow toward the ranch, I could hear the silvery clanging of the rake. It rose clean and sure in the still night. That was when I knew the tough kid was going to turn out all right.

The novel from which this story is excerpted, The Fancher Train, *was the recipient of the Western Writers of America's Spur Award for best western historical novel of 1958. This chronicle of a wagon train heading west demonstrates the librarian-historian author's deft dramatic touch, skillful characterization, and excellent interweaving of great amounts of carefully researched material. Even today the tensions between the whites and Indians depicted in this story are familiar ones with which readers can identify, and they will also be heartened by a resolution which says that people may respect and treat one another honorably regardless of racial barriers.*

The Warhorse
of Spotted Tail

AMELIA BEAN

Jed Smith felt driven to near murderous rage at the down-right viciousness that seemed to crop up so regularly with the Missouri bunch that had attached itself to the Fancher Wagon Train. When they weren't bragging around camp trying to egg someone into a brawl they thought up some other form of devilment. Like what they were up to, now.

Nightly they set up a dice game on a blanket. That was fairly harmless, when they gambled and fought drunkenly among themselves. But this night some Sioux braves had wandered into camp and the bunch had first got them drunk on uncut corn liquor, now they were gambling for their horses. The Indians were too drunk to notice when they switched to loaded dice. It was a twice-dirty deal, for a couple of the animals were not just Indian ponies, they were fine, good conformation.

Jed decided against speaking out. It wasn't his business, he'd only signed on to scout for the wagon train. But he settled in shadow, where he could watch. The Sioux were unarmed or they wouldn't have been let into camp, but one of them might pack a knife under his shirt and if they caught on, or were pushed too far . . .

By the time some woman, upset by the drunken squalling of the Indians, had complained to Captain Fancher, they'd won four of the five horses. All except a buckskin pony ridden by a tight-faced stripling who'd taken no part in the drinking or gambling. Likely he'd seen the older men get cheated, for the black eyes in his thin, proud face were smoldering.

Captain Fancher showed up but he stood perplexedly to one side. He was a man who hated trouble, God knows what it would take to get him on the prod, Jed thought. But then Fancher shared most white men's views on Indians. The emigrators didn't hold a redskin to be hardly more account than an animal, sure not to be considered same as a man. An awful lot of hair had been lifted off just such people.

The gambling blanket had been spread close enough to catch the light from a fire. Now one reeling, slobbering brave was using wide gestures, making some sort of protest. Jed, who understood Sioux talk, made out that the man hadn't understood what the stake was, this last time. He had not wagered the horse, it was the warhorse of Spotted Tail, his brother-in-law, and not his to lose. Spotted Tail was in the white man's prison in Leavenworth. It was a family honor trust that the horse be kept safe against his release. A war chief must have his warhorse and his brother-in-law would soon return to his lodge. The thing was a mistake, therefore he would take the horse now and return to his people. He reached an unsteady hand to the animal's bridle.

The hand was knocked aside and the sodden Indian found himself staring up into the contemptuous gaze of a big red-bearded man. Solomon Ward, heavily booted feet truculently spread, beefy hands on hips, sneeringly dared the Indian to start something. The red-beard's arms and shoulders were immense, his barrel chest wore a mat of thick red hair, which protruded though the opening of his dirty shirt. A wide leather belt rode below his bulging belly and supported a sheath which held a knife.

The Indian reeled, stared confusedly up at the man, and reached for the bridle again. Sol Ward grinned and put a hamlike hand on the Indian's chest and shoved, sending him sprawling. While he was down, Sol kicked him, hard. The other Indians clamored protestingly but now the other men, roaring with brutal mirth, joined in the fun. Kicking and shoving, they drove the Indians out of camp.

The watching youngster at the edge of light cast by the fire sat his pony, his gaze on the man, Sol Ward, who stood holding his belly as he laughed.

Jed saw that the set young face was murderous with hate and outrage. Good thing for Sol Ward that the young pup was unarmed, he'd likely been dead before he finished his belly laugh. The slitted black eyes memorized the look of the red-beard before he wheeled the buckskin and followed the staggering braves.

Jed followed along at a distance, wanting to make sure they got out of camp with no further trouble. He saw the boy rein up alongside the reeling group and help two of the kicked men onto the pony. Taking the halter rope, he led the horse away into the night, thin shoulders bowed under the weight of humiliation.

Jed returned to camp for a short, blunt word with Captain Fancher, with the result that more guards were dispatched to the horse herd and around the encamped train. Captain Fancher then notified the Missouri bunch that he would put up with no more gambling with Indians.

They had been noisily boasting over their winnings. Sol had won the warhorse—an unusually handsome animal. It was a "paint" horse, satiny black on the thickly muscled neck and shoulders with a white blaze between the eyes.

The powerful hindquarters were also black, there were white ovals on the belly, and the strong, nervous legs were deeply white-stockinged. From the thickness of the proud, arching neck Jed guessed it was a stallion in the prime of maturity, seven or eight years old. He could understand well the Indian's panic, there was nothing valued higher by a warrior than a spotted, trained-for-war horse.

Sol Ward's heavy face was quarrelsome, he did not like Captain Fancher's edict about their gambling. "Guess you didn't like our little game either, Smith," he said belligerently.

Jed shrugged. "One of 'em wasn't drunk, he knew how come they lost. They could give us trouble, if they're a mind to."

"Them stinkin' bastards?" Sol snorted. "Hell, they ain't hardly got enough spine to hold themselves up, not a one of 'em would stand and fight!" Sol was disgusted at having been done out of a brawl.

Jed bit back his anger. "Half the Sioux Nation is camped over there"—he waved toward the northern hills—"they're headin' for a big council in the Tetons. That little bunch that was here could likely find a hundred relatives anxious to help give us trouble."

"Well, hell, let 'em!" Sol was scornful. "We got enough rifles to take care of the whole damn pack of 'em!"

"You ain't likely been in a wagon-train fight, Ward, or you wouldn't just as soon start one. Trouble is, it ain't always the fightin' men gets it. Sometimes a woman or a little kid winds up with a bullet or arrow in 'em."

Among the listeners a woman muffled a scream and Jed went hastily on. "I don't think they'll attack the train—they ain't on the warpath, they've got their women and kids along. And they been mighty leery of exposin' their folks to trouble after what Squaw-killer Harney done. But they might jump the horse herd or figger out some way to even things up. Sioux warriors got a hell of a lot of pride. They get even when they can."

"Warriors? Hell, them draggle-tail punks didn't look like warriors to me!" Sol spat contemptuously.

Jed wanted to smash his fist into the sneering, bearded face but the echo of old Jim Bridger's advice slowed his anger. Bridger had gotten him the scouting job and he'd warned him he'd find emigrators a stupid, pigheaded lot, seldom willing to take the guidance they paid for. "But don't let an emigrator have room to rile you, boy," he'd said. "They don't any of 'em appear to have what you'd call horse sense. Just kinda nurse 'em along like a passel of idiots and pay no mind to what they say."

"They're warriors," Jed repeated, "one of 'em was Iron Shell and he's already packin' a grudge, his wife and son was killed by white soldiers. And the kid on the buckskin, I know of him. He's the son of Crazy Horse, the Oglala Holy Man. Nobody's got more influence in the tribes than a Holy Man."

Captain Fancher looked unhappily at the two men who faced each other, hard dislike evident on both of them. "Well," Fancher tried to put an end to the strain, "we put more guards out, all around. Maybe that'll do it. Anyway, what's done is done."

Jed spat and turned away. "That's right," he said, "it's done."

The next morning Jed scouted over toward where the Indian encampment had been, five or six miles from the wagon train. They had moved on and he returned, noticing he followed the tracks of the group which had visited the train. The tracks were deep in soft dirt, because of the double load the pony had carried. Jed saw that the buckskin left an odd left hind print. It splayed out a little, the hoof must have been split and healed a little crooked.

Since Jed had started courting Melissa Boller he was usually invited to eat supper with her and her brother, David. That night Jed informed Melissa that she must not ride her mare away from the wagon train for a spell, nor could she accompany him on his scouting, as she had been doing at times.

"You mean," Melissa sputtered, "that just because ol' Sol Ward cheated an Injun out of a horse that *I* can't ride out at all?"

"Yep."

"But *you* can look after me—"

"Not proper, you never know what might come up." He was nettled at her rebellious attitude, which seemed to question his judgment, but his gaze softened as he looked down at her. She was mighty pretty.

The ruby-red calico she wore with its rows of little ruffles across the bosom was becoming, flattering. The rich color made her cheeks rosy, her eyes seem darker. She had wound the thick blond braid into a coronet high on her head and it made her seem taller, more womanly.

"The Sioux are travelin' just a few miles north of us, Melissa," he said, "in the same direction. And some of the braves would take a lot of chances to even the score. I won't have you skylarkin' around on a horse, even close to the train. You stay on the wagon, hear?"

Melissa appealed to David but her brother only grinned, he was enormously tickled at Jed's assumption of authority and, knowing his headstrong little sister, interested in the outcome. David only shook his head. "Time for me to get on over to the herd," he said, "my turn to night-wrangle." He got lazily up and ambled off across the encampment.

Melissa switched tactics. Her slanting eyes teased up at Jed where he lounged against the wagon, sipping coffee. "Aw, please, Jed—" This was accompanied by her most promising smile.

He emptied the coffee grounds into the embers of the cook fire and set the cup down. "Nope."

"You're not running this train," Melissa flared, "or *me!* I guess I'll ride if I want to!"

"Just you do—" Jed said coldly, "and see what you get! You act like a little kid—and I'm liable to whip you—like a little kid!"

Melissa was infuriated because she believed that he actually would. "Or maybe like you'd whip a squaw?"

"Like I'd whip a squaw. Except I never knowed a squaw that would act that damn silly!"

"I guess you know a lot of squaws—"

"Yep."

"Well, I'm not a squaw, Jed Smith—and if you lay one dirty paw on me, I'll—I'll— I'm not your property!"

Jed did not answer, he looked at her, unsmiling, a long look from her small button shoes up her body to her face. She felt the intimacy of his stare like a searching hand and a scarlet wave of color crowded flushingly to her cheeks.

A deep knowing was in Jed as he looked at her. He was remembering all the women he had known but it was not until now that it was the one he wanted to keep. The others had been only to ease a momentary need, brighten a day, an hour. What he felt now, bound up in this small, strong-spirited girl, was the big thing that a man could search for all his life. And maybe never find.

The changing temper of Jed's thoughts matched a similar realization in Melissa. And she was glad to have it so, she knew a surge of fierce joy in his mastery but she dropped her eyes, unwilling to meet his gaze.

His hand reached for her chin, raised her face. "You'll do like I say—" he said. It was not command, nor question, but something between.

When she nodded he leaned and kissed her parted lips. He felt the tremor of response from her soft mouth and he grinned crookedly, tenderly. He was unaccountably pleased at the stormy nature of her.

The next few days Jed grew to feeling vaguely uneasy as he scouted ahead of the wagon train. Things were too peaceful but there were no signs, although he took to making ever widening circles. But no redskin, or the slightest sign of any, was to be found near the emigrant road. The hordes of Sioux had turned north, away from the trail, toward Bear Butte, where their Great Council was to be held.

Days later, when he scouted the first crossing of the Sweetwater, he came across the fresh hoofprints of an unshod horse—and the shape of an odd track leaped at him. The left hind hoofprint splayed out, it had been made by the little buckskin ridden by the son of Crazy Horse. And maybe now ridden by one of the men of the dishonored lodge of Spotted Tail.

Jed grinned, knowing now what had caused his uneasiness. That itching sensation along his spine, the watched feeling that'd caused him to make like a deer combing the wind with its nose. All the time he'd taken to riding wide, watching jumpy-like for sign, this lone buck had dogged him, more than likely anticipating his every move. They were damn cagey, Injuns, when it came to a deal like that. But he'd been raised by mountain men and he'd felt a prickling uneasiness, eying every clump of cover like a spooky squaw, swinging his gaze, hunting untoward movement. And not finding a thing that didn't belong. The quick, startled leap of antelopes maybe or the peevish flurry of sage hens—but nothing he hadn't kicked up himself.

The hair on his neck could stay down now, for the lone buck didn't have designs on Jed or he'd have jumped long ago, there'd been plenty of chance. He'd bet money on it that it was the warhorse he was after. And that was Sol Ward's lookout.

That night after the cook pots had been emptied Jed sought out Ward. The big man looked at him sourly. "Where you keepin' that paint horse nights?" Jed asked.

"With the horse herd. Why?"

"If I was you I'd sleep with him wrist-haltered, less'n you wanta take a chance on losin' him."

Sol stared suspiciously at the scout. "What makes you think I might lose him?"

"I seen sign at the Sweetwater ford this mornin'. Tracks of the buckskin that young'un was ridin' the night you got the paint."

Sol's look was first incredulous, then it hardened into a

sneer. "You seen sign—and you kin tell by a *track* it was the buckskin? So you want I should sleep with that big brute trompin' round my head? D'you take me to be a fool, Smith?"

Jed stiffened, he should have known better than to bother warning this stupid, pigheaded bully. "I don't take to you at all, Ward," he said flatly, "I got a heap better things to do than fret over you losin' a horse, specially one you got crooked. I've warned you. What you do, or don't do is your own lookout."

Jed turned away but Ward's heavy hand fell on his shoulder, violently swung him around. He shoved his coarse, bearded face up close. "I don't let no man call me crooked!" he prodded. "You'll take back the word—or stand and fight!"

Jed looked expressionlessly at the big man while he considered briefly. Then he nodded. Leaning his Hawken against a wagon wheel, he unbuckled his belt with its sheathed knife, hung it beside the rifle. He removed his buckskin shirt, hung that also on the wheel. Looking around to a dusty clearing lighted somewhat by a big fire, he motioned toward it. "Over there all right?" he asked.

An expression of almost unbelieving joy had come on Sol's brutal face. He hadn't thought for a minute the scout would dare take him up on it and the lean-built man looked like a cinch. There were no holds barred when Sol Ward fought, kicking, gouging, anything went. He took off his shirt, baring the huge shoulders and arms, the hairy barrel chest. His teeth gleamed through his red beard, nothing Sol enjoyed as much as a fight, especially when he had an edge on the outcome.

Jed knew what Ward was thinking—and knew also the way he would fight. Behind the casual, almost indifferent cast of his face Jed was calculating. The red-bearded giant had height and reach on him and possibly forty pounds of weight. But also at least fifteen years of age, and he was ponderous-moving as a fat bear, his bulging lard belly might not stand heavy punishment. And he was too sure of himself.

Sol might not have met up with a trick or two and obviously underestimated the strength of the lean arms and shoulders that were solid with hard layers of muscle. Jed's habitual easy slouch was very misleading. And fighting was second nature to the scout. His boyhood rough-and-tumble days had been spent with the Indians. He had been schooled in the peculiarly vicious Indian style of hand-to-hand combat, where the single motive was to kill, and quickly. Short of that, the goal was to maim, disable your opponent with no thought for anything as unrealistic as gallantry. Jed had survived several broken bones before the grim lessons were finished. The redskins didn't pamper their fledgling war hawks, the training was severe—and enormously effective. Now, slightly crouching, eyes on Sol's big hands, Jed waited.

As if by magic a crowd had gathered. Someone rushed off to get Captain Fancher to stop so unevenly matched a fight. Melissa and David were among those pushing through the forming circle. "David—" she cried, "don't let Jed— Stop them, David!"

David turned on her savagely. "Shut up!" he ordered, "and get back to the wagon—you got no business here."

She retreated from her brother but she didn't leave. She moved off to edge up and peer between two intently watching men. She was shaking with sickened fear.

David's stern face did not show that he, also, was afraid for Jed. He knew there could be no stopping of it, but David was resolved to interfere if things got too bad. There'd be help from another man or two, should Sol's cronies want the red-beard left unhindered.

David looked across the excited circle at Les Prichard, whose weasel face was a-grin with anticipation. Les was a measly sneak, always toadying around Ward and Jake Tibbetts, Sol's most constant companion. Tibbetts was there, stolidly watching, the usual dead expression on his hoglike face. He was an obscenely fat, dirty man, uncommunicative beyond grunts. Sol Ward did not bully Jake as he did Les, there was a viciousness about the lardlike man for all his seeming lethargy, he seemed capable of monstrosities.

Sol Ward laughed, a great bellow that shook his belly as he charged, bull-like, at the scout. One great fist struck out toward Jed's head, it would have been bone-shattering had it landed, but Jed moved fast, escaped with skin rubbed off one cheek. As the red-beard's arms flailed wide Jed's hands found a hold on Sol's belt. Using an Indian wrestling trick, he exploited the rushing weight and momentum of Sol's charge plus his own complete strength in a great, heaving throw. The astounded watchers saw Sol seem to dive across Jed's suddenly crouching form and land with terrible force on his belly, his face plowing dirt. It hurt Sol Ward, it was a punishing shock to his big body. Gasping for knocked out breath, brushing at dirt blinding his eyes, he scrambled up and located the scout, who was waiting for him, a half grin on his face. Sol charged again but more cautiously, the bear-like arms reaching. Jed maneuvered, feinting until Sol straightened, before he let the huge grip encircle him. The scout knew a moment of strangling panic as he experienced the powerful savagery of their crushing strength. But his shorter stature helped, he was able to work downward, bending his knees slightly. As Sol's brutal vise tightened, sought to bend him, crack his spine, the red-beard spread his legs to steady his stance. Like a steel spring, Jed's bony knee came up without mercy in Sol's groin.

Agony shot up through the thick body, loosened the hairy arms, and Jed's fists buried themselves piston-fast and hard in the protruding belly. While Sol reeled, rendered flaccid momentarily, Jed punished the belly again and again. The red-beard faltered to one knee, his shaking hands sought his tortured crotch, his shaggy head shaking. He raised blurred eyes to see the scout crouching, watching.

"Call it off, Ward?" Jed asked.

The terse question infuriated Sol beyond all reason. He drew a knife from his boot, the wicked blade glinting in the firelight.

A woman screamed, a low murmur growled through

the crowd. "Here, now—" It was Captain Fancher's voice, he had started forward. David was moving to interfere, also.

But like a swift, leaping cougar, the scout came in on Sol. As the red-beard came to his feet one moccasined toe shot out, connected with the knife hand. There was a cracking sound, the knife dropped, and Sol bellowed, reaching for his broken wrist as Jed's foot, toe rigid, came up again, deep into his lower belly. The huge man went back, his head thudded on the ground. And Jed kicked him again, in his thick neck just below the ear.

Sol shuddered once and lay still, his eyes rolled whitely under half-closed lids. A trickle of blood came from his mouth, seeped through his beard, and dripped onto the ground. Still in a crouch, Jed waited, his eyes on Sol. Then he straightened to glare around at the watchers. "Anybody want to take up for Ward?" he invited angrily.

No one answered. Jed reached a long arm, picked up Sol's knife. "Tell Ward when he comes to that I stopped fightin' for fun when I was still a kid. Tell him the next time he starts somethin', I'll kill him. I can use a knife some, too." He flung the knife and it struck so close to Sol's head that the shaggy hair parted to receive it. "I got no use for crooked gamblers," he said, "tell Ward I said it again—*crooked!*"

There was stunned silence as he reached for his shirt, took his rifle and belt from the wheel. There was respectful admiration in the eyes of the men who hastily moved back to allow him passage. Eyes shining, David watched him go and then turned a suddenly narrowed stare on Les and Jake. They had looked at the prone mound that had been their vaunted champion and now sent a planning, venomous glare after the scout. David stepped forward. "Anyone takin' it further with Jed Smith had best figger on me, too." The usually genial face of the stocky man was hard, dangerously set.

"Count me in on that." The drawl came from lanky Joel Mitchell, who stepped up to stand spraddle-legged alongside David. His cheerful bony face looked eagerly across at Les and Jake.

"And me!" Lawson Mitchell stood happily belligerent beside his brother.

The crafty faces turned sullen. "Aw, who's takin' it any further?" whined Les. "Come on, Jake, give me a hand here." Ungently heaving and hauling, they dragged the beaten man to his wagon. Sol's wife, Sairy, a thin, tired woman with a bitter face, surveyed him and malicious satisfaction appeared in her faded eyes as she took in the extent of the damage.

"One of these first days," she said sourly, "he's gonna have to learn to keep his big mouth shut. He's a-gettin' too old and fat to fight ever' tough young'un that calls his hand." She got a basin of water and rags and with untender thoroughness began to mop him off.

Melissa had pushed her way out of the crowd to run after Jed. He heard the quick pattering and turned as she came up with him. She was breathless. "Oh, Jed!" she gasped, "are you all right?"

He nodded, frowning at her. There was something about her appearance that startled him. "Were *you* there?" he asked disapprovingly.

"Oh, *yes!* And I was so scared, at first! But when you beat him, I—oh, *Jed!*"

Now he recognized the look of her. He'd seen this exultance in the faces of Indian women, welcoming their men home from battle. Fierce, proud-lusting, woman-strong, hungry to passionately reward a strong warrior.

Jed was surprised—and shocked. Squaws, now, they enjoyed a brawl, but he'd thought white women carried on, fainted, maybe, or something. This small one held surprises for him at every turn. She'd not only stood and watched, she was glorying in the winning, there was shared triumph in every line of her. Her hands raised now, brushed dirt from his bare chest, gently touched his bloody face. "You're bleeding, Jed, and it's dirty. Come over to the wagon—let me wash it—"

Her touch triggered away his control and his arms went swiftly around her, lifting her. The rifle, still in one hand, bruised her as she was held crushed against him, feet off the ground. Savagely his mouth came down on hers, which was still open and surprised—but instantly responded. One arm was pinned against him but the other went around his neck, clutching, holding on. The whole warm length of her answered, arching, pressing frantically closer. It was a long, hurting, glorying kiss and a wonder of ecstatic delight ran shaking through her body and legs.

Jed set her down on her feet, staring down at her with astounded eyes. Her face was flushed, lovely with adoration. She was smiling delightedly and moved to come closer in his arms again. But he held her off. "Get off to your wagon"— it was a husky growl, belied by the shine of his eyes, the tenderness of the crooked grin—"before I drag you off in the bushes like the bloody little squaw you are!"

Her smile was pixyish. "I'll go in the bushes with you, Jed," she announced, "you won't have to drag me!"

"I believe you would, you little hussy," he said, "and then I'd have your brother on my neck. Get off with you now —" His hand turned her, slapped at her calico rear. He hastily took off in the other direction, not daring to test his control by prolonging the contact.

Later, making his final round of the camp, Jed noticed that the paint warhorse had been picketed near the wagons, with the mounts used by the herders. He grinned mirthlessly, the horse's being picketed wouldn't likely hinder a horse stealer who'd proved so crafty thus far. But it just could be that the redskin was ready to make his try for the horse—there'd been no sign close to the emigrant road until this day.

Jed moved his bedroll to a place deep in the shadow of some willow bushes from where he could see the horse herd and also the picket line. It was a dark night, moonrise would be well after midnight. If the Indian made his try it would be after the camp settled down and before the moon made light. There was still movement in camp, some people sitting around fires, so Jed decided to catch a nap. He dropped off instantly, waking as though at an alarm when all was finally silent.

The night was inky black, thick with quiet. Jed's eyes adjusted, catlike, and sought the picket line. The warhorse stood quietly, head down, among the shadowy shapes of the other horses, but he was a big horse and his rump was higher than the others. Silently, Jed sat comfortably cross-legged, facing the herd and the picket line. The only sounds were the slow, muffled movement of hoofs, the somnolent crunching of leisurely jaws. He knew he would not hear anything unusual, but as his eyes made wide circles which began and ended with the warhorse, his ears strained for the slightest whisper of activity.

He sat motionless for well over an hour. Then his gaze riveted on the fringe of the quiet herd. Two animals grazed out a little apart from the rest. One of them seemed to be moving naturally, but gradually it was nearing the picket line. After a very long while the lone grazer cropped grass a few feet from the picketed horses.

Jed grinned with admiration, this redskin was truly an accomplished horse stealer. Not once had the scout glimpsed him, there had been no untoward movement, even to his practiced eyes. But Jed knew where the Indian now was, as if he looked full at him—behind the herd side of that grazing horse. His arm would be crooked around its neck, his hand reaching up under the mane. His head would be flattened against and below the ridge of the animal's shoulder. His moccasined feet moved only in synchronization with the horse's slow, infrequent stepping. The unalarmed horse would respond to the pressure and drift, apparently aimlessly, wherever directed.

This was indeed a master horse stealer—among the tribes it was an ancient, well-studied science and a proud skill, for it could only be acquired dangerously. Jed could knowledgeably appreciate the proficiency he was seeing, for he had learned the art from old Red Feather himself, long considered to be the greatest horse stealer of all time. Not only among the Flatheads, of whom he was chief, but among all the tribes.

When the exchange of horses took place, Jed caught his first glimpse of the Indian, and then only a shadowy figure that imperceptibly blended and was lost as the big warhorse commenced moving slowly, grazing back toward the herd.

Jed had stiffened with surprise. The shadow had been very small, slight. He frowned in puzzlement and then it dawned on him. By God, the thief was that youngster! That bitter-proud stripling with the banked embers of hate in his wild black eyes. The half-grown son of Crazy Horse!

Jed sat motionless, his mind racing, marveling, his heart suddenly full to suffocation with an emotion he could not down. That skinny, half-starved-looking kid. Well, by God!

The big horse and its invisible guide gained the fringes of the herd, mingled, and was lost in the shadowy outlines. Jed reached for his saddlebags, which he used as a pillow, and searched their contents. He checked the revolver he kept there, making sure all five chambers were filled.

The dark pool of shadow under the willows seemed unchanged but Jed no longer used their shelter. Quiet as a drifting hawk, he faded past the sleeping wagon train and its somnolent guards. Circling, he headed north and east toward a high, wooded knoll. He had probed the area all about the camp before sundown and knew without thinking about it that the buckskin was likeliest hid out on the highest point near the wagon encampment. Jed would have bet money on it that the youngster had likely watched the picketing of the warhorse.

Jed knew he had plenty of time to find the buckskin. The boy would graze the warhorse slowly along the edge of the herd, alert for the night guards as a stalking cougar. When he neared a line of trees along a little creek the horse would be slid past them at the moment the slow-moving guard was the farthest away. He'd walk the horse slowly, circling to come up the knoll on its far side. Then, with two mounts to alternate, he'd be fast, running miles beyond pursuit, come sunup. It was a good, well-thought-out plan—but the boy wouldn't have counted on Jed watching from the start.

The buckskin was there on the knoll, tethered under a tree, a hunting bow and quiver of arrows hung from a branch. The night was still black but the moon would soon rise, there was faintly lighter sky above the eastern hills. Jed moved off a ways from the patient little buckskin and settled in shadow to wait.

The rising moon had just bared a narrow curve above the mountains when Jed heard faint sounds. His mouth slitted into his crooked grin, the kid all but had the big brute of a warhorse tiptoeing. Then they appeared, the slight boy leading the slow-moving big horse. The boy halted and turned, put both arms about its neck, his face was hidden in its mane. Jed could see the deep sigh shudder across the bony young shoulders.

The scout made no more than a whisper of sound as he moved but the boy whirled like a cat, his hand whipping to the knife he carried. It gleamed wickedly before him as he half crouched, his slender muscles tight as a coiled steel spring.

Jed had taken only a couple of steps. He halted, stood with both hands extended, palm up. "The son of Crazy Horse," he said in the Sioux tongue, "goes lightly armed to make the big coup."

Seen close to, like this, the boy looked very young. His skin was pale for a Sioux, his hair was brown, not black, and Jed recalled that his boy-name in the tribes was "The Light-Haired One." Undersized for his fifteen years he might be, but not frail, Jed knew. Those lean muscles would have the swift lash of a whip, he was plenty dangerous. Jed hoped he wouldn't throw the knife before they could talk. The boy spoke.

"I take back the honor of my uncle, Spotted Tail!" It was a challenge, the manner of it. He remained crouched and ready; he'd fight to the death before relinquishing the warhorse.

"My younger brother," Jed said softly, "is indeed an

accomplished horse stealer. I saw him take the warhorse of
Spotted Tail from near the wagons. I, who was the pupil of
Red Feather, have never seen more skill than shown by the
son of the great Crazy Horse."

Surprise, confused uncertainty, crossed the thin face.
The term "younger brother" had great significance in the
tribes. The boy straightened a little from his threatening
crouch, his eyes were still wary but the frenzied defiance
had abated.

Jed spoke again. "I have heard of the Light-Haired One
from Hotoa-Quaihoois, Tall Bull, who is blood brother to Jim
Bridger, my foster father."

The boy knew him now, he sheathed his knife and ac-
knowledged the identification with a compliment delivered
with the dignity of a patriarch. "Word has reached my people of Jed Smith, pupil of Red Feather. Loud have been the
praises of Bridger and the Bad Hand."

Jed's grin crooked. Sure, Bad Hand Fitzpatrick, old
mountain man, now government agent to the Indians on the
upper Platte, would have bragged. He and Jim Bridger took
on big over anything Jed did passably—these two tough old
roosters had raised him from a pup.

The boy went on. "And there are still those among the
Old Ones who speak of Singing Ax. They say that his son,
Little Ax, now follows fittingly in his proud tracks."

Jed bowed his head with honest pride. Any place he set
foot the deeds of his father, mountain man Jedediah Strong
Smith, lived in legend and firelit chant. The proud title of
Singing Ax had been bestowed by his enemies. Old Jed had
been deeply religious—but a mighty fighter. Deadly in a
hand-to-hand fracas, his usual weapon was a short ax and
always, as he hewed mighty havoc, he chanted prayers for
the dying, whose demise he sought to make mercifully swift.
The deep bell of his voice ringing above the clamor of battle
had created mighty big medicine about his person and the
superstitious redskins took to avoiding a brush with mountain men if Singing Ax was known to be present. They be-

lieved that the powerful God of the white man sat on his big arm, breathing invincibility into him as he fought.

Ceremoniously Jed returned the compliment. "We have heard much of the son of Crazy Horse. His warrior-teacher, High Back Bone, has told that he killed his first buffalo before his head reached as tall as his father's shoulder. We have heard that his naming ceremony will soon give him the proud name of his holy father, Crazy Horse."

Now the moon cleared the heights and the two young men saw each other plainly, their eyes met with warmth and mutual respect. It grew late and Jed wanted the youngster away from here.

"The moon has risen to make light your path to the Great Council," he said. "I would send word to the tepee of your father, if you will carry it."

"The words of my brother, Little Ax, will be carried in my heart and spoken straight on my tongue."

"Say to your father," Jed ordered his message with care, "the wise and holy Crazy Horse, that some men of our race shame us all. The red-beard who cheated to win the war-horse is one of these. Say to Crazy Horse that Little Ax was made glad by the manner of the return of honor to the lodge of Spotted Tail. I send a token of friendship to Crazy Horse —and greetings to all in his lodge."

Jed took up his saddlebags and held out the revolver. "It carries five shots," he said, "for the enemies of Crazy Horse. In the saddlebags there is grain for the horses and some jerked meat. The Light-Haired One must eat, but he should not pause to hunt now."

It was most evident that the boy could have had little to eat during his days of stalking vigilance. About the breechclout and knife belt, which were all he wore, his ribs curved gauntly. He accepted the revolver with both hands, his eyes shining boyishly. He examined it with delight before sticking it carefully through his belt.

The boy placed a hand on Jed's shoulder, the smile on his high-boned thin face was wildly beautiful. "The lodge of my father, Crazy Horse, is the lodge of my brother, Little Ax, from this night forth. The day will be good when he brightens it with his coming to us."

He settled his bow and quiver back of his shoulder, slung through one arm. Jed untied the buckskin as, with one lithe movement, the boy mounted the warhorse. Jed slung the saddlebags across the pinto and handed him the halter line of the buckskin.

"Ride fast, younger brother," he said, "and take no thought for your back trail. Little Ax will not be able to discover any tracks and there be none down there"—with a scornful gesture toward the wagon train—"who could track a fat squaw through a snowbank."

A smile flashed white across the dusky, narrow face. "It will be as you say. And as I ride toward the rising of the Great One, I will sing a morning song for my brother."

Jed gave the black shoulder of the warhorse a farewell slap and stepped back. Wheeling the big animal, the buckskin trotting alongside, the boy rode out of the clearing, heading off the knoll toward the north and east.

Jed moved to the brow of the hill and watched. The slender rider was dwarfed, tiny on his powerful mount. They crossed into shadows at the base of the hill and then into a long meadow bathed, now, in moonlight. Jed saw the strides of the horses lengthen, reach swiftly out, flowing into a full run. Faintly as the echo of a drumbeat the rhythmic rumble of swinging hoofs came drifting back on the night wind. They had reached the far side of the meadow, now they rushed into enveloping trees and were gone from sight.

A shadow slipped down from the knoll and drifted toward the wagon train. Jed circled silently back toward his bedroll, pausing at the picket line. Tethered in place of the warhorse was a tall black gelding. Driven into the ground in front of its nose was a Sioux war arrow, its slender shaft ceremoniously dark with dried blood. The son of Crazy Horse had observed with warriorlike care all of the traditional details of the coup.

Jed thought, with some wistfulness, of the triumphant entry the boy would make into the encampment of his people. Proudly riding the great warhorse between the rows of tepees, startling them into rejoicing. He'd have given a lot to see it, maybe he'd one day hear tell of it from Tall Bull. It would be a story retold, of that he was sure, holding all the makings of great legend, always so dear to the Indian heart.

He felt a wave of great satisfaction over this night's business, he smiled up at the peaceful moon. And as he settled down to sleep he dreamed, his heart mounted and rode with fierce pride in the moonlight above the thundering hoofs of the warhorse of Spotted Tail.

Ann Ahlswede's fiction embodies the age-old struggle be-
tween the forces of good and evil—a struggle which she does
not always resolve in the harmonious manner typical of the
popular western. Her first two novels, Day of the Hunter
and Hunting Wolf *(both published in 1960), deal with a*
justice and revenge theme popular in western fiction; a
third, The Savage Land *(1962), experiments with this plot*
structure, showing how a good man can be destroyed by
traditional values which have gotten out of hand. In "The
Promise of the Fruit," which is Ahlswede's only published
short story, the author gives us a further variation on stan-
dard American ideals—a soldier returning from the Civil
War who wants only peace and finds he may have to die to
achieve it.

The Promise of the Fruit

ANN AHLSWEDE

He came home from the big war with only one yearning in his heart. He was as tired as any soldier of the Confederacy, he wanted to put aside forever all the clever ways men taught themselves to kill each other; but most of all, after so long and so hard a journey, young Cullen Brace only wanted peacefulness.

He entered the roadway where he knew each twist, each path and dooryard, and the dust was fine and the echoes rang like distant, frail music to the ghostly fall of confetti, to the laughter of young girls and children, and in the crush of earth and blossoms beneath the boots of the outgoing soldiers:

We are a band of brothers, and native to the soil . . .

Full and rich in memory came his own voice lifted with strength and insistence in the rightness of it all. And in the green-scented darkness the night before leave taking, Cullen Brace held Rachel and whispered to her, "You'll see! I'll come back when the fighting's over. No Yank'll ever kill Cullen Brace!" His whole body had been anguished with the sudden, piercing weight of love, and the burden of mortality, all felt whole, at once, as though he knew already what it was to die in battle, to love once in the rivergrass, experiencing only this and nothing beyond. Fervently he whispered to her, "I'll come home again!"

And he had, but never the way he had dreamed about it with her. His old boots stirred the dust in the awkward walk of a leg-wounded soldier with blue eyes and rough brown hair, and a stillness in his thinned, weather-aged face.

He stopped and stood bareheaded by the side of the road. The sun filtered down to him through the branches of a mulberry tree. In his nostrils was the smell of the dust and the papery smell of the leaves. He could almost hear the echoes coming sweetly again through the tarnish of time; *band of brothers* . . .

A dog barked. Cullen turned his head, shaking himself free of his reverie of the past as he looked outward to see and absorb all that he had hungered to see again, all things crowding into him sharp against his eyes and ears—the purple blossoms on the Jacaranda tree by the hardware store; the willow brush tangle down by the river crossing; town dogs lazy in the shade; a woman's voice lifted to call a child. Over the length of his hungry body came the familiar hot-weather lethargy of a day in early summer, and from the tavern by the road in front of him seeped the smell of ale and grease and coffee and worn dry wood. Over his head the young fruit of the mulberry hung small from milky green stems, flushed with the wine of approaching ripeness, and bees worked among the weed blossoms by the curb at his feet.

He brushed at the travel dust on his ragged clothing,

waiting for his mind to grow coolly shadowed with the certainty that the fighting was over at last, that he was finally home. He had walked from Missouri through Arkansas and on to this place by the river, this widening in the road. Before that he had ridden out of Texas when he should have died there after the trouble at Bonham. But he was still stubbornly alive as much by accident as any other man who had come through it all; and now he was home.

He straightened, ready, conscious of the clumsiness of his leg. Some day he'd be used to it, he supposed, and forget about it and step out expecting his leg to carry him easily as it always had. But it took a man a long time to give up part of himself even when he knew it was a fact. He even dreamed about running sometimes.

The pistol pressed against his body where he'd wedged it under his belt earlier in the day. The sudden fierce wave of loathing that rose in him at the thought of it, was so intense, so violent, that he was sick and miserable with it. He yanked the pistol from his belt and stared at it. Ugly thing, death and destruction, no way to count its terrible toll. It stood for everything he was finished with and wanted to forget, everything that blackened his soul; because there had to be a time when men walked without death in their hands, there had to be a choice between that and the black, blind destiny of worms.

He looked around him, searching for a place. He looked up into the tree and found the fork, and laid the gun up there where the leaves and the shadows and the hanging fruit almost hid it. Let the gun grow rusty and forgotten, let the tree smother it until it was gone.

The planks of the walk were hot beneath the soles of his boots. An old granny woman shuffled past in front of him. His smile began in the faintest recognition but she went by without looking up, a lump-filled gunnysack clutched to her breast. Roots and greens from the riverbank and the meadows and the swamps, he thought, with a quick, dark pity for the woman. Food for hungry people without recourse, the poultices of the earth for the old and ailing and the defeated. Her dim eyes stared down vacantly to each feeble step as she rustled through the curb weeds and out into the afternoon sunlight.

He started on, and stopped again when two boys bolted by, jolting him backwards. He caught at an awning post to keep from falling, and looked after them, at their quick legs, at the fishing poles they carried down to the river, at the hound dogs trailing languidly.

The planks vibrated as others passed, and no one noticed him in his old clothes and his boney hunger because there were still thousands of others like him wandering the long roads, old young men with the same look in their faces. He wanted to say, I'm home. I belong here. But he went on into the shade of the tavern, feeling foolish with so much hidden gladness.

The shadowed inner stillness of the room wrapped around him soothingly. Motes of dust hovered in the quiet light. His body seemed to part them like dry waves as he limped slowly to the bar, and stopped. He reached down into his gritty pocket, searching out the last coin saved for this.

A celebration, a triumph without a name. Glory Hallelujah! I'm home! He wanted to spend his coin grandly on one cool drink.

"Beer!" he ordered. The coin rang brightly on the wooden bar.

"Young Cullen Brace, ain't it?" the innkeeper asked. "Widow Brace's boy?"

"Yes sir?" Cullen answered. He did not recognize this man with one arm gone, but he grinned because this man had recognized him.

"Don't you all remember old Ed Zoel, boy?"

"Zoel?" Cullen echoed. Then laughter bubbled up inside of him and he saw the same kind of crazy, wild mirth twist Ed Zoel's mouth into a grin. "Ed Zoel," Cullen marveled, because he had not thought of Ed Zoel in all the years and now he was back, and Ed Zoel was back too.

"Yes sir," Zoel answered triumphantly. "It's me all right. I made it too."

Sighs and sniffling and throat clearing came from the far corner of the room where two old men haggled softly over the pawns on a chess board. The corner was dim as twilight. Cullen turned his head to stare at them, seeing bent spines and white, tufted hair and withered hands reaching out to touch the pawns with such anxiety that life and death hovered over the board, and each breath was a shallow jealous effort. Time dribbled away between their withered fingers.

Cullen turned his back on them again, suddenly angry.

It was like looking into a room closed away from life for a century. Like looking into a darkened, tarnished mirror filled with unwanted images.

In a twist of savage bitterness he hated the old men because they were so substanceless, so horribly invisible in the midst of life.

He, Cullen Brace, had fought to come home; he had bled, he was filled with the blood and pain of living, and it throbbed insistently through him with each stubborn heartbeat, making him live on with the sting of its pricelessness.

He would not see himself in the old men; he could not believe that life could be so pastel; so filled with melancholy patience. Time could never be so meaningless, no by God, not to him, or the others like him who had suffered so much just to draw another breath.

He sighed, letting the anger drain away, telling himself to drink the beer and forget the rest. But he thought of Ed Zoel, with an arm lost. Hadn't he once shod Cullen's horse over at Jackson's smithy? How could he shoe a horse now, how could he ever go back to what he was once, whole and strong and full of humble purpose?

And why was the old granny woman out foraging in the fields? Was there no one left to take care of her? A morbid picture of his own mother came into his mind. He imagined her, before she died, grubbing and digging in the dirt for the roots in the earth.

Think of better things, he told himself. Forget all that and think of something good, something cool and filled with endless peace . . .

Go down to the river and wash in the green water, wash away the stink of war; remember when you had a pole and bobber, and went barefoot in the mud, carefree in the world? . . .

"Things is changed," Ed Zoel said. He tucked a glass under the stump of his right arm and held it there while he dried it with his left hand. He tipped his head back to look up at the ceiling beams where dusty cobwebs looped down motionless in the hot air. He entered a dark and thoughtful contemplation of change with bitterness and wonder so old that it no longer showed in his moist, softening features. "Yes sir, things do change."

The stirring of light and air told Cullen that someone had entered the tavern from the afternoon outside. He drank his beer and remembered the river, miles of green banks and softly flowing water; he thought of the boys fishing there in the summer haze.

"You're in early," Ed Zoel said.

"I don't mind," a woman's voice answered. She walked around the end of the counter and lifted a shawl from her shoulders, leaving them chalky white in the gloom. She wore a faded dress of lavender satin that flashed garishly with each movement of her body. Her hair was the maple red of fall leaves. Cullen turned his head and looked at her hair and at her face, and the shock reached him slowly through his good dreams. "Rachel—?"

Her red curls swung as she turned to look at him, a smile on her lips. Then recognition froze the smile. She seemed to shrink before his eyes until the lavender satin hung loose over her small breasts and the hot black stockings sagged over her knees.

"Look who's home, Rae," Ed Zoel said to her.

Cullen pulled up straighter at the bar, reaching to his full height, balancing to make up for his crippled leg. Still he did not feel tall enough, not as tall and tree-straight as he once had been. But as he waited for her to say the first word and the excitement grew with tumbling thoughts and emotions, he saw the dress and understood what it meant. Seconds late with his comprehension, he stared at the dress and the dark blood flushed into his face. "What're you doing, what're you wearing that thing for?"

Rachel Danton straightened pridefully. The silence strained between them as she stood there in the ugly hurdy-gurdy dress and glared back at Cullen Brace as though she thought herself something rare, something marvelous to gaze at. Then her lips opened, red lips he'd kissed when they were only pink. "Well, so the big war hero comes home at last. Well, I declare!" Her high heels clacked against the floor as she walked closer to him. Her eyes gleamed like jewels in the merciful light which made her white face seem wonderfully alluring. "Well, I declare," she cried, for all the world to hear her astonishment. "Look who's here! It's Cullen Brace come home again like a poor lost sheep!"

"I see you didn't wait for me, Rachel Danton!"

"Wait?" she cried in wonder. "Wait forever?" An edge of misery crumbled her voice. "Wait forever like I had a thousand years to live, Cullen Brace? Wait while I lost everything I ever had and went hungry and . . ."

She broke off and turned sharply away from him as two men entered the tavern and stepped up to the bar, bringing silence into the room with them.

The old ones in the corner fretted over their game. Ed Zoel served beer to his customers, lifting his glance aimlessly over the room.

The bitter thoughts seethed through Cullen's mind.

It was the least a woman could do while her man was off. The least. Just wait.

But who could wait forever, like she said?

Like they all had a thousand years to live, and there was no hurry?

Like he hadn't changed, himself, and hadn't done things he was ashamed of?

Oh God, yes! Things he was ashamed of.

All right then. He had to tell her he wanted to understand all this; more than anything he wanted to understand, and not let other things matter—nothing in all the world but Rachel Danton and Cullen Brace, off in the clinging search for what they had once known.

"Oh, you righteous man," she accused in a bitter whisper. She leaned toward him from behind the bar, and their faces were close, and he forgot everything he wanted to say to her, every fearful, eager hope, every tenderness, for the brittle words spilled too quickly from her mouth. *"You saint! You sinless boy.* Your Ma's dead, you know that? You know she died all alone on the farm like some poor old sick creature with no one to look after her and no one even knowing, and the land's gone now—"

"Rachel . . ." he began, and the morbid picture of his mother came back again, filled with shadow and abandonment.

"No, you listen for once, Cullen Brace!" Rachel cried. "I know she's dead."

"You don't know everything, you—"

"Leave be, can't you? I know she's gone!"

"But you're too late now, too late for me, too late for her, too late for everything!"

"She died before it was over, I didn't even hear till six months later!" The blood throbbed hotly in his face with the injustice of her accusation. "If I'd walked down that road the day Lee surrendered it wouldn't have made her rise up out of her grave, Rachel Danton!"

"It's been a year, a whole year—and I stood in that doorway watching, and I looked for you with the ones that came down that road, and you weren't ever there, you just never came!"

"I couldn't get back . . ."

"Why not?" She slashed the words at him triumphantly. "Because you'd been off burning and murdering with that Quantrill? Oh, don't you look so surprised, Cullen Brace. We heard. Is that what you were doing, soldier boy? Running wild? Is that why you didn't get home till now?"

He was aware of the others in the room listening to each word. He could hear how this would sound to them now when it was all over, and easy to look back on, because if there'd ever been any glory shining from Quantrill's name in the early days, it had died forever into the butcher deeds of a man the Confederacy wouldn't honor with a commission, who made his war a personal vendetta and cut his way through Lawrence, Kansas, in search of enemies; and on to Baxter Springs in '63 and then south in flight into east Texas and the last bitter pretense of a soldier's war at Bonham . . .

Oh yes, there were things Cullen Brace was ashamed of.

"Look at you," Rachel's voice broke across his bleak memories. Her eyes searched over him for all the newness, all the brightness he had once possessed. Suddenly she clawed at the paint on her own face. "Look at me!" She flung her hand out in a gesture of misery. "Look at this place— look at everything!"

At the end of the bar Ed Zoel polished a glass and looked idly up at the rafters. The old men paused in their game, foolishly bewildered by the intrusion of wretchedness not their own. The two customers, caught innocently in this scene, finished their drinks and walked out into the afternoon once more.

"But the fighting's over," Cullen Brace said to Rachel. He spoke the vital words he had nourished in his own heart, he offered them to Rachel, the highest of his hope, the best of himself. "The fighting is done with."

Rachel laughed.

"And a man don't need to carry weapons in his hands," he insisted stubbornly, blindly, because he would not believe in her disbelief.

"Don't he?" she countered. "Is that what you think down in your heart?"

"Yes ma'am, I believe it. Because it's so."

"You and your notions. Notions don't change things from what they are. All those notions don't turn dirt into dreams."

His mouth tightened, aging his face with a harsh, enduring expression. "You think I don't know what's real? Maybe I don't have half a leg left? Is that just a notion too?"

"Half—" she faltered. For an instant she looked child-young and woundable beneath the mask of paint. Her eyes rounded and glittered with a rush of tears. "You never said . . . oh my, you never said."

He caught her hand, his face lighting with new eagerness. "Oh, I didn't mean to go and make it sound that bad. It ain't off or anything, it's just lame. It gives me fits, sometimes."

She looked searchingly into his face, the tears pooled in her eyes. "You are so thin."

Her hand was tight and warm in his, a life-line grasp straining between them. He waited, all age and harshness drained from his face in the eagerness and the anxiety of his waiting.

"You say it's over," she said. The tears spilled quietly down over her cheeks. Her lips were wooden with the effort for control. "Make me believe it then. Make me believe it too."

The tavern doorway darkened suddenly.

Rachel looked past Cullen's shoulder. All at once her expression hardened again. Before Cullen's eyes she became too wise, too unbelieving.

"Oh, no, Cullen Brace. No, it just ain't so!" Angrily she pulled back from him, drawing away when he would have held her and weakened her with his belief.

"Why?" he demanded. "Why ain't it so?"

She laughed again. "Because here comes that Tooley Jackson looking to shoot you."

* * *

Tooley Jackson was a great, strong man in the very prime of his life. There were streaks of premature gray in his hair. Lines of past hardships made his face almost ugly, so bold and open were they for the world to see. His mouth was large and calm, his nostrils wide, his dark eyes burning with some great purpose. He stood in the doorway with the afternoon light bright behind him, and stared at Cullen while quiet deepened in the tavern.

"I'm looking for a feller calls himself Cullen something-or-other," Tooley Jackson said. His mouth formed a single word with care. "You?"

Cullen looked around uncertainly. He frowned, because Rachel's words made no sense to him. The worry line deepened between his brows. "Yes sir," he answered. "That's my name."

"You the boy that rode with Will Quantrill?"

Cullen felt a coldness sink into him. He looked around at the others again, wondering what all this meant, where it was taking him. He saw that the room had begun to fill with people, people he had known all his life, and he heard not one greeting and saw no smile of recognition. He hesitated, bewildered by the silent weight of their hostility.

"Well?" Jackson spoke the round, full word quietly.

Cullen looked at Rachel. He answered, "Yes sir. I guess I rode with him."

A tremor passed over Tooley Jackson's face. "You one of them plundering killers who called theirselves *Irregulars*?"

"No sir, I was a *soldier*," Cullen answered quickly.

"You one of them loyal boys who robbed their own and killed their own for the money and the pleasure of it?" Tooley Jackson's voice grew louder with each breath, thundering across Cullen's answer.

"No, listen to me . . ."

"You one of the four hundred that raided in Kansas?"

"No!"

"Them that looted Lawrence and massacred every man there?"

"I wasn't at Lawrence, I joined up afterwards!"

"You rode with Will Quantrill, didn't you?" Tooley Jackson shouted. "Didn't you?"

"Yes I did! But not at Lawrence!"

"You rode with him!"

Cullen's mouth was suddenly cotton dry. He looked around, tearing his stare from Jackson's; he looked into Ed Zoel's empty face, and beyond to the two old men who had stopped their game to gape uncomprehendingly. He saw the young boys push through the circle closing around him, back from the river and the afternoon's whim. He saw Rachel, and all the others, watching, listening all around him.

A hunger like that of starvation moved in his body, a hunger to be heard, to tell someone. "Listen . . . will you just listen? I never raided at Lawrence, my God no. I was a soldier. When we attacked Helena in Arkansas I got hit in the leg. It was July of '63." The words spilled out, reaching out to these people, this great bitter man. "They started to cut off my leg right then but I said no, like hell they would, and then they told me if I didn't die anyway I'd be all through with the war afterwards." He felt their eyes go down to his legs, prying and hunting for the long, ugly scars. "There was a war on yet," he explained urgently. "Only I couldn't fight it any more and there wasn't anything else, nothing but fighting, that's all there was. Just fighting and being scared of getting killed or torn up in some stinking shell burst, or being caught and put in Rock Island Prison. Or losing like we hadn't fought with everything we had." He paused breathlessly because this was so terribly important. They had to understand how it was to be left useless with a cause still burning in your heart. Had they forgotten, themselves? Had they never felt the wrath in defeat? "I was sick with my leg," he went on, trying to strike through their stony silence to the things that were common in all of them. "I don't remember where I was, I just kept walking. I couldn't go fast. There wasn't any place to stop. It didn't make sense. I kept thinking we were really losing, like some people said, I kept thinking all the dying'd been *wasted*."

He stopped at last, dismayed, failing, exposed, for he had bared the melancholy in his own soul. But the people only watched him coldly. None of this mattered. He wet his lips. His anger was deep and chagrined. "All right! Maybe that don't matter, maybe yes and no is all you want to hear. Quantrill raided Lawrence in August, didn't he? Well I heard about it afterwards and then that Yankee General Ewing put out the order that burned the Missouri border to get back at Quantrill for going into Kansas."

"There was Southerners in Lawrence too," Tooley Jackson challenged.

"I don't know nothing about Lawrence!" Cullen answered. "Will you let me tell it?"

"I already know all I need to know."

"You asked did I ride with Quantrill and I'm telling you why!" He waited, glaring at Jackson and the others. They'd asked and now he'd make them listen. "So I set out looking for Quantrill. He was still fighting. It took me a month because I couldn't walk fast but I went on looking because he was *still fighting.* It was a way to keep on. That's why I rode with him, only I didn't join up until the end of September. After Lawrence!"

"You lie."

"I don't lie, I'm telling you true only you won't listen. I joined him just before Baxter Springs!"

"What about Bonham, Texas?"

"I was laid up with my leg again after we went into Texas. I rode with him at Baxter Springs against a Union detachment—against soldiers! But before God I never raided in Texas with the others."

"Listen to him," Tooley Jackson cried. "Talking himself out of all the wrong." His eyes glittered with the hard tears of grief and anger. "We was a sizeable family but the war took us down right off at Bull Run and Cedar Mountain. Then Will Quantrill came looking for that Yankee Red-Leg Senator Jim Lane, and Lane ran out the window and hid in the woods, then Quantrill killed every man and boy he could find, every one! He shot my old pa and he shot my two brothers and he shot my only boy, while I was off to the fighting, and now I'm all that's left. I'm the last one."

The silence was grieved, shared, weighted with debt.

"But I wasn't there," Cullen said to them. He looked around, begging for belief. "I wasn't even there!"

"You are a stinking Quantrill butcher and I am going to kill you now," Tooley Jackson said. "Get ready."

Cullen stared at the others, stunned by the suddenness of this. "D'you believe him?" he asked them furiously. "Is this what you want? What're we supposed to do, kill each other?" He paused, panting. "Why? What good'll it do now, what's it supposed to prove? He kills me and I kill him and what's left? What's it mean? That it just keeps going on till there's nobody left?" He waited for an answer but they only watched him, their faces blunt, secretive, dull with what seemed like a great weariness of mankind itself, a great indifference. Cullen felt cold, abandoned; he felt as though he were the last man on earth. "This ain't the war at all," he charged them bitterly. "What d'you want me for! Ain't you had enough yet?"

Tooley Jackson answered him quietly, "I am no big gun fighter and I never fought a duel nor killed a man except on the line like any soldier following orders. But I know I'll make out today because it's a debt that's owed me, it's a justice."

"You going to kill them all?" Cullen asked with a wild twist of mirth. He laughed. "All four hundred men who rode into Lawrence?"

"I'll start with you."

"No, sir. I won't fight you!"

Silence seeped through the room like a gray, chill mist. Coward, it said. Yellow coward. "I wasn't there," Cullen repeated. He pointed at Tooley Jackson and spoke to the others. "I don't even *know* him! I never killed his people. I

never made war on anybody but soldiers! Now he stands
there wanting to make a fight, dying to kill me, and he's
wrong! He's wrong. It's all for nothing." They did not answer
him and he shouted, "Can't you hear? Can't you talk?" Still
he saw no flicker of response, no willingness. His hand
dropped to his side as he began to believe that nothing he
said would matter. "I won't fight him!"

Tooley Jackson said, "Then I will purely shoot you down
where you stand."

Cullen's heart beat rapidly. How could this be what he
had returned to when he had come searching for things far
from the streams of chaos and calamity?

He felt the force of their waiting silence. He scarcely
believed all this was happening to him.

He had dared to hope for work to do and food to eat and
peacefulness, and moments to stand in idle contemplation
beneath a mulberry tree and smell its greenness, and look
forward to its summer fruit.

Now Tooley Jackson would shoot him where he stood
and maybe he wouldn't ever feel the bullet, and no one
would stop it; then later they'd lay him out in his rags and
bury him prayerlessly on the graveyard hill.

Their waiting hurried him in his floundering thought.
How could you set out to try to kill a man you didn't know
when you'd sworn you were done forever with all of that,
sick to death of it all, seeing its pointlessness? Clinging to a
last tenacious faith even when your own ignorance and uncertainty overwhelmed you—

"You want to die like a dog?"

"I don't want to die any way at all!"

"Make your choice."

"You're wrong, you're wrong . . ."

"Make your choice!"

Cullen looked into Ed Zoel's passive face, searching,
appealing, waiting for some word. But all he saw was the
wonder of time and change. Beside him were the two old
men drifting effortlessly, unimportantly toward death. And

only a step beyond in the living circle were the boys, a curious innocence in their faces as they watched and did not understand, and waited to be shown.

Cullen wanted to run; he wanted to close his eyes and open them, and find that this was only a nightmare rising cruelly out of the travail of war.

But he remembered that he could not run any more, that each step he took was now and forever more an effort of will, and pain, and hardheaded faith.

A breeze outside rustled the leaves of the mulberry, a breath of river coolness brushing across the heat of the afternoon laden with the spice of meadows and pines and sunlight.

"I am through waiting," Tooley Jackson said.

Cullen straightened. His throat felt thick, and he cleared it and said the soft, hollow words. "I left my weapon outside."

"Then let's get to it."

The crowd followed at his back as he entered the afternoon again. The day seemed strangely unchanged, as though no time had passed.

He limped to the tree and reached up through its leaves to the fork. His fingers touched the gun even as he breathed the greenness of the leaves and the bitter sweet promise of the fruit. He hesitated. He tore one of the berries loose and put it in his mouth. A flood of sourness came from the unripe fruit. It was too soon; too green. He had known it. Yet ripeness hovered; the taste, the promise, lingered hauntingly.

He limped out into the open of the roadway. He stood there, looking at the Goliath figure of Tooley Jackson. He could not believe it was happening, and yet he knew.

The fighting is over, he had told Rachel with such certainty. It has to be sometime.

But when? When!

His own faltering shook him; he was more afraid than he had ever been.

* * *

Make me believe it, too, Rachel Danton had begged him.

He squeezed his fingers around the grips of the old gun, torn with a last urgent indecision. The muscles of his hand contracted with paralyzing tightness.

Make me believe it.

I . . . But I came so far . . .

A spurt of fear shot all through him then as he saw Tooley Jackson move, and the time diminished to nothing and he thought wildly, I can't, I can't!

In all of Cullen's life no sound was so loud as the thunder of Tooley Jackson's shot. He heard it as he felt the great bewildering blow of the ball striking him, and the thundering blast surrounded him and lifted him, and he fell brokenly, his limbs awkward in the dirt of the roadway. He did not know if he had fired the gun; in the waves of shock he didn't know. He tried to get up again but his limbs were oppressively burdened, his movements grotesque. He fell back and tasted dust in his mouth and saw it in his eyes; he saw the sky beyond, far above him.

One by one the faces came to peer down at him. He saw the people he had known all his life. They stared, and still their silence was unbroken as they watched him breathing desperately. He waited to see Tooley Jackson there among them because the wrongful debt wasn't yet paid in full. Urgently he tried to remember if he had fired his gun; he had to know this. His fingers moved in the dust, searching feebly, finding only themselves in the granules of earth; his hand was empty. He could feel his hand's vast emptiness.

"Why didn't you shoot it, boy?" Ed Zoel asked from the circle above him.

Cullen did not try to answer him. The relief streamed flooding clean and bitter sweet all through him, as sweet and bitter to his spirit as the juices of the unripe berries had been to his mouth.

But up there against the blue of the sky the faces of the two boys looked down at him, and the sweetness died, crushed, a terrible agonized loss; only the bitter remained. Because maybe this was the end of their last innocence with the sight and the stink of blood running out in the dirt.

At last he saw Tooley Jackson again. The great man loomed so high and so far above that he shut out the sky from Cullen, and dwarfed the people in his towering rightness.

Pain began to reach Cullen's brain. He struggled in the ultimate wonder of whether Tooley Jackson would fire again, because he did not know even yet if a man could live on without a weapon in his hand, although he knew how marvelously easy it was for a man to die weaponless, with only a longing for peacefulness clutched in his fists.

"No," someone said from the circling faces above.

"No more," a dull voice insisted. "No more!"

"It's enough."

Tooley Jackson stared down at Cullen. The day went endlessly on with birdsong and the blooming of flowers and the blowing of wind while Tooley Jackson looked down at the man at his feet.

He lifted the gun again, and held in his palm the dark before Genesis, the dark of nothing.

Cullen waited for the answer. He felt nothing, and then he felt an innocence like that of the boys; then that too was gone.

"Oh damn you boy," Tooley Jackson whispered at last. His long shaking sigh was like the wind in the river trees, as thwarted, as lonely. He dropped the gun from his hand and let it lie there, near the place where Cullen's gun had fallen. His fingers held its shape in a lingering echo. Then that passed and he turned away. He parted the people with his hands. They moved aside and closed in after him once more, pressing and circling in a wall of flesh around Cullen Brace and his red place in the dust.

A passing warmth and abrasion touched Cullen's face. The boney fingers of an old man plucked at dirt embedded in the sweat and cold of his shock. He sensed a chaos of motion and sound all around him and above him, a restless stirring as though some paralytic isolation had been broken.

"Take him inside," a woman's voice pleaded. "Please. Let me take care of him now."

A piping boy's voice asked, "He going to die, Mr. Zoel?"

"No, damn it! No he ain't. Not now. Can't you see?"

The words lifted a helpless worry from Cullen. Relief flowed through him, because he had come such a long, hard way. He closed his eyes tiredly.

It wasn't just for nothing then, and that was a relief too. And maybe men like himself, and all the others, fools, heroes, men who dared to hope, maybe they were more than tearless, bloodless pawns played in a game they'd never understand . . .

The light was yellow-bright against his lids. He felt quick hands grasp him in islands of feeling all along the awkward length of his body; children's hands, the hands of the old and the crippled, all of them straining, bearing up the burden.

The theme of racial conflict between whites and Indians is a familiar one in western fiction, but seldom do we see portrayals of the tension between whites and blacks. In "A Season for Heroes," Carla Kelly explores the relationship among a white cavalry officer, his black sergeant, and the white man's wife. Her sensitive treatment of the material, seen retrospectively through the eyes of the white family's daughter, reinforces the concept of egalitarianism on the frontier, showing how man's—or woman's—capacity for friendship and love transcends mere barriers of color. Kelly, who began writing while working as a ranger-historian at the Fort Laramie National History Site in Wyoming, was awarded the Western Writers of America's Golden Spur Award for this short story in 1978; a subsequent story, "Kathleen Flaherty's Long Winter," received the same award in 1981.

A Season for Heroes

CARLA KELLY

Ezra Freeman died yesterday. I don't usually read the obituaries, at least I didn't until after Pearl Harbor. With four grandsons in the service now and one of them missing over a place called Rabaul, or some such thing, I generally turn to the obituaries after the front page and the editorials.

There it was, right at the bottom of the column, in such small print I had to hold the paper out at arm's length ... Ezra Freeman. There was no date of birth listed, probably because even Ezra hadn't known that, but it did mention there were no surviving relatives and the deceased had been a veteran of the Indian Wars.

And when I thought about Ezra Freeman, I ended up thinking about Mother and Father. Still carrying the newspaper, I went into my bedroom and looked at the picture of Mother and Father and Company D hanging on the wall next to the window. It was taken just before Father was assigned to 10th Cav headquarters, so he is still leaning on a cane in the picture. Mother is sitting on a bench holding quite a small baby and next to her, his shoulders thrown back and his feet together, is Sergeant Ezra Freeman.

The picture was taken at Ft. Bowie, Arizona Territory. I was ten or eleven then and that garrison was the first memory that really stuck in my mind. It was where Dad nearly got killed and my little brother was born, and where I discovered a few things about love.

But first, something about my parents.

My mother was what people call lace-curtain Irish. She was born Kathleen Mary Flynn. Her father owned a rather successful brewery in upstate New York and Mother was educated in a convent where she learned to speak French and make lace. She never owned up to learning anything else there, although she wrote a fine copperplate hand and did a lot of reading when Father was on campaign. The nuns taught her good manners and how to pour tea the right way. Father could always make her flare up by winking at her and saying in his broadest brogue, "What'll ye hev to dhrink now, Kate Flynn?"

She had beautiful red hair that curled every which way. Little springs of it were forever popping out of the bun she wore low on her neck. She had a sprinkling of light brown freckles which always mystified the Indians. I remember the time an old reservation Apache stopped us as we were walking down Tucson's main street. He spoke to Father in Apache. Dad answered him, and we could see he was trying to keep a straight face.

We pounced on him when the Indian nodded and walked away.

"What did he say, Dad? What did he say?"

Father shook his head and herded us around the corner where he leaned against the wall and laughed silently until tears shone on his eyelashes. Mother got exasperated.

"What *did* he say, John?"

"Oh, Kate Flynn," he wheezed and gasped, "he wanted to know . . . Oh, God . . ." He went off into another quiet spasm.

"John!"

Mother didn't approve of people taking the Lord's name in vain (which made garrison life a trial for her at times).

"Sorry, Kathleen," Dad looked at her and winked. I could feel Mother stiffening up. "He wanted to know if you had those little brown dots all over."

We children screamed with laughter. Mother blushed. A lesser Victorian lady would have swooned, but Tucson's streets were dusty then, and Father was laughing too hard to catch her on the way down.

Mother and Father met after Father's third summer at West Point. He had been visiting friends of his family in Buffalo and Mother had been a guest of one of the daughters. They had spent a week in each other's company, then Mother had gone back to the convent. They had corresponded for several months, then Father proposed during Christmas furlough and they were married after graduation in June.

There had been serious objections from both sides of the family. Papa Flynn made Father promise to raise any children as Catholics, and Grandpa Stokes wanted to be assured that he and Grandma wouldn't be obliged to call on the Flynns very often.

Father agreed to everything and he would have raised us as Catholics, except that we seldom saw a priest out on the plains; besides, Mother wasn't a very efficient daughter of the church. I think she figured she'd had enough, what with daily Mass at the convent for six years straight. But she always kept her little ebony and silver rosary in her top drawer under her handkerchiefs and I only saw her fingering it once.

I don't really remember what my father looked like in those early years. I do remember that he wasn't too tall (none of the horse soldiers were) and that the other officers called him Handsome Johnny. Mother generally called him "the Captain" when we were around. "The Captain says you should do this, Janey," or "Take the Captain's paper to him, Gerald." When he was promoted, she called him "the Major," and the last name before he died was "the Colonel." Fifteen years later, just before she died, she had started over and was calling him "the Lieutenant" again.

I was born in Baton Rouge about a year after they were married, where the 10th Cavalry was serving Reconstruction duty. Pete came along two years later at Ft. Sill and Gerald was born at Ft. Robinson in the Black Hills.

When I was ten, we were assigned to Ft. Bowie, Arizona Territory. That was in the fall of 1881, more than sixty years ago.

Dad commanded Company D of the 10th Cavalry. The 9th and 10th Cavalry were composed entirely of Negro enlisted men, serving under white officers. The Indians called them Buffalo Soldiers, I suppose because their kinky black hair reminded them of the hair of a buffalo. Father always swore they were the best troops in the whole U.S. Army and said he was proud to serve with them, even though some of his fellow officers considered such duty a form of penance.

My favorite memory of Company D was listening to them riding into Ft. Bowie after duty in the field. They always came in singing. The only man who couldn't carry a tune was my father. I remember one time right before Christmas when they rode out of Apache Pass singing "Star of the East." Even Mother came out on the porch to listen, her hand on my shoulder.

Company D had two Negro sergeants. Master Sergeant Albert Washington was a former slave from Valdosta, Georgia. He was a short, skinny little man who never said very much, maybe because he was married to Clara Washington who did our washing and sewing, and who had the loudest, strongest voice between the Mississippi and the Pacific.

The other sergeant was Ezra Freeman. Ezra wasn't much taller than my father and he had the biggest hands I ever saw. They fascinated me because he was so black and the palms of his hands were so white.

Ezra had a lovely deep voice that reminded me of chocolate pudding. I loved to hear him call the commands to the troops during Guard Mount and I loved to watch him sit in his saddle. My father was a good horseman but he never sat as tall as Ezra Freeman, and Father's shoulders got more and more stooped as the years passed. Not Ezra. Last time I saw him, sitting in his wheelchair, his posture was as good as ever, and I think he would have died before he would have leaned back.

Once I asked Ezra about his childhood. He said that he had been raised on a plantation in South Carolina. At the age of twelve, he and two sisters and his mother and father had been sold at the Savannah auction to help pay off his master's gambling debts. He never saw any of them again.

He was bought by a planter from Louisiana and stayed a field hand until Admiral Farragut steamed up the Mississippi and ended that. He sometimes spoke a funny kind of pidgin French that made my mother laugh and shake her head.

But she never got too close to Ezra, or to any of Father's other troopers. None of the other white ladies of the regiment did either. Mother never would actually pull her skirts aside when the colored troopers passed, as some of the ladies did, but she had a formality about her in the presence of the Buffalo Soldiers that we weren't accustomed to. At least, she did until the summer of 1882, when we came to owe Ezra Freeman everything.

That was the summer Ignacio and his Apaches left the San Carlos Agency and raided, looted, burned and captured women and children to enslave or sell in Mexico. The troops garrisoned at Bowie knew that Ignacio's activities would touch them soon, and the early part of the summer was spent in refitting and requisitioning supplies and ordnance in preparation for the orders they knew would come.

Mother was not receiving any callers that summer. That was how we put it then. Or we might have said that she was "in delicate health." Now, in 1942, we say "she is expecting," or "she is in the family way." But back then, that would have been altogether too vulgar and decidedly low class.

Neither of them told us. I just happened to notice Mother one morning when I burst into her room and caught her in her shift. She bulged a little in the front and I figured we were going to have another baby brother sometime. They never seemed to have girls after me. She didn't say anything then and I didn't either. Later on in the week, when we were polishing silver, she paused, put her hand on her middle and stared off in space for a few moments, a slight smile on her face.

At breakfast a few mornings later, Father asked Mother if she wanted to go home for the summer to have the baby. The railroad had been completed between Bowie and Tucson, and it would be a much less difficult trip.

"Oh, no, I couldn't, John," she had replied.

"Well, why not? I'll probably be gone all summer anyway." Dad wiped up the egg on his plate with one swipe of his toast and grinned when Mother frowned at him.

"Oh, I just couldn't, John," she repeated, and that was the end of that.

About two weeks later, three of the cavalry companies and two of the infantry were detached from Bowie to look for Ignacio.

Mother said her goodbyes to Father inside their bedroom. As I think of it, very few of the wives ever saw their husbands off from the porch, except for Lieutenant Grizzard's wife, and everyone said she was a brassy piece anyway.

But we kids followed Father out onto the porch. My little brother Pete wore the battered black felt hat Dad always took on campaign and Gerald lugged out the sabre, only to be sent back into the house with it. Father let me bring out his big Colt revolver and I remember that it took both hands to carry it.

He took the gun from me and pushed it into his holster. He put his hand on my head and shook it back and forth. Then he knelt down and kissed me on both cheeks.

"Keep an eye on Mother for me, Janey," he said.

I nodded and he stood up and shook my head again. He plucked the black hat off Pete's head and swatted him lightly with it. He knelt down again, and both Pete and Gerald clung to him.

"Now you two mind Janey. She's sergeant major."

Company D rode out at the head of the column after Guard Mount, and the corporal who taught school for the officers' children was kind enough to dismiss us for the day.

Summers are always endless to children, but that summer of 1882 seemed to stretch out like cooling taffy. One month dragged by and then two, and still the men didn't return. In fact, another company was sent out and Bowie had only the protection of one understrength troop of infantry and the invalids in the infirmary.

The trains stopped running between Bowie and Tucson because of Ignacio and his warriors, and I recall how irritated Mother was when the last installment of a serial in Frank Leslie's *Illustrated Weekly* never showed up. The only mail that got through was official business the couriers brought in.

But then Mother was irritated with many things that summer. She usually didn't show at all until the eighth month, but this time she had Clara Washington sew her some new Mother Hubbards before her sixth month was over. And her ankles were swollen too. I rarely saw Mother's legs, but once I caught her out on the back porch one evening with her dress up around her knees.

"Oh, Mama!" was all I said.

It startled her and she dropped her skirts and tucked her feet under the chair.

"Jane, you shouldn't spy on people!" she scolded, and

then she smiled when she saw my face. "Oh, I'm sorry, Jane. And don't look so worried. They'll be all right again soon."

Toward the middle of August we began to hear rumors in garrison. Ordinarily we just shrugged off rumors, but the men were now quite overdue and still Ignacio hadn't been subdued. One rumor had the troops halfway across Mexico pursuing Apaches, and another rumor had them in San Diego waiting for a troop train back.

On the 18th of August (I remember the date because it was Gerald's fifth birthday), the rumor changed. A couple of reservation Apaches slouched in on their hard-bitten ponies to report a skirmish to the south of us, hard on the Mexican border. Captain Donelly, B Company, 4th Infantry, was senior officer of the fort then and he ignored the whole thing. The Indians weren't scrupulous about the truth and they often confused Mexican and U.S. soldiers.

I mentioned the latest rumor to Mother, who smiled at me and gave me a little shake. I went back outside to play but I noticed a look in her eyes that hadn't been there before.

Two days later the troops rode in. They were tired, sunburned and dirty, and their mounts looked mostly starved. Mother came out on the porch. She leaned on the porch railing and stood on one foot and then the other. I saw that she had taken off her wedding ring and Dad's West Point ring that she wore on her first finger. Her hands looked swollen and tight.

The troops assembled on the parade ground and some of the women and children ran out to them. We looked hard for Company D but it wasn't there. Mother sat down on the bench under the parlor window.

Several of the officers dismounted and stood talking together. One of them gestured our way and Mother got up quickly. When Major Connors started walking over to our quarters, she backed into the house and jerked me in with her.

"Listen to me, Jane Elizabeth," she hissed and her

fingers dug into my shoulders until I squirmed in her grasp. "You take their message."

"But Mother," I whined, trying to get out of her grip. "Why don't you?"

"It's bad luck," she said, and turned and went into the parlor, slamming the door behind her.

Major Connors didn't seem too surprised that Mother wouldn't come out to talk to him. I backed away from him a little myself, because he smelled so awful.

"Jane, tell your mother that Company D and A are both a bit overdue but not to worry because we expect them anytime."

After he left I told Mother, but she wouldn't come out of the parlor until supper time.

Several days passed, and then a week and still no sign of either company. None of the other officers' wives said anything to Mother about it but several of them paid her morning calls and brought along baked goods.

"Why are they doing this, Mama?" I asked her, after Captain O'Neill's wife left an eggless custard.

Mother murmured something about an early wake. I asked her what she meant but she shook her head. My brothers and I downed all the pastries and pies but Mother wouldn't eat any of it.

One night when I couldn't sleep because of the heat, I crept downstairs to get a drink of water from the pump. Mother was sitting on the back porch, rocking slowly in the moonlight. She heard me and closed her fist over something in her lap, but not before I'd seen what it was . . . the little ebony rosary she kept in her drawer. I could tell by the look in her eye that she didn't want me to say anything about it. She rocked on and I sat down near her on the porch steps.

"Mother, what happens if he doesn't come back?"

I hadn't meant to say that. It just came out. She stopped rocking. I thought she might be angry with me but she wasn't.

"Oh, we just manage, Jane. It won't be as much fun, but we'll just manage."

She rocked on in silence and I could hear above the creak of the rocking chair the click of the little ebony beads. I got up to go and she took my hand.

"You know, Jane, there's one terrible thing about being a woman."

I looked down at her. Her ankles and hands were swollen, her belly stretched against the nightgown that usually hung loose on her and her face was splotched.

"What's that, Mama?"

"The waiting, the waiting."

She didn't say anything else, so I went back upstairs and finally fell asleep after the duty guards had called the time from post to post all around the fort.

Another week passed and still no sign of the companies. The next week began as all the others had. The blue sky was cloudless and the sun beat down until the whole fort shimmered. Every glance held a mirage.

It was just after Stable Call that I heard the singing. The sound came up faintly from the west, and for a few moments I wasn't sure I heard anything except the wind and the stable noises to the south of us. But there it was again, and closer. It sounded like "Dry Bones," and that had always been one of Dad's favorite songs.

I turned to call Mother, but she was standing in the doorway, her hand shading her eyes as she squinted toward Apache Pass.

People popped out of houses all along Officers Row, and the younger children began pointing and then running west past headquarters and the infirmary.

There they were, two columns of blue filing out of the pass, moving slowly. The singing wasn't very loud and then it died out as the two companies approached the stables.

Mother took her hand away from her eyes and walked over to the edge of the porch.

"He's not there, Jane," she whispered.

I looked again. I couldn't see Father anywhere.

She stood still on the porch and shaded her eyes again, then she gave a sob and began running.

So many nights in my dreams I've seen my mother running across the parade ground. She was so large and clumsy then, and as I recall, she was barefoot, but she ran as lightly as a young child, her arms held out in front of her. In my dream she runs and runs until I wake up.

I was too startled to follow her at first and then I saw her run to the back of the column and drop down on her knees by a travois one of the horses was pulling. The animal reared back and then nearly kicked her but I don't think she even noticed. Her arms were around a man lying on the travois. As I ran closer, I could see him raise his hand slowly and put it on her hair.

I didn't recognize my father at first. His hair was matted with blood and it looked as though half his head had been blown away. There was a bloody, yellowish bandage over one eye and his whole face was swollen.

He turned his head in my direction and I think he tried to smile, but he only bared his teeth at me and I stepped back. I wanted to turn and run and I didn't see how Mother could stand it.

But there she was, her head on his chest. She was saying something to him but I couldn't hear, and all the while he was stroking her hair with that filthy, bruised hand.

I backed up some more and bumped into Ezra Freeman. I tried to turn and run but he held me.

"Go over to him, Janey," he urged and gave me a push. "He wants you."

I couldn't see how Ezra could interpret the slight movement of Father's hand but he kept pushing me toward the travois.

"Pa? Pa?" I could feel tears starting behind my eyelids.

He said something that I couldn't understand because it sounded as if his mouth was full of mashed potatoes. I leaned closer. He smelled of blood, sweat, dirt and wood-smoke. As I bent over him, I could see under the bandage on his face and gasped to see teeth and gums where his cheek should have been.

Mother was kneeling by him now, her hand on his splinted leg. She took my hand in her other hand and placed it on his chest. He tried to raise his head and I leaned closer. I could make out the words "Janey" and "home," but what he was saying was unimportant. All of a sudden I didn't care what he looked like. He was my father and I loved him more than words could say.

He must have seen my feelings in my eyes because he lay back again and closed his eyes. His hand relaxed and let go of mine.

I helped Mother to her feet and we stood back as two orderlies lifted him off the travois and onto a stretcher. He moaned a little and Mother bit her lip.

They took him to the infirmary and Ezra Freeman walked alongside the stretcher, steadying it. Mother would have followed him but the post surgeon took one look at her and told her to go lie down, because he didn't have time to deliver a baby just then. Mother blushed and the two of us walked back to our quarters hand in hand.

Mother spent an hour that evening in the infirmary with Father. She came home and reported he looked a lot better and was asleep. We went upstairs then and, while she tucked Gerald and Pete in bed, I sat on the rag rug by Pete's army cot, and she told us what happened.

"The two companies had separated from the main detachment and, after a couple days, they found an Apache rancheria. It was at the bottom of a small canyon near Deer Spring; when they tried to surround it before daybreak, they were pinned down by rifle fire from the rim of the canyon."

Mother paused and I noticed that she had twisted her fingers up in the afghan at the foot of Pete's bed. He sat up and prodded her.

"And what happened, Ma? What happened?"

He pulled on her arm a little and his eyes were shining. He had been down at the creek that afternoon and hadn't seen Father yet. The whole thing was still just a story to him.

While the candle on the night stand burned lower and lower, Mother told how Father had been shot down while trying to lead the men back to the horses. He had lain on an exposed rock all morning until Ezra Freeman had crawled out and pulled him to safety. The two companies had stayed in a mesquite thicket, firing at the Apaches until the sun went down. They withdrew in the dark.

Pete was asleep by then but Mother went on to say that the men had holed up for several days about sixty miles south of us because they were afraid Father would die if they moved him. When it looked like he would make it, they started for the fort.

Gerald fell asleep then and as Mother pulled the sheet up around him, she said to me,

"I can't understand it, Jane. Everyone else thought the Captain was dead. Why did Sergeant Freeman do it?"

Then she tucked me in bed.

But I couldn't sleep. Every time I closed my eyes, I kept seeing Father on that travois and the look in Mother's eyes as she knelt by him. I got out of bed and started into Mother's room.

She wasn't there. The bed hadn't even been slept in. I tiptoed down the stairs, stepping over the third tread because it always squeaked. As I groped to the bottom in the dark, I saw the front door open and then close quietly.

I waited a few seconds, then opened it and stood on the porch. Mother was dressed and wrapped in a dark shawl, despite the heat, and walking across the parade ground. She wasn't going toward the infirmary so I trailed her, skirting around the parade and keeping in the shadow of the officers' quarters. I didn't know where she was going but I had a feeling that she would send me back if she knew I was following her.

She passed the quartermasters buildings and the sta-

bles, pausing to say something to the private on guard, who
saluted her and waved her on. I waited until he had turned
and walked into the shadow of the blacksmith shop before
I continued.

I could see now that she was heading to Suds Row,
where the enlisted and their families lived. She walked to
the end of the row and kept going, toward the Negro soldiers' quarters at the edge of the fort. Halfway down the row
of attached quarters she stopped and knocked on one of the
doors. I ducked behind the row until I came to the back of
the place where she had knocked. There was a washtub in
the yard and I dragged it to the window and turned it over
and climbed up.

It was Ezra Freeman's quarters. He lived there with his
friend Jackson Walter of Company A, Jackson's wife Chloe
and their two children.

Mother and Ezra were standing in the middle of the
room. She had taken off her shawl. Freeman offered her the
chair he had been sitting in but she shook her head. I could
see Chloe in the rocking chair by the kitchen, knitting.

Mother was silent for a few moments. Then,

"I just wanted to say thank you, Sergeant Freeman,"
she said finally. Her voice sounded high and thin, like it did
after Grandpa Flynn's funeral three years before.

"Oh . . . well . . . I . . . Jeez, ma'am, you're welcome,"
stammered Ezra.

She shrugged her shoulders and held her hands out in
front of her, palms up. "I mean, Sergeant, you didn't even
know if he was alive and you went out there anyway."

He didn't say anything. All I could hear was the click of
Chloe's bone needles. I barely heard Mother's next word.

"Why?"

Again that silence. Ezra Freeman turned a little and I
could see his face. His head was down and he had sucked in
his lower lip, and he was crying. The light from the kerosene
lamp was reflected in his tears and they shone like diamonds
on his black face.

"Well, hell, ma'am . . . he's the only man I ever served of my own free will." He paused. "And I guess I love him."

Mother put her hands to her face and I could see her shoulders shaking. Then she raised her head and I don't think she ever looked more beautiful.

"I love him too, Ezra. Maybe for the same reasons."

Then she sort of leaned against him and his arms went around her and they held onto each other, crying. She was patting him on the back, like she did when Father hugged her, and his hand was smoothing down her hair where it curled at the neck.

I am forever grateful that the white ladies and gents of Ft. Bowie never saw the two of them together like that, for I'm sure they would have been scandalized. But as I stood there peeking in the window, I had the most wonderful feeling of being surrounded by love, all kinds of love, and I wanted the moment to last and last.

But the moment soon passed. They both backed away from each other and Mother took out a handkerchief from the front of her dress and blew her nose. Ezra fished around in his pocket until he found a red bandanna and wiped his eyes. He sniffed and grinned at the same time.

"Lord almighty, ma'am. I ain't cried since that Emancipation Proclamation."

She smiled at him and put her hand on his arm, but didn't say anything. Then she nodded to Chloe, put her shawl around her head again and turned to the door.

"Good night and thank you again," she said before she went outside.

I jumped off the washtub and ran down the little alley behind the quarters. Staying in the shadows and watching out for the guards, I ran home. I wanted to be home before Mother because I knew she would look in on us before she went to sleep.

She did. She opened the door a crack, then opened it wider and glided in. I opened my eyes a little and stretched, as if she had just wakened me. She bent down and kissed me, then kissed Gerald and Pete. She closed the door and soon I heard her getting into bed.

One week later a couple of troopers from Company D carried Father home on a stretcher. The doctor insisted on putting him in the second parlor on the daybed because he didn't want him climbing the stairs.

The post surgeon had done a pretty good job on Father's face. The bandages were off so the air could get to his cheek, which was a crisscross maze of little black sutures. He had lost his left eye and wore a patch over the socket. (Later on he tried to get used to a glass eye but never could get a good fit. He gradually accumulated a cigar box-full of glass eyes, and we used to scare our city cousins with them and play a kind of lopsided marbles game.)

His mouth drooped down at one corner and made him look a little sad on one side, and none of the other officers called him Handsome Johnny again.

The day after he had been set up in the second parlor, Mother went into labor. The post surgeon tried to stop him but Father climbed the stairs—slowly, hand over hand on the railing and sat by Mother until their third boy was born.

An hour later the doctor motioned me and my brothers into the room. Mother was lying in the middle of the bed, her red hair spread around the pillow like a fan. Her freckles stood out a little more than usual, but she was smiling. Father sat in an armchair near the bed, holding the baby, who had a red face and hair to match.

"What are you going to name him?" I asked, after giving him a good look.

Mother hesitated a moment, then looked over at the baby and Father.

"Ezra Freeman Stokes," she replied quietly, her eyes on Father.

He said something to her that I couldn't understand because his face was still swollen. But Mother kept her eyes on his and snapped back at him in a low voice that sent shivers down my back.

"I don't give a damn what the garrison thinks! He's going to be Ezra Freeman!"

None of us had ever heard Mother swear and Father nearly dropped the baby.

So that was how Ez got his name.

About a month later Father was promoted to major and given the Medal of Honor for "meritorious gallantry under fire at Deer Spring." I remember how he pushed that little medal around in its plush velvet case, then closed the box with a click. "I'm not the one who should be getting this," he murmured. No one could ever prevail upon him to wear it. Even when he was laid out in his coffin years later, with his full dress uniform and all his medals, I never saw that one.

Father was transferred to 10th Cavalry headquarters, then in San Antonio, and given a desk job. We didn't see much of Ezra Freeman after that and never did correspond with him because he couldn't read or write. But somehow we always heard about him from the other officers and men of Company D, and every year at Christmas, Mother sent him a dried apple fruit cake and socks she had knitted. We knew when he retired twenty-five years later and learned in 1915 that he had entered the Old Soldiers' Home in Los Angeles.

Before Father's stroke, he paid him one visit there. I remember that it was 1919 and Father went to tell him that Captain Ezra F. Stokes had died in France of Spanish influenza.

"You know, Janey," he told me after that visit, "Ez may have been my son but I ended up comforting Sergeant Freeman. I almost wish I hadn't told him."

After Father passed away, Mother paid Ezra the yearly visit. She insisted on going alone on the train up from San Diego but when her eyesight began to fade, she finally relented and let me come with her once.

As it turned out, it was her last trip. I think she knew it.

Sergeant Freeman was in a wheelchair by then and, after giving me a nod and telling me to wait there, Mother pushed Ezra down the sidewalk to a little patio under the trees. She sat next to him on a bench and they talked together. After about half an hour she took an object out of her purse, leaned toward Ezra and put something on the front of his robe. I couldn't see what it was but I could tell that Ezra was protesting. He tried to push her hands away, but she went ahead and put something on him. It flashed in the sunlight but I was too far away to make out what it was.

Then she took a handkerchief out of her pocket and wiped his eyes. She sat down again beside him and they sat there together until his head nodded forward and he fell asleep. She wheeled him back to the far entrance of the building and I never had a chance to say good-bye.

She was silent on the trip home; after we got to my house, she said, "Jane, I feel tired," and went to bed. She drifted in and out of sleep for the next two days and then she died.

After the funeral I was going through her things when I came across the plush velvet case containing the Medal of Honor Father had been awarded at Ft. Bowie. I snapped it open but the medal was gone. I think I know where it went.

And now Ezra's dead. Well.

I can see that I've spent more time on this than I intended. I hear the postman's whistle outside. I hope there's a letter from my daughter Ann. Her oldest boy Steve has been missing over the Solomons for more than a month now. I don't suppose I can give her much comfort but I can tell her something about waiting.

Marcia Muller has received considerable acclaim for two series of mystery novels, one featuring a female San Francisco private investigator, Sharon McCone (Games to Keep the Dark Away, Leave a Message for Willie), *and the other starring a Chicana museum curator in Santa Barbara, Elena Oliverez* (The Tree of Death, Legend of the Slain Soldiers). *She also has a sure hand with other types of fiction, particularly the western story, as is amply demonstrated by this wryly amusing and ironic tale of a pioneer woman and her problems with a persistent suitor.*

Sweet Cactus Wine

MARCIA MULLER

The rain stopped as suddenly as it had begun, the way it always does in the Arizona desert. The torrent had burst from a near-cloudless sky, and now it was clear once more, the land nourished. I stood in the doorway of my house, watching the sun touch the stone wall, the old buckboard and the twisted arms of the giant saguaro cacti.

The suddenness of these downpours fascinated me, even though I'd lived in the desert for close to forty years, since the day I'd come here as Joe's bride in 1866. They'd been good years, not exactly bountiful, but we'd lived here in quiet comfort. Joe had the instinct that helped him bring the crops—melons, corn, beans—from the parched soil, an instinct he shared with the Papago Indians who were our neighbors. I didn't possess the knack, so now that he was gone I didn't farm. I did share one gift with the Papagos, however—the ability to make sweet cactus wine from the fruit of the saguaro. That wine was my livelihood now—as well as, I must admit, a source of Saturday-night pleasure—and the giant cacti scattered around the ranch were my fortune.

I went inside to the big rough-hewn table where I'd been shelling peas when the downpour started. The bowl sat there half full, and I eyed the peas with distaste. Funny what age will do to you. For years I'd had an overly hearty appetite. Joe used to say, "Don't worry, Katy. I like big women." Lucky for him he did, because I'd carried around enough lard for two such admirers, and I didn't believe in divorce anyway. Joe'd be surprised if he could see me now, though. I was tall, yes, still tall. But thin. I guess you'd call it gaunt. Food didn't interest me any more.

I sat down and finished shelling the peas anyway. It was market day in Arroyo, and Hank Gardner, my neighbor five miles down the road, had taken to stopping in for supper on his way home from town. Hank was widowed too. Maybe it was his way of courting. I didn't know and didn't care. One man had been enough trouble for me and, anyway, I intended to live out my days on these parched but familiar acres.

Sure enough, right about suppertime Hank rode up on his old bay. He was a lean man, browned and weathered by the sun like folks get in these parts, and he rode stiffly. I watched him dismount, then went and got the whiskey bottle and poured him a tumblerful. If I knew Hank, he'd had a few drinks in town and would be wanting another. And a glassful sure wouldn't be enough for old Hogsbreath Hank, as he was sometimes called.

He came in and sat at the table like he always did. I stirred the iron pot on the stove and sat down too. Hank was a man of few words, like my Joe had been. I'd heard tales that his drinking and temper had pushed his wife into an early grave. Sara Gardner had died of pneumonia, though, and no man's temper ever gave that to you.

Tonight Hank seemed different, jumpy. He drummed his fingers on the table and drank his whiskey.

To put him at his ease, I said, "How're things in town?"

"What?"

"Town. How was it?"

"Same as ever."

"You sure?"

"Yeah, I'm sure. Why do you ask?" But he looked kind of furtive.

"No reason," I said. "Nothing changes out here. I don't know why I asked." Then I went to dish up the stew. I set it and some corn bread on the table, poured more whiskey for Hank and a little cactus wine for me. Hank ate steadily and silently. I sort of picked at my food.

After supper I washed up the dishes and joined Hank on the front porch. He still seemed jumpy, but this time I didn't try to find out why. I just sat there beside him, watching the sun spread its redness over the mountains in the distance. When Hank spoke, I'd almost forgotten he was there.

"Kathryn"—he never called me Katy; only Joe used that name—"Kathryn, I've been thinking. It's time the two of us got married."

So that was why he had the jitters. I turned to stare. "What put an idea like that into your head?"

He frowned. "It's natural."

"Natural?"

"Kathryn, we're both alone. It's foolish you living here and me living over there when our ranches sit next to each other. Since Joe went, you haven't farmed the place. We could live at my house, let this one go, and I'd farm the land for you."

Did he want me or the ranch? I know passion is supposed to die when you're in your sixties, and as far as Hank was concerned mine had, but for form's sake he could at least pretend to some.

"Hank," I said firmly, "I've got no intention of marrying again—or of farming this place."

"I said I'd farm it for you."

"If I wanted it farmed, I could hire someone to do it. I wouldn't need to acquire another husband."

"We'd be company for one another."

"We're company now."

"What're you going to do—sit here the rest of your days scratching out a living with your cactus wine?"

"That's exactly what I plan to do."

"Kathryn . . ."

"No."

"But . . ."

"No. That's all."

Hank's jaw tightened and his eyes narrowed. I was afraid for a minute that I was going to be treated to a display of his legendary temper, but soon he looked placid as ever. He stood, patting my shoulder.

"You think about it," he said. "I'll be back tomorrow and I want a yes answer."

I'd think about it, all right. As a matter of fact, as he rode off on the bay I was thinking it was the strangest marriage proposal I'd ever heard of. And there was no way old Hogsbreath was getting any yesses from me.

He rode up again the next evening. I was out gathering cactus fruit. In the springtime, when the desert nights are still cool, the tips of the saguaro branches are covered with waxy white flowers. They're prettiest in the hours around dawn, and by the time the sun hits its peak, they close. When they die, the purple fruit begins to grow, and now, by midsummer, it was splitting open to show its bright red pulp. That pulp was what I turned into wine.

I stood by my pride and joy—a fifty-foot giant that was probably two hundred years old—and watched Hank come toward me. From his easy gait, I knew he was sure I'd changed my mind about his proposal. Probably figured he was irresistible, the old goat. He had a surprise coming.

"Well, Kathryn," he said, stopping and folding his arms

across his chest, "I'm here for my answer."

"It's the same as it was last night. No. I don't intend to marry again."

"You're a foolish woman, Kathryn."

"That may be. But at least I'm foolish in my own way."

"What does that mean?"

"If I'm making a mistake, it'll be one I decide on, not one you decide for me."

The planes of his face hardened, and the wrinkles around his eyes deepened. "We'll see about that." He turned and strode toward the bay.

I was surprised he had backed down so easy, but relieved. At least he was going.

Hank didn't get on the horse, however. He fumbled at his saddle scabbard and drew his shotgun. I set down the basket of cactus fruit. Surely he didn't intend to shoot me!

He turned, shotgun in one hand.

"Don't be a fool, Hank Gardner."

He marched toward me. I got ready to run, but he kept going, past me. I whirled, watching. Hank went up to a nearby saguaro, a twenty-five footer. He looked at it, turned and walked exactly ten paces. Then he turned again, brought up the shotgun, sighted on the cactus, and began to fire. He fired at its base over and over.

I put my hand to my mouth, shutting off a scream.

Hank fired again, and the cactus toppled.

It didn't fall like a man would if he were shot. It just leaned backwards. Then it gave a sort of sigh and leaned farther and farther. As it leaned it picked up momentum, and when it hit the ground there was an awful thud.

Hank gave the cactus a satisfied nod and marched back toward his horse.

I found my voice. "Hey, you! Just what do you think you're doing?"

Hank got on the bay. "Cactuses are like people, Kathryn. They can't do anything for you once they're dead. Think about it."

"You bet I'll think about it! That cactus was valuable to me. You're going to pay!"

"What happens when there're no cactuses left?"

"What? What?"

"How're you going to scratch out a living on this miserable ranch if someone shoots all your cactuses?"

"You wouldn't dare!"

He smirked at me. "You know, there's one way cactuses *aren't* like people. Nobody ever hung a man for shooting one."

Then he rode off.

I stood there speechless. Did the bastard plan to shoot up my cacti until I agreed to marry him?

I went over to the saguaro. It lay on its back, oozing water. I nudged it gently with my foot. There were a few round holes in it—entrances to the caves where the Gila woodpeckers lived. From the silence, I guessed the birds hadn't been inside when the cactus toppled. They'd be mighty surprised when they came back and found their home on the ground.

The woodpeckers were the least of my problems, however. They'd just take up residence in one of the other giants. Trouble was, what if Hank carried out his veiled threat? Then the woodpeckers would run out of nesting places—and I'd run out of fruit to make my wine from.

I went back to the granddaddy of my cacti and picked up the basket. On the porch I set it down and myself in my rocking chair to think. What was I going to do?

I could go to the sheriff in Arroyo, but the idea didn't please me. For one thing, like Hank had said, there was no law against shooting a cactus. And for another, it was embarrassing to be in this kind of predicament at my age. I could see all the locals lined up at the bar of the saloon, laughing at me. No, I didn't want to go to Sheriff Daly if I could help it.

So what else? I could shoot Hank, I supposed, but that was even less appealing. Not that he didn't deserve shooting, but they could hang you for murdering a man, unlike a cactus. And then, while I had a couple of Joe's old rifles, I'd never been comfortable with them, never really mastered the art of sighting and pulling the trigger. With my luck, I'd miss Hank and kill off yet another cactus.

I sat on the porch for a long time, puzzling and listening to the night sounds of the desert. Finally I gave up and went to bed, hoping the old fool would come to his senses in the morning.

He didn't, though. Shotgun blasts on the far side of the ranch brought me flying out of the house the next night. By the time I got over there, there was nothing around except a couple of dead cacti. The next night it happened again, and still the next night. The bastard was being cagey, too. I had no way of proving it actually was Hank doing the shooting. Finally I gave up and decided I had no choice but to see Sheriff Daly.

I put on my good dress, fixed my hair and hitched up my horse to the old buckboard. The trip into Arroyo was hot and dusty, and my stomach lurched at every bump in the road. It's no fun knowing you're about to become a laughingstock. Even if the sheriff sympathized with me, you can bet he and the boys would have a good chuckle afterwards.

I drove up Main Street and left the rig at the livery stable. The horse needed shoeing anyway. Then I went down the wooden sidewalk to the sheriff's office. Naturally, it was closed. The sign said he'd be back at two, and it was only noon now. I got out my list of errands and set off for the feed store, glancing over at the saloon on my way.

Hank was coming out of the saloon. I ducked into the shadow of the covered walkway in front of the bank and watched him, hate rising inside me. He stopped on the sidewalk and waited, and a moment later a stranger joined him. The stranger wore a frock coat and a broad-brimmed black hat. He didn't dress like anyone from these parts. Hank and the man walked toward the old adobe hotel and shook hands in front of it. Then Hank ambled over to where the bay was tied, and the stranger went inside.

I stood there, frowning. Normally I wouldn't have been

curious about Hank Gardner's private business, but when a man's shooting up your cacti you develop an interest in anything he does. I waited until he had ridden off down the street, then crossed and went into the hotel.

Sonny, the clerk, was a friend from way back. His mother and I had run church bazaars together for years, back when I still had the energy for that sort of thing. I went up to him and we exchanged pleasantries.

Then I said, "Sonny, I've got a question for you, and I'd just as soon you didn't mention me asking it to anybody."

He nodded.

"A man came in here a few minutes ago. Frock coat, black hat."

"Sure. Mr. Johnson."

"Who is he?"

"You don't know?"

"I don't get into town much these days."

"I guess not. Everybody's talking about him. Mr. Johnson's a land developer. Here from Phoenix."

Land developer. I began to smell a rat. A rat named Hank Gardner.

"What's he doing, buying up the town?"

"Not the town. The countryside. He's making offers on all the ranches." Sonny eyed me thoughtfully. "Maybe you better talk to him. You've got a fair-sized spread there. You could make good money. In fact, I'm surprised he hasn't been out to see you."

"So am I, Sonny. So am I. You see him, you tell him I'd like to talk to him."

"He's in his room now. I could . . ."

"No." I held up my hand. "I've got a lot of errands to do. I'll talk to him later."

But I didn't do any errands. Instead I went home to sit in my rocker and think.

That night I didn't light my kerosene lamp. I kept the house dark and waited at the front door. When the evening shadows had fallen, I heard a rustling sound. A tall figure slipped around the stone wall into the dooryard.

I watched as he approached one of the giant saguaros in the dooryard. He went right up to it, like he had the first one he'd shot, turned and walked exactly ten paces, then blasted away. The cactus toppled, and Hank ran from the yard.

I waited. Let him think I wasn't to home. After about fifteen minutes, I got undressed and went to bed in the dark, but I didn't rest much. My mind was too busy planning what I had to do.

The next morning I hitched up the buckboard and drove over to Hank's ranch. He was around back, mending a harness. He started when he saw me. Probably figured I'd come to shoot him. I got down from the buckboard and walked up to him, a sad, defeated look on my face.

"You're too clever for me, Hank. I should have known it."

"You ready to stop your foolishness and marry me?"

"Hank," I lied, "there's something more to my refusal than just stubbornness."

He frowned. "Oh?"

"Yes. You see, I promised Joe on his deathbed that I'd never marry again. That promise means something to me."

"I don't believe in . . ."

"Hush. I've been thinking, though, about what you said about farming my ranch. I've got an idea. Why *don't* you farm it for me? I'll move in over here, keep house and feed you. We're old enough everyone would know there weren't any shenanigans going on."

Hank looked thoughtful, pleased even. I'd guessed right; it wasn't my fair body he was after.

"That might work. But what if one of us died? Then what?"

"I don't see what you mean."

"Well, if you died, I'd be left with nothing to show for all that farming. And if I died, my son might come back from

Tucson and throw you off the place. Where would you be
then?"

"I see." I looked undecided, fingering a pleat in my
skirt. "That *is* a problem." I paused. "Say, I think there's a
way around it."

"Yeah?"

"Yes. We'll make wills. I'll leave you my ranch in mine.
You do the same in yours. That way we'd both have something to show for our efforts."

He nodded, looking foxy. "That's a good idea, Kathryn.
Very good." I could tell he was pleased I'd thought of it
myself.

"And, Hank, I think we should do it right away. Let's go
into town this afternoon and have the wills drawn up."

"Fine with me." He looked even more pleased. "Just let
me finish with this harness.

The will signing, of course, was a real solemn occasion. I
even sniffed a little into my handkerchief before I put my
signature to the document. The lawyer, Will Jones, was a
little surprised by our bequests, but not much. He knew I
was alone in the world, and Hank's son John was known to
be more of a ne'er-do-well than his father. Probably Will
Jones was glad to see the ranch wouldn't be going to John.

I had Hank leave me off at my place on his way home.
I wanted, I said, to cook him one last supper in my old house
before moving to his in the morning. I went about my prepa-
rations, humming to myself. Would Hank be able to resist
rushing back into town to talk to Johnson, the land developer? Or would he wait a decent interval, say a day?

Hank rode up around sundown. I met him on the porch,
twisting my handkerchief in my hands.

"Kathryn, what's wrong?"

"Hank, I can't do it."

"Can't do what?"

"I can't leave the place. I can't leave Joe's memory. This
whole thing's been a terrible mistake."

He scowled. "Don't be foolish. What's for supper?"

"There isn't any."

"What?"

"How could I fix supper with a terrible mistake like this on my mind?"

"Well, you just get in there and fix it. And stop talking this way."

I shook my head. "No, Hank, I mean it. I can't move to your place. I can't let you farm mine. It wouldn't be right. I want you to go now, and tomorrow I'm going into town to rip up my will."

"You what?" His eyes narrowed.

"You heard me, Hank."

He whirled and went toward his horse. "You'll never learn, will you?"

"What are you going to do?"

"What do you think? Once your damned cactuses are gone, you'll see the light. Once you can't make any more of that wine, you'll be only too glad to pack your bags and come with me."

"Hank, don't you dare!"

"I do dare. There won't be a one of them standing."

"Please, Hank! At least leave my granddaddy cactus." I waved at the fifty-foot giant in the outer dooryard. "It's my favorite. It's like a child to me."

Hank grinned evilly. He took the shotgun from the saddle and walked right up to the cactus.

"Say good-bye to your child."

"Hank! Stop!"

He shouldered the shotgun.

"Say good-bye to it, you foolish woman."

"Hank, don't you pull that trigger!"

He pulled it.

Hank blasted at the giant saguaro—one, two, three times. And, like the others, it began to lean.

Unlike the others, though, it didn't lean backwards. It gave a great sigh and leaned and leaned and leaned forwards. And then it toppled. As it toppled, it picked up momentum. And when it fell on Hank Gardner, it made an awful thud.

I stood quietly on the porch. Hank didn't move. Finally I went over to him. Dead. Dead as all the cacti he'd murdered.

I contemplated his broken body a bit before I hitched up the buckboard and went to tell Sheriff Daly about the terrible accident. Sure was funny, I'd say, how that cactus toppled forwards instead of backwards. Almost as if the base had been partly cut through and braced so it would do exactly that.

Of course, the shotgun blasts would have destroyed any traces of the cutting.

Jeanne Williams has won no fewer than three WWA Spur Awards, two for best juvenile novel—The Horse Talker *(1960) and* Freedom Trail *(1973)—and one for best adult novel,* The Valiant Women *(1980). She was also the 1962 recipient of the Levi Strauss Golden Saddleman Award. Author of more than forty historical novels, a third of them for young readers, she is noted for (among other fictional attributes) the strong feminist element in her works. "The Debt," a low-key portrait of an Iowa family on their way to Oregon by wagon train, demonstrates both her feminism and her considerable narrative talent.*

The Debt

JEANNE WILLIAMS

One of the articles agreed to by all members of the McBride Company when it was forming up in Iowa was that anyone who killed another member of the party during the trip to Oregon was to be tried and hanged. So when, a day west of Split Rock, Jed Hoffman shot Harry Drew in a card game, Jed didn't beg, though his tanned young face went pale and haggard when the other men found no way to call what he'd done anything but murder. Harry had a foul mouth, but it shouldn't have been answered with a gun.

Jed was well liked and it was a shame that his wife, Mary Ann, was big with their second child, but the articles had to be followed. Make exceptions and the fifteen interdependent families would lose all order, perhaps fatally, long before they got to Oregon. So Jed was hanged with the best rope they had to the best tree they could find along the sulky Sweetwater.

After he kissed Mary Ann and four-year-old Billy, Jed looked at his friends. "I know you got to do this. But since you're taking me, you owe it to Mary Ann to get her to Oregon."

"We'll do it," promised Tam McBride, the captain, a stocky man with a grizzled spade beard and brown eyes that were merry except when he had something like this to do.

Mary Ann didn't beg, either, but though Mrs. McBride tried to lead her away, she stood and watched Jed hang. She was thin, weathered past her twenty years by farm work and the wind and sun of the trail, but her eyes were like a mountain lake, blue-green and fathomless beneath dark brows that winged up at the sides, a strange contrast to hair the pale shade of the underleaf of a cottonwood.

She kept Billy's face buried in her skirt while the women murmured with shock and pity. When Jed's legs hung slack and his poor face was something no one should see and some of the men were sick and old Mrs. Steubens fainted, Mary Ann got a knife to cut Jed down.

Talt Braden took the knife and did it for her. Rangy, broad in the shoulder, Talt had straight black hair, a lean rock-hard face, eyes like a summer storm, and a half smile that seemed to mock the world. It was whispered that he'd been a squaw man, a trapper on the Yellowstone, till his woman died. He'd joined the company at Fort Laramie and knew a lot more about the country than the little Emigrants' Guide Tam McBride had previously relied on.

Not that there was much chance of losing the way. It was a devastated swath several miles wide in places, marked with dead oxen, horses and cattle, discarded furniture and belongings that had proved too heavy for the long ordeal, and a few graves. In order to prevent looting by Indians, most burials were made in the trail and driven over so that they were obliterated.

This was how Jed and the man he'd killed were buried, wrapped first in blankets because there was no wood for coffins. Talt helped cover the graves before he came over to Mary Ann.

"I'll drive your wagon."

She stared at him as if waking from a deep sleep. Her bewildered gaze moved over the hurrying company who were eager to get away from what they had done.

"I—I can't travel with these people."

"You can't stay here!"

"I can wait till another train comes along."

He swore. "That might be a week. Indians don't bother trains much but they're always ready for easy pickings." When she said nothing, Talt demanded roughly, "What about the kid? Think of him if you don't care about yourself."

She stroked Billy's blond head as he still clung to her. "I don't want to be beholden to anyone who had a hand in—in this."

"You won't be." Talt frowned. "It's something we owe." And without allowing her further argument, he lifted her up on the seat and put Billy beside her.

Mary Ann had always been one for keeping to herself. She had no real friends in the company and, with the reproach of Jed's death on them, people were relieved that Talt had taken on the responsibility of looking after the dead man's family. It took away the awkwardness of trying to talk to her when, no matter how friendly or matter-of-fact a body tried to be, Mary Ann just looked through you and wouldn't say anything past yes or no. She got even chillier after the children started teasing Billy.

"Your pa wet his pants when he died!" they'd taunt, when out of earshot of their elders. "His eyes booged out and his tongue was purple!"

Talt dragged a few of the boys by the scruffs of their necks over to their folks and saw they got whomped, but there's no way to stop a thing like that. Billy quit playing with the other youngsters and stuck close to his mama. Talt made him a willow flute and carved him a whole menagerie of bone animals, buffalo, horses, bear, antelope, beaver and coyotes. Billy had them march to funny little whistle tunes or made up long stories about them as he moved them around on the wagon seat or the ground. Folks began to wonder if he was touched in the head but they didn't dare talk to Mary Ann about it. When Mrs. McBride ventured a question to Talt, he just rared back on his heels and stared at her till she turned redder than a turkey gobbler's wattles.

"My God, woman!" That was all he said.

So, though Mary Ann's wagon moved along with the company, she and her little son were more like some kind of ghosts. They made everyone uneasy, squelched the jokes and laughter that helped ease such a grinding, monotonous journey. Still, it was an obligation to get Mary Ann to Oregon. No one questioned that.

For sure, if she'd had any appetite, she could have eaten better with Talt than ever she had with Jed. Talt was far and away the best hunter in the company and when Mary Ann couldn't fancy even hump or tongue of buffalo, he brought in sage grouse or caught fish to broil till they were a mouth-watering gold. After camp was made of an evening, he often took Billy to hunt for berries and wild turnips and onions. They often had a swim before they came back and if Billy's short legs were worn out. Talt brought him back on his shoulders.

"You're good to Billy," Mary Ann said one night after the boy had gone to sleep with the bone animals arranged close to him.

Talt shrugged. "Never had any folks. I know a kid can get lonesome."

She regarded him with the first real interest she'd shown in anything. "I was an orphan, too. My aunt raised me, talked on how Christian she was while she worked me like a slave. Couldn't get out of there fast enough—"

Her voice trailed off. She'd never said how she'd felt about her husband and she didn't say now. Just stared at the sunlit snow on top of the Wind Rivers to the north of where the company would cross the Continental Divide at South Pass, that broad, high plain that stretched for miles between the ranges.

At Pacific Springs, where water could for the first time be seen flowing toward the Pacific, the company found what seemed to be an abandoned wagon, amid signs of a hastily broken big encampment. Tam McBride went over to look and came back in a hurry, brown eyes wide with fright.

"Cholera!" he choked. "Woman's dead and the man's close to it." This was supposed to be the night's halting place, but he gave orders to move on. Most of the drivers were already ahead of him.

"Hold on!" called Talt. "One of you come drive Mrs. Hoffman."

"Why?" demanded McBride.

Talt was climbing down as he spoke, and his storm-colored eyes had lightning in them. "Man shouldn't die alone when there are people."

"He's out of his head," McBride argued. "And you could pick up the contagion." Talt didn't answer, just started for the death wagon. "You poke around here, man, and we don't want you rejoining the company!" McBride warned, sweat popping out on his seamed forehead. "Hell, it could take away every soul of us!"

"Don't worry," said Talt. "I'll pass you up and have my land staked before you cross the Snake."

He went on toward the wagon. McBride scowled, looked unhappily at Mary Ann, and then bellowed for one of the single men to come drive her. There was a scramble. Women were scarce out west and all the bachelors had been waiting for some hint in Mary Ann's behavior that would show she had properly decided she needed a man for herself and a father for her kids. No one had pushed. Talt had the inside track there. But at this opportunity, Mary Ann could have had her pick of the unmarried fellows.

Not even looking at them as they hustled around her

wagon, she said to McBride, "I'll wait for Mr. Braden."

"You can't do that!" Tam growled.

"I will."

His eyes fell under her strange blue-green ones. "But you might catch the sickness! Little Billy might! Looky here, Mrs. Hoffman, this party owes it to you—"

She made a gesture with her hand as if she were throwing something away. "I'm sick of you and your whining about a debt! Do you think you can give back a man's life? I'm sick of being tied to you on account of your duty. Go along!"

Mrs. McBride made a helpless gesture. "Now, Mrs. Hoffman, Mary Ann—" Her voice thinned to a whisper. "You can't be wicked enough to risk your little boy! Let us take him."

"So the boys can make mock of him again?" Mary Ann hugged her child against the swell of the one that was coming. "If he can't make it with us, he'd be better off dead than being kicked around like a stray cur! You better go fast. The wind might blow the cholera your direction!"

The McBrides paled and swung their wagon. One by one, under Mary Ann's sightless stare, the young single men, muttering, went back to their horses.

"Play with your animals," Mary Ann told Billy.

Heavily, she climbed down from the wagon. Talt, going for water, stopped in his tracks and shouted at her, "Go on with the others!"

She shook her head.

"You fool woman! Hurry up and rejoin the company."

"Reckon I owe you something."

"Is that the only word anyone knows? Owe?" He must have realized he couldn't budge her. "All right, wait if you're crazy enough! But you keep away from this wagon and me. If I don't come down with it in a week or two, I'd reckon we could travel along. Drive over to those willows and set up camp."

Talt dug a grave for the dead woman that afternoon. He brewed some herb drink for the man and got quite a lot of it down him but the sick man passed with next morning's dawn. Talt dug his grave, too, and burned the wagon and tainted possessions. He made his camp in sight of Mary Ann and the boy, but didn't go near them. For their meat, though, he managed to shoot a pronghorn a hundred yards from the wagon, which Mary Ann laboriously skinned and butchered. Talt shot another for himself and feasted.

He also kept constant watch for Indians. South Pass was a favorite spot for various tribes to skirmish with each other or just come looking for excitement. Shoshoni, Sioux, Snake and Crow. He sighed, wishing he'd told Mary Ann that. Then he reflected that if cholera wouldn't send her with the company, nothing could have. She smiled sometimes at Billy. Talt wished that she would smile at him.

Five mornings after the abandoned man had died, Mary Ann climbed off the shuck mattress in the wagon and glanced toward Talt's camp. Usually, he'd wave at her, shout a greeting. This morning, he lay in his blankets.

Fear gripped and squeezed her heart. *He's just tired,* she told herself stoutly. *Man has a right to sleep late if he's not going anywhere.* And because this just had to be the answer, she got breakfast before she'd let herself look over at Talt.

He hadn't moved.

"Talt!" she shouted. There was a panicky note in her cry. Little Billy gave a whimper and ran to her. That made her get hold of herself, forced herself to think.

She'd heard that about half the people who got cholera died of it, some in a day, others taking closer to a week of terrible retching agony, fever and chills. Talt Braden, if she had anything to do with it, was going to be one of those who got well.

But Billy—

What if she got the sickness, too? Terror swirled over

her but she fought it down. Surely a wagon train would be along soon, it was just a fluke that none had passed while they were camped by the springs. She had often doubted there was a God. Now she had to pray that there was and that He would take care of her son.

"Billy," she said, kneeling, swallowing to steady her voice and keep it calm and reassuring. "Talt may be sick and I have to take care of him. You've got to be a big boy and take care of your animals here at the wagon. I baked bread yesterday and there's cooked meat and that I've been smoking. You can gather berries but don't get out of sight of the wagon."

His mouth trembled and his blue eyes were bewildered. "But, Mama—"

"You can see me," she assured him. "We can wave at each other and you can play some tunes on your whistle. But you mustn't come over where you could get sick." She gave him a fierce squeeze. "Whatever happens, keep away from us till I tell you it's all right."

"Talt get well?" he pleaded, tightening his grip on her dress. Gently, she unpried the chubby brown fingers, dimpled so sweetly at the knuckles.

"Yes. He's going to get well. But you have to help. Go see if you can find some berries. If you do, put them right over there by that biggest sagebrush. Then I can give them to Talt."

"I'll get a lot of berries!" Billy promised. Clutching his whistle, he went off at a trot with a little bucket.

Mary Ann gathered up things she would need and moved across the space to Talt.

Talt's sunken eyes stared at her without recognition as she coaxed him to drink the tea she'd made from the herbs left from treating the stranger. She got a few swallows down him before he convulsed in long shuddering cramps. He threw up a thin, stinking bile, kept heaving when nothing more would come. When he collapsed, she bathed him, taking off his shirt and wondering where a white scar in the shoulder had come from.

The stomach cramps tortured him again. She heated their skillets and applied them to Talt's abdomen, wrapped in one of his shirts. His legs twitched and strained. She rubbed them, trying to work out the massed rigidity of spasmed muscles. It seemed an eternity that the cramps continued. She applied heat, rubbed his arms and legs, and talked, hoping that beneath his delirium, he could know someone was there.

Billy's whistle sounded after a time. She glanced up to see that he was cautiously depositing berries on a plate by the big sagebrush.

"For Talt!" he shouted.

Rising, she waved at him and went to get the fruit. Billy looked very small and vulnerable, standing uncertainly by the wagon. "Why don't you get some nice long grass for Midge and Sam?" she called.

The oxen were finding ample graze, but Billy would feel better if he had something to do. "Billy find good grass," he promised, and trotted off.

Mary Ann crushed the berries into water and got some of the thickened juice down Talt. She was encouraged when he didn't vomit at once, but within the hour, hideous cramps contorted the body which seemed to be shrinking before her eyes.

More heated skillets, more rubbing till her hands and shoulders ached. Sometimes his contortions and retching were so violent that she thought they must kill him, but his breath labored on. And thinking he surely needed fluid to replace all he was losing, she would wait for half an hour or so after a bout of retching and then get him to take tea or broth or the fruit drink.

Several times that long, hot day, Billy sounded his whistle. Mary Ann would walk as near the wagon as she dared and tell him how much the berries seemed to be helping Talt and make sure the boy was eating. Seeing her even for a few minutes seemed to reassure Billy and he would go back to playing with his animals, moving them up and down the wagon tongue.

As the setting sun made rose-gold of the high peaks of the Wind Rivers, Mary Ann looked down at Talt and thought he was resting easier. Or perhaps he was simply exhausted, slipping over that line between sleep and death?

Raising him against her breast, she gave him the rest of the fruit juice. At this altitude, the air cooled rapidly after sundown. She wrapped him warmly, went back to call goodnight to Billy.

"Do you have your animals all ready to sleep?"

"All but bear. Bear's going to stand guard. He'll watch out for you and Talt, too, Mama."

"Thank him, honey. Now you cuddle up in the blankets and sleep sound."

"Talt sleep sound?"

"He's a lot better. Maybe you can find him some more berries tomorrow."

"I will." She heard him talking to his bear. Dear God, what if he should be left with only his toy animals for comfort? It didn't stand thinking about.

She wrapped up in her blankets, close enough to wake if Talt stirred much, and dropped instantly into slumber.

Twice that night, Talt's threshings roused her. She heated skillets, rubbed the knotting muscles, and got him to drink. He slept late next morning, face haggard and dark with whiskers that made his cheeks seem even more hollowed. But the dreadful vomiting and the worst cramping seemed to be over.

Billy brought more berries, and today Talt could relish their tart sweetness whole. Mary Ann enriched the broth with bits of meat and bread. Most of that day, Talt slept, but once when she was slipping berries into his mouth, his eyes looked full at her, no longer glazed.

"You're a stubborn woman," he mumbled.

"I pay my debts."

His eyebrows lifted but he was too weak to argue and lapsed back into a drowse.

He improved steadily after that. Within a week, he said he could travel though he wasn't yet up to a full day. They burned his bedding and clothes and what Mary Ann had worn while nursing him. Then, before going to Billy, they both scrubbed themselves thoroughly in water from the spring, using strong lye soap, and washing their hair as well.

"Want me to wash your back for you?" Talt called softly through the willows.

Mary Ann blushed in spite of the chuckle in his voice, but she was glad he felt good enough to be a little pesky. "I washed yours often enough," she retorted.

"But I couldn't enjoy it, ma'am. Why don't you be real sweet and do it again?"

"You—you *man!*"

He seemed to be coming through the bushes. She made for the wagon as fast as her condition permitted and stood behind it while she dried off and got into clean clothing. Then she rummaged his extra garments out of the wagon and deposited them on the willows.

"Now you can get decent," she called primly, and fled as she saw him approaching shamelessly through the wispy trees. His laughter followed her. Drat the man! Weak with cholera, he'd been safe, but now it seemed she was going to have to fight him off! It was purely ridiculous when she was big as a barn.

The baby kicked within her and she put her hands over it as if to soothe it. Anyhow, it seemed she'd escaped cholera and she didn't see any way Billy could have caught it. But her labor was before her. If only there was a woman around since there couldn't be a doctor! She'd have to deliver with no one to help but a man who was, after all, a stranger.

They got stuck in Big Sandy. In spite of Talt's warnings, Mary Ann helped push, and an hour after they were back on the road, her pains began. She hoped the birthing would hold off till they stopped for the day. Talt's sickness had made them late and every day counted now in getting through the mountains before the snows. But the muted pangs grew harsher, closer together, and within another hour, Mary Ann was chewing her lips and perspiring cold sweat.

"What's the matter?" Talt shot a sidelong glance at her involuntary moan, gasped, and stopped the oxen. "The baby?"

She nodded, panted and squeezed her eyes shut as a great hand seemed to grip the inside of her belly and wrench it around. Billy squealed and grabbed her.

"Listen, son," said Talt, lifting him down. "Your mama's going to be fine but we need some hot water. How's about you bringing in lots of sagebrush and any dried chips you can find? And then you go play over in that draw till I call you to see your new brother or sister."

"Billy want brother."

"I'll see what I can do," Talt promised. "But sometimes the good Lord decides we need a woman so there'll always be plenty of mamas. Scoot, now!"

Mary Ann wanted to lie down but Talt wouldn't let her. "You'll have that baby a lot faster if you keep walking around."

"How do you know?"

"That's how Indian women do."

"Damn you, I'm not an Indian!"

"Well, you're going to have this baby like you were, lady, because that's the only way I know how to help—and from what I've seen, it sure works better than the white way."

He made her walk while he built a fire and put water to boil. Then he drove two poles into the ground and tied a braided rawhide rope between them. "Kneel in the middle," he said, "and hang onto the rope. It'll help you push."

She was still skewered by dizzying surges of black-red pain but gradually she found that being able to push down and encourage the pains made her feel better than if she'd been lying prone amid a flock of anxious women, passively enduring her labor rather than urging it on.

Talt brought her hot tea frequently. When she was so exhausted that her sweating hands slipped from the rope, he gripped her wrists and supported her in a squat. She screamed, strangled the sound in her throat so Billy wouldn't be scared. She was splitting, being torn apart—She faded into soft darkness, conscious only of Talt's hands.

When she roused, she felt something at her breast. Wonderingly, she touched her stomach, found it flat. Bending her neck, she gazed down at a silk black head, a funny little squished-up visage.

"That's brother?" Billy was saying in disgust. "Mama, he's too little!"

"He'll grow," Talt promised.

"Bear won't like him much."

"He will later. Now why don't you and bear go find some berries?"

Billy loped off. Mary Ann sighed, blissful at being free from pain and the cumbering bigness, and drifted off to sleep.

She lay on the mattress next day as they traveled on. The baby was fretful and didn't suck much. By the fourth day, when real milk should have replaced the clear fluid, she realized that her right breast was hard and swollen, increasingly painful. By night, the other breast was caked, too, and she had to confess her condition to Talt before the baby starved.

"Fool woman!" he growled, something like panic leaping into his eyes. "Why didn't you tell me this morning?"

He made hot compresses applied with mullein leaves, made her drink herbal teas and eat, and insisted that she let the infant suck, agonizing as it was. "He won't get any milk to speak of but it'll help break up that abscess."

"He needs milk!"

"He'll get it from you when you get straightened out. Till then, don't you worry. I'll make him such a nice broth that he may not want milk, ever."

* * *

That didn't happen, but the baby stayed alive on broth till Talt's stern regime righted the misery in Mary Ann's breasts. As she cradled the child and relaxed to the sweetly painful tugging of his little jaws, it seemed natural enough for Talt to stand there watching them.

"Strong little guy. What you going to call him?"

Vaguely, she had planned to name a boy baby after Jed, but it seemed now that she had known the father of this child countless years ago, almost in another life. She had married Jed in the excitement of her first courtship and to escape her aunt, but had she ever loved him? He had been a habit. She was too honest to let the tragedy of his death blind her.

Looking up at Talt, she said quietly, "If—if you don't mind, I'd like to name him for you. He wouldn't be alive if you hadn't taken care of us."

"You owe it to me?"

She started to lash out at him. Then she saw a sort of hunger deep in his eyes, a look curiously like Billy's when he occasionally worried that the baby might supplant him. "I'm mighty tired of all these debts," she said levelly. "Maybe I pulled you through the cholera. You for sure saved my baby. Let's call it even."

He took a deep breath. The fire in his eyes sent a sweetness rushing through her, a sunny warmth she had never felt before. "Does that mean—well, that we're starting fresh?"

"Fresh as we can after all we've been through."

"Guess we acted like we were married—except for the best parts. Mary Ann, you reckon it's about time you got a daddy for these boys?"

She nodded. He leaned over and kissed her above the nursing baby, his kiss a promise of all they were going to share. Billy stepped out of the shadows and climbed into Talt's lap. "Bear wants someone to hold him, too!"

"Bear's come to the right place," Talt said. "And so have I."

Above the yellow head, his eyes met Mary Ann's.

Dorothy M. Johnson is one of the foremost writers of western fiction, and her work shows great understanding of the forces that shaped the American West. The critical recognition she has received includes a Western Writers of America Spur Award for her short story "Lost Sister" in 1956, the Levi Strauss Golden Saddleman Award in 1976, the Western Heritage Wrangler Award in 1978, and the Western Literary Association Distinguished Achievement Award in 1981. Johnson is also beloved by the people about whom she writes, as evidenced by the fact that she is an adopted member of the Blackfeet Indian tribe and honorary police chief of her hometown, Whitefish, Montana. Three motion pictures have been based on her work: A Man Called Horse *(1970);* The Man Who Shot Liberty Valance *(1962); and* The Hanging Tree *(1959), adapted from the excellent story which follows. In these pages Johnson shows us the gold camp of Skull Creek and the delicate and complex structure of society there, as embodied in the relationship among three of its more unusual residents.*

The Hanging Tree

DOROTHY M. JOHNSON

I

Just before the road dipped down to the gold camp on Skull Creek, it crossed the brow of a barren hill and went under the out-thrust bough of a great cottonwood tree.

A short length of rope, newly cut, hung from the bough, swinging in the breeze, when Joe Frail walked that road for the first time, leading his laden horse. The camp was only a few months old, but someone had been strung up already, and no doubt for good cause. Gold miners were normally more interested in gold than in hangings. As Joe Frail glanced up at the rope, his muscles went tense, for he remembered that there was a curse on him.

Almost a year later, the boy who called himself Rune came into Skull Creek, driving a freight wagon. The dangling length of rope was weathered and raveled then. Rune

273

stared at it and reflected, If they don't catch you, they can't hang you.

Two weeks after him, the lost lady passed under the tree, riding in a wagon filled with hay. She did not see the bough or the raveled rope, because there was a bandage over her eyes.

Joe Frail looked like any prospector, ageless, anonymous and dusty, in a fading red shirt and shapeless jeans. His matted hair, hanging below his shoulders, would have been light brown if it had been clean. A long mustache framed his mouth, and he wore a beard because he had not shaved for two months.

The main difference between Joe Frail and any other newcomer to Skull Creek was that inside the pack on his plodding horse was a physician's satchel.

"Now I wonder who got strung up on that tree," remarked his partner. Wonder Russell was Joe Frail's age—thirty—but not of his disposition. Russell was never moody and he required little from the world he lived in. He wondered aloud about a thousand things but did not require answers to his questions.

"I wonder," he said, "how long it will take us to dig out a million dollars."

I wonder, Joe Frail thought, if that is the bough from which I'll hang. I wonder who the man is that I'll kill to earn it.

They spent that day examining the gulch, where five hundred men toiled already, hoping the colors that showed in the gravel they panned meant riches. They huddled that night in a brush wickiup, quickly thrown together to keep off the rain.

"I'm going to name my claim after me when I get one," said Wonder Russell. "Call it the Wonder Mine."

"Meaning you wonder if there's any pay dirt in it," Joe Frail answered. "I'll call mine after myself, too. The Frail Hope."

"Hell, that's unlucky," his partner objected.

"I'm usually unlucky," said Joe Frail.

He lay awake late that first night in the gulch, still shaken by the sight of the dangling rope. He remembered the new-made widow, six years ago, who had shrieked a prophecy that he would sometime hang.

Before that, he had been Doctor Joseph Alberts, young and unlucky, sometimes a prospector and sometimes a physician. He struck pay dirt, sold out and went back East to claim a girl called Sue, but she had tired of waiting and had married someone else. She sobbed when she told him, but her weeping was not because she had spoiled her life and his. She cried because she could not possess him now that he was rich.

So he lost some of his youth and all his love and even his faith in love. Before long he lost his riches, too, in a fever of gambling that burned him up because neither winning nor losing mattered.

Clean and new again, and newly named Frail—he chose that in a bitter moment—he dedicated himself to medicine for a winter. He was earnest and devoted, and when spring came he had a stake that would let him go prospecting again. He went north to Utah to meet a man named Harrigan, who would be his partner.

On the way, camped alone, he was held up and robbed of his money, his horse and his gun. The robbers, laughing, left him a lame pinto mare that a Digger Indian would have scorned.

Hidden in a slit in his belt for just such an emergency was a twenty-dollar gold piece. They didn't get that.

In Utah he met Harrigan—who was unlucky, too. Harrigan had sold his horse but still had his saddle and forty dollars.

"Will you trust me with your forty dollars?" Joe Frail asked. "I'll find a game and build it bigger."

"I wouldn't trust my own mother with that money," Harrigan objected as he dug into his pocket. "But my mother don't know how to play cards. What makes you think you do?"

"I was taught by an expert," Joe Frail said briefly.

In addition to two professions, doctor and miner, he had two great skills: he was an expert card player and a top hand with a pistol. But he played cards only when he did not care whether he won or lost. This time winning was necessary, and he knew what was going to happen—he would win, and then he would be shattered.

He found a game and watched the players—two cowboys, nothing to worry about; a town man, married, having a mildly devilish time; and an older man, probably an emigrant going back East with a good stake. The emigrant was stern and tense and had more chips before him than anyone else at the table.

When Doc sat in, he let the gray-haired man keep winning for a while. When the emigrant started to lose, he could not pull out. He was caught in some entangling web of emotions that Doc Frail had never felt.

Doc lost a little, won a little, lost a very little, began to win. Only he knew how the sweat ran down inside his dusty shirt.

The emigrant was a heavy loser when he pulled out of the game.

"Got to find my wife," was his lame excuse. But he went only as far as the bar and was still there, staring into the mirror, when Doc cashed in his chips and went out with two hundred dollars in his pockets.

He got out to the side of the saloon before the shakes began.

"And what the hell ails you?" Harrigan inquired. "You won."

"What ails me," said Doc with his teeth chattering, "is that my father taught me to gamble and my mother taught me it was wicked. The rest of it is none of your business."

"You sound real unfriendly," Harrigan complained. "I was admiring your skill. It must be mighty handy. The way you play cards, I can't see why you waste your time doctoring."

"Neither can I," said Doc.

He steadied himself against the building. "We'll go someplace and divide the money. You might as well have yours in your pocket."

Harrigan warned, "The old fellow, the one you won from, is on the prod."

Doc said shortly, "The man's a fool."

Harrigan sounded irritated. "You think everybody's a fool."

"I'm convinced of it."

"If you weren't one, you'd clear out of here," the cowboy advised. "Standing here, you're courting trouble."

Doc took that as a challenge. "Trouble comes courting me, and I'm no shy lover."

He felt as sore as raw meat. Another shudder shook him. He detested Harrigan, the old man, himself, everybody.

The door swung open and the lamplight showed the gray-haired emigrant. The still night made his words clear: "He cheated me, had them cards marked, I tell you!"

Salt stunk unbearably on raw meat. Doc Frail stepped forward.

"Are you talking about me?"

The man squinted. "Certainly I'm talking about you. Cheating, thieving tin horn—"

Young Doc Frail gasped and shot him.

Harrigan groaned, "My God, come on!" and ducked back into darkness.

But Doc ran forward, not back, and knelt beside the fallen man as the men inside the saloon came cautiously out.

Then there was a woman's keening cry, coming closer: "Ben! Ben! Let me by—he's shot my husband!"

He never saw her, he only heard her wailing voice: "You don't none of you care if a man's been killed, do you! You'll let him go scot free and nobody cares. But he'll hang for this, the one who did it! You'll burn in hell for this, the lot of you—"

Doc Frail and Harrigan left that place together—the

pinto carried both saddles and the men walked. They parted company as soon as they could get decent horses, and Doc never saw Harrigan again.

A year or so later, heading for a gold camp, Doc met the man he called Wonder, and Wonder Russell, it seemed to him, was the only true friend he had ever had.

But seeing him for the first time, Joe Frail challenged him with a look that warned most men away, a slow, contemptuous look from hat to boots that seemed to ask, "Do you amount to anything?"

That was not really what it asked, though. The silent question Joe Frail had for every man he met was "Are you the man? The man for whom I'll hang?"

Wonder Russell's answer at their first meeting was as silent as the question. He smiled a greeting, and it was as if he said, "You're a man I could side with."

They were partners from then on, drifting through good luck and bad, and so finally they came to Skull Creek.

They built more than one wickiup in the weeks they spent prospecting there, moving out from the richest part of the strike, because that was already claimed.

By September they were close to broke.

"A man can go to work for wages," Wonder Russell suggested. "Same kind of labor as we're doing now, only we'd get paid for it. I wonder what it's like to eat."

"You'll never be a millionaire working someone else's mine," Doc warned.

"I wonder how a man could get a stake without working," his partner mused.

"I know how," Joe Frail admitted. "How much have we got between us?"

It added up to less than fifty dollars. By morning of the following day, Joe Frail had increased it to almost four hundred and was shuddering so that his teeth chattered.

"What talent!" Wonder Russell said in awe. He asked no questions.

Four days after they started over again with a new supply of provisions, they struck pay dirt. They staked two claims, and one was as good as the other.

"Hang on or sell out?" Joe Frail asked.

"I wonder what it's like to be dirty rich," Wonder mused. "On the other hand, I wonder what it's like to be married?"

Joe Frail stared. "Is this something you have in mind for the immediate future, or are you just dreaming in a general kind of way?"

Wonder Russell smiled contentedly. "Her name is Julie and she works at the Big Nugget."

And she already has a man who won't take kindly to losing her, Joe Frail recollected. Wonder Russell knew that as well as he did.

She was a slim young dancer, beautiful though haggard, this Julie at the Big Nugget. She had tawny hair in a great knot at the back of her neck, and a new red scar on one shoulder; it looked like a knife wound and showed when she wore a low-necked dress.

"Let's sell, and I'll dance at your wedding," Joe Frail promised.

They sold the Wonder and the Frail Hope on a Monday and split fifteen thousand dollars between them. They could have got more by waiting, but Wonder said, "Julie don't want to wait. We're going out on the next stage, Wednesday."

"There are horses for sale. Ride out, Wonder." Doc could not forget the pale, cadaverous man called Dusty Smith who would not take kindly to losing Julie. "Get good horses and start before daylight."

"Anybody'd think it was you going to get married, you're in such a sweat about it," Wonder answered, grinning. "I guess I'll go tell her now."

A man should plan ahead more, Joe Frail told himself. I planned only to seek for gold, not what to do if I found it, and not what to do if my partner decided to team up with someone else.

He was suddenly tired of being one of the anonymous, bearded, sweating toilers along the creek. He was tired of being dirty. A physician could be clean and wear good clothes. He could have a roof over his head. Gold could buy anything—and he had it.

He had in mind a certain new cabin. He banged on the door until the owner shouted angrily and came with a gun in his hand.

"I'd like to buy this building," Joe Frail told him. "Right now."

A quarter of an hour later, he owned it by virtue of a note that could be cashed at the bank in the morning, and the recent owner was muttering to himself out in the street, with his possessions on the ground around him, wondering where to spend the rest of the night.

Joe Frail set his lantern on the bench that constituted all the cabin's furniture. He walked over to the wall and kicked it gently.

"A whim," he said aloud. "A very solid whim to keep the rain off."

Suddenly he felt younger than he had in many years, light-hearted, completely carefree, and all the wonderful world was his for the taking. He spent several minutes leaping into the air and trying to crack his heels together three times before he came down again. Then he threw back his head and laughed.

Lantern in hand, he set out to look for Wonder. When he met anyone, as he walked toward the Big Nugget, he lifted the lantern, peered into the man's face, and asked hopefully, "Are you an honest man?"

Evans, the banker, who happened to be out late, answered huffily, "Why, certainly!"

Wonder Russell was not in the saloon, but tawny-haired Julie was at the bar between two miners. She left them and came toward him smiling.

"I hear you sold out," she said. "Buy me a drink for luck?"

"I'll buy you champagne if they've got it," Joe Frail promised.

When their drinks were before them, she said. "Here's more luck of the same kind, Joe." Still smiling gaily, she whispered, "Go meet him at the livery stable." Then she laughed and slapped at him as if he had said something especially clever, and he observed that across the room Dusty Smith was playing cards and carefully not looking their way.

"I've got some more places to visit before morning," Joe Frail announced. "Got to find my partner and tell him we just bought a house."

He blew out the lantern just outside the door. It was better to stumble in the darkness than to have Dusty, if he was at all suspicious, be able to follow him conveniently.

Wonder was waiting at the livery stable corral.

"Got two horses in here, paid for and saddled," Wonder reported. "My war sack's on one of 'em, and Julie's stuff is on the other."

"I'll side you. What do you want done?"

"Take the horses out front of the Big Nugget. They're yours and mine, see? If anybody notices, we bought 'em because we made our pile and we've been drinking. Hell, nobody'll notice anyway."

"You're kind of fidgety," Joe Frail commented. "Then what?"

"Get the horses there and duck out of sight. That's all. I go in, buy Julie a drink, want her to come out front and look at the moon."

"There isn't any moon," Joe warned him.

"Is a drunk man going to be bothered by that?" Wonder answered. "I'll set 'em up for the boys and then go show Julie the moon while they're milling around. That's all."

"Good luck," Joe Frail said, and their hands gripped. "Good luck all the way for you and Julie."

"Thanks, partner," Wonder Russell said.

And where are you going, friend? Joe Frail wondered.

Your future is none of my business, any more than your past.

He staggered as he led the horses down the gulch, in case anyone was watching. A fine performance, he told himself; too bad it is so completely wasted. Because who's going to care, except Dusty Smith, if Julie runs off and gets married?

He looped the lines over the hitch rail so that a single pull would dislodge them. Then he stepped aside and stood in the shadows, watching the door.

Wonder Russell came out, singing happily: "Oh, don't you remember sweet Betsy from Pike, who crossed the big desert with her lover Ike?"

Another good performance wasted, Joe Frail thought. The lucky miner with his claim sold, his pockets full of money, his belly full of whiskey—that was Wonder's role, and nobody would have guessed that he was cold sober.

Wonder capped his performance by falling on the steps and advising them to get out of the way and let a good man pass. Joe grinned and wished he could applaud.

Two men came out and, recognizing Russell, loudly implored him to let some golden luck rub off on them. He replied solemnly, "Dollar a rub, boys. Every little bit helps." They went away laughing as he stumbled through the lighted doorway.

Joe Frail loosened his guns in their holsters and was ready in the shadows. The best man helps the happy couple get away, he remembered, but this time not in a shower of rice with tin cans tied to the buggy and bunting on the team!

Wonder Russell was in the doorway with Julie beside him, laughing.

"Moon ain't that way," Russell objected. "It's over this way." He stepped toward the side of the platform where the saddled horses were.

Inside the lighted room a white-shirted gaunt man whirled with a gun in his hand, and Dusty Smith was a sure target in the light for three or four seconds while Joe Frail stood frozen with his guns untouched. Then the noise inside the saloon was blasted away by a gunshot, and Wonder Russell staggered and fell.

The target was still clear while Dusty Smith whirled and ran for the back door. A pistol was in Joe Frail's right hand, but the pistol and the hand might as well have been blocks of wood. He could not pull the trigger—until the miners roared their shock and anger and Dusty Smith had got away clean.

Joe Frail stood frozen, hearing Julie scream, seeing the men surge out the front door, knowing that some of them followed Dusty Smith out the back.

There were some shots out there, and then he was no longer frozen. His finger could pull the trigger for a useless shot into the dust. He ran to the platform where Julie was kneeling. He shouldered the men aside, shouting, "Let me by. I'm a doctor."

But Wonder Russell was dead.

"By God, Joe, I wish you'd have come a second sooner," moaned one of the men. "You could have got him from the street if you'd been a second sooner. It was Dusty Smith."

Someone came around the corner of the building and panted the news that Dusty had got clean away on a horse he must have had ready out back.

Joe Frail sat on his heels for a long time while Julie held Wonder's head in her arms and cried. One of the little group of miners still waiting asked, "You want some help, Joe? Where you want to take him?"

He looked down at Julie's bowed head.

My friend—but her lover, he remembered. She has a better right.

"Julie," he said. He stooped and helped her stand up. "Where do you want them to take him?"

"It doesn't matter," she said dully. "To my place, I guess."

Joe Frail commissioned the building of a coffin and bought burying clothes at the store—new suit and shirt that Wonder had not been rich long enough to buy for himself. Then, carrying a pick and shovel, he climbed the hill.

While he was digging, another friend of Wonder's came, then two more, carrying tools of the same kind.

"I'd rather you didn't," Joe Frail told them. "This is something I want to do myself."

The men nodded and turned away.

When he stopped to rest, standing in the half-dug grave, he saw another man coming up. This one, on horseback, said without dismounting, "They got Dusty hiding about ten miles out. Left him for the wolves."

Joe Frail nodded. "Who shot him?"

"Stranger to me. Said his name was Frenchy Plante."

Joe went back to his digging. A stranger had done what he should have done, a stranger who could have no reason except that he liked killing.

Joe Frail put down his shovel and looked at his right hand. There was nothing wrong with it now. But when it should have pulled the trigger, there had been no power in it.

Because I shot a man in Utah, he thought, I can't shoot any more when it matters.

Julie climbed the hill before the grave was quite finished. She looked at the raw earth, shivering a little in the wind, and said, "He's ready."

Joe stood looking at her, but she kept her eyes down.

"Julie, you'll want to go away. You'll have money to go on—all the money for his claim. I'll ride with you as far as Elk Crossing, so you'll have someone to talk to if you want to talk. I'll go with you farther than that if you want."

"Maybe. Thanks. But I kind of think I'll stay in Skull Creek."

She turned away and walked down the hill.

Sometime that night, Julie cut her throat and died quietly and alone.

II

Elizabeth Armistead, the lost lady, came to Skull Creek the following summer.

About four o'clock one afternoon, a masked man rode out of the brush and held up a stage coach some forty miles south of the diggings. Just before this, the six persons aboard the stage were silently wrapped in their separate thoughts, except the stage line's itinerant blacksmith, who was uneasily asleep.

A tramp printer named Heffernan was dreaming of riches to be got by digging gold out of the ground. A whiskey salesman beside him was thinking vaguely of suicide, as he often did during a miserable journey.

The driver, alone on his high seat, squinted through glaring light and swiped his sleeve across his face, where sand scratched the creases of his skin. He envied the passengers, protected from the sand-sharp wind, and was glad he was quitting the company. He was going back to Pennsylvania, get himself a little farm. Billy McGinnis was fifty-eight years old on that last day of his life.

The sick passenger, named Armistead, was five years older and was planning to begin a career of schoolteaching in Skull Creek. He had not intended to go there. He had thought he had a good thing in Elk Crossing, a more stable community with more children who needed a school. But another wandering scholar had got there ahead of him, and so he and his daughter Elizabeth traveled on toward the end of the world.

The world ended even before Skull Creek for Mr. Armistead.

His daughter Elizabeth, aged nineteen, sat beside him with her hands clasped and her eyes closed but her back straight. She was frightened, had been afraid for months, ever since people began to say that Papa was dishonest. This could not be, must not be, because Papa was all she had to look after and to look after her.

Papa was disgraced and she was going with him into exile. She took some comfort from her own stubborn, indignant loyalty. Papa had no choice, except of places to go. But Elizabeth had had a choice—she could have married Mr. Ellerby and lived as she had always lived, in comfort.

If Papa had told her to do so, or even suggested it, she would have married Mr. Ellerby. But he said it was for her to decide and she chose to go away with Papa. Now that she had an idea how harsh life could be for both of them, she was sick with guilt and felt that she had been selfish and willful. Mr. Ellerby had been willing to provide Papa with a small income, as long as he stayed away, and she had deprived him of it.

These two had no real idea about what the gold camp at Skull Creek would be like. The towns they had stopped in had been crude and rough, but they were at least towns, not camps. Some of the people in them intended to stay there, and so made an effort toward improvement.

Mr. Armistead was reasonably certain that there were enough children in Skull Creek for a small private school, and he took it for granted that their parents would be willing to pay for their education. He assumed, too, that he could teach them. He had never taught or done any other kind of work, but he had a gentleman's education.

He was bone-tired as well as sick and hot and dusty, but when he turned to Elizabeth and she opened her eyes, he smiled brightly. She smiled back, pretending that this endless, unendurable journey to an indescribable destination was a gay adventure.

He was a gentle, patient, hopeful man with good intentions and bad judgment. Until his financial affairs went wrong, he had known no buffeting. Catastrophe struck him before he acquired the protective calluses of the spirit that accustomed misfortune can produce.

All the capital they had left was in currency in a small silk bag that Elizabeth had sewed under her long, full traveling dress.

Elizabeth was wondering, just before the holdup, whether her father could stand it to travel the rest of the day and all night on the final lap of the journey. But the stage station would be dirty and the food would be horrible—travel experience had taught her to be pessimistic—and

probably it would be better if they went on at once to Skull
Creek where everything, surely, would be much, much
pleasanter. Papa would see to that. She could not afford to
doubt it.

Billy McGinnis, the driver, was already in imagination
in Pennsylvania when a masked rider rode out of scanty
timber at his right and shouted, "Stop there!"

Billy had been a hero more than once in his career, but
he had no leanings that way any more. He cursed dutifully
but hauled on the lines and stopped his four horses.

"Drop that shotgun," the holdup man told Billy. He
obeyed, dropping the weapon carefully, making no startling
movement.

"Everybody out!" yelled the masked man. "With your
hands up."

The printer, as he half fell out of the coach (trying to
keep his hands up but having to hang on with one of them),
noted details about the bandit: tall from the waist up but sort
of short-legged, dusty brown hat, dusty blue shirt, red bandanna over his face.

The whiskey salesman stumbled out hastily—he had
been through this a couple of times before and knew better
than to argue—and wondered why a man would hold up a
stage going into a gold camp. The sensible thing was to hold
up one going out.

The blacksmith, suddenly wide awake, was the third to
descend. He accepted the situation philosophically, having
no money with him anyway, and not even a watch.

But Mr. Armistead tried to defend his daughter and all
of them. He warned her, "Don't get out of the coach."

As he stepped down, he tried to fire a small pistol he had
brought along for emergencies like this.

The bandit shot him.

Billy McGinnis, jerking on the lines to hold the frightened horses, startled the masked man into firing a second
shot. As Billy pitched off the seat, the team lit out running,
with Elizabeth Armistead screaming in the coach.

She was not in it any more when the three surviving men found it, overturned, with the frantic horses tangled in the lines, almost an hour later.

"Where the hell did the lady go to?" the blacksmith demanded. The other two agreed that they would have found her before then if she had jumped or fallen out during the runaway.

They did the best they could. They shouted and searched for another hour, but they found no sign of the lost lady. At the place where the coach had turned over, there was no more brush or scrubby timber by the road, only the empty space of the Dry Flats, dotted with greasewood.

One of the horses had a broken leg, so the whiskey salesman shot it. They unhitched the other three, mounted and searched diligently, squinting out across the flats, calling for the lost lady. But they saw nothing and heard no answering cry.

"The sensible thing," the printer recommended, "is to get on to the station and bring out more help."

"Take the canteen along?" suggested the whiskey salesman.

"If she gets back here, she'll need water," the blacksmith reminded him. "And she'll be scared. One of us better stay here and keep yelling."

They drew straws for that duty, each of them seeing himself as a hero if he won, the lady's rescuer and comforter. The blacksmith drew the short straw and stayed near the coach all night, with the canteen, but the lady did not come back.

He waited alone in the darkness, shouting until he grew hoarse and then voiceless. Back at the place of the holdup, Billy McGinnis and Mr. Armistead lay dead beside the road.

Doc Frail was shaving in his cabin, and the boy called Rune was sullenly preparing breakfast, when the news came about the lost lady.

Doc Frail was something of a dandy. In Skull Creek,

cleanliness had no connection with godliness and neither did anything else. Water was mainly used for washing gold out of gravel, but Doc shaved every morning or had the barber do it.

Since he had Rune to slave for him, Doc had his boots blacked every morning and started out each day with most of the dried mud brushed off his coat and breeches. He was a little vain of his light brown curly hair, which he wore hanging below his shoulders. Nobody criticized this, because he had the reputation of having killed four men.

The reputation was unearned. He had killed only one, the man in Utah. He had failed to kill another, and so his best friend had died. These facts were nobody's business.

Doc Frail was quietly arrogant, and he was the loneliest man in the gold camp. He belonged to the aristocracy of Skull Creek, to the indispensable men like lawyers, the banker, the man who ran the assay office, and saloon owners. But these men walked in conscious rectitude and carried pistols decently concealed. Doc Frail wore two guns in visible holsters.

The other arrogant ones, who came and went, were the men of ill will, who dry-gulched miners on their way out with gold. They could afford to shoulder lesser men aside.

Doc Frail shouldered nobody except with a look. Where he walked, other men moved aside, greeting him respectfully: "Morning, Doc. . . . How are you, Doc? . . . Hear about the trouble down the gulch, Doc?"

He brandished no pistol (though he did considerable target practice, and it was impressively public) and said nothing very objectionable. But he challenged with a look.

His slow gaze on a stranger, from hat to boots, asked silently, "Do you amount to anything? Can you prove it?"

That was how they read it, and why they moved aside.

What he meant was, "Are you the man I'm waiting for, the man for whom I'll hang?" But nobody knew that except himself.

By Skull Creek standards, he lived like a king. His cabin

was the most comfortable one in camp. It had a wood floor and a half partition to divide his living quarters from his consulting room.

The boy Rune, bent over the cookstove, said suddenly, "Somebody's hollering down the street."

"That's a fact," Doc answered, squinting in his shaving mirror.

Rune wanted, of course, to be told to investigate, but Doc wouldn't give him the satisfaction and Rune wouldn't give Doc the satisfaction of doing anything without command. The boy's slavery was Doc's good joke, and he hated it.

There was a pounding on the door and a man's voice shouting, "Doc Frail!"

Without looking away from his mirror, Doc said, "Well, open it," and Rune moved to obey.

A dusty man shouldered him out of the way and announced, "Stage was held up yestiddy, two men killed and a lady lost track of."

Doc wiped his razor and permitted his eyebrows to go up. "She's not here. One of us would have noticed."

The messenger growled. "The boys thought we better warn you. If they find her, you'll be needed."

"I'll keep it in mind," Doc said mildly.

"They're getting up a couple posses. I don't suppose you'd care to go?"

"Not unless there's a guarantee I'd find the lady. What's the other posse for?"

"To get the road agent. One of the passengers thinks he'd recognize him by the build. The driver, Billy McGinnis, was shot, and an old man, the father of the lost lady. Well, I'll be going."

The messenger turned away, but Doc could not quite let him go with questions still unasked.

"And how," he inquired, "would anybody be so careless as to lose a lady?"

"Team ran off with her in the coach," the man answered triumphantly. "When they caught up with it, she wasn't in it any more. She's lost somewheres on the Dry Flats."

The boy Rune spoke unwillingly, unable to remain silent and sullen: "Kin I go?"

"Sure," Doc said with seeming fondness. "Just saddle your horse."

The boy closed down into angry silence again. He had no horse; he had a healing wound in his shoulder and a debt to Doc for dressing it. Before he could have anything he wanted, he had to pay off in service his debt to Doc Frail— and the service would end only when Doc said so.

Doc Frail set out after breakfast to make his rounds— a couple of gunshot wounds, one man badly burned from falling into his own fire while drunk, a baby with colic, a miner groaning with rheumatism, and a dance-hall girl with a broken leg resulting from a fall off a table.

The posses were setting out then with considerable confusion and some angry arguments over the last of the horses available at the livery stable.

"You can't have that bay!" the livery stable man was shouting. "That's a private mount and I dassent rent it!"

"You certainly dassent," Doc agreed. "The bay is mine," he explained to three scowling men. The explanation silenced them.

Doc had an amusing thought. Rune would sell his soul to go out with the searchers.

"Get the mare ready," Doc said, and turned back to his cabin.

"I've decided to rent you my horse," he told the sullen boy. "For your services for—let's see—one month in addition to whatever time I decide you have to work for me anyway."

It was a cruel offer, adding a month to a time that might be endless. But Rune, sixteen years old, was a gambler. He blinked and answered, "All right."

"Watch yourself," Doc warned, feeling guilty. "I don't

want you crippled." The wound was two weeks old.

"I'll take good care of your property," the boy promised. "And the horse too," he added, to make his meaning clear. Doc Frail stood back, smiling a little, to see which crowd Rune would ride with. There was no organized law enforcement in the gravel gulches of Skull Creek, only occasional violent surges of emotion, with mob anger that usually dissolved before long.

If I were that kid, thought Doc, which posse would I choose, the road agent or the lady? He watched the boy ride to the milling group that was headed for the Dry Flats and was a little surprised. Doc himself would have chosen the road agent, he thought.

So would Rune, except that he planned to become a road agent himself if he ever got free of his bondage.

Rune dreamed, as he rode in the dust of other men's horses, of a bright, triumphant future. He dreamed of a time when he would swagger on any street in any town and other men would step aside. There would be whispers: "Look out for that fellow. That's Rune."

Doc Frail's passage in a group earned that kind of honor. Rune, hating him, longed to be like him.

Spitting dust, the boy dreamed of more immediate glory. He saw himself finding the lost lady out there on the Dry Flats in some place where less keen-eyed searchers had already looked. He saw himself comforting her, assuring her that she was safe now.

He was not alone in his dreaming. There were plenty of dreams in that bearded, ragged company of gold-seekers (ragged even if they were already rich, bedraggled with the dried mud of the creek along which sprawled the diggings). They were men who lived for tomorrow and the comforts they could find somewhere else when, at last, they pulled out of Skull Creek. They were rough and frantic seekers after fortune, stupendously hard workers, out now on an unaccustomed holiday.

Each man thought he was moved by compassion, by

pity for the lost and lovely and mysterious lady whose name most of them did not yet know. If they went instead because of curiosity and because they needed change from the unending search and labor in the gravel gulches, no matter. Whatever logic moved them, they rode out to search, fifty motley, bearded men, each of whom might find the living prize.

Only half a dozen riders had gone over the sagebrush hills to look for the road agent who had killed two men. The miners of Skull Creek gambled for fortune but, except when drunk, seldom for their lives. About the worst that could happen in looking for the lost lady was that a man might get pretty thirsty. But go looking for an armed bandit—well, a fellow could get shot. Only the hardy adventurers went in that posse.

When the sun went down, nobody had found anybody, and four men were still missing when the rest of the lady's seekers gathered at the stage line's Station Three. The state company superintendent permitted a fire to be set to a pile of stovewood (freighted in at great expense, like the horse feed and water and everything else there) to make a beacon light. The missing men came in swearing just before midnight. Except for a few provident ones, most of the searchers shivered in their broken sleep, under inadequate and stinking saddle blankets.

They were in the saddle, angry and worried, before dawn of the day Elizabeth Armistead was found.

The sun was past noon when black-bearded Frenchy Plante stopped to tighten his cinch and stamp his booted feet. He pulled off a blue kerchief that protected his nose and mouth from the wind-borne grit, shook the kerchief and tied it on again. He squinted into the glare and, behind a clump of greasewood, glimpsed movement.

A rattler, maybe. Might as well smash it. Frenchy liked killing snakes. He had killed two men, too, before coming to Skull Creek, and one since—a man whose name he found out later was Dusty Smith.

He plodded toward the greasewood, leading his horse, and the movement was there—not a rattler but the wind-whipped edge of a blue skirt.

"Hey!" he shouted, and ran toward her.

She lay face down, with her long, curling hair, once glossy brown, dull and tangled in the sand. She lay flat and drained and lifeless, like a dead animal. Elizabeth Armistead was not moving. Only her skirt fluttered in the hot wind.

"Lady!" he said urgently. "Missus, here's water."

She did not hear. He yanked the canteen from his saddle and pulled out the stopper, knelt beside her and said again, "Lady, I got water."

When he touched her shoulder, she moved convulsively. Her shoulders jerked and her feet tried to run. She made a choking sound of fear.

But when he held the canteen to her swollen, broken lips, she had life enough to clutch at it, to knock it accidentally aside so that some of the water spilled on the thankless earth. Frenchy grabbed the canteen and set it again to her lips, staring at her face with distaste.

Dried blood smeared it, because sand cut into the membranes of the nose like an abrasive. Her face was bloated with the burn of two days of sun, and her anguished lips were shapeless.

Frenchy thought, I'd rather be dead. Aloud he said, "No more water now for a minute. Pretty soon you can have more, Missus."

The lost lady reached blindly for the canteen, for she was blind from the glaring sun, and had been even before she lost her bonnet.

"You gotta wait a minute," Frenchy warned. "Don't be scared, Missus. I'm going to fire this here gun for a signal, call the other boys in. We'll get you to the stage station in no time."

He fired twice into the air, then paused. Two shots meant "found dead." Then he fired the third that changed the pattern and told the other searchers, listening with their mouths open slightly, that the lady had been found living.

The first man to get there was tall, fair-haired Rune, aching with sunburn and the pain of his wound, which had pulled open. When Frenchy found the lady, Rune had been just beyond a little rise of barren ground, stubbornly dreaming as he rode.

I should have been the one, he thought with dull anger. I should have been the one, but it's always somebody else.

He looked at the lady, drained and half dead, dull with dust. He saw the frail and anxious hands groping for the canteen, clutching it as Frenchy guided it to her mouth. He saw the burned, blind face. He said, "Oh, God!"

Frenchy managed a friendly chuckle.

"You're going to be all right, Missus. Get you to a doctor right away. That's a promise, Missus. Frenchy Plante's promise."

He put his name on her, he staked his claim, Rune thought. Who cares? She's going to die anyway.

"I'll go for Doc," Rune said, turning his horse toward the stage station.

But he couldn't go for Doc, after all. He took the news to Station Three; he had that much triumph. Then there was vast confusion. The stage line superintendent ordered a bed made up for the lady, and it was done—that is, the stock-tender took the blankets off his bunk and gave them a good shaking and put them back on again. Riders began to come in, shouting, "How is she? Who found her?"

By the time Frenchy Plante arrived, with the lady limp in his arms, and an escort of four other searchers who had gone in the direction of his signal shots, it was discovered that nobody at all had started for Skull Creek to get the doctor.

Rune sat on the ground in the scant shade of the station with his head bowed on his knees, as near exhausted as he had ever been in his life. His shoulder wound hurt like fury, and so did his stomach whenever he remembered how the lost lady looked.

Frenchy Plante was the hero again. He borrowed a fresher horse and rode on to Skull Creek.

He found Doc Frail at home but occupied with a patient, a consumptive dancer from the Big Nugget. With her was another woman, who looked up scowling, as Doc did, when Frenchy came striding in.

"Found the lady, Doc," Frenchy announced. "Want you to come right away."

"I have a patient here," Doc said in controlled tones, "as you will see if you're observant. This lady also needs me."

The consumptive girl, who had seldom been called a lady, was utterly still, lying on Doc's own cot. Her friend was holding her hands, patting them gently.

"Come out a minute," Frenchy urged, "so I can tell you."

Doc closed the door behind him and faced Frenchy in the street.

Frenchy motioned toward the door. "What's Luella doing in your place?"

"Dying," Doc answered. "She didn't want to do it where she works."

"How soon can you come? The lost lady's real bad. Got her to the stage station, but she's mighty sick."

"If she's as sick as this one," Doc said, "it wouldn't do her any good for me to start out there anyway."

"Damned if you ain't a hard-hearted scoundrel," commented Frenchy, half shocked and half admiring. "You ain't doing Luella no good, are you?"

"No. Nobody ever has. But I'm not going to leave her now."

Frenchy shrugged. "How long'll it be?"

"Couple hours, maybe. Do you expect me to strangle her to hurry it along?"

Frenchy's eyes narrowed. "I don't expect nothing. Get out there when you feel like it. I done my duty anyhow."

Was that a reminder, Doc wondered as he watched Frenchy ride on to the Big Nugget, that once you did a duty that should have been mine? That you killed Dusty Smith—a man you didn't even know—after I failed?

Doc Frail went back into his cabin.

A few hours later, Luella released him by dying.

It was dawn when he flung himself off a rented horse at the station and stumbled over a couple of the men sleeping there on the ground.

The lost lady, her face glistening with grease that the stocktender had provided, was quiet on a bunk, with a flickering lamp above her on a shelf. Cramped and miserable on his knees by the bunk was Rune, whose wrist she clutched with one hand. Her other arm cradled Frenchy's canteen.

There was a spot of blood on Rune's shoulder, soaked through Doc's neat dressing, and he was almost too numb to move, but he looked up with hostile triumph.

"She let me be here," he said.

"Now you can go back to Skull Creek," Doc told him, stating a command, not permission. "I'll stay here until she can be moved."

Dispossessed, as he had often been before, but triumphant as he had longed to be, Rune moved away, to tell the sleepy, stirring men that Doc had come. He was amused, when he started back to the gold camp a little later, by the fact that he still rode Doc's mare and Doc would be furious when he discovered it.

The searchers who delayed at Station Three because of curiosity were relieved at the way Doc Frail took charge there. The lost lady seemed to be glad of his presence, too. He treated her burns and assured her in a purring, professional tone, "You'll get your sight back, madam. The blindness is only temporary, I can promise you that."

To the clustering men, he roared like a lion: "Clean this place up—she's got to stay here a few days. Get something decent for her to eat, not this stage-line diet. That's enough to kill an ox. Clean it up, I say—with water. Don't raise a lot of dust."

The superintendent, feeling that he had done more

than his duty by letting the stocktender feed the search posse, demurred about wasting water.

"Every drop has to be hauled clear from Skull Creek," he reminded Doc, who snapped back, "Then hitch up and start hauling!"

The stocktender was caught between Doc's anger and the superintendent's power to fire him. He said in a wheedling voice, "Gonna make her some good soup, Doc. I shot a jackrabbit and had him in the pot before he quit kicking."

"Get out of here," snarled Doc. He bent again to the burned, anguished lady.

"You will be able to see again," he promised her. "And your burns will heal."

But your father is dead and buried, and Skull Creek is no place for you, my dear.

III

Frenchy Plante was still around when Rune got back to Skull Creek. Frenchy swaggered, as he had a right to do, being the man who had found the lost lady. But he spent only half a day or so telling the details over. Then he went back to the diggings, far up the gulch, to toil again in the muck and gravel. He had colors there, he was making wages with a small sluice, he had high hopes of getting rich. It had happened before.

The curious of Skull Creek left their own labors to stand by and get the story. When Frenchy was out of the way, Rune became the belligerent center of attention. He had just finished applying a bunchy bandage to his painful shoulder when he jumped guiltily at a pounding on Doc's door. He finished putting his shirt on before he went to take the bar down.

"Doc ain't back yet?" the bearded caller asked.

Rune shook his head.

"Expecting him?" the man insisted.

"He don't tell me his plans."

The man looked anxious. "Look here, I got a boil on my neck needs lancing. Don't suppose you could do it?"

"Anybody could do it. Wrong, maybe. Doc could do it right—I guess."

The man sidled in. "Hell, you do it. Ain't he got some doctor knives around, maybe?"

Rune felt flattered to have someone show confidence in him.

"I'll find something," he offered. He did not know the name of the thing he found, but it was thin and sharp and surgical. He wiped it thoroughly on a piece of clean bandage and, after looking over the boil on the man's neck, opened it up with a quick cut.

The patient said, "Wow!" under his breath and shuddered. "Feels like you done a good job," he commented. "Now tie it up with something, eh?"

He stretched out his booted legs while he sat back in Doc's best chair and waited for Rune to find bandaging material that pleased him.

"You was right on the spot when they found her, I hear," he hinted.

"I was second man to get there," Rune answered, pretending that to be second was nothing at all, but knowing that it was something, knowing that the man's boil could have waited, or that anyone could have opened it.

"Heard she's a foreigner, don't talk no English," the man hinted.

"She didn't say nothing to me," Rune answered. "Couldn't talk any language. She's an awful sick lady."

The man touched his bandage and winced. "Well, I guess that fixes it. Your fee the same as Doc Frail's, I suppose?"

As coolly as if he were not a slave, Rune nodded, and the man hauled a poke from his pocket, looking around for the gold scales.

For a little while after he had gone, Rune still hated him, even with the man's payment of gold dust stowed away in his pocket. So easy to get a doctor—or somebody with a knife, anyway—when you had the dust to pay for it! So easy to enter servitude if you were penniless and had to have a shoulder wound dressed and thought you were going to die!

Before the morning was half done, another visitor came. This time it was a woman, and she was alone. The ladies of Skull Creek were few and circumspect, armored with virtue. Rune guessed that this one, wife of Flaunce the storekeeper, would not have visited Doc Frail's office without a companion if she had expected to find Doc there.

But she asked in her prissy way, "Is the doctor in?" and clucked when Rune shook his head.

"Well, I can see him another day," she decided. "It was about some more of that cough medicine he gave me for my little ones."

And what for do they need cough medicine in warm weather? Rune would have liked to ask her. He said only, "He ain't here."

"He's out at the stage station, I suppose, with the poor lady who was rescued. Have you heard how she's getting along?"

"She's alive but blind and pretty sick," he said. "She'll get her sight back afterwhile."

"I don't suppose anyone knows why she was coming here?" the woman probed.

"Was with her pa, that's all I know. He's dead and she can't talk yet," Rune reported, knowing that what Flaunce's wife really wanted to know was, Is she a lady or one of those others? Was he really her father?

"Dear me," she asked, "is that blood on your shirt?"

Another one, then, who did not know his shame.

"I shot a rabbit, ma'am," he lied. That satisfied her, even though a man would not normally carry a freshly killed rabbit over his shoulder.

The woman decided the cough medicine could wait and minced up the deep-rutted street of the gulch, carefully looking neither to the right nor left.

At the store, buying supplies for Doc's account, Rune inquired, "Any news of the other posse? Them that was after the road agent?"

"It's bigger'n it was, now they found the lost lady. Some of the men figure there's got to be a lesson taught."

"If they catch him, that is," Rune suggested, and the storekeeper nodded, sighing, "If they catch him."

In Doc's absence, Rune carried out a project he had in mind, now that there was no fear of interruption by Doc himself. He searched with scrupulous care for the place where Doc hid his gold.

There should be some in the cabin somewhere. Doc had much more than a physician's income, for he had grub-staked many miners, and a few of them had struck it rich. Doc could afford to be careless with his little leather pokes of nuggets and dust, but apparently he wasn't careless. Rune explored under every loose board and in every cranny between the logs, but he didn't find anything. He did not plan to take the gold yet anyway. It could wait until he was free to leave.

And why don't I pull out now? he wondered. Two men that morning had asked if he wanted to work for wages, and he had turned them down.

It was not honor that kept him there—he couldn't afford the luxury of honor. It was not his wound; he knew now he wasn't going to die of that. The reason he was going to stay, he thought, was just because Doc expected him to run out. He would not give his master that much satisfaction.

He was Rune, self-named, the world's enemy. The world owed him a debt that he had never had much luck in collecting.

He thought he was going to collect when he came to Skull Creek in triumph driving a freight team and carrying his whole fortune—eighty dollars in gold—inside a canvas belt next to his skin. He drew his pay, had a two-dollar meal, and set out for the barber shop.

There was music coming from the Big Nugget. He went

in to see the source. Not for any other purpose; Rune spent no money that he didn't have to part with. He did not mean to gamble, but while he watched, a miner looked up and said, scowling, "This is a man's game."

He began to lose, and he could not lose, he must not lose, because if you did not have money you might as well be dead.

When he left the saloon, he was numb and desperate and dead.

Toward morning he tried to rob a sluice. He was not yet hungry, but he would be hungry sometime. He had been hungry before and he was afraid of it. He lurked in shadows, saw the sluice had no armed guard. He was scrabbling against the lower riffles, feeling for nuggets, when a shot came without warning. He fell, pulled himself up and ran, stumbling.

Twenty-four hours later he came out of hiding. He was hungry then, and his shoulder was still bleeding. By that time, he knew where the doctor lived, and he waited, huddling outside the door, while the sun came up.

Doc, in his underwear, opened the door at last to get his lungs full of fresh air and, seeing the tall boy crouching on the step, said, "Well!" Noticing the blood-stiffened shirt he stepped back, sighing, "Well, come in. I didn't hear you knock."

Rune stood up carefully, trying not to move the injured shoulder, holding it with his right hand.

"I didn't knock," he said, hating this man of whom he must ask charity. "I can't pay you. But I got hurt."

"Can't pay me, eh?" Doc Frail was amused. "Guess you haven't heard that the only patients who didn't pay me are buried up on the hill."

Rune believed his grim joke.

"You've been hiding out with this for quite a spell," Doc guessed, as he teased the shirt away from the wound, and the boy shuddered. "You wouldn't hide out without a reason, would you?"

He was gentle from habit, but Rune did not recognize gentleness. He was being baited and he was helpless. He gave a brazen answer:

"I got shot trying to rob a sluice."

Doc, working rapidly, commented with amusement, "So now I'm harboring a criminal! And doing it for nothing, too. How did you figure on paying me, young fellow?"

The patient was too belligerent, needed to be taken down a peg.

"If I could pay you, I wouldn't have tackled the sluice, would I?" the boy demanded. "I wouldn't have waited so long to see you, would I?"

"You ask too damn many questions," Doc grunted. "Hold still. . . . Your wound will heal all right. But of course you'll starve first."

Sullen Rune made no answer.

Doc Frail surveyed him. "I can use a servant. A gentleman should have one. To black his boots and cook his meals —you can cook, I hope?—and swamp out the cabin."

Rune could not recognize kindness, could not believe it, could not accept it. But that the doctor should extract service for every cent of a debt not stated—that he could understand.

"For how long?" he bargained, growling.

Doc Frail could recognize what he thought was ingratitude.

"For just as long as I say," he snapped. "It may be a long time. It may be forever. If you bled to death, you'd be dead forever."

That was how they made the bargain. Rune got a home he needed but did not want to accept. Doc got a slave who alternately amused and annoyed him. He resolved not to let the kid go until he learned to act like a human being—or until Doc himself became too exasperated to endure him anymore. Rune would not ask for freedom, and Doc did not know when he would offer it.

There was one thing that Rune wanted from him: skill

with a gun. Doc's reputation as a marksman trailed from him like a tattered banner. Men walked wide of him and gave him courtesy.

But I won't lower myself by asking him to teach me, Rune kept promising himself. There were depths to which even a slave did not sink.

A letter came from Doc Frail the day after Rune returned to Skull Creek. It was brought by a horseback rider who came in from Station Three ahead of the stage.

Rune had never before in his life received a letter, but he took it as casually as if he had had a thousand. He turned it over and said, "Well, thanks," and turned away, unwilling to let the messenger know he was excited and puzzled.

"Ain't you going to read it?" the man demanded. "Doc said it was mighty important."

"I suppose you read it already?" Rune suggested.

The man sighed. "I can't read writing. Not that writing, anyhow. Print, now, I can make out with print, but not writing. Never had much schooling."

"He writes a bad hand," Rune agreed, mightily relieved. "Maybe the store man, he could make it out."

So there was no need to admit that he could not read, either. Even Flaunce, the storekeeper, had a little trouble, tracing with his finger, squinting over his glasses.

Doc had no suspicion that his servant could not read. He had never thought about the matter. If he had known, he might not have begun the letter, "White Sambo."

Hearing that, his slave reddened with shame and anger, but the store man merely commented, "Nickname, eh? White Sambo: Miss Elizabeth Armistead will arrive in Skull Creek in three or four days. She is still weak and blind. She must have shelter and care. I will provide the care, and the shelter will have to be in the cabin of the admirable and respectable Ma Fisher across the street from my own mansion.

" 'Convey my regards to Mrs. Fisher and make all the necessary arrangements. Nothing will be required of Mrs.

Fisher except a temporary home for Miss Armistead, who will of course pay for it.' "

The storekeeper and the messenger stared at Rune.

"I'm glad it ain't me that has to ask Ma Fisher a thing like that," the messenger remarked. "I'd as soon ask favors of a grizzly bear."

Flaunce was kinder. "I'll go with you, son. She wants a sack of flour anyhow, over to the restaurant. I'll kind of back you up—or pick up the pieces."

Ma Fisher served meals furiously in a tent restaurant to transients and miners who were tired of their own cooking in front of the wickiups along the gulch. She seldom had any hired help—too stingy and too hard to get along with, it was said. Her one luxury was her cabin, opposite Doc's, weather-tight and endurable even in cold weather. Most of the population, willing to live miserably today in the hope of a golden tomorrow, housed itself in shacks or lean-to's or caves dug into the earth, eked out with poles and rocks and sods.

Ma Fisher fumed a little when she was informed that the lost lady would be her guest, but she was flattered, and besides she was curious.

"I won't have time to wait on her, I want that understood," she warned. "And I won't stand for no foolishness, either."

"She's too sick for foolishness, I'd say," the storekeeper said soothingly. "Hasn't got her sight back yet. She mighty near died out there, you know."

"Well," Ma Fisher agreed without enthusiasm. "Well."

The first words Elizabeth Armistead spoke in the stage station were, faintly, "Where is Papa?"

"Your father is dead," Doc Frail answered gently. "He was shot during the holdup."

Why didn't she know that? She had seen it happen.

She answered with a sigh: "No." It was not an exclamation of shock or grief. It was a soft correction. She refused to believe, that was all.

"They buried him there by the road, along with the driver," Doc Frail said.

She said again, with more determination, "No!" And after a pause she pleaded, "Where is Papa?"

"He is dead," Doc repeated. "I am sorry to tell you this, Miss Armistead."

He might as well not have told her. She did not accept it.

She waited patiently in darkness for someone to give a reasonable explanation for her father's absence. She did not speak again for several hours because of her weakness and because of her swollen, broken lips.

Doc wished he could give her the comfort of a sponge bath, but he did not dare offend her by offering to do so himself, and she was not strong enough to move her arms. She lay limp, sometimes sleeping.

When he judged that the girl could better bear the trip to Skull Creek in a wagon than she could stand the stage station any longer, he explained that she would stay at Mrs. Fisher's—a very respectable woman, she would be perfectly safe there—until she could make plans for going back East.

"Thank you," the lost lady answered. "And Papa is in Skull Creek waiting?"

Doc frowned. The patient was beginning to worry him. "Your father is dead, you know. He was shot in the holdup."

She did not answer that.

"I will try again to comb your hair," Doc offered. "Tomorrow you can wash, if you want to try it. There will be a blanket over the window, and one over the door, and I will be outside to make sure no one tries to come in."

Her trunk was there, brought from the wrecked coach. He searched out clean clothes that she could put on, and carefully he combed her long, dark, curling hair. He braided it, not very neatly, and wound the two thick braids up over her head.

IV

The wagon was slow, but Doc Frail preferred it for his patient; she could ride easier than in the coach. He ordered the wagon bed well padded with hay, and she leaned back against hay covered with blankets. He had a canvas shade rigged to protect her from the sun. The stage-line superintendent himself was the driver—mightily relieved to be getting this woman to Skull Creek where she would be no more concern of his.

Doc Frail had not looked ahead far enough to expect the escort that accompanied them the last mile of the journey. He sat with the lost lady in the wagon bed, glaring at the curious, silent miners who came walking or riding or who stood waiting by the road.

None of them spoke, and there was no jostling. They only stared, seeing the lady in a blue dress, with a white cloth over her eyes. From time to time, the men nearest the wagon fell back to let the others have their turn.

Once, Doc got a glimpse of the boy, Rune, lanky and awkward, walking and staring with the rest. Doc scowled, and the boy looked away.

For a while, the doctor closed his eyes and knew how it must be for the girl who could hear but could not see. The creak of the wagon, the sound of the horses' hoofs—too many horses; she must know they were accompanied. The soft sound of many men's feet walking. Even the restless sound of their breathing.

The lady did not ask questions. She could not hide. Her hands were clasped tightly together in her lap.

"We have an escort," Doc murmured. "An escort of honor. They are glad to see that you are safe and well."

She murmured a response.

At the top of the hill, where the road dipped down to the camp, they lost their escort. The riders and the walkers stepped aside and did not follow. Doc Frail glanced up as the wagon passed under the great, out-thrust bough of the gnarled tree and felt a chill tingle the skin along his spine.

Well, the fellow deserved the hanging he would get. Doc regretted, however, that the mob that would be coming in from the north would have to pass Ma Fisher's cabin to reach the hanging tree. He hoped they would pass in decent silence. But he knew they would not.

Rune waited near the tree with the other men, torn between wanting to help the lost lady into the cabin and wanting to see the road agent hang. Whichever thing he did, he would regret not having done the other. He looked up at the great bough, shivered, and decided to stay on the hill.

He could see Doc and the stage superintendent help Miss Armistead down from the wagon. As they took her into Ma Fisher's cabin, he could see something else: dust in the distance.

A man behind him said, "They're bringing him in."

Rune had two good looks at the road agent before he died and one brief, sickening glance afterward. The angry miners were divided among themselves about hanging the fellow. The men who had pursued him, caught him, and whipped him until his back was bloody were satisfied and tired. Four of them even tried to defend him, standing with rifles cocked, shouting, "Back! Get back! He's had enough."

He could not stand; men pulled him off his horse and held him up as his body dropped and his knees sagged.

But part of the crowd roared, "Hang him! Hang him!" and shoved on. The mob was in three parts—those for hanging, those against it, and those who had not made up their minds.

Rune glimpsed him again through the milling miners beneath the tree. The posse men had been pushed away from him, their guns unfired, and men who had not pursued him were bringing in a rope.

The black-bearded giant, Frenchy Plante, tied the noose and yanked the road agent to his feet. Frenchy's roar came over the rumbling of the mob: "It's his fault the lost lady pridnear died! Don't forget that, boys!"

That was all they needed. Order came out of chaos. Fifty men seized the rope and at Frenchy's signal "Pull!" jerked the drooping, bloody-backed road agent off the ground. Rune saw him then for the third time, dangling.

A man beside him said knowingly, "That's the most humane way, really—pull him up all standing."

"How do you know?" Rune sneered. "You ever get killed that way?"

With the other men, he walked slowly down the hill. He waited in Doc's cabin until Doc came in.

"You had to watch," Doc said. "You had to see a man die."

"I saw it," Rune growled.

"And the lost lady might as well have. She might as well have been looking, because Ma Fisher kindly told her what the noise was about. And was offended, mind you, when I tried to shut her up!"

Doc unbuckled his gun belt and tossed it on his cot.

"You're going to wait on Miss Armistead," he announced. "I told her you would do her errands, anything that will make her a little easier. Do you hear me, boy? She keeps asking for her father. She keeps saying, 'Where is Papa?' "

Rune stared. "Didn't you tell her he's dead?"

"Certainly I told her! She doesn't believe it. She doesn't remember the holdup or the team running away. All she can remember is that something happened so the coach stopped, and then she was lost, running somewhere, and after a long time a man gave her a drink of water and took the canteen away again."

"Did she say where she's going when she gets her sight back?" Rune asked.

Doc let out a gusty breath. "She has no place to go. She says she can't go back because she has to wait for Papa. He was going to start a school here, and she was going to keep house for him. She has no place to go, but she can't stay alone in Skull Creek. It's unthinkable."

Ma Fisher came flying over to get Doc.

"The girl's crying and it'll be bad for her eyes," she said.

Doc asked coolly, "And why is she crying?"

"I'm sure I don't know," Ma answered, obviously injured. "I wasn't even talking to her. She started to sob, and when I asked her what was the matter, she said, 'Papa must be dead, or he would have been waiting here to meet me.' "

"Progress," Doc growled. "We're making progress." He went out and left Ma Fisher to follow if she cared to do so.

Doc was up before daylight next morning.

"When Ma Fisher leaves that cabin," Doc told Rune, when he woke him, "you're going to be waiting outside the door. If the lady wants you inside for conversation, you will go in and be as decently sociable as possible. If she wants to be alone, you will stay outside. Is that all perfectly clear?"

It was as clear as it was hateful. Rune would have taken delight in being the lady's protector if he had had any choice. (And Doc would, too, except that he wanted to protect her reputation. It wouldn't look good for him to be in the cabin with her except on brief professional visits.)

"Nursemaid," Rune muttered sourly.

Ma Fisher scowled when she found him waiting outside her door, but Miss Armistead said she would be glad of his company.

The lost lady was timid, helpless, but gently friendly, sitting in the darkened cabin, groping now and then for the canteen that had been Frenchy's.

Rune asked, "You want a cup to drink out of?" and she smiled faintly.

"I guess it's silly," she answered, "but water tastes better from this canteen."

Rune kept silent, not knowing how to answer.

"Doctor Frail told me your first name," the lost lady said, "but not your last."

"Rune is all," he answered. He had made it up, wanting to be a man of mystery.

"But everybody has two names," she chided gently. "You must have another."

She was indeed ignorant of frontier custom or she would not make an issue of a man's name. Realizing that, he felt infinitely superior and therefore could be courteous.

"I made it up, ma'am," he told her. "There's lots of men here go by names they wasn't born with. It ain't a good idea to ask questions about folks' names." Then, concerned lest he might have offended her, he struggled on to make conversation:

"There's a song about it. 'What was your name in the States? Was it Johnson or Olson or Bates?' Goes that way, sort of."

The lady said, "Oh, my goodness. Doctor Frail didn't make up his name, I'm sure of that. Because a man wouldn't take a name like that, would he?"

"A man like Doc might," Rune decided. The idea interested him. "Doc is a sarcastic fellow."

"Never to me," Miss Armistead contradicted softly. "He is the soul of kindness! Why, he even realized that I might wish for someone to talk to. And you are kind, too, Rune, because you came."

To get her off that subject, Rune asked, "Was there any errands you'd want done or anything?"

"Doctor Frail said he would send my meals in, but I am already so much obligated to him that I'd rather not. Could you cook for me, Rune, until I can see to do it myself?"

"Sure," he agreed. "But I cook for Doc anyhow. Just as easy to bring it across the street."

"No, I'd rather pay for my own provisions." She was firm about that, with the pathetic stubbornness of a woman who for the first time must make decisions and stick to them even if they are wrong.

"I have money," she insisted. "I can't tell what denomination the bills are, of course. But you can tell me."

Poor, silly lady, to trust a stranger so! But Rune honestly identified the bills she held out.

"Take the five dollars," she requested, "and buy me whatever you think would be nice to eat. That much money should last for several days, shouldn't it?"

Rune swallowed a protest and murmured, "Kind of depends on what you want. I'll see what they got at Flaunce's." He backed toward the door.

"I must be very businesslike," Miss Armistead said with determination. "I have no place to go, you know, so I must earn a living. I shall start a school here in Skull Creek."

Arguing about that was for Doc, not for his slave. Rune did not try.

"Doc's going in his cabin now," he reported, and fled across the street for instructions.

The storekeeper's inquisitive wife got in just ahead of him, and he found Doc explaining, "The lady is still too weak for the strain of entertaining callers, Mrs. Flaunce. The boy here is acting as amateur nurse, because she needs someone with her—she can't see, you know. But it would not be wise for anyone to visit her yet."

"I see," Mrs. Flaunce said with cold dignity. "Yes, I understand perfectly." She went out with her head high, not glancing at the cabin across the street.

Doc thus cut the lost lady off from all decent female companionship. The obvious conclusion to be drawn— which Mrs. Flaunce passed on to the other respectable women of the camp—was that the doctor was keeping the mysterious Miss Armistead. Ma Fisher's stern respectability was not enough to protect her, because Ma herself was strange. She chose to earn her living in a community where no sensible woman would stay if she wasn't married to a man who required it.

When Mrs. Flaunce was gone, Rune held out the greenback.

"She wants me to buy provisions with that. Enough for several days, she says."

Doc's eyebrows went up. "She does, eh? With five dollars? Why, that'd buy her three cans of fruit, wouldn't it? And how much is Flaunce getting for sugar, say?"

"Dollar a pound."

Doc scowled thoughtfully. "This is a delicate situation.

We don't know how well fixed she is, but she doesn't know anything about the cost of grub in Skull Creek. And I don't want her to find out. Understand?"

Rune nodded. For once, he was in agreement with his master.

Doc reached into his coat pocket and brought out a leather poke of dust.

"Put that on deposit to her account at the store," he ordered.

"Lady coming in on the stage wouldn't have gold in a poke, would she?" Rune warned.

Doc said with approval, "Sometimes you sound real smart. Take it to the bank, get currency for it, and take the currency to Flaunce's. And just pray that Ma Fisher doesn't take a notion to talk about the price of grub. Let the lady keep her stake to use getting out of here as soon as she's able."

A week passed before he realized that Elizabeth Armistead could not leave Skull Creek.

V

Elizabeth could find her way around the cabin, groping, stepping carefully so as not to fall over anything. She circled sometimes for exercise and to pass the long, dark time and because she did not feel strong enough to think about important matters.

The center of her safe, circumscribed world was the sagging double bed where she rested and the table beside it, on which was the water bucket. She still clung to Frenchy Plante's canteen and kept it beside her pillow but only when she was alone so that no one would guess her foolish fear about thirst. But every few minutes she fumbled for the dipper in the bucket. She was dependent on strangers for everything, of course, but most important of them was Rune, who filled the water bucket at the creek that he said was not far outside the back door.

She had explored the cabin until she knew it well, but its smallness and scanty furnishings still shocked her. Papa's house back East had had nine rooms, and until his money began to melt away, there had been a maid as well as a cook.

She moved cautiously from the table a few steps to the front door—rough planks with a strong wooden bar to lock it from the inside; around the wall to a bench that Rune had placed so she would not hurt herself on the tiny stove; then to the back door.

But the need for decision gnawed at her mind and made her head ache.

"You must go back East just as soon as you can travel," Doctor Frail had said—how many times?

But how could she travel again when she remembered the Dry Flats that had to be crossed? How could she go without Papa, who was dead, they kept telling her?

The cabin was uncomfortably warm, but she could not sit outside the back door, where there was grass, unless Rune was there. And she must not open the door unless she knew for sure who was outside.

She could not go back East yet, no matter what they said. To stay in Skull Creek was, of course, an imposition on these kind people, but everything would work out all right after a while—except for Papa, who they said was dead.

She remembered what Papa had said when his investments were dwindling.

"We do what we must," he had told her with his gentle smile when he made the hard decision to go West. And so his daughter would do what she must.

I must find a place for the school, she reminded herself. Perhaps Mrs. Fisher will let me use this cabin. I must offer her pay, of course, very tactfully so she will not be offended.

It was a relief to keep her mind busy in the frightening darkness, safe in the cabin with an unknown, raucous settlement of noisy men just outside the door. There were women, too; she could hear their laughter and screaming sometimes from the saloon down the street. But ladies did not think about those women except to pity them.

They were very strange, these people who were looking after her—Doc, who sounded strained and cross: Rune, whose voice was sullen and doubtful; Mrs. Fisher, who talked very little and came to the cabin only to groan into bed. Elizabeth was a little afraid of all of them, but she reminded herself that they were really very kind.

There was cautious knocking on the door, and she called out, "Yes?" and turned. Suddenly she was lost in the room, not sure of the position of the door. Surely the knocking was at the back? And why should any of them come that way, where the little grassy plot went only down to the creek?

She stumbled against a bench, groping. The knocking sounded again as she reached the door. But she was cautious. "Who is it?" she called, with her hand on the bar.

A man's voice said, "Lady! Lady, just let me in."

Elizabeth stopped breathing. The voice was not Doc Frail's nor Rune's. But it was cordial, enticing: "Lady, you ever seen a poke of nuggets? I got a poke of gold right here. Lady, let me in."

She trembled and sank down on the floor in her darkness, cowering. The voice coaxed, "Lady? Lady?"

She did not dare to answer. She did not dare to cry. After a long time the pounding and the coaxing stopped.

She could not escape any more by planning for the school. She was remembering the long horror of thirst, and the noise the mob had made, going past to hang a man on a tree at the top of the hill. She hid her burned face in her trembling hands, crouching by the barred door, until a familiar and welcome voice called from another direction, "It's me, Rune."

She groped to the front door, reached for the bar. But was the voice familiar and therefore welcome? Or was this another importunate, lying stranger? With her hand on the unseen wooden bar, she froze, listening, until he called again. His voice sounded concerned: "Miss Armistead, are you all right in there?"

This was Rune. She could open the door. He was not offering a poke of nuggets, he was only worried about her welfare.

"I was frightened," she said as she opened the door.

"You're safer that way in Skull Creek," he said. "Anything you want done right now?"

"You are so kind," she said gently. "No, there is nothing. I have plenty of drinking water in the bucket. Oh—if you go to the store, perhaps there would be some potatoes and eggs?"

After a pause he said, "I'll ask 'em." (A month ago there had been a shipment of eggs; Doc had mentioned it. There had not been a potato in camp since Rune came there.)

"Doc says to tell you you'll have your unveiling this evening, get your eyes open. I got to go find him now, give him a message from the Crocodile."

"The—what?"

"Ma Fisher, I mean." She could hear amusement in his voice.

"Why, it's not nice to speak of her so. She is very kind to me, letting me share her home!"

There was another pause. He said, "Glad to hear it," and "I'll go find Doc now. He went to get a haircut."

Doc's haircut was important. He went often to the barbershop for a bath, because he could afford to be clean, but never before in Skull Creek had he let scissors touch his hair, hanging in glossy waves below his shoulders.

A miner might let his hair and whiskers grow, bushy and matted, but Doc Frail was different. His long hair was no accident, and it was clean. He wore it long as a challenge, a quiet swagger, as if to tell the camp, "You may make remarks about this if you want trouble." Nobody did in his presence.

Except the barber, who laughed and said, "I been wantin' to put scissors to that, Doc. You gettin' all fixed up for the lost lady to take a good look?"

Doc had dignity even in a barber's chair. "Shut up and tend to business," he advised. There was no more conversation even when the barber handed him a mirror.

Rune had too much sense to mention the reformation. The tall boy glanced at him, smiled tightly, and reported, "Ma Fisher wants to see you. She's tired of having the lost lady underfoot."

Doc snorted. "Ma has no weariness or distaste that a poke of dust won't soothe." He turned away, but Rune was not through talking.

"Can I come when you take the bandage off her eyes?"

"No. Yes. What do I care?" Doc strode away, trying to put his spirits into a suitably humble mood to talk business with Ma Fisher.

The girl was a disturbing influence for him, for Rune, for the whole buzzing camp. She must get out in a few days, but she must not be made any more miserable than she already was.

He did not wait for Ma Fisher to attack, from her side of the dirty wooden counter in her tent restaurant. He spoke first: "You would no doubt like to be paid for Miss Armistead's lodging. I will pay you. I don't want you to get the idea that I'm keeping her. My reason for wishing to pay is that I want her to keep thinking the world is kind and that you have welcomed her."

Ma Fisher shrugged. "You can afford it. It's an inconvenience to me to have her underfoot."

Doc put a poke on the counter. "You can heft that if you want to. That's dust you'll get for not letting her know she's unwelcome. You'll get it when she leaves, in a week or so."

Ma lifted the leather sack with an expert touch. "All right."

Doc swept it back again. "One compliment before I leave you, Mrs. Fisher: you're no hypocrite."

"Two-faced, you mean? One face like this is all a woman can stand." She cackled at her own wit. "Just the same, I'd like to know why you're willing to pay good clean dust to keep the girl from finding out the world is cruel."

"I wish I knew myself," he answered.

I'll take off the dressings now, he decided, and let her get a glimpse of daylight, let her see what she's eating for a change.

He crossed the street and knocked, calling, "Doc Frail here." Rune opened the door.

Elizabeth turned her face toward him. "Doctor? Now will you let me see again? I thought if you could take the dressings off now, you and Rune might be my guests for supper."

You and Rune. The leading citizen and the unsuccessful thief.

"I'll be honored," Doc replied. "And I suppose Rune realizes that it is an honor for him."

He removed the last dressings from her eyes and daubed the closed lids with liquid.

"Blink," he ordered. "Again. Now try opening them."

She saw him as a blurred face, close up, without distinguishing characteristics. The one who protected in the darkness, the one who had promised to bring light. The only dependable creature in the world. There was light again, she had regained her sight. She must trust him, and she could. He had not failed her in anything.

But he was a stranger in a world of terror and strangers. He was too young. A doctor should be old, with a gray chin beard.

"Hurts a little?" he said. "You can look around now."

He stepped aside and she was lost without him. She saw someone else, tall in the dimness; that was Rune, and he was important in her life. She tried to smile at him, but she could not tell whether he smiled back.

Doc said, "Don't look in a mirror yet. When your face is all healed, you will be a pretty girl again. Don't worry about it."

Unsmiling, she answered, "I have other things to concern me."

Elizabeth tried to make conversation as they ate the

supper Rune had cooked. But now that she could see them dimly, they were strangers and she was lost and afraid.

"It's like being let out of jail, to see again," she offered. "At least I suppose it is. When may I go outside to see what the town is like?"

"There is no town, only a rough camp," Doc told her. "It's not worth looking at, but you may see it tomorrow. After sunset, when the light won't hurt your eyes."

The following day, after supper, when she heard knocking on the front door, she ran to answer. Dr. Frail had changed his mind about waiting until later, she assumed. He must have come back sooner than he had expected from a professional call several miles away.

She swung the door wide—and looked up through a blur into the black-bearded, grinning face of a stranger. Then she could not shut it again. A lady could not do a thing so rude as that.

The man swept off his ragged hat and bowed awkwardly. "Frenchy Plante, ma'am. You ain't never seen me, but we sure enough met before. Out on the Dry Flats."

"Oh," she said faintly. He looked unkempt and she could smell whiskey. But he had saved her life. "Please come in," she said, because there was no choice. She hoped he did not notice that she left the door open. With this man in the cabin, she wanted no privacy.

He remembered to keep his hat in his hand but he sat down without waiting to be invited.

"Figure on doing a little prospecting, ma'am," he said jovially. "So I just dropped in to say good-by and see how you're making out."

Frenchy was well pleased with himself. He was wearing a clean red shirt, washed though not pressed, and he had combed his hair, wanting to make a good impression on the lost lady.

"I have so much to thank you for," Elizabeth said earnestly. "I am so very grateful."

He waved one hand. "It's nothing, lady. Somebody

would of found you." Realizing that this detracted from his glory, he added, "But of course it might have been too late. You sure look different from the first time I seen you!"

Her hands went up to her face. "Doctor Frail says there won't be any scars. I wish I could offer you some refreshment, Mr. Plante. If you would care to wait until I build up the fire to make tea?"

Doc Frail remarked from the doorway, "Frenchy would miss his afternoon tea, I'm sure."

There were a few men in the camp who were not afraid of Doc Frail—the upright men, the leading citizens, and Frenchy Plante.

Frenchy had the effrontery to suggest, "Come on in, Doc," but the wisdom to add, "Guess I can't stay, ma'am. Going prospecting, like I told you."

Doc Frail stood aside so as not to bar his progress in leaving. "I thought your claim was paying fairly well."

Frenchy made an expansive gesture. "Sold it this morning. I want something richer."

Elizabeth said, "I hope you'll find a million dollars, Mr. Plante."

"With a pretty lady like you on my side, I can't fail, can I?" replied the giant, departing.

Elizabeth put on her bonnet. With her foot on the threshold, she murmured, "Everyone is so kind." She took Doc's arm as he offered it.

"To the left," he said. "The rougher part of the camp is to the right. You must never go that way. But this is the way you will go to the hotel, where the stage stops. Next week you will be able to leave Skull Creek."

She did not seem to hear him. She trembled. She was staring with aching eyes at the rutted road that led past Flaunce's store and the livery stable, the road that took a sudden sweep upward toward a cottonwood tree with one great out-thrust bough.

"You are perfectly safe," Doc reminded her. "We will not go far this time. Only past the store."

"No!" she moaned. "Oh, no!" and tried to turn back.

"Now what?" Doc demanded. "There is nothing here to hurt you."

But up there where she had to go sometime was the hanging tree, and beyond was the desert. Back all that distance, back all alone—a safe, quiet place was what she must have now, at once.

Not here in the glaring sun with the men staring and the world so wide that no matter which way she turned she was lost, she was thirsty, burning, dying.

But there must be some way out, somewhere safe, the cool darkness of a cabin, if she could only run in the right direction and not give up too soon—

But someone tried to keep her there in the unendurable sun glare with the thirst and endless dizzying space—someone held her arms and said her name urgently from far away as she struggled.

She jerked away with all her strength because she knew the needs of her own anguished body and desperate spirit—she had to be free, she had to be able to hide.

And where was Papa, while this strange and angry man carried her back to the cabin that was a refuge from which she would not venture forth again?

And who was this angry boy who shouted, "Doc, if you've hurt her, I'll kill you!"

When she was through with her frantic crying and was quiet and ashamed, she was afraid of Doc Frail, who gripped her wrists as she lay on Ma Fisher's bed.

"What was it, Elizabeth?" he demanded. "Nothing is going to hurt you. What did you think you saw out there?"

"The Dry Flats," she whispered, knowing he would not believe it. "The glaring sun on the Dry Flats. And I was lost again and thirsty."

"It's thirty miles to the Dry Flats," he told her brusquely. "And the sun went down an hour ago. It's getting dark here in the gulch."

She shuddered.

"I'll give you something to make you sleep," he offered.

"I want Papa," she replied, beginning to cry again.

Back in his own cabin, Doc walked back and forth, back and forth across the rough floor boards, with Rune glaring at him from a corner.

Doc Frail was trying to remember a word and a mystery. Someone in France had reported something like this years ago. What was the word, and what could you do for the suffering patient?

He had three books in his private medical library, but they treated of physical ailments, not wounds of the mind. He could write to Philadelphia for advice, but—he calculated the weeks required for a letter to go East and a reply to come back to Skull Creek.

"Even if they know," he said angrily, "we'll be snowed in here before the answer comes. And maybe nobody knows, except in France, and he's probably dead now, whoever he was."

Rune spoke cuttingly. "You had to be in such a hurry to make her start back home!"

Doc said, "Shut your mouth."

What was the word for the mystery? Elizabeth remembered nothing about the runaway of the coach horses, nothing about the holdup that preceded it, only the horror that followed.

"Hysteria?" he said. "Is that the word? Hysteria? But if it is, what can you do for the patient?"

The lost lady would have to try again. She would have to cross the imaginary desert as well as the real one.

VI

I will not try to go out for a few days, Elizabeth told herself, comforted by the thought that nobody would expect her to try again after what had happened on her first attempt.

The desert was not outside the cabin, of course. It was only a dreadful illusion. She realized that, because she could look out and see that the street was in a ravine. Nothing like the Dry Flats.

Next time, she assured herself, it will be all right. I will not look up toward the tree where they—no, I will simply not think about the tree at all, nor about the Dry Flats. Other people go out by stage and nothing happens to them. But I can't go right away.

Doctor Frail did not understand at all. He came over the next morning, implacable and stern.

"I have a patient to see down at the diggings," he said, "but he can wait half an hour. First you will walk with me as far as Flaunce's store."

"Oh, I couldn't," she answered with gentle firmness. "In a few days, but not now. I'm not strong enough."

He put his hat on the table and sat on one of the two benches.

"You will go now, Elizabeth. You have got to do it now. I am going to sit here until you are ready to start."

She stared at him in hurt surprise. Of course he was a doctor, and he could be expected to be always right. He was a determined man, and strength came from him. It was good, really, not to make a decision but to have him make it, even though carrying it out would be painful. Like the time Papa made her go to a dentist to have a tooth pulled.

"Very well," she replied with dignity. She put her bonnet on, not caring that there was no mirror.

"You are only going for a walk to the store," he told her, offering his arm at the door. "You will want to tell your friends back home what a store in a gold camp is like. You will have a great many things to tell your friends."

She managed a laugh as she walked with her eyes down, feeling the men staring.

"They would not believe the things I could tell them," she agreed.

The sun was not yet high over the gulch and the morning was not warm but she was burning and thirsty and could not see anything for the glare and could not breathe because she had been running, but he would not let her fall. He was speaking rapidly and urgently, telling her she must go on. He was not Papa because Papa was never angry; Papa would never have let her be afraid and alone in the glare and thirsty and going to die here, now, if he would only let her give up and fall. . . .

She was lying down—where? On the bed in the cabin? And turning her head away from something, the sharp odor of something the doctor held under her nose to revive her.

The men had seen her fall, then, the staring men of Skull Creek, and she had fainted, and they must think she was insane and maybe she was.

She was screaming and Doc Frail was slapping her cheek, saying, "Elizabeth! Stop that!"

Then she was crying with relief, because surely now nobody would make her go out again until she was ready. The doctor was angry, a cruel man, a hateful stranger. Angry at a helpless girl who needed only to be let alone until she was stronger!

She said with tearful dignity, "Please go away."

He was sarcastic, too. He answered, "I do have other patients," and she heard the door close.

But she could not lie there and cry as she wanted to do, because she had to bar the door to keep out fear.

At noontime she was calmer and built a fire in the little stove and brewed some tea to eat with a cold biscuit of the kind Rune called bannock. Nobody came, and in the afternoon she slept for a while, exhausted, but restless because there was a great deal of racket from down the gulch.

Rune leaned against a building with his thumbs in his belt, watching two drunk miners trying to harness a mule that didn't want to be harnessed. Rune was amused, glad to have something to think about besides Doc Frail's cruelty to the lost lady.

"Leave her strictly alone till I tell you otherwise," Doc had commanded.

Rune was willing, for the time being. She had cold grub

in the cabin and the water bucket was full. He didn't want to embarrass her by going there anyway. He had seen her stumble and struggle and fall. He had watched, from Doc's shack, as Doc carried her back to the cabin, had waited to be called and had been ignored.

The plunging mule kicked one of the miners over backward into the dust, while a scattering of grinning men gathered and cheered.

The other drunk man had a long stick, and as he struck out with it, the mule went bucking, tangled in the harness. A man standing beside Rune commented with awe and delight, "Right toward Ma Fisher's restaurant! Now I'd admire to see that mule tangle with her!"

He shouted, and Rune roared with him. A roar went up from all the onlookers as the far side of Ma Fisher's tent went down and Ma came running out on the near side, screaming. The mule emerged a few seconds behind her, but the drunk miner was still under the collapsed, smoke-stained canvas.

There was a frenzied yell of "Fire!" even before Rune saw the smoke curl up and ran to the nearest saloon to grab a bucket.

They kept the flames from spreading to any buildings, although the lean-to behind the tent was badly charred and most of the canvas burned.

Ma Fisher was not in sight by the time they got the fire out. Rune slouched away, grinning.

Ma Fisher made only one stop on the way from her ruined restaurant to the cabin. She beat with her fist on the locked door of the bank until Mr. Evans opened it a few inches and peered cautiously out.

"I want to withdraw all I've got on deposit," she demanded. "I'm going to my daughter's in Idaho."

He unfastened the chain on the inside and swung the door open.

"Leaving us, Mrs. Fisher?"

"Sink of iniquity," she growled. "Of course I'm leaving. They've burned my tent and ruined my stove, and now they can starve for all I care. I want to take out every dollar.

"But you needn't think I want to carry it with me on the stage," she warned. "I just want to make the arrangements now. Transfer it or whatever you do, so's I can draw on it in Idaho."

"Will you need some for travel expenses?" the banker asked, opening his ledger.

"I've got enough dust on hand for that. Just let me sign the papers and get started."

Rune, lounging in Doc's doorway, saw Ma Fisher jerk at her own door handle and then beat angrily with her fist, yelling, "Girl, you let me in! It's Ma Fisher."

She slammed the door behind her, and Rune grinned. He worried a little though, wondering how her anger would affect the gentle Miss Armistead. But he had his orders not to go over there. His own opinion was that the lost lady was being mighty stubborn, and maybe Doc Frail was right in prescribing the let-alone treatment till she got sensible.

Elizabeth listened with horror to Ma Fisher's description of the wrecking of her restaurant. Ma paced back and forth across the floor and she spat out the news.

"How dreadful!" Elizabeth sympathized. "What can I do to help you?"

Ma Fisher stopped pacing and stared at her. It was a long time since anyone had offered sympathy. Having had little of it from anyone else, she had none to give.

"I don't need nothing done for me," she growled. "I'm one to look after myself. Oh, laws, the cabin. I've got to sell this cabin."

"But then you'll have no place to live!" Elizabeth cried out.

"I'm going to Idaho. But I got to get my investment out of the cabin. You'll have to leave, Miss. I'm going tomorrow on the stage."

She was pacing again, not looking to see how Elizabeth was affected by the news, not caring, either.

"Man offered me five hundred dollars in clean dust for

it not long ago, but I turned it down. Had to have a place to live, didn't I? Now who was that? Well, it won't be hard to find a buyer.... You've got your things all over the place. You better start packing. Could come on the same stage with me if you're a mind to."

Out in to the open, away from refuge? Out across the Dry Flats—and before that, under the hanging tree? When she could not even go as far as Flaunce's store!

There was no one to help her, no one who cared what became of her. The doctor was angry, the boy Rune had deserted her, and this hag, this witch, thought only of her own interests. Papa had said, "We do what we must."

"I will give you five hundred dollars for the cabin," Elizabeth said coolly.

Doc Frail did not learn of the transaction until noon the next day. He had been called to a gulch ten miles away to care for a man who was beyond help, dying of a self-inflicted gunshot wound. Crippled with rheumatism, the man had pulled the trigger of his rifle with his foot.

Doc rode up to his own door and yelled, "Rune! Take care of my horse."

Rune came around from the back with the wood-chopping axe in his hand.

"Hell's broke loose," he reported. "Old lady Fisher left on the stage this morning, and the girl must be still in the cabin, because she didn't go when Ma did."

Doc sighed.

"Fellow that came by said she's bought Ma's cabin," Rune said, watching to see how Doc Frail would take that news.

Doc disappointed him by answering, "I don't care what she did," and went into his own building.

But while Rune was taking the mare to the livery stable, Doc decided he did care. He cared enough to cross the road in long strides and pound on the door, shouting, "Elizabeth, let me in this instant."

She had been waiting for hours for him to come, to tell her she had done the right thing, the only thing possible.

But he said, "If what I hear is true, you're a fool. What are you going to do in Skull Creek?"

She stepped back before the gale of his anger. She drew herself up very straight.

"Why, I am going to start a school for the children," she replied. "I have been making plans for it all morning."

"You can't. You can't stay here," Doc insisted.

"But I must, until I am stronger."

Doc glared. "You'd better get stronger in a hurry then. You've got to get out of this camp. You can start by walking up to the store. And I'll go with you. Right now."

Elizabeth was angry too. "I thank you for your courtesy," she said. "I must look out for myself now, of course." Looking straight into his eyes, she added. "I will pay your fee now if you will tell me what I owe."

Doc flinched as if she had struck him.

"There is no charge, madam. Call on me at any time."

He bowed and strode out.

He told Rune, "The order to leave her alone still stands," and told him nothing else.

Rune endured it for twenty-four hours. The door across the street did not open. There was no smoke from the chimney.

She's got just about nothing in the way of grub over there now, Rune fretted to himself. Ain't even building a fire to make a cup of tea.

But when Rune crossed the street, he did not go for pity. He had convinced himself that his only reason for visiting Elizabeth was that Doc had forbidden him to go there.

He knocked on the slab door but no answer came. He pounded harder, calling, "Miss Armistead!" There was no sound from within, but there was a waiting silence that made his skin crawl.

"It's Rune!" he shouted. "Let me in!"

A miner, passing by, grinned and remarked, "Good luck, boy. Introduce me sometime."

Rune said, "Shut your foul mouth," over his shoulder just as the door opened a crack.

Elizabeth said coolly, "What is it?" Then, with a quick-drawn breath like a sob, "Rune, come in, come in."

As she stepped away from the entrance, her skirt swung and he saw her right hand with a little derringer in it.

"The gun—where'd you get it?" he demanded.

"It was Papa's. They brought it to me with his things after—" Remembering that she must look after herself, not depending on anyone else, she stopped confiding. "Won't you sit down?" she invited formally.

"I just come to see—to see how everything is. Like if you needed something."

She shook her head, but her eyes flooded with tears. "Need something? Oh, no. I don't need a thing. Nobody can do anything for me!"

Then she was sobbing, sitting on a bench with her face hidden in her hands, and the little gun forgotten on the floor.

"Listen, you won't starve," he promised. "I'll bring your grub. But have you got money to live on?" He abased himself, admitting, "I ain't got anything. Doc don't pay me. If I had, I'd help you out."

"Oh, no. I will look after myself." She wiped her eyes and became very self-possessed. "Except that for a while I should appreciate it if you will go to the store for me. Until I am strong enough to walk so far by myself."

But Doc had said she was strong enough, and Doc Frail was no liar. Rune scowled at Elizabeth. He did not want to be bound to her by pity. It was bad enough to be bound to Doc by debt.

This tie, at least, he could cut loose before it became a serious burden.

"You got to get out of Skull Creek," he said harshly. "Unless you've got a lot of money."

"I have sufficient," she said.

Now she was playing the great lady, he thought. She was being elegant and scornful.

"Maybe where you come from, folks don't talk about such things," he burst out with bitterness. "It ain't nice, you think. Don't think I'm asking you how much you got. But you don't know nothing about prices here. You ain't been paying full price for what you got, not by a long ways. You want to know?"

She was staring at him wide-eyed and shocked.

"Sugar's ninety cents a pound at Flaunce's," he told her. "It went down. Dried codfish—you're tired of it, I guess, and so's everybody—it's sixty cents. Dried apples—forty cents a pound last time they had any. Maybe you'd like a pound of tea? Two and a half, that costs you. Potatoes and eggs, there ain't been any in a long time. Fresh meat you can't get till another bunch of steers come in. Now how long will your money last you if you stay in Skull Creek?"

She had less than five hundred dollars left after buying the cabin. Stage fare—that was terribly high. She had never had to handle money, and only in the last year had she even had to be concerned about it, since Papa's affairs had gone so badly.

But she said coolly, "I have a substantial amount of money, thank you. And I am going to start a school. Now tell me, please, who paid for my supplies if I didn't?"

Rune gulped. "I can't tell you that."

"So it was Doctor Frail," Elizabeth said wearily. "I will pay him. Tell him that."

"He'd kill me," Rune said. "Remember, I never said it was him."

Between two dangers, the lesser one seemed to be telling Doc himself. He did so at the first opportunity.

Doc did not explode. He only sighed and remarked, "Now she hasn't even got her pride. How much money has she got to live on?"

"She didn't tell me. Won't tell you, either, I'll bet."

"And she thinks she can make a fortune teaching school!" Doc was thoughtful. "Maybe she can earn part of her living that way. How many children are there in camp, anyway?" He scrabbled for a sheet of paper and began writing the names of families, muttering to himself.

"Go to the livery stable," he said without looking up, "and get a string of bells. They've got some. Then figure out a way to hitch them over her door with a rope that she can pull from inside her cabin."

"What for?" Rune demanded.

"So she can signal for help next time somebody tries to break in," Doc explained with unusual patience.

And what will I do to protect her when the time comes? Doc Frail wondered. Look forbidding and let them see two guns holstered and ready? That will not always be enough.

The noted physician of Skull Creek can outshoot anyone within several hundred miles, but will he fire when the target is a man? Never again. Then his hand and his eye lose their cunning, and that is why Wonder Russell sleeps up on the hill. If I could not pull the trigger to save the life of my friend, how can I do it for Elizabeth? I must have a deputy.

Rune was on his way out when Doc asked, "Can you hit a target any better than you dodge bullets?"

Rune hesitated, torn between wanting to boast and wanting to be taught by a master. If he admitted he was no marksman, he was not a complete man. But a slave didn't have to be.

He answered humbly, "I never had much chance to try. Target practice costs money."

"Stop at the store and get a supply of ammunition," Doc ordered. "I'm going to give you the world's best chance to shoot me."

Rune shrugged and went out, admitting no excitement. He was going to have his chance to become the kind of man from whose path other men would quietly step aside.

Doc watched him go, thinking, Are you the one for whom I'll hang? Put a gun in your hand, and skill with it, and there's no telling. But your lessons start tomorrow.

"I wish the school didn't matter so much to her," Doc muttered. "I wish she wasn't so set on it."

He had made some calls early that morning and was

back in his cabin, scowling across the street at Elizabeth's, with its door standing open to welcome the children of Skull Creek.

Her floor was scrubbed; the rough plank table was draped with an embroidered cloth, and her father's books were on it. She visualized the children: shy, adorable, anxious to learn. And their mothers: grateful for a school, full of admonitions about the little ones' welfare, but trusting the teacher.

Doc turned to Rune, saw the rifle across his knees.

"You planning to shoot the children when they come?" he demanded.

"Planning to shoot any miner that goes barging in there with her door open," Rune answered. "Because I don't think there's going to be any children coming to school."

Doc sighed. "I don't either. After all the notes she wrote their mothers, all the plans she made."

At eleven o'clock, they saw Elizabeth shut her door. No one had crossed the threshold.

Doc growled, "Bring my mare. I've got a patient up the gulch. Then go see about getting her dinner."

Rune muttered, "I'd rather be shot."

Elizabeth had the derringer in her hand, hidden in a fold of her skirt, when she unbarred the door. She did not look at him but simply stepped aside.

"I don't care for anything to eat," she said faintly.

"If you don't eat nothing, I don't either."

She sipped a cup of tea, but she set it down suddenly and began to cry.

"Why didn't anybody come?" she wailed.

"Because they're fools," he told her sturdily.

But he knew why. He had guessed from the way the women acted when he delivered the notes. Elizabeth Armistead, the lost lady, was not respectable. She had come under strange circumstances, and the protection of Doc Frail was like a dark shadow upon her.

"I thought I would teach the children," she said hopelessly. "I thought it would be pleasant."

Rune drew a deep breath and offered her all he had—his ignorance and his pride.

"You can teach me," he said. "I ain't never learned to read."

The look of shock on her face did not hurt quite so much as he had supposed it would.

VII

Early cold came to Skull Creek, and early snow. Halfway through one gloomy, endless morning, someone knocked at Elizabeth's door, but she had learned caution. She called, "Who is it?"

A voice she did not know said something about books. When she unbarred the door, the derringer was in her hand, but she kept it decently hidden in the folds of her skirt.

He was a big man with a beard. He swept off a fur cap and was apologetic.

"I didn't mean to frighten you, ma'am. Please don't be afraid. I came to see if you would rent out some of your books."

Elizabeth blinked two or three times, considering the matter. "But one doesn't rent books!" she objected. "I have never heard of renting books. . . . It's cold, won't you come in so I can close the door?"

The man hesitated. "If you're sure you will let me come in, ma'am. I swear I'll do you no harm. It's only for books that I came. Some of the boys are about to go crazy for lack of reading matter. We drew straws, and I got the short one. To come and ask you."

It's my house, Elizabeth told herself. And surely no rascal would care for books.

This man happened not to be a rascal, though he acted so fidgety about being in there that Elizabeth wondered who he thought might be chasing him.

"They call me Tall John, ma'am," he said in introduction, cap in hand. "Any book would do, just about. We've worn out the newspapers from the States and we're tired of reading the labels on canned goods. And the winter's only just begun."

He paid five dollars apiece for the privilege of keeping three books for a month. (His listeners, when he read aloud in a hut of poles and earth, were a horse thief, a half-breed Arapaho Indian and the younger son of an English nobleman.)

Doc scolded Elizabeth for letting a stranger in, although he admitted that Tall John was a decent fellow.

"He was a perfect gentleman," she insisted. What bothered her was that she had accepted money for lending books.

Rune complained bitterly because his book supply was cut by three.

"Listen, boy," Doc said, "you can read like a house afire, but can you write? Your schooling isn't even well begun. Do you know arithmetic? If you sold me eight head of horses at seventy dollars a head, how much would I owe you?"

"I wouldn't trust nobody to owe me for 'em," Rune told him earnestly. "You'd pay cash on the barrel head, clean dust, or you wouldn't drive off no horses of mine."

But thereafter his daily lessons in Elizabeth's cabin included writing, spelling and arithmetic. When the only books she had left were readers through which he had already ploughed his impetuous way, he was reduced to sneaking a look at the three medical books in Doc's cabin—Doc's entire medical library.

When Rune boasted of how much he was learning in his classes at the lost lady's cabin, Doc listened and was pleased.

"Each week, you will take her a suitable amount of dust for tuition," Doc announced. "I will have to decide how much it's going to be."

"Dust? Where'm I going to get dust?" Rune was frantic; the only delight he had was being barred from him, as everything else was, by his poverty.

"From me, of course. I can properly pay for the education of my servant, surely?"

"The lady teaches me for nothing," Rune said in defense of his privilege. "She don't expect to get paid for it."

"She needs an income, and this will help a little." Doc felt lordly. He was doing a favor for both his charges, Rune and the pathetic girl across the street. "If you don't care to accept a favor from me," he told Rune, "you'd better get used to the idea." With a flash of insight, he explained, "It is necessary sometimes to let other people do something decent for you."

That is, he considered, it is necessary for everybody but me. And I have a sudden very excellent idea about the uses of gold.

He had an interest in several paying placer claims, which he visited often because the eye of the master fatteneth the cattle, and the eye of an experienced gold miner can make a shrewd guess about how many ounces there should be on the sluice riffles at the weekly cleanup. His various partners seldom tried to cheat him any more.

With the ground and the streams frozen, placer mining had come to a dead stop, but Dr. Frail's professional income had dwindled only a little, and there was so much dust to his credit with the bank that he had no financial problems anyway.

He strode up the street to visit Evans, the banker.

"Your dealings with your customers are strictly confidential, are they not?" he inquired.

"As confidential as yours," Evans replied stiffly.

"I want to make a withdrawal. The dust is to be put into leather pokes that can't be identified as the property of anyone around here. Old pokes, well worn."

"Very well," said Evans, as if it happened every day

"Weigh it out in even pounds," Doc instructed, and Evans' eyebrows went up. "I want—oh, six of them. I'll be back for them this afternoon."

He sat with Elizabeth just before supper, drinking tea,

listening to the sounds Rune made chopping firewood outside the back door. Rune had the bags of gold and orders to
conceal them in the woodpile to be found accidentally.

"And remember, I know very well how much is in
there," Doc had warned him. "I know how much she's supposed to find when she does find it."

Rune had glared at him in cold anger, replying, "Did
you think I would steal from *her?*"

Tall John's shack burned when he built the fire too hot on
a bitter cold day. The three men who shared it with him
were away. He ran out, tried to smother the flames with
snow, then ran back to save what he could, and the roof fell
in on him.

When help came, he was shouting under the burning
wreckage. His rescuers delivered him to Doc's office with a
broken leg and serious burns on his shoulders and chest.

Doc grumbled, "You boys think I'm running a hospi-
tal?" and started to work on the patient.

"He's got no place to go; our wickiup burned," the horse
thief apologized. "The rest of us, we can hole up someplace,
but John can't hardly."

"He needs a roof over his head and conscientious nursing," Doc warned.

"I could sort of watch him," Rune suggested, wondering
if they would sneer at the idea.

"Guess you'll have to," Doc agreed. "All right, he can
have my bunk."

Then there was less company to help Elizabeth pass the
time. Rune bought her supplies and carried in firewood, but
he was always in a hurry. There were no more interesting
evenings with Doc and Rune as her guests for supper, because Doc never stayed with her more than a few minutes.

Winter clamped down with teeth that did not let go.
Elizabeth began to understand why Tall John had found it
necessary to borrow books—she was reading her father's
books over and over to pass the time. She began to under-

stand, too, why a man of pride must pay for such borrowing.

She sewed and mended her own clothes until there was no more sewing to do. Doc commissioned her to make him a shirt and one for Rune. She finished them and was empty-handed again.

Then she peeled every sliver of bark from the logs that made her prison.

Rune came dutifully twice a day to bring supplies, and do her chores, but he no longer had lessons.

"Tall John's teaching me," he explained.

"And what are you studying?" she asked with some coolness.

"Latin. So I can figure out the big words in Doc's books."

"Now I wonder whether Papa brought his Latin grammar," she cried, running to look at the books she could not read.

"You ain't got one," Rune said. "I looked. We get along without. Sometimes we talk it."

"I didn't think anybody talked Latin," Elizabeth said doubtfully.

"Tall John can. He studied it in Rome. Told me where Rome is, too."

Elizabeth sighed. Her pupil had gone far beyond her.

She faced the bleak fact that nobody needed her at all any more. And Doc said there would be at least another month of winter.

"I don't want to impose on you, now that you're so busy," she told Rune with hurt dignity. "Hereafter I will bring in my own firewood and snow to melt for water. It will give me something to do."

"Don't hurt yourself," he cautioned. He didn't seem to see anything remarkable in her resolve to do hard physical labor. Elizabeth had never known any woman who carried water or cut wood. She felt like an adventurer when she undertook it.

Rune told Doc what she was planning, and Doc smiled.

"Good. Then you won't have to find what's in her wood-pile. She can find it herself."

He visited her that evening, as he did once a day, briefly. She was a little sulky, he noticed, and he realized that she deserved an apology from him.

"I'm sorry not to spend more time in your company," he said abruptly. "There is no place I'd rather spend it. But for your own protection, to keep you from being talked about—do you understand why I'd rather not be here when Rune can't be here too?"

Elizabeth sniffed. "Have I any good name left to protect?"

The answer was No, but he would not say it.

"Rune says you're going to do your own chores," he remarked.

"Beginning tomorrow," she said proudly, expecting either a scolding or a compliment.

Doc disappointed her by saying heartily, "Good idea. You need some exercise."

Then he wondered why she was so unfriendly during the remainder of his visit.

Her venture into wood cutting lasted three days. Then, with a blister on one hand and a small axe cut in one shoe —harmless but frightening—she began to carry in wood that Rune had already chopped and piled earlier in the winter.

She was puzzled when she found a leather bag, very heavy for its size, and tightly tied. Unable to open the snow-wet drawstring with her mittened hands, she carried the bag into the house and teased the strings open with the point of a knife.

She glimpsed what was inside, ran to the shelf for a plate, and did not breathe again until the lovely yellow treasure was heaped upon it.

"Oh!" she said. "Oh, the pretty!" She ran her chilled fingers through the nuggets and the flakes that were like fish scales. "Maybe it belongs to Ma Fisher," she said angrily to the emptiness of the cabin. "But I bought the place and it's mine now. And maybe there's more out there!"

She found them all, the six heavy little bags, and completely demolished the neat woodpile.

Then she ran to the rope of the warning bells and pulled it for the first time, pulled it again and again, laughing and crying, and was still pulling it when Rune came shouting.

She hugged him, although he had a cocked pistol in his hand. She did not even notice that.

"Look!" she screamed. "Look what I found in the woodpile!"

Doc came to admire, later in the day, and stayed for supper, but Elizabeth was too excited to eat—or to cook, for that matter. The table was crowded, because all the golden treasure was on display in plates or cups. She kept touching it lovingly, gasping with delight.

"Now you know," Doc guessed, "why men search for that. And why they kill for it."

"I know," she crooned. "Yes, I understand."

He leaned across the table. "Elizabeth, with all that for a stake, you needn't be afraid to go out next spring, go home."

She caressed a pile of yellow gold. "I suppose so," she answered, and he knew she was not convinced.

The woodpile was a symbol after that. She restored the scattered sticks to make a neat heap, but did not burn any of them. She went back to chopping wood each day for the fire.

She was hacking at a stubborn, knotty log one afternoon, her skirts soggy with snow, when a man's voice not far behind her startled her into dropping the axe.

He was on the far side of the frozen creek, an anonymous big man bundled up in a huge and shapeless coat of fur.

"It's me, Frenchy," he shouted jovially. "Looks like you're working too hard for a young lady!"

Elizabeth picked up the axe. When the man who once saved your life speaks to you, you must answer, she decided.

Especially when you had nobody to talk to any more.

"I like to be in the fresh air," she called.

He waded through the snow. "Let me do that work for you, little lady."

Elizabeth clung to the axe, and he did not come too close.

"Sure having a cold spell," he commented. "Been a bad winter."

This is my own house, Elizabeth told herself. This man saved my life on the Dry Flats.

"Won't you come in and thaw out by the stove?" she suggested. "Perhaps you'd like a cup of tea."

Frenchy was obviously pleased. "Well, now, a day like this, a man can sure use something hot to drink."

Elizabeth felt guilty, ushering him into her cabin by the back way, as if trying to hide her doings from her guardians across the street. But he had come the back way, and not until later did it occur to her that his choice of routes had been because he wanted to avoid being seen.

He sat across the table from her, affable and sociable, waiting for the tea to steep. When his clothing got warmed, he smelled, but a lady could not tell a guest that he should go home and take a bath.

Frenchy had in mind to tell a fine big lie and perhaps to get himself a stake. The lost lady, he guessed, had brought lots of money with her. For her Rune bought the very best supplies available. She was strange, of course, about staying in her cabin all the time, and he had seen her almost fall down in a kind of struggling fit when she went outside. But she was very pretty, and she was nice to him. Doc Frail was her protector, but Frenchy had a strong suspicion that Doc Frail was frail indeed.

Frenchy went into his lie.

"Just can't hardly wait for a warm spell. I got the prettiest little claim you ever seen—colors galore. I'm going to be the rich Mr. Plante, sure enough. That is," he sighed, "if I can just keep eating till the ground thaws."

He blew politely into his tea to cool it.

"Yes, sir," mused Frenchy, "all I need is a grubstake. And whoever stakes me is going to be mighty lucky. That's how Doc Frail made his pile, you know. Grubstaking prospectors."

He did not ask her for anything. He did not suggest that she stake him. She thought of it all by herself.

"Tell me more, Mr. Plante," she said. "Maybe I will stake you."

He argued a little—couldn't possibly accept a stake from a lady. She argued—he must, because she owed him her life, and she would like to get rich. How much did he need?

Anything, anything—but with prices so high—and he'd have to hire labor, and that came high, too—

She calculated wildly. Six pokes of gold, a pound in each one. She had no basis for computing how much a prospector needed.

"I will give you half of what I have," she offered. "And you will give me half of the gold you find. I think we should have some sort of written contract, too."

Frenchy was dazzled. He had nothing to lose. He did not expect to have any gold to divide. His luck had been bad for months, and he intended to leave Skull Creek as soon as the weather permitted travel.

He dictated the contract as Elizabeth wrote in her prettiest penmanship, and both of them signed.

"The contract's yours to keep," he told her. It was a valid grubstake contract—if the holder could enforce it.

"I'll name the mine after you," he promised, vastly cheerful. "A few weeks from now—next summer anyway—you'll have to get gold scales to keep track of your take. When you see me again, you can call me Solid Gold Frenchy!"

At the Big Nugget, Frenchy took care to stand at the end of the bar nearest the table where Doc Frail was killing time in a card game.

The bartender was polite to Frenchy because business was poor, but his tone was firm as he warned, "Now, Frenchy, you know you ain't got no more credit here."

Frenchy was jovial and loud in his answer: "Did I say a word about credit this time? Just one drink, and I'll pay for it." He pulled out a poke.

Doc Frail was paying no attention to Frenchy and not much to the game. He took care to be seen in public most evenings, in the vain hope of weakening the camp's conviction that the lost lady was his property. He succeeded only in confusing the men, who felt he was treating her badly by leaving her in solitude.

Frenchy held up his glass and said with a grin, "Here's to the gold that's there for the finding, and here's to my grubstake partner."

Doc could not help glancing up. Frenchy had worn out three or four stakes already. Doc himself had refused him and did not know of a single man in camp who was willing to give him another start.

He looked up to see Frenchy grinning directly at him.

A challenge? Doc wondered. What's he been up to?

A suspicion of what Frenchy had been up to was like a burning coal in his mind.

Are you the man? he thought. Are you, Frenchy Plante, the man for whom I'll hang?

He stayed on for half an hour, until Frenchy had gone. He found Elizabeth in a cheerful mood, mending one of his shirts.

"The tea's been standing and it's strong," she apologized, getting a cup ready for him.

Drinking it, he waited for her to say that Frenchy had been there, but she only asked about Tall John's health.

Finally Doc remarked, "Frenchy Plante has suddenly come into comparative riches. He's got a grubstake from somewhere."

Elizabeth said mildly, "Is that so?"

"He said so when he bought a drink just now," Doc added, and Elizabeth was indignant.

"Is that what he's doing with it—drinking it up? I declare, I don't approve. I grubstaked him, if that's what you're trying to find out. But that was so he wouldn't starve and could go on mining when the weather moderates."

Doc said sadly, "Oh, Elizabeth!"

"It was mine," she maintained. "I simply invested some of it. Because I have plenty—and I want more."

Frenchy went on a prolonged, riotous and dangerous drinking spree. He was so violent that Madame Dewey, who kept the rooms above the Big Nugget, had him thrown out of there—at some expense, because two men were injured in removing him.

When he was almost broke, he really did go prospecting.

Doc and Rune treated Elizabeth with distant courtesy, mentioning casually the less scandalous highlights of Frenchy Plante's orgy. They did not scold, but their courtesy was painful. She had no friends any more, no alternately laughing and sarcastic friend named Joe Frail, no rude but faithful friend named Rune. They were only her physician and the boy who did her errands. She lived in a log-lined, lamplit cave, and sometimes wished she were dead.

There was a window by her front door; Rune had nailed stout wooden bars across it on the inside. For privacy, an old blanket was hung over the bars. She could peek through the small hole in the blanket for a narrow glimpse of the street, but nothing ever happened that was worth looking at. To let in daylight by taking the blanket off the window was to invite stares of men who happened to pass by—and sometimes the curious, yearning, snow-bound miners were too drunk to remember that Doc Frail was her protector, or if they remembered, too drunk to care.

One of them, who tried to get in one evening in mid-April, was cunning when he made his plans. He was sober enough to reconnoiter first.

He knew where Doc Frail was—playing cards at the Big Nugget, bored but not yet yawning. Rune was in Doc's cabin with a lamp on the table, bent over a book. Tall John was limping down the gulch with a lantern to visit friends. And Frenchy Plante, who had some right to the lady because he had found her, was somewhere out in the hills.

The intruder felt perfectly safe about the warning bells. If the lady pulled the rope, there would be no noise, because he had cut the rope.

Elizabeth was asleep on her bed, fully clothed—she slept a great deal, having nothing else to do—when knuckles rapped at the back door and a voice not quite like Doc's called, "Miss Armistead! Elizabeth!"

She sat up, frozen with fright. Then the pounding was louder, with the slow beats of an axe handle. She did not answer, and with senseless anger the man began to chop at the back door.

She ran and seized the bell rope. It slumped loose in her hands. She heard the dry wood crack and splinter. She did not even try to escape by the front door. She reached for the derringer that had been her father's, pointed it blindly and screamed as she pulled the trigger.

Then she was defenseless, but there was no more chopping, no sound at all, until she heard Rune's approaching shout. She was suddenly calm and guiltily triumphant. Making very sure that Rune was indeed Rune, she unbarred the front door and let him in.

"I fired the little gun!" she boasted.

"You didn't hurt anybody," Rune pointed out. The bullet had lodged in the splintered back door. "We'll just wait right here till Doc comes."

But Doc solved no problems when he came. He sat quietly and listened to Elizabeth's story.

"I don't know," Doc said hopelessly. "I don't know how to protect you." He motioned toward the shattered, splintered door. "Rune, fix that. I'll repair the bell rope."

Rune nailed the back door solid again and was noisy outside at the woodpile for a few minutes. When he came back, he said briefly, "Nobody will try that entrance again tonight. I'm going to bring blankets and sleep on the woodpile."

In Doc Frail's cabin he bundled blankets together. He straightened up and blurted out a question: "How much time do I still owe you?"

"Time? That old nonsense. You don't owe me anything. I just wanted to cut you down to size."

"Maybe somebody will cut you down to size sometime," Rune said. "I suppose you were never licked in your life. The great Joe Frail, always on top of the heap. It's time you got off it."

Doc said, "Hey! What's this sudden insurrection?"

"All you do is boss Elizabeth around. Why don't you get down on your knees instead? Didn't it ever dawn on you that if you married her, you could take her out of here to some decent place?" Rune was working himself up to anger. "Sure, she'd say she couldn't go, but you could make her go —tie her up and take her out in a wagon if there's no other way. How do you know the only right way to get her out of Skull Creek is to make her decide it for herself? Do you know everything?"

Doc answered, "No, I don't know everything," with new humility. He was silent for a while. "Don't think the idea is new to me. I've considered it. But I don't think she'd have me."

Rune picked up his blankets. "That's what I mean," he said. "You won't gamble unless you're sure you'll win." He slammed the door behind him.

VIII

When Doc set out to court Elizabeth Armistead, he put his whole heart into it, since this was what he had been wanting to do for a long time anyway. He was deferential and suitably humble. He was gentle. He was kind. And Elizabeth, who had never had a suitor before (except old Mr. Ellerby, who had talked across her head to her father), understood at once what Doc's intentions were.

He crossed the street more often and stayed longer. He came at mealtime, uninvited, and said he enjoyed her cooking. He even cut and carried in firewood. He brought his socks to be mended. They sat in pleasant domesticity at the table, while Elizabeth sewed and sometimes glanced across at him.

In his own cabin, Rune studied with the patient, Tall John.

And fifteen miles away, Frenchy Plante panned gravel. The ground had thawed, and rain made his labors miserable, but Frenchy had a hunch. Ninety-nine times out of a hundred, his hunches didn't pan out, but he trusted them anyway.

On a slope by a stream there was a ragged old tree. Beside it he had a pit from which he had dug gravel that showed occasional colors. He groaned out of his blankets one gray dawn, in his ragged tent, to find that the tree was no longer visible. Its roots washed by rain, it had fallen headfirst into his pit.

Frenchy swore.

"A sign, that's what it is," he growled. "A sign there wasn't nothing there to dig for. Damn tree filled up my pit. Going to leave here, never go back to Skull Creek."

But he had left a bucket by the tree, and he went for the bucket. The tree's head was lower than its roots, and the roots were full of mud, slick with rain. Mud that shone, even in the gray light.

He tore at the mud with his hands. He shelled out chunks like peanuts, but peanuts never shone so richly yellow. He forgot breakfast, forgot to build a fire, scrabbled in the oozing mud among the roots.

He held in his hand a chunk the size of a small crabapple, but no crabapple was ever so heavy.

He stood in the pouring rain with a little golden apple in his muddy hands. He threw his head back so the rain came into his matted beard, and he howled like a wolf at the dripping sky.

He staked his claim and worked it from dawn to dusk for a week, until he was too exhausted by labor and starva-

tion to wash gravel any more. He might have died there in
the midst of his riches, because he was too weak to go back
to Skull Creek for grub, but he shot an unwary deer and
butchered it and fed. The discovery that even he could lose
his strength—and thereby his life and his treasure—frightened him. He caught his horse, packed up, and plodded
toward Skull Creek, grinning.

He slogged down the gulch at dusk, eager to break the
news to Elizabeth Armistead, but he had another important
plan. He shouted in front of a wickiup built into the side of
the gulch: "Bill, you there? It's Frenchy."

The wickiup had been his until he sold it for two bottles
of whiskey. Bill Scanlan looked out and said without enthusiasm, "Broke already? Well, we got beans."

A man known as Lame George, lying on a dirty blanket,
grunted a greeting.

"Crowded here," he murmured. "But we can make
room."

"Anything happening?" Frenchy asked, wolfing cold
fried pork and boiled beans.

"Stages ain't running yet. This camp's played out.
What'd you find?"

"Some good, some bad. Mostly bad." That was honest,
not that honesty mattered much, and not that prospectors
expected it even among friends. "I was thinking about that
time the boys drove the mules through the old lady's tent.
I bet there ain't been a funny joke like that for a long time."

Lame George said sadly, "There ain't, for a fact. Nothing much to do, nothing to laugh about. We been digging
but couldn't raise a color."

"I got a good idea for a funny joke," Frenchy hinted.
"On Doc Frail."

Lame George snorted. "Nobody jokes him."

"I'd make it worth a man's while," Frenchy said with
great casualness, and Lame George sat up to demand,
"What'll you do it with? You find something?"

"What you got, Frenchy?" Scanlan asked tensely.

"The joke," Frenchy reminded them. "What about the joke on Doc?"

"Hell, yes!" Lame George exploded. "Let us in on something good and we'll take our chances on Doc." He glanced at Scanlan, who nodded agreement.

"All I want," Frenchy explained, spreading his hands to show his innocent intentions, "is to make a social call on the lady, Miss Armistead, without getting my head blowed off. Is Tall John still living at Doc's?"

"He got better and moved to a shack. Rune still lives with Doc. But what," Lame George demanded with justifiable suspicion, "do you want with the lady?"

"Wouldn't hurt her for the world. Won't lay a hand on her. Just want to talk to her." Frenchy added with a grin, "Just want to show her something I found and brought back in my pocket."

They swarmed at him, grabbed his arms, their eyes eager. "You made a strike, Frenchy? Sure you did—and she grubstaked you!"

Elizabeth sat at the table, mending by lamplight. Doc was across from her, reading aloud to their mutual contentment. He sat in comfort, in his shirt sleeves, his coat and gun belt hanging on a nail by the front door. The fire in the cookstove crackled, and the teakettle purred.

Doc chose his reading carefully. In an hour and a half, he worked through portions of the works of Mr. Tennyson and Mr. Browning and, apparently by accident, looked into the love sonnets of William Shakespeare—exactly what he had been aiming at from the beginning.

"Why," Elizabeth asked, "are you suddenly so restless? Are you tired of reading to me?"

Doc discovered that he was no longer sitting. He was walking the floor, and the time had come to speak.

"My name," he said abruptly, "is not really Frail."

She was not shocked. "Why did you choose that one, then?"

"Because I was cynical. Because I thought it suited me.

Elizabeth, I have to talk about myself. I have to tell you some things."

She said, "Yes, Joe."

"I killed a man once."

She looked relieved. "I heard it was four men!"

He frowned. "Does it seem to you that one does not matter? It matters to me."

She said gently, "I'm sorry, Joe. It matters to me, too. But one is better than four."

And even four killings, he realized, she would have forgiven me!

He bent across the table.

"Elizabeth, I enjoy your company. I would like to have it the rest of my life. I want to protect you and work for you and love you and—make you happy, if I can."

"I shouldn't have let you say that," she answered quietly. Her eyes were closed, and there were tears on her cheeks. "I am going to marry a man named Ellerby. And I expect I'll make his life miserable."

He said teasingly, "Does a girl shed tears when she mentions the name of a man she really plans to marry? I've made you cry many a time, but—"

He was beside her, and she clung as his arms went around her. He kissed her until she fought for breath.

"Not Ellerby, whoever he is, my darling. But me. Because I love you. When the roads are passable—soon, soon —I'll take you away and you'll not need to set foot on the ground or look at—anything."

"No, Joe, not you. Mr. Ellerby will come for me when I write him, and he will hate every mile of it. And I will marry him because he doesn't deserve any better."

"That's nonsense," Doc Frail said. "You will marry me."

Across the street, a man with a bad cold knocked at Doc's door. He kept a handkerchief to his face as he coughed out his message to Rune:

"Can Doc come, or you? Tall John's cut his leg with an axe, bleeding bad."

"I'll come," gasped Rune, and grabbed for Doc's bag.

He knew pretty well what to do for an axe cut; he had been
working with Doc all winter. "Tell Doc—he's right across
the street."

"Go to Tall John's place," the coughing man managed
to advise. As far as Rune knew, he went across the street to
call Doc. Rune did not look back; he was running to save his
patient.

When he was out of sight, another man who had been
standing in the shadows pounded on Elizabeth's door, calling frantically, "Doc, come quick! That kid Rune's been
stabbed at the Big Nugget!"

He was out of sight when Doc Frail barged out, hesitated a moment, decided he could send someone for his bag,
and ran toward the saloon.

He tripped and, as he fell, something hit him on the
back of the head.

He did not lie in the mud very long. Two men solici-
tously carried him back in the opposite direction and laid
him in the slush at the far side of Flaunce's store. They left
him there and went stumbling down the street, obviously
drunk.

Frenchy Plante did not use force in entering Elizabeth's cabin. He knocked and called out, "Miss Armistead,
it's Frenchy." In a lower tone, he added, "I got good news
for you!"

She opened the door and demanded, "Is Rune hurt
badly? Oh, what happened?"

"The boy got hurt?" Frenchy was sympathetic.

"Someone called Dr. Frail to look after him—didn't you
see him go?"

Frenchy said good-humoredly, "Miss, I'm too plumb
damn excited. Listen, can I come in and show you what I
brought?"

She hesitated, too concerned to care whether he came
in or not.

"Remember," he whispered, "what I said once about
Solid Gold Frenchy?"

She remembered and gasped. "Come in," she said.

Doc reeled along the street, cold, soaking wet, and with his head splitting. He would have stopped long enough to let his head stop spinning, but he was driven by cold fear that was like sickness.

What about Elizabeth alone in her cabin? Where was Rune and how badly was he hurt? Doc was bruised and aching, tricked and defeated. Who had conquered him was not very important. Skull Creek would know soon enough that someone had knocked the starch out of Doc Frail without a shot being fired.

Rune, wherever he was, would have to wait for help if he needed it.

At Elizabeth's door Doc listened and heard her voice between tears and laughter: "I don't believe it! I don't think it's really true!"

The door was not barred. He opened it and stood watching with narrowed eyes. Elizabeth was rolling something crookedly across the table, something yellow that looked like a small, misshapen apple. When it fell and boomed on the floor boards, he knew what it was.

He asked in a controlled voice, "Has the kid been here?"

Elizabeth glanced up and gasped. She ran to him, crying, "Joe, you're hurt—what happened? Come sit down. Oh, Joe!"

Frenchy Plante was all concern and sympathy. "My God, Doc, what hit you?"

Doc Frail brushed Elizabeth gently aside and repeated, "Has the kid been here?"

"Ain't seen him," Frenchy said earnestly. "Miss Armistead was saying you'd been called out, he was hurt, so we thought you was with him."

Doc turned away without answering. He ran, stumbling, toward the Big Nugget. He stood in the doorway of the saloon, mud-stained, bloody and arrogant. He asked in a voice that did not need to be loud, "Is the kid in here?"

Nobody answered that, but someone asked, "Well, now, what happened to you?" in a tone of grandfatherly indulgence.

They were watching him, straight-faced, without concern, without much interest, the way they would look at any other man in camp. But not the way they should have looked at Doc Frail. There was nothing unusual in their attitudes, except that they were not surprised. And they should have been. They expected this, he understood.

"I was informed," Doc said, "that Rune had been knifed in a fight here."

The bartender answered, "Hell, there ain't been a fight here. And Rune ain't been in since he came for you two-three days ago."

Doc was at bay, as harmless as an unarmed baby. He turned to the door—and heard laughter, instantly choked.

Outside, he leaned against the wall, sagging, waiting for his head to stop spinning, waiting for his stomach to settle down.

There was danger in the laughter he had heard. And there was nothing he could do. Frail, Frail, Frail.

He realized that he was standing on the spot where Wonder Russell stood when Dusty Smith shot him, long ago.

He began to run, lurching, toward Elizabeth's cabin.

She was waiting in the doorway. She called anxiously, "Joe! Joe!"

Frenchy said, "I kept telling her you'd be all right, but I figured it was best to stay here with her in case anything else happened."

Doc did not answer but sat down, staring at him, and waited for Elizabeth to bring a pan of water and towels.

"Is Rune all right?" she demanded.

"I presume so. It was only a joke, I guess."

Golden peas and beans were on the table with the little golden apple. When Doc would not let Elizabeth help him clean the blood off his face, she turned toward the table slowly as if she could not help it.

"He named the mine for me," she whispered. "He calls it the Lucky Lady." Her face puckered, but she did not cry. She laughed instead, choking.

Rune came in at that moment, puzzled and furious, with Doc's bag.

"They said Tall John was hurt," he blurted out, and stopped at sight of Doc Frail.

"The way I heard it," Doc said across the towel, "you were knifed at the saloon. And somebody hit me over the head."

Rune seemed not to hear him. Rune was staring at the nuggets, moving toward them, pulled by the same force that had pulled Elizabeth.

Frenchy chortled, "Meet the Lucky Lady, kid. I got a strike, and half of it is hers. I'll be leaving now. No, the nuggets are yours, Miss, and there'll be more. Sure hope you get over that crack on the head all right, Doc."

Doc's farewell to Elizabeth was a brief warning: "Bar the door. From now on, there'll be trouble."

He did not explain. He left her to think about it.

She did not go to bed at all that night. She sat at the table, fondling the misshapen golden apple and the golden peas and beans, rolling them, counting them. She held them in her cupped hands, smiling, staring, but not dreaming yet. Their value was unknown to her; there would be plenty of time to get them weighed. They were only a token, anyway. There would be more, lots more.

She hunted out, in its hiding place, a letter she had written to Mr. Ellerby, read it through once, and burned it in the stove.

The golden lumps would build a wall of safety between her and Mr. Ellerby, between her and everything she didn't want.

She sat all night, or stood sometimes by the front window, smiling, hearing the sounds she recognized although she had never heard the like before: the endless racket of a gold rush. Horses' hoofs and the slogging feet of men, forever passing, voices earnest or anxious or angry, the creak of wagons. She listened eagerly with the golden apple cupped in her hand.

Even when someone pounded on her door, she was not afraid. The walls are made of gold, she thought. Nobody can break them down. A man called anxiously, "Lucky Lady, wish me luck! That's all I want, lady, all in the world I want."

Elizabeth answered, "I wish you luck, whoever you are," and laughed.

But when, toward morning, she heard an angry racket outside the back door, she was frightened for Rune. She ran to listen.

"I've got a gun on you," he was raging. "Git going, now!" And men's voices mumbled angrily away.

She spoke to him through the closed back door.

"Rune, go and get Doc. I have been making plans."

The three of them sat at the table before dawn. Coffee was in three cups, but only Rune drank his.

Doc listened to Elizabeth and thought, This is some other woman, not the lost lady, the helpless prisoner. This is the Lucky Lady, an imprisoned queen. This is royalty. This power. She has suddenly learned to command.

"I would like to hire you, Rune, to be my guard," she began.

Rune glanced at Doc, who nodded. Rune did not answer. Elizabeth did not expect him to answer.

"I would like you to buy me a gold scale as soon as possible," she continued. "And please find out from Mr. Flaunce what would be the cost of freighting in a small piano from the States."

Doc said wearily, "Elizabeth, that's defeat. If you order a piano and wait for it to get here, that means you're not even thinking of leaving Skull Creek."

"When I thought of it, thinking did me no good," she answered, and dismissed the argument.

"Rune, please ask Mr. Flaunce to bring over whatever

bolts of dress material he has—satin, in a light gray. I shall have a new dress."

Rune put down his coffee cup. "You could build a lean-to on the back here. I'd ought to stay pretty close, and I don't hanker to sleep on that woodpile often."

She nodded approval. "And another thing: grubstaking Frenchy brought me luck. Other miners will think of the same thing, and I will grubstake them, to keep my luck."

Rune growled, "Nonsense. Hand out a stake to every one that asks for it, and you'll be broke in no time. Set a limit—say every seventh man that asks. But don't let anybody know it's the seventh that gets it."

Elizabeth frowned, then nodded. "Seven is a lucky number."

Doc picked up his cup of cool coffee.

A handful of gold has changed us all, he thought. Elizabeth is the queen—the golden Queen Elizabeth. Rune is seventeen years old, but he is a man of sound judgment—and he is the second best shot in the territory. And I, I am a shadow.

Doc said gently, "Elizabeth, there may not be very much more gold for Frenchy to divide with you. You are planning too much grandeur."

"There will be a great deal more," she contradicted, serenely. "I am going to be very rich. I am the Lucky Lady."

IX

At the end of a single week, the fragility of the Skull Creek gold camp was plain. The town was collapsing, moving to the new strike at Plante Gulch.

The streets swarmed and boomed with strangers—but they were only passing through. Flaunce's store was open day and night to serve prospectors replenishing grub supplies and going on to the new riches. Flaunce was desperately trying to hire men to freight some of his stock on to diggings to set up another store before someone beat him to it.

Doc Frail lounged in his own doorway waiting for Rune to come from Elizabeth's cabin, and watched the stream of men passing by—bearded, ragged, determined men on foot or on horseback, leading donkeys or mules, driving bull teams with laden wagons, slogging along with packs on their shoulders. Almost all of them were strangers.

Let's see if I'm what I used to be, Doc thought, before Frenchy tricked me and got me hit over the head.

He stepped forward into the path of a pack-laden man, who was walking fast and looking earnestly ahead. When they collided, Doc glared at him with his old arrogance, and the man said angrily, "Damn you, stay out of the way," shoved with his elbow, and went on.

No, I am not what I used to be, Doc admitted silently. The old power, which had worked even on strangers, was gone, the challenge in the stare that asked, Do you amount to anything?

Rune came weaving through the crowd, and Doc saw in him power that was new. Rune looked taller. He wore new, clean clothing and good boots, although the gun in his holster was one Doc had given him months before. Rune was no longer sullen. He wore a worried frown, but he was sure of himself.

Doc pointed with his thumb to a vacant lot, and Rune nodded. It was time for his daily target practice, purposely public. In the vacant space where nobody would get hurt, Doc tossed an empty can, and Rune punctured it with three shots before it fell. The steady stream of passing men became a whirlpool, then stopped, and the crowd grew.

Someone shouted, "Hey, kid," and tossed another can. Doc's pistol and Rune's thundered a duet, and the crowd was pleased.

When Rune's gun was empty, Doc kept firing, still with his right hand but with his second gun, tossed with a flashing movement from his left hand as the first weapon dropped to the ground. No more duet, but solo now, by the old master. He heard admiration among the men around them, and that was all to the good. It was necessary that strangers should know the Lucky Lady was well protected. The border shift, the trick of tossing a loaded gun into the hand that released an empty one, was impressive, but Rune had not yet perfected it enough for public demonstration.

That was all there was to the show. The crowd moved on.

"Go take yourself a walk or something," Doc suggested. "I'll watch Elizabeth's place for a while."

"There's a crazy man in town," Rune said. "Did you see him?"

"There are hundreds of crazy men in town. Do you mean that fanatical preacher with red whiskers? I've been on the edge of his congregation three or four times but never stopped to listen. I wouldn't be surprised if the camp lynched him just to shut him up."

"He scares me," Rune admitted, frowning. "They don't like him, but he gets everybody mad and growling. He don't preach the love of God. It's all hell fire and damnation."

Doc asked, suddenly suspicious, "Has he been to Elizabeth's?"

"He was. I wouldn't let him in. But when I said he was a preacher, she made me give him some dust. She'd like to talk to him, figuring she'd get some comfort. He's not the kind of preacher that ever comforted anybody. Go listen to him when you have time."

"I have more time than I used to," Doc Frail admitted. Two new doctors had come through Skull Creek, both heading for the booming new settlement at Plante Gulch.

Doc had an opportunity to listen to the preacher the next afternoon. The piano player at a dance hall far down the street threw his back out of kilter while trying to move the piano. Doc went down to his shack, gave him some pain killer and with a straight face prescribed bed rest and hot bricks.

The man squalled, "Who'll heat the bricks? And I can't stay in bed—we're moving this shebang to Plante Gulch soon as they finish laying a floor."

"They need a piano player when they get there," Doc reminded him. "I'll tell the boss to see to it you get the hot bricks. You are an important fellow, professor."

"Say, guess I am," the man agreed. "Unless they get a better piano player."

Doc left the proprietor tearing his hair because of the threatened delay, then went out to the street. It was crowded with men whose movement had been slowed by curiosity, for across the street on a packing box the red-haired man was preaching.

His eyes were wild, and so were his gestures, and his sermon was a disconnected series of uncompleted threats. He yelled and choked.

"Oh, ye of little faith! Behold I say unto you! Behold a pale horse: and his name that sat on him was Death, and Hell followed with him! Verily, brethren, do not forget hell—the eternal torment, the fire that never dieth. And I heard a great voice out of the temple saying to the seven angels, go your ways, and pour out the vials of the wrath of God upon the earth.

"Lo, there is a dragon that gives power unto the beast, and you worship the dragon and the beast, saying, 'Who is like unto the beast?' And the dragon is gold and the beast is gold, and lo, ye are eternally damned that seek the dragon or the beast."

The preacher was quoting snatches of Revelation, Doc realized, with changes of his own that were not exactly improvements. But gold may be a dragon and a beast, indeed.

A man in the crowd shouted, "Aw, shut up and go dig yourself some beast!" and there was a roar of approving laughter.

"Remember Sodom and Gomorrah!" screamed the red-haired man. "For their wickedness they were burned—yea, for their sin and evil! Lo, this camp is wicked like unto those two!"

Doc Frail was caught in an impatient eddy in the moving crowd, and someone growled, "Give that horse a lick or we'll never get out of Sodom and on to Gomorrah by dark!"

The preacher's ranting stirred a kind of futile anger in Joe Frail. What makes him think he's so much better than his congregation? Doc wondered. There's a kind of hatred in him.

"A sinful nation," shouted the preacher. "A people laden with iniquity, the seed of evildoers, children that are corrupters. Hear the word of the Lord, ye rulers of Sodom; give ear unto the law of our God, ye people of Gomorrah!"

The Book of the Prophet Isaiah, reflected Joe Frail, who was the son of a minister's daughter. Immediately the red-haired man returned to Revelation:

"There is given unto me a mouth speaking great things, and power is given unto me to continue forty and two months!"

A man behind Joe Frail shouted, "We ain't going to listen that long."

"If any man have an ear, let him hear! He that leadeth into captivity shall go into captivity; he that killeth with the sword must be killed with the sword."

Joe Frail shivered in spite of himself, thinking, And he that killeth with a pistol?

In that moment a man's voice said behind him, *"That is the man,"* and Doc went tense as if frozen, staring at the red-haired madman.

"That's the man I told you about," the voice went on, moving past him. "Crazy as a loon. His name is Grubb."

How could it be? Doc wondered. How could that be the man for whom I'll hang?

After a few days, the madman went on to Plante Gulch.

By August, Elizabeth Armistead was rich and getting richer. The interior log walls of her cabin were draped with yards of white muslin, her furniture was the finest that could be bought in Skull Creek, her piano had been ordered from the East, and she dressed in satin. But only a few men ever saw her, only every seventh man who came to beg a grubstake from the Lucky Lady, and Frenchy Plante when he came to bring her half the cleanup from the mine.

This is Saturday, Doc Frail remembered. Cleanup day at the sluices. Frenchy will be in with the gold. And I will spend the evening with Elizabeth, waiting for him to come. The Lucky Lady hides behind a golden wall.

He found Elizabeth indignantly arguing with Rune.

"Frenchy sent a man to say they have a big cleanup this time," she told Doc. "And they want a man with a reputation to help guard it on the way in. But Rune refuses to go!"

"I don't get paid to guard gold," Rune said. "I hired out to guard you."

"Half of it's mine," she argued.

"And half of it's Frenchy's. He'll look after it. The bank's going to open up whenever he comes. But I'm going to be right here."

Doc said without a smile, "Young lady, you seem to have a sensible fellow on your payroll," and was pleased to see Rune blush.

By George, he thought, that's probably the first decent thing I ever said to him!

"I'll be here, too," Doc promised. "Just making a social call."

He was too restless to sit down and wait. He stood in the doorway, looking out, thinking aloud: "The month is August, Elizabeth. The day is lovely, even in this barren cleft between barren hills. And you are young, and I am not decrepit. But you're a prisoner." He turned toward her and asked gently, "Come for a walk with me, Elizabeth?"

"No!" she whispered instantly. "Oh, no!"

He shrugged and turned away. "There was a time when you couldn't go because you didn't have any place to go or enough money. Now you can afford to go anywhere, but you've got a pile of nuggets to hide behind."

"Joe, that's not it at all! I can't go now for the same reason I couldn't go before."

"Have you tried, Elizabeth?"

She would not answer.

He saw that Rune was watching him with slitted eyes and cold anger in the set of his mouth.

"Maybe your partner will bring you some new and unusual nuggets," Doc remarked. "I wonder where he gets them from."

"From his mine, of course," Elizabeth answered. Her special nuggets were not in sight, but Doc knew they were in the covered sugar bowl on the table.

"Madam, I beg to differ. The Lucky Lady is a placer operation. Water is used to wash gold out of dirt and gravel. Most of your nuggets came from there, all right. But— spread them out and I'll show you."

Unwillingly, she tipped the sugar bowl. It was packed with gold; she had to pry it out with a spoon. And this was not her treasure, but her hobby, the private collection she kept just because it was so beautiful.

Doc touched a golden snarl of rigid strands. "That's wire gold, hardened when it cooled. It squeezed through crevices in rock. Rock, Elizabeth. That's hard-rock gold, not placer, and it never came from diggings within a couple of hundred miles from here. Neither did those sharp-edged nuggets with bits of quartz still on them. That gold never came from the mine Frenchy named for you."

Elizabeth stared, fascinated and frightened. "It was in with some other lumps he brought. Where did he get it?"

"He sent for it, to give you. Some men go courting with flowers. Frenchy gives his chosen one imported gold nuggets."

"Don't talk that way! I don't like it."

"I didn't suppose you would, but it was time to tell you."

Frenchy was cleverly succeeding in two purposes: to please Elizabeth and to taunt Joe Frail.

And we are harmless doves, both of us, Doc thought.

"I wish you'd keep those grubstake contracts at the bank," Doc remarked. Four of them were paying off, and some of the others might. "Why keep them in that red box right here in your cabin?"

"Because I like to look at them sometimes," she said stubbornly. "They're perfectly safe. I have Rune to guard me."

Doc smiled with one corner of his mouth, and she hastened to add, "And I have you, too."

"As long as I live, Elizabeth," he said gently.

Rune tried to clear the air by changing the subject. "I hear the preacher, Grubb, is back."

"Then I would like to talk to him," said Elizabeth. "If he comes to the door, please let him in."

"No!" Doc said quite loudly. "Rune, do not let him in. He's a lunatic."

Elizabeth said coolly, "Rune will let him in. Because I want to talk to him. And because I say so!"

Doc said, "Why, Elizabeth!" and looked at her in astonishment. She sat stiff-backed with her chin high, pale with anger, imperious—the queen behind the golden wall, the Lucky Lady, who had forgotten how vulnerable she was. Doc Frail, newly vulnerable and afraid since the great joke Frenchy had played on him, could not stare her down.

"Rune," he began, but she interrupted, "Rune will let him in because I say so."

Rune looked down at them both. "I will not let him in, and not because Doc says to keep him out. I won't let him in—because he shouldn't get in. And that's how it is."

Doc smiled. "The world has changed, Elizabeth. That's how it is. Rune holds all the winning cards—and nobody needs to tell him how to play them."

Rune guessed dimly in that moment that, no matter how long he lived or what he accomplished to win honor among men, he would never be paid any finer compliment.

"Guess I'll go see what's doing around town," he said, embarrassed.

"Both of you can go!" Elizabeth cried in fury.

To her surprise, Doc answered mildly, "All right," and she was left alone. The nuggets from the sugar bowl were scattered on the table. She touched them, fondled them, sorted them into heaps according to size and shape. She began to forget anger and imprisonment. She began to forget that she was young and far from home.

Doc Frail was only a hundred yards away from the cabin when a messenger on a mule hailed him: "Hey, Doc! My partner Frank's hurt up at our mine. There's three men trying to get him out, or hold up the timbering anyway."

He flung himself off the mule and Doc, who had his satchel, leaped into the saddle. He knew where the mine was.

"Send some more men up there," he urged, and started for it.

Rune, strolling, saw him go and turned at once back to the Lucky Lady's cabin. He did not go in. He hunkered down by the front door and began to whittle.

Down beyond the Big Nugget, the red-haired man was preaching a new sermon, lashing himself to fury—and attracting a more favorably inclined audience than usual. His topic was the Lucky Lady. There was no more fascinating topic in Skull Creek, for she was young and desirable and mysterious, and she represented untold riches, even to men who had never seen her, who knew her only as a legend.

"Lo, there is sin in this camp, great sin!" Grubb was intoning. "The sin that locketh the door on deliverance, that keepeth a young woman prisoner against her will. There is a wicked man who shutteth her up in a cabin, that she escape not, and putteth a guard before her door that righteousness may not enter!"

His listeners were strangers. They believed him, because why not?

One nudged another and murmured, "Say, did you know that?" The other shook his head, frowning.

"She cannot be delivered from evil," intoned Grubb, "because evil encompasseth her round about. She has no comfort within those walls because the servant of the Lord is forbidden to enter."

Someone asked, "Did you try?"

Grubb had tried just once, weeks earlier. But he remembered it as today, and anger was renewed in him. He began to yell.

"Verily, the servant of the Lord tried to enter, to pray with her for deliverance, to win her from evil. But the guard at the door turned him away and bribed him with nuggets. Lo, the guard is as evil as the master, and both of them are damned!"

His audience saw what he saw, the arrogant doctor who would not let the Lucky Lady go, and the young man who idled at her doorway to keep rescuers away. His audience stirred and murmured, and someone said, "By damn, that's a bad thing!" His audience increased, and Grubb, for once delivering a message to which men listened without reviling him, went on screaming words that he convinced himself were true.

One man on the edge of the crowd walked away—the horse thief who was a friend of Tall John, and of Doc who had cured him, and of Rune who had nursed him. The horse thief passed the barbershop and observed that Frenchy Plante was inside, getting his hair cut. Frenchy's mule was hitched in front, and the gold from the weekly cleanup was no doubt in the pack on the mule. But Frenchy was watching from the barber chair with a rifle across his knees, so the horse thief did not linger.

Walking fast, but not running, he paused in front of the Lucky Lady's cabin and spoke quietly to Rune:

"The red-haired fellow is raising hell, working the men up. Saying the girl could get away if it wasn't Doc pays you to keep her locked up. Don't act excited, kid. We're just talking about the weather. I think there's going to be hell to pay, and I'll go tell Tall John. Where's Doc?"

"Went on a call, on Tim Morrison's mule—to Tim's mine, I guess. Thanks."

Unhurried, Rune entered the Lucky Lady's cabin and sat down.

The horse thief, who did not happen to possess a horse

just then, went to the livery stable and rented one. At a trot, he rode to the place where Tall John was washing gravel. Tall John dropped his pick and said, "Go look for Doc." He himself started back toward Elizabeth's cabin at a brisk limp.

Tall John observed that a fairly large crowd had gathered down beyond the Big Nugget, and occasionally a shout came from it.

If they ever get into her cabin, he told himself, they'll have to kill the boy first—and if that happens, she won't care to live either. He and I, between us, will have to keep Frenchy out. Heaven forbid that he should be her rescuer!

Tall John knocked on Elizabeth's door and after he identified himself, Rune let him in. He sat down to chat as if he had come only for a friendly visit.

The horse thief met Doc Frail walking. The man trapped in the cave-in had died. He was still trapped.

"There's trouble," the horse thief said bluntly, and told him what the trouble was.

"I'll take that horse, please," Doc replied. He rode at a trot; he did not dare attract attention by going faster. And he did not know what he was going to do when he got to the cabin—if he got there.

It is too late to try to take her out of Skull Creek now, he realized. I wonder how much ammunition Rune has. I haven't much—and what can I do with it anyway, except to shoot through the roof and make a noise?

He heard Frenchy shout "Hey Doc!" from down the street, but he did not turn.

The crowd beyond the Big Nugget was beginning to stir and to scatter on the edges. Rune, watching from a peephole in the blanket on the window, let Doc in before he had a chance to knock.

The three inside the cabin were still as statues. Elizabeth said, "They've just told me. Joe, I'll go out when they come in and I'll tell Grubb it isn't so."

"You'll stay right here," Doc answered. "I hope you will

not think I am being melodramatic, but I have to do something that I have been putting off for too long. Tall John, can I make a legal will by telling it to you? There's not time to write it. I want to watch that window."

Elizabeth gasped.

Tall John said, "Tell me. I will not forget."

"My name is Joseph Alberts. I am better known as Joseph Frail. I am of sound mind but in imminent danger of death. I bequeath two thousand dollars in clean gulch gold to—Rune, what's your name?"

Rune answered quietly, "Leonard Henderson."

"To Leonard Henderson, better known as Rune, to enable him to get a medical education if he wants it. Everything else I leave to Elizabeth Armistead, called the Lucky Lady."

"Oh, so lucky!" she choked.

He did not say that he wanted Rune to take her away from Skull Creek. It was not necessary.

"That mob is getting noisier," Doc commented. "Tall John, you'd better go out by the back door."

"I will not forget," Tall John promised. He left the cabin, not stopping even to shake hands.

Just outside the window, Frenchy shouted, "Lucky Lady! I got gold for you! Open the door for Frenchy, Lucky Lady."

No one inside the cabin moved. No one outside could see in.

Frenchy hiccuped and said, "Aw, hell, she ain't home." He rode on, then shouted, "But she's always home, ain't she?"

Doc spoke rapidly. "If I go out this door, both of you stay inside—and bar it. Do you understand?"

"I get it," Rune replied. Elizabeth was crying quietly.

Frenchy's voice came back. "Doc, you in there? Hey, Doc Frail! Come on out. You ain't scared, are you?"

Joe Frail went tense and relaxed with an effort of will.

"You wouldn't shoot me, would you, Doc?" Frenchy teased. "You wouldn't shoot nobody, would you, Doc?" He laughed uproariously, and Doc Frail did not move a muscle.

He heard the muttering mob now, the deep, disturbed murmur that he had heard from the hill on the day the road agent swung from a bough of the great tree.

He heard a shrill scream from Grubb, who saw Frenchy coaxing at the window and had seen Frenchy enter the cabin before.

Grubb's topic did not change, but his theme did, as he led his congregation. His ranting voice reached them:

"Wicked woman! Wicked and damned! Will all your gold save you from hell fire? Wanton and damned—"

Doc forgot he was a coward. He forgot a man lying dead in Utah. He forgot Wonder Russell, sleeping in a grave on the hill. He slammed the bar upward from the door and stepped into the street.

His voice was thunder: "Grubb, get down on your knees!"

Grubb was blind to danger. He did not even recognize Doc Frail as an obstacle. Clawing the air, he came on, screaming, "Babylon and the wicked woman—"

Doc Frail gasped and shot him.

He did not see Grubb fall, for the mob's wrath downed him. The last thing he heard as he went down under the deluge was the sound he wanted to hear: the bar falling shut inside the cabin door.

X

The rabble. The rabble. The first emotion he felt was contempt. Fear would come later. But no; fear had come. His mouth was cotton-dry.

He was bruised and battered, had been unconscious. He could not see the men he heard and despised. He lay face down on dirty boards and could see the ground through a crack. On a platform? No, his legs were bent and cramped. He was in a cart. He could not move his arms. They were bound to his body with rope.

The rabble shouted and jeered, but not all the jeering

was for him—they could not agree among themselves. He knew where he was: under the hanging tree.

A voice cried furiously, "A trial! You've got to give the man a trial!"

Another shout mounted: "Sure, try him—he shot the preacher!"

This is the place and this is the tree, Joe Frail understood, and the rope must be almost ready. Grubb was the man, and I hardly knew he existed.

There was nothing that required doing. Someone else would do it all. There was something monstrous to be concerned about—but not for long.

And there was Elizabeth.

Joe Frail groaned and strained at the rope that bound him, and he heard Frenchy laugh.

"Let the boys see you, Doc," Frenchy urged. "Let 'em have a last good look!"

Someone heaved him to his feet and he blinked through his hair, fallen down over his eyes. The mob turned quiet, staring at a man who was as good as dead.

There was no need for dignity now, no need for anything. If he swayed, someone supported him. If he fell, they would stand him on his feet again. Everything that was to be done would be done by someone else. Joe Frail had no responsibilities any more. (Except—Elizabeth? Elizabeth?)

"Hell, that's no decent way to do it," someone argued with authority, not asking for justice but only for a proper execution. "The end of the cart will catch his feet that way. Put a plank across it. Then he'll get a good drop."

There was a busy delay while men streamed down the hill to get planks.

Joe Frail threw back his head with the old arrogant gesture and could see better with his hair tossed away from his eyes. He could see Skull Creek better than he wanted to, as clearly as when he first walked under the tree with Wonder Russell.

Elizabeth, Elizabeth. He was shaken with anger. When

a man is at his own hanging, he should not have to think of anyone but himself.

And still, he understood, even now Joe Frail must fret helplessly about Elizabeth. Who ever really died at peace except those who had nothing to live for?

Men were coming with planks—four or five men, four or five planks. They busied themselves laying planks across the cart to make a platform so they could take satisfaction in having hanged him decently and with compassion. And from the side, Frenchy was bringing up a team of horses to pull the cart away.

Someone behind him slipped a noose down over his head, then took it off again, testing the length of the rope. Above, someone climbed along the out-thrust bough of the tree to tie it shorter. Joe Frail stood steady, not looking up, not glancing sideways at the horses being urged into position.

The crowd was quieter now, waiting.

Just as the team came into position in front of the cart, he saw movement down in the street of Skull Creek and strained forward.

Elizabeth's door had opened and Rune had come out of her cabin.

No! No! You damn young fool, stay in there and do what you can to save her! By tomorrow, they'll slink off like dogs and you can get her away safely. You fool! You utter fool!

What's he carrying? A red box.

No, Elizabeth! Oh, God, not Elizabeth! Stay in the cabin! Stay out of sight!

But the Lucky Lady had emerged from her refuge and was walking beside Rune. Walking fast, half running, with her head bent. Don't look, Elizabeth! My darling, don't look up! Turn back, turn back to the cabin. Tomorrow you can leave it.

A man behind Doc remarked, "Well, would you look at that!" but nobody else seemed to notice.

Doc said sharply, "What the hell are you waiting for?"

Suddenly he was in a hurry. If they finished this fast enough, she would go back—Rune would see to it.

She was leaning forward against the wind of the desert that was thirty miles away. She was stumbling. But she did not fall. She had got past Flaunce's store.

The red box Rune is carrying? The box she keeps her gold in. Go back. Go back.

Someone slipped the noose down over his head again and he groaned and was ashamed.

She was struggling up the first slope of the barren hill, fighting the desert. Her right arm was across her eyes. But Doc could see Rune's face. Rune was carrying the heavy box and could not help the Lucky Lady, but the look on his face was one Doc had seen there seldom. It was pity.

The team was ready, the platform was prepared, the noose was around the condemned man's neck. The Lucky Lady stopped halfway up the hill.

There was almost no sound from the rabble except their breathing. Some of them were watching Elizabeth. She lifted her right hand and fired a shot from the derringer into the air.

Then they all watched her. The silence was complete and vast. The men stared and waited.

Rune put the red box on the ground and opened it, handed something to Elizabeth—a poke, Doc thought. She emptied it into her hand and threw nuggets toward the silent mob.

No one moved. No one spoke or even murmured.

Why, Rune has no gun, Doc saw. It is a long time since I have seen him with no holster on his hip. And Elizabeth has fired into the air the one shot her pistol will hold. They are unarmed, helpless. As helpless as I am.

The voice he heard was his own, screaming, "Go back! Go back!"

A man behind him rested a hand on his shoulder without roughness, as if to say, Hush, hush, this is a time for silence.

Elizabeth stooped again to the box and took out something white—the sugar bowl. She flung the great, shining nuggets of her golden treasure, two and three at a time, toward the motionless men on the slope. Then they were not quite motionless, there was jerky movement among them, instantly ceasing, as they yearned toward the scattered treasure but would not yield.

Elizabeth stood for a while with her head bent and her hands hanging empty. Joe Frail saw her shoulders move as she gulped in great breaths of air. Rune stood watching her with that look of pity twisting his mouth.

She bent once more and took out a folded paper, held it high, and gave it to the wind. It sailed a little distance before it reached the ground. She waited with her head bowed, and the mob waited, stirring with the restless motion of puzzled men.

She tossed another paper and another. Someone asked the air a question: "Contracts? Grubstake contracts?"

And someone else said, "But which ones?"

Most of the contracts had no meaning any more, but a very few of them commanded for the Lucky Lady half the golden treasure that sifted out of paying mines.

Frenchy's voice roared with glee: "She's buying Doc Frail! The Lucky Lady is buying her man!"

Joe Frail quivered, thinking, This is the last indignity. She has gambled everything, and there will be nothing for her to remember except my shame.

All the contracts, one at a time, she offered to the mob, and the wind claimed each paper for a brief time. All the nuggets in the sugar bowl. All the pale dust in the little leather bags that made the red box heavy.

Elizabeth stood at last with her hands empty. She touched the box with her foot and Rune lifted it, turned it upside down to show that it held nothing more, and let it fall.

Frenchy's shout and Frenchy's forward rush broke the mob's indecision. He yelled, "Come and git it, boys! Git your share of the price she's paying for Doc Frail!"

Frenchy ran for the scattered papers, tossed away one after another, then held one up, roaring, and kissed it.

The rabble broke. Shouting and howling, the mob scattered, the men scrabbled for gold in the dust. They swarmed like vicious ants, fighting for the treasure.

A jeering voice behind Doc said, "Hell, if she wants you that bad!" and cut the rope that bound him. The knife slashed his wrist and he felt blood run.

The Lucky Lady was running up the slope to him, not stumbling, not hesitating, free of fear and treasure, up toward the hanging tree. Her face was pale, but her eyes were shining.